Blind Suspicion

4.25 stars. With the first book ending on a cliffhanger, I was very much looking forward to reading this sequel and it was so satisfying. Lynn Miller knows how to keep things interesting and I'm learning that the different volumes in her series never feel repetitive.

Let me start by saying that these books have to be read in order. It's all about the family dynamics of the Castle family. In book one you learn about William Castle, who's spearheading the Castle luxury resort chain, and his children, Alex, and her brother Andrew, who are fighting to gain his favor and be second in line. And there is so much more going on in this family, it is complex, but a lot of fun, I like a bit of soap opera drama and these books have it in spades. The second part of the book is where the actual sleuthing starts, and the stakes are high. In summary, drama, romance, and mystery what's not to like? I hope to see more books in this series.

-Meike V., *NetGalley*

Honestly? Stacy Lynn Miller is probably one of the better authors I've come across in the last few years. If you want something fresh, gripping, entertaining and keeps you guessing to the end, this author is for you. *Blind Suspicion* is the sequel to *Despite Chaos*, another fantastic read, I recommend you read it first.

-Jo R., *NetGalley*

This novel is a very enticing and captivating story full of love, drama, loyalty, family dynamics (both good and bad ones), romance, mystery and so many other things…

-Laurie D., *NetGalley*

Despite Chaos

I honestly do not know what to say! Fantastic story. Everything I've read by Stacy Lynn Miller has been entertaining, engaging and gripping. *Despite Chaos* is yet another amazing story, it's a must book to own in 2022. It's a 5/5. And with a cliffhanger like that... can't wait for that sequel.

-Emma S, *NetGalley*

4.25 Stars. Stacy Lynn Miller has a great ability to write messy, complicated people that are easy to like. With this first book in the "Falling Castles" series, she does it again with Alexandra Castle and Tyler Falling.

-Colleen C., *NetGalley*

This is a well-written, slow-burn romance. There's romance, competition, blackmail, embezzlement and jealousy. The story was fast-paced, and I enjoyed every minute of it. The love, support and understanding of Tyler's husband was astounding. Hands down a great read and I recommend getting a copy. 4.5 stars.

-Bonnie K., *NetGalley*

Beyond the Smoke

This was really good! This is the third book in Miller's Manhattan Sloane Thriller series and is the best written book of the series. I was caught up in the mystery, it kept me turning the pages, but so did the romance.

-Lex Kent's Reviews, *goodreads*

I loved the first two novels, but I think this one might be the best yet...I've enjoyed all the mystery, excitement, action, and intrigue in the plots of these books, but I've fallen in love with these characters, and want to know what's happening in their lives. This is the mark of an exceptionally talented author.

-Betty H., *NetGalley*

From the Ashes

I have been looking forward to reading *From the Ashes* by Stacy Lynn Miller since I read her first Manhattan Sloane novel back in April. I fell in love with Sloane, Finn, and all the other characters in this story while reading the first book, and I wanted more, especially since the story didn't completely end with the first novel. I'm happy to say I loved this book as much as the first one.

In this second tale, we find Sloane still struggling with her grief over her wife's death as she also deals with her growing love for Finn. Nothing is ever easy for Sloane and Finn, since the head of the drug cartel they battled in the first book is now looking for revenge, and he's quite willing to target Sloane and Finn's loved ones.

This is an action-packed story with a complex plot. Most of the characters in this book were introduced in the first one, so they are already well developed and we learn more about the different members of the drug cartel and their motivations. This is definitely a character-driven tale, and Ms. Miller has done an excellent job of creating realistic characters, both good and bad.

I enjoyed seeing the romance grow between Sloane and Finn, even with all the obstacles that could come between them. The author did a wonderful job weaving this romance into all the action and suspense in the overall story.

As I mentioned above, this book is the second in the Manhattan Sloane series and takes up where the first novel, *Out of the Flames*, ended. These books really need to be read together and in order to get the most enjoyment out of the story. I highly recommend both novels, though, so get them both. You won't be disappointed.

-Betty H., *NetGalley*

This was the sequel to this author's very good debut book, *Out of the Flames*.

I enjoyed how the author developed this sequel with realistic problems the characters faced after the loss of loved ones. The author also provided more answers to the car accident that killed Sloane's parents. This was a very emotional moment for those involved. The way it was described, I couldn't help but feel for those characters.

Similar to the previous book, there was a lot of drama when the characters dealt with the cartels. These scenes quickened the pace of the story and allowed for more anxious moments. The secondary characters, both good and bad, increased this story's emotional depth.

Since this was a sequel, I recommend reading the first book to get an overall understanding of the characters and their backgrounds. The author did allow some past events to resurface, but the emotional scenes from the first book were too good not to read and experience.

This book was very engaging with tense moments, emotional breakdowns and recovery, and most of all, tender loving scenes.

-R. Swier, *NetGalley*

From the Ashes is the sequel to *Out of the Flames* with SFPD Detective Manhattan Sloane and DEA [Agent] Finn Harper. They're chasing after a Mexican drug cartel that is ultimately responsible for killing Sloane's wife. Sloane and Harper had a connection in high school but they were torn apart after Sloane's parents were killed in a car accident. Then they were thrown together on this case as the drug cartel seeks revenge for the death of one of their own. Miller is a wonderful storyteller and this story had me sitting on the edge of my seat from start to finish. The first book in the series, *Out of the Flames*, was a 5-star read and *From the Ashes* is the same as it ducks and weaves and thrills and spills all the way to the end. The chemistry between Sloane and Harper is palpable...Miller certainly knows how to write angst into her characters. This book is a thrill a minute and I can't wait for the next one.

-Lissa G., *NetGalley*

I read Stacy Lynn Miller's debut novel *Out of the Flames* back in May, and couldn't wait to read the sequel to learn what happens to San Francisco police detective Manhattan Sloane and DEA Agent Finn Harper's relationship as well as the drug cartel they were chasing. *From the Ashes* resumes from the point that *Out of the Flames* ended.

The book was fast-paced with quite a few anxious and emotional moments. I don't think that you have to read the first book to enjoy this one, but I recommend it since it is a good story and it will introduce the background and characters in a more complete manner. I'd definitely recommend both books to other readers.

-Michele R., *NetGalley*

Out of the Flames

This is the debut novel of Stacy Lynn Miller and it's very, very good. The book is a roller coaster of emotion as you ride the highs and lows with Sloane as she navigates her way through her life which is riddled with guilt, self blame, and eventually love. It's easy to connect with all the main characters and sub-characters, most of them are all successful strong women so what's not to love? The story line is really solid.

-Lissa G., *NetGalley*

If you are looking for a book that is emotional, exciting, hopeful, and entertaining, you came to the right place. There are characters you will love, and characters you will love to hate. And the important thing is that Miller makes you care about them so, yes, you might need the tissues just like I did. I see a lot of potential in Miller and I can't wait to read book two.

-Lex Kent's 2020 Favorites List.
Lex Kent's Reviews, *goodreads*

If you are looking for an adventure novel with mystery, intrigue, romance, and a lot of angst, then look no further.

...I'm really impressed with how well this tale is written. The story itself is excellent, and the characters are well-developed and easy to connect with.

-Betty H., *NetGalley*

AMID
SECRETS

STACY LYNN MILLER

Other Bella Books by Stacy Lynn Miller

A Manhattan Sloane Thriller
Out of the Flames
From the Ashes
Beyond the Smoke

Falling Castle Series
Despite Chaos
Blind Suspicion

About the Author

A late bloomer, Stacy Lynn Miller took up writing after retiring from the Air Force. Her twenty years of toting a gun and police badge, tinkering with computers, and sleuthing for clues as an investigator form the foundation of her Lexi Mills and Manhattan Sloane thriller series. She is visually impaired, a proud stroke survivor, mother of two, tech nerd, chocolate lover, and terrible golfer with a hole-in-one. When you can't find her writing, she'll be golfing or drinking wine (sometimes both) with friends and family in Northern California.

For more information about Stacy, visit her website at stacylynnmiller.com. You can also connect with her on Instagram @stacylynnmiller, Twitter @stacylynnmiller, or Facebook @ stacylynnmillerauthor

AMID
SECRETS

STACY LYNN MILLER

BELLA
BOOKS

2023

Bella Books, Inc.
P.O. Box 10543
Tallahassee, FL 32302

Printed in the United States of America on acid-free paper.

First Edition - 2023

Editor: Medora MacDougall
Cover Designer: Heather Honeywell

ISBN: 978-1-64247-432-9

PUBLISHER'S NOTE

Acknowledgments

Thank you, Louise, Kristianne, Diane, Sue, and Sabrin. This incredible crew of beta readers pushes me to be a better writer.

Thank you, Linda and Jessica Hill, for believing in my work and making a dream come true.

Thank you, Medora MacDougall, my editor who brings out the best in me.

Finally, to my family. Thank you for loving me.

Dedication

To Barbara Gould
My best friend and plotting partner in crime.
She teaches me every day the meaning of selflessness.

PROLOGUE

Manhattan, New York, 2007

Faint voices from the other side of Georgia Cushing's closed office door woke her from a short power nap. The dark sky outside her twenty-third-floor window, though, told her it had lasted a lot longer than intended. She couldn't blame herself for being so tired. She'd worked nonstop since her morning meeting with William Castle that had left her feeling used again. She'd done what he'd asked, and like he'd done every other time her accounting findings reflected poorly on his heirs, he'd closed ranks. *"You are to tell no one about what you've found. Since all the money is back in place, I'll handle the matter personally."*

William Castle had brushed her off for the last time, and her nearly thirty-seven-year stretch of forgiving him was over. His son was an embezzler, and his daughter had covered it up. Those were crimes, and Alexandra and Andrew needed to be punished, not have their father reward them with keys to the Castle empire of hotels that she'd been part of since its first day. If William didn't have the fortitude to do the right thing, Georgia would.

She'd spent the rest of the day digging deeper through Castle Resorts' accounting records to document every irregularity. Now it was time to get back to work. Shaking off the fog of sleep, she thought she heard someone yell, "You son of a bitch." Male or female? She couldn't tell. Moments later, footsteps tore past her office and down the hallway and, if she heard correctly, out of the main suite. She checked her watch and silently chided herself. It was nearly nine thirty. She'd been asleep for hours.

Curiosity got the best of her. She opened the office door to an empty hallway. The earlier lightning storm having passed, the only visible light there came from William's office suite at the far end of the corridor. The entire floor was utterly silent, and the soft carpet in the hallway masked the sound of her heels hitting the floor as she made her way toward the light source.

Walking through the thick wooden doors of William's executive office, Georgia got the fright of her life. William was lying motionless on the floor, face up, near his desk. She darted toward him and knelt, avoiding the blood pooling around his head. She felt for signs of life, a pulse, but she couldn't be sure she detected one. She put her hand on his chest. A slight intake of air confirmed he still clung to life.

She rose as quickly as her aging body allowed and started for the phone on the desk. A weak groan stopped her in her tracks and forced her to turn back. William moved his head from left to right, so she returned to his side, intending to comfort him. She knelt again and grasped his right hand. She was about to call out his name when her instinct to render aid gave way to the memories of how horribly he'd treated her. He'd strung her along for years, only to marry another woman once he'd finally rid himself of his first wife. The awful situation he'd forced her into years ago was another act she hadn't forgiven.

She slowly released his hand, struggled to her feet again, and sank into the guest chair closest to him. She leaned back to grasp fully the opportunity that was unfolding in front of her eyes, cocking her head from one side to the other as she stared at him. She leaned forward, ready to release decades of pent-up anger.

"Why did I love you for so long? Our on-again-off-again affair was such a mixed bag over the years. A never-ending cycle of joy and sorrow and pleasure and pain. Every time we started up, you were attentive, playful, and erotic. But then something would happen. Your wife's birthday, an anniversary, or Christmas would approach, and you'd turn all business and treat me like any other employee. But I wasn't just a subordinate! I was your lover. I was your confidant. I was the one you came to when your wife turned cold in bed. I was the one you came to with excitement when you wanted to expand the business. I was your sounding board, in the office and the bedroom."

She took in a deep breath to say what needed saying for thirty-five years. "You're a heartless beast. Before you die, you should know I took care of things my way, not yours."

William opened his eyes, and a single tear fell down his cheek. He then turned his face to look up into the heavens and took one last breath. Without any more blood to pump, his heart stopped. He was dead.

Georgia had wondered how she would feel when her former lover and long-term employer finally passed away. Would she feel sadness or joy or regret or satisfaction? To her surprise, she felt relieved. His death meant he would never again enjoy his favorite seared steak or bottle of fifty-year-old scotch. He would never see another beautiful sunset or feast his eyes on historical buildings he'd spent decades preserving. But most importantly, William would never again break her heart.

"Burn in Hell, William Castle."

Georgia pushed up from her chair. As she lifted the telephone to call 911, several black and white photographs strewed atop the desk caught her eye. Her lip turned up, her first glance having revealed what she could only describe as pornography—two women in various stages of undress or wholly naked and engaged in unspeakable sexual acts. Closer inspection confirmed to her the identity of Alex Castle and solidified Georgia's loathing of her. Of course, she would pose for such depravity.

Georgia had long thought William's twins were unworthy

of his trust and had never understood why he consistently defended their actions, even when they proved unreliable. These photographs represented everything she hated about the Castle family. She didn't know how yet, but she would see that these pictures marked the end of Alexandra's control of Castle Resorts.

She grabbed the photos, left William lying in a pool of his blood, and calmly returned to her office. Gathering her things, she thought about the police investigation that would commence once someone found William's body. Instead of riding the elevator down and risking being recorded by its surveillance camera, she slowly descended the twenty-three floors via the stairwell, where sheets of plastic had blocked the building's security cameras during construction work. Once out of the building, just like she did every night after work, albeit usually hours earlier than tonight, she made her way to the subway station two blocks away, rode the train to Brooklyn, and walked the rest of the way home. There she carefully tucked the photographs away in a shoebox and placed the box on the top shelf of her closet for safekeeping.

Enjoy your time at Castle Resorts, Alex, Georgia thought. *You won't have the reins for long.*

CHAPTER ONE

Bedford Hills, New York, 2010

A soothing male voice drifted from the train's intercom, announcing, "This is the Mount Kisco station. Next stop Bedford Hills." Georgia stirred from the trance induced by her early morning trip from Brooklyn, a journey that had started with a half-hour ride on Line Five to Grand Central before segueing into an hour on this northbound Harlem line train. The sound of the train's wheels rocking along the half-century-old metal rails would've lulled her into a pleasant sleep if not for the twenty-three stops, the constant coming and going of passengers, and the anger brewing inside her.

One more stop to go, Georgia thought. She spent the next few minutes mulling over how she would entice a long-term resident at the Bedford Hills Correctional Facility for Women into providing her information. Hopefully, this woman would supply the golden bullet that would allow her to repay Alex Castle and her older sister, Sydney Barnette, for destroying her life and setting in motion plans that would force her out of the only home she'd known for four decades.

Georgia had loathed William's oldest child the longest. Sydney had held her back from promotion for years because of Georgia's affair with her father. Then she'd fired her for tipping off the press about Alex Castle's falling out with her father shortly before his death, a death Georgia had hastened by not lifting a finger to help. Her unemployment had reduced Georgia to pinching pennies until she could start collecting Social Security without penalty. Those lean times, ones like no others she'd experienced, were nothing like those now facing her. In six months, Castle Resorts would sell Georgia's house, the one William had promised her rent-free for life for keeping their secret, leaving her homeless on a fixed retiree income in a city too expensive for her to live in.

She had a plan in mind, though it would take months to pull off and require her to be patient and commit to the long haul. For it to work, however, she needed to gather more information and to find someone with a particular set of skills and flexible morals. In other words, she needed a criminal. What better place to find a criminal than a prison?

The train came to a stop. Georgia stepped onto the station platform, a robust gust of warm summer wind nearly knocking her over. She steadied herself by grabbing onto a nearby lamppost, silently cursing her reality. *I should be at my desk at Castle Resorts Headquarters, not holding on to this dirty train platform for dear life.*

Making her way to the main entrance, she flagged the only taxi idling curbside and directed the driver, "To the prison, please." The facility was only a mile away, but at her age, she wasn't up for a long windy hike. Thankfully, the cab was clean and free of the faint vomit smell that plagued many New York City cabs.

The crusty cab driver craned his head over his shoulder in her direction, rolling his eyes. "Which one, lady?" Remaining anonymous and unremarked being paramount, Georgia ignored his boorish behavior. She'd forgotten that the tiny hamlet of Bedford Hills was home to not one but two New York state prisons for women. Taconic was a medium-security prison for minor offenders. Bedford Hills was a maximum-security prison for violent and career criminals. According to *The New York Times*, the prisoner she needed to see had pleaded guilty to manslaughter and had already served three years of a minimum twenty-year stretch. That meant only one destination. "I'm sorry. Bedford."

Minutes later, the driver made a sharp right turn and maneuvered through the prison parking lot, stopping at the foot of a short path leading to a temporary trailer marked by a weather-beaten sign labeled Visitors.

Georgia paid the cab fare and politely thanked the driver for the ride. Steps inside the trailer, she judged her visit would be a day-long affair. The room, filled with a dozen visitors and two uniformed guards, had the feel of a crowded DMV office and a bureaucracy running at a leisurely pace.

She approached the four-foot-high reception desk, where an overweight, job-weary-looking male correctional officer, likely nearing retirement, presented her with a clipboard with two forms attached. "Fill these out and pull out two forms of ID."

Georgia carefully read and completed the forms, specifying who she was and who she intended to visit. Once she produced her valid New York State identification card and an expired passport she never used, the officer read through the forms at an agonizingly slow pace, made a few annotations, and directed, "Take a seat. We'll call your name soon."

During the next half hour, Georgia sized up the other visitors. Most had brought newspapers or books to pass the time—obvious frequent flyers here. The only things she had to read were the government signs lining the trailer walls. They provided no insight into the visitation process but warned of the penalties for bringing contraband into the prison. Given that the staff hadn't yet ushered a single visitor out of the waiting room, it didn't seem like that was much of a likelihood. At this rate the guards' sloth-like speed might well make her miss the last train back to the city when she finished her business here.

Following a full hour-long wait, a younger correctional officer entered the room, his baby face and slim frame screaming recent high school graduate. He buried his nose in a clipboard he'd brought with him and announced several names. Georgia's was among them. He instructed, "Bring only one form of picture ID and no more than seventy-five dollars in cash. All other belongings must be stowed in a locker."

Like a well-trained herd of cattle, the called-up visitors shuffled to the lockers. Georgia stored her purse, minus the required items, and fell in line with the others. The group exited to a hallway where everyone, even the children, underwent a search. Though intrusive in its own way, the pat-down and a run through the metal detector didn't approach the degrading full-body searches she'd read were forced upon prisoners. That was one positive aspect of this otherwise dismal experience.

The baby-faced guard marched the herd up a hill in the wind and heat toward a building a hundred yards away. Signs identified it as the "Main Visitors Center." The challenging conditions winded Georgia, the group's oldest member by far, causing her to lag behind the main gaggle. She considered calling for help, but again, remaining unmemorable was key to her visit, so she pushed on.

When it was her turn to sign in with the desk sergeant, he scanned her forms and entered some information into the computer terminal before looking up. "You're in luck. She was released from isolation yesterday." Georgia simply smiled, keeping her thoughts to herself. What on earth did this woman do to earn a stint in isolation? The sergeant then asked, "Do you want a commissary envelope?"

Georgia had heard stories from parishioners in her church who had family members in prison. They'd explained that while the state provided bare minimum clothing and items for personal care, each prison operated an on-site commissary, selling various preapproved items to brighten a prisoner's otherwise dreary existence. She figured the prospect of potato chips, playing cards, or a bit of mascara might break the ice.

"Yes, please." She completed the form printed on the envelope and placed fifty dollars inside—the maximum allowed per month according to the instructions. The other twenty-five dollars she pocketed.

"Table six." The sergeant gestured toward the middle of the room and the dozen round elementary-school-like tables with four chairs surrounding each one.

Georgia acknowledged with a nod but waited to observe the other visitors. Several, one by one, took a seat at their assigned table, keeping their backs to the correctional officers at the desk. Others lined up at the vending machines to purchase snacks and drinks. When the line dwindled, Georgia bought two soft drinks and a bag of popcorn then sat at her assigned table with her back to the guard. After setting up her goodies, she glanced at the weather-stained, barred windows. They reinforced the oppressive nature of her surroundings and the fact that it was crucial that her plan to take down the Castle family not leave a trail of evidence that linked back to her. She'd rather die in a blaze of glory than spend one day behind bars.

Minutes had passed before a door on the wall opposite the check-in desk opened. Inmates filed in one by one. Spotting their visitors, they would smile, wave, and approach their assigned table. But once the children saw their mother, or who Georgia presumed was their mother, emerge from the inmate door, they darted straight toward her. The guards looked the other way without enforcing the rule forbidding running or contact.

Having never met the prisoner she'd come to visit, Georgia was relying on pictures from the newspaper at the time of her arrest to recognize her. She expected the woman to appear plain and frazzled, of course, compared to the Hollywood red carpet look she sported in the *Times* photos documenting her arrest and prosecution.

The woman Georgia had come to see was the last to emerge through the inmate door. She was dressed in the same dark-green jumpsuit as the other prisoners and appeared confused, scanning the room, clearly searching for someone she might recognize. Georgia stood and waved her arm as if hailing a cab. "Over here."

She gave Georgia a quizzical look, scrunching her brow without a hint of recognition. She sat at the table, facing the guards like the other inmates, and grabbed a can of soda. Taking a big gulp, she ran a green sleeve across her mouth, clearing away the dribble on her chin. "Not that I'm ungrateful for the Coke, but who the hell are you?"

"Now, that's not the proper way to greet your old friend," she replied just as a correctional officer passed by, sticking to her cover story on the forms she'd filled out earlier, where she'd identified herself as a friend of the prisoner. Once the officer moved out of earshot, she continued, "Miss Thatcher, I believe we have a common enemy by the name of Alex Castle. I need your help in giving the woman her just due."

Georgia couldn't be sure if Alex's name caught her attention. Kelly seemed more interested in the bag of vending machine popcorn Georgia had microwaved and placed on the table, eying it as if it were a canteen of fresh water discovered after a week lost in the desert. "Are you going to eat that?" Kelly asked.

Georgia gestured toward the bag. "Help yourself. I wasn't sure what you'd like." After Kelly inhaled a few handfuls, she continued, "Is there something else you would prefer? It's on me."

"Can we look at what they have? You're my first visitor."

"Of course, dear."

Georgia led Kelly to the row of vending machines, where Kelly eyed the offerings like a child scanning a mesmerizing menu of thirty-one ice cream flavors. If Georgia was indeed her first visitor, she'd had nothing but jail and prison food since the night she confessed to a crime that they both had a hand in. That was three years ago.

Kelly stepped forward but came to a screeching halt when a guard yelled, "Inmate, stay behind the black line."

"Let me, dear," Georgia offered. "Just tell me what you want."

Georgia hoped Kelly's choice of empty calories wasn't indicative of her mental acuity. So far, nothing this woman had said or done convinced her she had the wits to contribute to a multifaceted plan such as the one Georgia had concocted. She'd have to call on Kelly's baser instincts to draw her out.

Back at the table, Georgia said, "As I was saying, I have a proposal."

"How do you know Alex?" Kelly's narrowed eyes made her appear skeptical. The speculation in the local rags about her and Alex's stormy relationship, however, had made Georgia confident that it would be a low hurdle to clear.

"I worked at Castle Resorts for thirty-seven years, ever since the door-opening at Times Square."

"And what's your beef with her?"

"She's the reason I lost my job and will soon lose my home."

"So, she's finally turned into her father. They both deserve—" Kelly checked her comment when another guard strolled past their table. If the lip snarl and flushed cheeks were an accurate barometer, the thought of William Castle made Kelly's blood boil, as it did Georgia's.

"So, he manipulated your life as well. He was a master at it." Georgia bit back memories of how William had used her for gratification only to cut her off emotionally and physically when she rightly expected more of him. "I'm here to make sure the business he built suffers along with his undeserving heirs."

Kelly cocked an eyebrow and a corner of her mouth turned upward, broadcasting that Georgia had struck the right chord—revenge. "What do you have in mind?"

The question was exactly what Georgia needed to hear. She had Kelly on the hook. "I've come to possess certain photos of you and Alex." Georgia gauged Kelly's reaction, and Kelly didn't disappoint her. The lack of surprise or confusion meant Kelly was ripe for the pickings. "I see you know what photos I'm referring to. They are quite lovely. As far as what I have in mind, for starters, I was wondering if there were any more current or telling photos."

"What's in it for me?" And there it was. Georgia had successfully tapped into Kelly's base instincts.

"I've heard how bleak conditions can be here. I'd like to make it easier for you."

"I'm listening." If Kelly was trying to appear stone-faced, her penchant for wearing her emotions on her sleeve explained why she was wearing green and Georgia was in her Sunday best.

"I'm sure by now you know of the prison commissary." Georgia paused when Kelly nodded in the affirmative. "I'm prepared to contribute one hundred dollars if you can help me find what I'm looking for. As a show of good faith, I've already added the first fifty to your account."

Kelly stuffed her face with more snacks and took another swig of soda. "There might be something more current and more telling, as you put it, but you said, 'for starters.' What else are you looking for?"

"First things first. Now, about Alex."

"All right. That bitch totally deserves what's coming to her. Alex must have had a hidden camera on her when she came over to my place that night. We had just gotten into things, if you know what I mean, when the cops broke down my door."

"And I assume the police have this tape," Georgia surmised. If the tape was salacious enough, it could pack a more potent punch than a sixteen-year-old set of photographs.

Kelly nodded. "My alleged confession is on that tape because of that bitch."

The video was Georgia's golden ticket, but it was of little use sitting in a police evidence locker. She'd have to figure out a way to get it out of official hands and into hers. In the meantime, she needed a Plan B. "This could be helpful, Kelly, but that tape might be hard to get. Is there anything else you can think of?"

Kelly gobbled down more of her salty and sugary snacks. "Alex wrote me a letter several years ago. In it, she lists every bad thing I ever did to her and every bad thing we did together. In my opinion, she was just whining."

"Do you still have that letter?" Georgia curbed her bursting enthusiasm, hoping she wasn't letting on that this was the bombshell she'd been dreaming of. If she could lay her hands on something that juicy, she could not only bring down Alex Castle a few notches but humiliate her enough to never show her face in public again.

"It's at my mother's house with my other childhood stuff." Kelly hardened her gaze. "Just so you know, if my next fifty doesn't show up in my account on the first of the month, I'm writing Alex a letter about our little discussion here today."

Kelly's fixation on money didn't surprise Georgia in the least. There were two types of people who gravitated toward

Alex Castle—those who had money and those who wanted it. Kelly didn't appear the type who could hold on to a dollar long enough to make a penny in interest.

"Very well. How can I reach your mother?"

Kelly passed along her mother's address before complaining, "She hasn't even visited me and has taken only one of my calls. Something about being too ashamed."

The next item of business that brought Georgia to Bedford Hills would require a bit more finesse. More buttering up was in order. "That's such a shame, dear. A mother should never turn her back on her own flesh and blood." Georgia swallowed hard. She regretted the choices she'd made out of desperation, but she'd done just that, hadn't she? "Now that my business regarding Alex is out of the way, I have one more item to discuss."

"What's that?"

"I read the newspaper accounts of your legal predicament and colorful past. Your work experience might be of some help with another item. I'm looking for someone of flexible morals who might have expertise in the wine or bottling business."

A devilish grin formed on Kelly's lips. "You must have a beef with Syd too."

"I do. Let's just say it's personal."

"I might know someone who has contacts in the beverage business."

"Who is this person and how can I reach them?"

"You make it fifty dollars a month until I'm out of here, and I'll give you his address."

Georgia wasn't about to dip into her savings to pay off this parasite. She'd earmarked that money for something more sinister. It took some haggling, but in the end, she negotiated a deal to get the name and number of her contact in exchange for sending Kelly twenty-five dollars each month. She left out the part where she only intended to pay until her plan worked. After that, she didn't care what Alex found out about her dealings with Kelly. It was a small price to shell out for keeping Kelly silent until Georgia could finally make Alex and Syd pay dearly for ruining her life.

On the southbound Metro train headed for Brooklyn, Georgia calculated that her visit with Kelly had put her in a position to take the next steps to set her plan in motion. Next on her checklist was traveling to Philadelphia to retrieve Alex's letter and to talk to Kelly's contact in the beverage industry. She jotted down the numbers of Kelly's mother and contact as best as she recalled, unconcerned about memorizing them since Kelly mentioned, "They're in the book."

Georgia let a sly grin build, settling into a comfortable position and giving thanks that Kelly Thatcher was a convenient and gullible patsy.

* * *

Philadelphia, Pennsylvania

The chatter of a hundred hungry patrons and the clatter of cutlery scraping across ceramic plates filled the busy café, making it impossible to discern a single thing being said at other tables. It was the perfect setting in which to pitch a plot of revenge that would require that several laws be broken.

Georgia was halfway through her brunch when a man in his thirties with a business cut and three-day stubble stopped at her table.

"Are you Georgia?" he asked.

Georgia wiped the corner of her mouth with a cloth napkin before extending her hand. "You must be Nick Castor."

Nick shook her hand and sat in the chair directly across from her. "You said you have a proposition for me."

A server approached with a coffee carafe and asked Nick, "Can I get you anything?"

"Just coffee." After the server poured him a cup and scurried off, Nick turned his attention to Georgia. "What's this proposition of yours?"

"I believe we both have a common thorn in our side who goes by the name of Alex Castle. I understand she is the reason Indra Kapoor fired you from PopCo and later got you ostracized from gaining a corporate position anywhere in the industry."

Kelly's willingness to fill in the blanks had saved Georgia money and countless hours of research.

Nick sneered. "Alex Castle is the reason I'm hawking entertainment systems at Best Buy instead of pulling in a six-figure salary." The veins in his neck popped a rosy shade brighter.

"I see your dislike for Alex hasn't waned."

"Not in the least," Nick replied with a searing stare. He added several sugar packets and mini creamers to his coffee and sucked it down like it was soda pop. *Ironic*, Georgia thought.

"Lovely. I want to pay her back for ruining my life, just as I suppose you would aspire to do," Georgia said.

"What exactly do you have in mind?"

"Bankrupt the family businesses, humiliate Alex Castle to force her out on her ear, and put an end to her happily ever after."

Nick's slow-forming grin meant she had hooked him. "You have my interest. What do you need me to do?"

"Kelly has helped with a critical piece of the plan. I believe you're familiar with a particular set of compromising photographs." Georgia continued following his affirmative nod. "Well, there's a similarly compromising video."

Nick laughed and slammed his hands on the table. "It's about fucking time Alex Castle got what's coming."

"Humiliation and no more happy family is just half of the plan. You, my friend, have the experience I need to bankrupt her sister's business as well."

"What business is that?"

"Winery. I understand you got your start in the beverage business by inventing an energy drink."

"I did," he said.

"Her sister's winery supplies most of the wine served at every Castle Resort. It's their signature wine. I intend to substitute her highly coveted wines at the eastern resorts with off-the-shelf rotgut and ruin the company's reputation. To make this worth your while, you may keep the original wine and do with it what you will."

"Is this expensive wine?"

Georgia nodded. "Some varieties fetch six hundred dollars a bottle."

"How many bottles and shipments are we talking about?"

"Two shipments, one month apart, totaling four thousand bottles."

"Producing the counterfeit wine is easy enough. My uncle operates a small water bottling company I could access. The cheapest method would be using the existing bottles and replacing the cork and foil seal. Getting access to the original bottles without being caught is the tricky part."

"I worked in Accounting for Castle Resorts for thirty-seven years. I know every supplier, trucking company, and warehouse they use. If you're as resourceful as Kelly made you seem, you should have no trouble greasing the right palms at the warehouse. It's right here in town."

"If it's in Philly, I can make it happen, but it's going to take about twenty grand in startup money."

"The money isn't a problem." Her savings would be well spent taking down the Castles. She'd rather go broke than see Alex and Syd flourish one day longer than necessary. "Right now, I need to know if you're in or out. I want both facets of the plan, bankruptcy and humiliation, to go down simultaneously so Alex won't know what hit her. Deal?"

Nick stuck out his hand and they shook, sealing their partnership.

CHAPTER TWO

Manhattan, New York, 2011

A hundred voices blended, creating a constant loud hum one step into Lara's, Castle Resorts Times Square's newly rebranded restaurant. The full crowd was the sign Alex Castle was looking for. Her business was on the mend, but would it pick up enough worldwide to stem the bleeding of the last several years?

Patrons had packed Lara's, and the wait time for a Friday lunch was over an hour. It had been like this since last week's midweek grand opening. The staff was still working out the kinks, as evidenced by a thundering crash of dishes on the newly laid floor, but the reviews in *The New Yorker* meant her best friend's connection there had paid off in spades.

"This is amazing, Alex," Syd Barnette, Alex's older half-sister, marveled. It had been nearly a year since she was last here, when the restaurant makeover was still in the planning stages. "How in the world did you ever convince Lara Prescott to open a restaurant in the resort?"

"Two words: Harley Spencer."

They followed a trim brunette hostess, dressed in a cropped black tux, to their reserved table with Alex bringing up the rear.

Syd had changed little since last year. Her arms and shoulders were still well-defined from working at the winery. Their eleven-year age gap, though, had finally caught up with her; considerably more gray was cutting through her shoulder-length brown hair.

Along the way to their table, Syd scanned the room to appreciate the restaurant's transformation into a unique five-star establishment which had turned out far better than Alex had envisioned. The room was the perfect blend of modern Italian and Asian design, complementing its featured Italian-Asian fusion cuisine.

Alex sat at her traditional seat at the corner table near the back, expressly reserving the table closest to the kitchen. Its location, with the constant traffic flow to and from the bustling heart of the restaurant, made for the least favorable dining experience in the room, but better the owner and her guests sit there than a customer who was visiting for the first time. Alex turned her head toward the hostess. "Thanks, Terry. Can you let Lara know I'm here?"

"Of course, Ms. Castle." Terry headed back to the kitchen.

"Harley?" Syd ended her question with a curious uptick.

"That's right. She and Lara have been hush-hush about things. They met at Lara's restaurant in London about seven months ago and have been seeing each other ever since."

"You're kidding. Harley dating a woman for more than six weeks? This has to be a first."

Like Alex's, Harley's first love had broken her heart by falling into bed with someone else with more money. They'd both sworn two things as a consequence—to never become the other woman and to never get burned like that again. Alex couldn't blame Harley for her proclivity to savor every drop of a woman for weeks and then let her down gently before things got serious. She didn't fully understand, though, how Harley found the strength to let go time and time again. Doing so would've turned her into a cynic, but not Harley. Alex had remained optimistic that she'd find "the one"—and she had.

"It is a first," Alex agreed. "I couldn't be happier for her. Lara is her perfect match."

"I can't wait to meet her." Syd opened the menu Terry had laid in front of her. "And to sample her food."

The door leading to the kitchen swung open. Lara, a forty-two-year-old redhead dressed smartly in a crisp white chef's uniform, emerged and walked straight to their table. "Alex, I'm glad you made it today."

"Lara, I'd like you to meet my sister, Syd." Alex gestured toward her. "Syd, this is Lara Prescott. She's the one who's been putting a smile on Harley's face for months."

Lara blushed as she shook Syd's hand. "It's a pleasure to put a face to the name. Alex has sung your praises endlessly."

"All exaggeration, I'm sure." Syd winked.

"Are we all set for Monday?" Alex asked Lara.

"I believe so. I'll check on the food we have planned for the party over the weekend. Tyler must be so proud of Erin."

"We both are." Though Erin wasn't her daughter, Alex was as proud of her as if she were. She'd followed in her mother's footsteps in both talent and drive for excellence, as evidenced by her Dean's List mention every semester. "But you're not to lift a finger once you get there. You're our guest. I'd never hear the end of it from Tyler if I had you working at Erin's graduation party."

Lara soon excused herself, returning to her duties in the kitchen. Not long after Alex and Syd ordered, a woman's familiar voice drew Alex's attention. "Sorry I'm late, Alex. Court went longer than expected." Jesse Simmons looked very lawyerly in her best tailored dark-gray suit and perfectly cut collar-length light brown hair without a strand out of place. She looked across the table and added, "Hey, Syd. It's been too long."

Syd gave Jesse one of her signature bear hugs. "It sure has. I haven't seen you since your wedding last year." When they both sat, Syd added, "How's Ethan?"

Picking up the menu, Jesse replied, "He's doing great. His private investigation firm is booming, and he's so excited to see Erin walk across that stage at Yale."

A second familiar voice caught Alex's ear. "There you are, boss."

Alex pivoted toward the voice. Destiny Scott was her chief accountant at Castle Resorts Headquarters, having worked her way up the ranks faster than her predecessors. She'd dug into every company asset during the great recession and found creative ways to come up with cash, including discovering a Brooklyn residential property that Alex's father had purchased forty years ago and kept in the company name. Its sale next month once the city finalized Georgia Cushing's eviction should bring in close to a million dollars. That amount wouldn't solve their problems, but every bit helped. The sale would also have the added benefit of twisting the knife into her father's backstabbing former paramour. She'd nearly tanked Castle Resorts by leaking to the media that Alex had reason to kill her father, and watching her struggle would be the icing on the cake.

Destiny was between Syd's and Alex's age, but she looked younger than Alex. She had been working as an exotic dancer when Alex met her in jail, something that had kept her in top shape. Her skin tone was exotic too, a light brown that suggested Mediterranean roots, as did her long, dark hair and piercing brown eyes. Alex wished she had skin like that, like that of her father, who always tanned so beautifully.

Destiny briefly rested a hand on Alex's shoulder. "I need you to sign this loan paperwork so I can submit it to the bank before the close of business today."

Alex cringed when Syd cocked her head at the word "loan." Like her and John's winery, Castle Resorts needed periodic infusions of money to stay afloat during the recession, but Alex didn't want her sister to know exactly how dire their situation had become. Things were beginning to bounce back but not fast enough yet. Lara's new restaurant would help the bottom line at Times Square but wouldn't come close to offsetting the running deficits at the rest of the resorts.

"Of course, Destiny." Alex briefly palmed her hand. Destiny was still reeling from learning of the death of her estranged mother last Friday, but today appeared less frazzled and more like the put-together woman she'd first met three years ago.

Destiny handed Alex several papers before greeting Syd. "It's nice seeing you again, Mrs. Barnette. I can't thank you enough for taking a chance and moving me up to corporate."

"First, please call me Syd." She paused at Destiny's reluctant nod. "Alex saw something in you back then, and I have to say you haven't disappointed either of us. I didn't stay onboard as acting CEO very long, but I could see right off you were a natural."

Alex signed the papers, patting Destiny on the forearm before returning them. "The bank won't close for hours. Why don't you join us for lunch?"

"I should get back to the office." Destiny's drive had mirrored Alex's; she spent virtually every waking hour putting out fires. Without her help, the company might have shuttered its doors months ago.

"Nonsense." Syd pulled out the fourth chair. "Sit your butt down."

Destiny sat, but not without looking pleased that the Castle sisters had convinced her to stay. Their server returned and took Jesse's order before turning her attention to Destiny.

Destiny asked Alex, "Did you order the Asian-braised short rib sliders and caponata?"

Alex smiled her reply. She and Destiny had sampled several dishes in the weeks leading up to the grand opening, but not that particular entrée and side dish. They were both eager to try them. Destiny turned toward the server. "Make that two."

While the kitchen prepared their food orders, the four women settled into light conversation, focusing primarily on work and family.

Alex turned to Jesse. "Since your firm has the inside track on the Marriage Equality Act introduced in the Assembly earlier this month, what's your take on its chances?" Syd and Destiny looked on with interest as Alex filled them in. "Jesse's firm was hired to draft the legislation Assemblyman O'Donnell introduced, and Jesse is spearheading the legal arguments for its support."

As two servers delivered their meals, Syd said, "Good for you, Jesse. With you behind the scenes of this historic piece of legislation, it's bound to pass yet this year."

"Thanks, Syd. We have momentum on our side. With Massachusetts, Vermont, New Hampshire, Connecticut, and DC paving the way, I honestly believe it has an excellent chance of doing just that."

Syd glanced at Alex, who let a grin grow. "I recognize that look, baby sis. What are you cooking up now?"

Alex reached into her purse and pulled out a distinctive red jewelry box. Her heart beat a little faster when she opened it, exposing the elegant black velvet lining with white lettering spelling out "Cartier." The bottom cradled a stunning engagement ring featuring a brilliant round diamond at the center of a diamond-encrusted halo and diamond accents all along the shank.

"I've had this since 2009 when we thought the Same-Sex Marriage Act was going to pass. As soon as it does, I'm going to ask Tyler to marry me."

All three women whistled their approval. Jesse said, "You certainly have good taste. Why not just marry in a state where it's legal now? New York recognizes out-of-state same-sex marriages."

"I seriously considered proposing a thousand times, but I'm a born and bred New Yorker. It's silly, I suppose, but I want to marry in my home state. Though, if it doesn't pass this time, I might consider it. I don't think I can wait another year."

"It's about time," Syd said. "I bet Father will turn in his grave. Are you going to ask Abby to give you away?"

Alex laughed her agreement. "Definitely. She's been like a mother to me since I was five, ever since Mom died. I wouldn't have it any other way."

Destiny's expression fell, her smile fading. Wincing at her misstep, Alex reached out and placed a hand on top of hers. "I'm so sorry, Destiny. That was insensitive of me. I know this is a tough time for you."

"It's all right, Alex. We weren't particularly close, not since I was eighteen." Destiny turned to the others to explain. "My mother passed away from breast cancer last week."

Syd and Jesse expressed their sympathy through pursed lips.

"She was quite strict when I was growing up," Destiny said. "I couldn't wait to move out. I tried making it on my own for a year, holding down two or three jobs, but I still couldn't make ends meet. That's when I became an exotic dancer. Fast forward sixteen years to when I met Alex in a holding cell and she put me on the fast track at Castle Resorts."

"If you don't mind my prying," Syd said. "If you two weren't that close, I'm guessing something else has you upset."

"Thank you for asking. You're right," Destiny started, arousing Alex's curiosity. Other than sharing the news about her mother's cancer, Destiny rarely had mentioned her over the years. "The night before she died, my mother told me I was adopted." She grimaced. "I hadn't a clue. The thought that another woman gave birth to me and that I have no idea who she is has me rattled."

Alex reached out again. "Do you want to find her?"

Destiny's expression brightened, but then her shoulders slumped as if the idea defeated her before it had gotten off the ground. "I'd like to, but I have no idea where to start."

"If I weren't so busy with this legislation, I'd help you," Jesse said. "But my husband is a private investigator. He finds people for a living."

"And he's an excellent one at that," Alex said. "If anyone could solve this mystery, Ethan Falling could."

Jesse continued, "I'm sure he'd be willing to help you get started."

Following a quick exchange of phone numbers, Syd leaned over to Alex, asking, "Could you ask your staff to bring us some of our 2008 cabernet? John and I had it delivered several weeks ago. It should be in storage waiting for its official release this weekend."

"Of course." Alex got Terry's attention. She promptly returned with four glasses and a bottle of the requested wine. The server first offered a sample to Alex. She sipped but expected a completely different taste. It was missing the hints of blueberries, cedar, and dark chocolate from the first time she tasted it at Syd's home. Instead, the wine had a distinct sharpness, and she thought she recognized the faint taste of oak and maybe plum. Overall, the wine was lifeless, without character—nothing like a Barnette vintage should taste. It reminded her of the Two Buck Chuck bottle Tyler once had her try in California. Alex inspected the glass, narrowing her eyes. If memory served her correctly, the wine she just tasted was ten times worse.

"Do you mind?" Syd handed her glass to the server and then sampled the small pour. Her lips pursed in clear disappointment. "Show me the bottle." She inspected the bottle the server handed her, giving the contents a long sniff. "Something is wrong with this wine." She turned her attention to Alex. "You need to pull every bottle in every hotel until we can sort this out."

"What's going on, Syd?" Not since their father's death had Alex seen her sister this upset.

"I don't know. It doesn't taste spoiled, just inferior, like a cheap table wine."

Alex read the alarm on Syd's face and in her voice. This was serious. Like Castle Resorts, Barnette Winery had been bleeding money since the beginning of the recession, and Alex doubted it could survive a disaster. Once word got around about the substandard quality, stores and wholesalers would demand a refund. Sales of the Barnette premiere blend would promptly drop to nothing. That would force Syd and John to drop their unit price on the next vintage release to coax buyers back.

The future of the Barnette Winery appeared bleak. This was a disastrous convergence, forming the perfect storm. When the 2008 cabernet testing had shown it was their best wine in a decade, Syd and John had created a buzz around it, resting the lot of their winery on it. If this vintage didn't pay off, this could be the final nail in the coffin and force the Barnette Winery to shutter its operations.

Alex rested a comforting hand on her sister's. "Whatever happened, we'll get to the bottom of this together."

CHAPTER THREE

An inviting wave of garlic and oregano floated through the air, wafting from the kitchen to the main room of Alex and Tyler's home. It drew murmurs from the two dozen partygoers there to celebrate Erin's Yale graduation.

After relocating to William Castle's Fifth Avenue mansion in 2007, Alex and Tyler had transformed it into a cozy home, blending both their decorating tastes. Every piece was functional, which pleased Tyler, yet each room had a warm, welcoming feeling, which pleased Alex. But it was Harley's critical eye for paintings and sculptures that truly brought each room to life. The month Alex and Tyler spent visiting small, out-of-the-way galleries on weekends with Harley, scavenging for the right pieces, had the added effect of reviving Alex's appreciation for art. It had brought her more satisfaction than the years she'd spent at the helm of Castle Resorts, planting some interesting thoughts about what she might do in the future, should it become necessary.

"Great party, baby sis." Syd sidled up to Alex's flank, nursing a glass of 2008 Barnette cabernet from Alex's private stock.

"You should compliment Tyler. She planned everything." That realization gnawed at Alex's conscience. She should have pried herself away from the office long enough to help in some small measure. Well, she couldn't remedy that now. She could, however, help her sister. She held her glass next to Syd's. "How is it that my bottles of cabernet are just fine?"

"I sent those out to you personally, not through the shipping company we use for Castle Resorts."

"Do you think we should ask for Ethan's help in this? He's going with Destiny to track down her birth parents in Massachusetts tomorrow, but I'm sure he'd be happy to help after he returns."

"Not yet," Syd said. "We don't know the extent of it. It may just be a transportation issue. John wants to talk to the trucking company after he returns to Napa tomorrow. Since I'm staying until the state releases Andrew from prison later this week, I'll use my time here to check the supplies at the other resorts."

At the mention of Andrew's name, Tyler appeared and rubbed the small of Alex's back. The show of affection was well-timed but failed to stave off the emotion collecting at the back of Alex's throat. The last time she'd seen her brother was at his court pleading four years ago for embezzling from Castle Resorts. The cold, steely look he gave her as the officer had whisked him away to begin his five-year sentence was sharp and heartbreaking. It was as if they were never brother and sister, never twins, but she'd expected nothing less from him.

She'd once pitied Andrew over their father's favoritism, but his excessive jealousy had gotten out of control. Trying to buy Kelly's blackmail photos to use against Alex and then pointing the finger at her to the police following their father's death were cruel acts. However, his swiping of their mother's Leica camera, Alex's most cherished memory of her, a decade ago at their father's bidding, was indefensible. It was too much to forgive or to attempt mending fences while he was in prison. It had been three years, and Alex had yet to figure out how she felt about her twin. His parole next week and the likelihood of seeing him again meant she needed to decide if reconciling was even a possibility.

John approached, rubbing his belly, with his cousin, Ethan, by his side. "Mmm. Everything smells good."

Ethan popped a strawberry in his mouth and swallowed before replying, "Wait until you taste it."

"That good?" John asked.

"Better," Ethan replied. "Lara Prescott is a culinary genius. She does this fusion thing with Italian and Asian that is out of this world."

When Alex heard Lara's name, she scanned the room. She located Harley but not Lara. The two were usually attached at the hips these days, so wherever Lara had disappeared to, it must have to do with something she loved as much as Harley—cooking. She gently squeezed Tyler's hand and kissed her on the cheek. "I'm going to make sure Lara isn't knocking herself out in the kitchen."

Tyler looked around the room before narrowing her right eye. "Drag her out of there if you have to."

Alex offered a military-like salute. "Yes, ma'am."

On her way to the kitchen, Alex whispered into Harley's ear, "Your woman better not get me into trouble today."

Harley rolled her eyes and locked arms with Alex. "Let's ensure she doesn't."

When Alex and Harley entered the kitchen, Lara was at the state-of-the-art oven, pulling out a fresh batch of the main entrée and giving her two-person staff last-minute instructions. Once Lara put the hot baking dish on the granite countertop, Harley sneaked up behind her, wrapped her arms around her slim waist, and said loud enough for Alex to hear, "Darling, if you don't let your staff do their job, Alex will be forced to sleep alone on the couch tonight."

Sadly, Harley didn't know that of late a version of sleeping alone had become an unintended consequence of Alex's excessive work hours. Too many nights in the last six months, she had arrived home late from work to find Tyler asleep. More often than not, she'd opted to slip into her side of the bed without curling up to Tyler, who was a light sleeper. In fact, she couldn't remember the last time they went to bed at the same time and did more than give each other a kiss goodnight.

"I just need to—"

Lara started to defend her need to oversee every detail of the food preparation, but Harley slid her hands down Lara's outer thighs and huskily replied, "The only thing you need to do right now is to kiss me."

Lara stopped fussing with the food on the counter and released a moan before turning to press her lips against Harley's. She deepened the kiss, caressing Harley's cheeks and making Alex feel like a voyeur.

Alex cleared her throat with the subtlety of one of Cher's stage get-ups—loud and attention-getting. "I'm sorry to break this up, but I have orders to drag you out of here if necessary."

Lara broke away. "I'm sorry, Alex. I wanted to try out a new cheese blend on the lasagna rolls for Erin. She should love them."

Alex understood Lara's drive and her unwillingness to loosen the reins with work. She was the same way. Since taking over as CEO of Castle Resorts, she focused all her energy on making the company better than it was when her father was in control. So, like Lara, she spent many long hours at the office, especially throughout the tough, lean years during and following the global financial crisis.

Harley tugged on the belt loops on either side of Lara's hip huggers and said in a determined voice, "Bailey and Grace are more than capable of handling things from here. It's time to go, beautiful."

Following Lara's sullen sigh, Harley led her out of the sleek kitchen with Alex following closely behind. Lara commented, "I love your kitchen, Alex," when they entered the hallway leading to the main room. "It's a chef's dream."

Once in the room, Alex replied, "It is, isn't it? It was mostly Tyler's touch. She insisted on high-tech functionality."

Harley added, "You two did a fantastic job. It looks nothing like it did when William was alive. And the art pieces you picked out pulled it all together."

While successful at stripping away the visual reminders of her father, the house's transformation failed to bury the memory of him. Perhaps it was the daily reminder of living in a place in which he took so much pride. Today was particularly difficult. Despite a house full of guests celebrating Tyler's oldest daughter's college graduation, Alex still felt echoes of her father's presence. Memories of her own graduation party lingered within these walls, as did the thought of the gift William had given her that day—her old West Village townhouse, now owned by Ethan and Jesse. She missed the coziness of that old house and the personal touches she'd added to it, but she never regretted moving here. She was with Tyler, and that was all that mattered.

Tyler looked up when she heard Alex's and Harley's compliments on the renovation, relieved that Lara had emerged from the kitchen and would finally enjoy herself as a guest. Holding her tongue on the subject, she said, "We can't take all the credit, babe. Indra was a great help in many of the design decisions. She has such a great eye."

"I couldn't agree more," Abby chimed in, handing Indra a small plate of her favorite hors d'oeuvres. "Her personal touches have made our home warm and cozy." Abby gave Indra a light yet intimate kiss on the lips. "Thank you."

"Do you miss the city?" Jesse asked.

Without a hint of hesitation, Abby said, "Not one bit. Greenwich is my home now. And now that Harley has taken over the foundation and my old penthouse, the only occasion I find myself on the busy streets of Manhattan is for special celebrations such as this one for our young Erin."

"Thanks, Abby." Erin smiled. "The time I spent with you and Indra at the estate the last four years has meant a lot to me. I consider you two the grandparents I never had."

"We're quite fond of you, young lady," Indra said. "We hope you'll continue popping by the occasional weekend during grad school. Otherwise, Moonlight might miss you."

"Count on it."

Tyler recalled the few times she and Alex joined Erin and her girlfriend at the Greenwich estate on the weekend, riding horses, swimming, and picnicking at the pond. She needed more weekends like that with Alex. But how could she convince her of it? Keeping Castle Resorts afloat had her singularly focused for months, even years.

Bailey and Grace served the lasagna rolls Erin was so fond of, along with several other hot dishes they'd prepared according to Lara's instructions. Erin grabbed her girlfriend, Connor Edwards, by the hand and dragged her to the food table. "Ooohhh, lasagna rolls."

Laughing, Jesse shook her head at Ethan and John, who were racing each other to the table. The competition between the two was one Tyler had witnessed for decades.

"Those guys and food. You'd never know they ate a few hours ago," Jesse said.

Syd laughed. "You've barely gotten a dose of those two. Wait until you've been married to one of them for seven years. You'll become immune to their antics."

Jesse raised her wineglass until Syd clinked it with hers. "Only six to go."

"Wait until you get to eighteen." Tyler smiled, leaned in, and said just loud enough for Jesse to hear, "If you ever want to put either of those two in their place, ask about Francis Boyle."

Jesse gave Tyler a curious look. "Who's Francis Boyle?"

Having never heard the entire story, Tyler shrugged. "I'm not sure. All I know is that she grew up with them, and whenever either of them mentions her name, the other gets that 'don't you dare' look and clams up."

"Good to know." Jesse's sly grin was clearly her way of tucking it away for future leverage.

Tyler did a double take. Those three words were her ex-husband's signature response. "Ethan must be rubbing off on you." She smiled again. "You sound like him."

Jesse smiled. "It must be love."

Ethan walked up behind Jesse, wrapping an arm around her waist before kissing her on the cheek. "It sure is."

Seeing those two happy and in love made Tyler nostalgic for a time before Castle Resorts took over Alex's life. Alex had been spending virtually every waking minute staying on top of the markets and suppliers to keep her company afloat, not for her sake, but for the eleven thousand employees counting on her leadership. Unfortunately, her dedication had come at a cost. Love was still there, but instead of feeling it in Alex's daily kiss and touch, Tyler had to find it most days in a call, FaceTime, or text message. To her credit, Alex had become a master at expressing love and seduction over those mediums. Still, all Tyler wanted was to fall asleep next to her every night and to have Alex staring lovingly at her when she opened her eyes.

Connor interrupted Tyler's reminiscing with a youthful quip. "Tell it like it is, Mr. F." She wrapped an arm around Erin's waist and kissed her on the cheek. "It sure is love."

Tyler enjoyed seeing the blush on Erin's cheeks, especially after what she'd been through. She marveled again at how the two had met. For her junior year, Erin, who was majoring in graphic design, had enrolled in an upper-level humanities class, something she'd done based on Alex's recommendation that it would help her to better understand human behavior. That was where Erin met Connor, and they'd dated since.

Bree, busy on her new iPhone, looked up from the couch in time to see both couples kiss. "Ewww! Get a room, guys."

Entertained by Bree's discomfort, Tyler played along. She walked up beside Alex, wrapped an arm around her waist, and kissed her on the cheek. "Sure is."

Alex's iPhone buzzed. She pulled it from her hip pocket, looking at the number on the screen. The deflated look on her face meant it was work. Again. She pecked Tyler on the cheek and said, "I have to take this." She swiped the screen to accept the call and walked toward the hallway. "Gretchen…"

Tyler let out a sigh when Alex left. That damn cell phone of hers had triggered too many sighs lately. Every time they'd set aside an hour or two of family time, that phone would ring, and something at work inevitably pulled her away.

Ethan maneuvered beside Tyler but remained silent. She knew what he was up to. He was gauging her mood. But even she wasn't sure if she was angry or fed up.

He finally broke his silence. "I can't blame her. Castle Resorts almost went under last year. Thousands of families would have been affected if she didn't work her ass off."

"Well, she's affecting *this* family," Tyler said, a bit of an edge to her voice, thinking of the many family dinners and softball games Alex had missed over the past year. "It's like she feels the weight of the world on her shoulders and can't focus on anything else."

"She doesn't trust anyone enough to delegate things to." Leave it to Ethan to cut through the crap and get to the core of an issue. That was what made him an excellent investigator.

"How do I fix that?" Tyler asked.

"You don't. Alex does," he said bluntly. "Talk to her, Tyler. She may not realize how much she's missing out on or how much her absence bothers you."

Tyler sighed again, realizing she had resorted to her old ways, bottling up her emotions instead of dealing with them. She'd kept silent on the subject far too long. "You're right, Ethan. You're always right."

"Being told that never gets old." Ethan rubbed his hands together in a satisfying motion. "My work is done here."

Before Ethan could rejoin his wife, Bree had ripped herself away from her iPhone long enough to approach her parents. "Hey, Mom. Dad. Before you say 'no,' hear me out."

Bree's choice of words made it easy for Tyler to forecast what this was about. Bree had turned sixteen last week. Tyler had expected for months that she'd bring up the topic, though she'd secretly hoped that their living in Manhattan would have diminished her interest. She stared stone-faced at her daughter, waiting for the bombshell to drop.

"I want to get my driver's license." Bree paused as if gauging her parents' response. A glance toward Ethan confirmed Tyler's suspicion. No shake of the head. No smile. Not a thing. Just awkward silence, neither of them offering her an answer.

Bree glanced over to her stepmother. Jesse gave her an encouraging nod and mouthed the words, "Go ahead."

Bree nodded back before returning her attention to her parents. "Let me make my case," she started with a shaky voice. She raised a hand and counted with her fingers as she made each supporting point.

"First, just because I live in Manhattan and primarily use the subway to get around doesn't automatically mean I don't need a driver's license. Second, with a license, I could drive myself to Greenwich on weekends for my weekly riding lesson at Abby and Indra's instead of making you drive me. Third, since you allowed Erin to get her license at sixteen, it is only fair that I'm allowed the same privilege. Fourth, I'm very responsible, as evidenced by my completed weekly chores at home and straight A's at school. Lastly, I've already studied for the permit test and scheduled an appointment for Thursday if you'll take me."

Bree took a deep breath. Her and Jesse's matching smiles explained how it was that she was so well-prepared to plead her case so eloquently. The two thumbs-up Bree flashed toward Jesse and the returned wink and Jesse mouthing, "Good job," confirmed it.

Tyler was stunned. She'd never been prouder of her daughter. Never had Bree expressed herself so clearly and concisely and defended her desire for something. At that moment, despite the obvious coaching she'd received from Jesse, Tyler knew she and Ethan had done their jobs as parents. They'd raised this girl to be strong, confident, and well-spoken. A very proud moment, indeed.

A few moments of awkward silence passed.

Tyler broke the silence with a single word. "Okay."

Ethan added, "But I'm taking you."

"Thank you, thank you, thank you," Bree shouted, hugging her mom and dad. She turned on her heel and did a double fist pump in victory as she returned to the couch and her iPhone. Jesse was all smiles.

After taking that vital business call that couldn't wait, Alex emerged from the hallway and returned to Tyler's side. "Sorry, T. I hope I didn't miss much."

Tyler came short of tossing Alex a glare but refused to hold her tongue any longer. "You missed a lot." She used a tight tone to send the message that something was wrong, or, more to the point, that Alex shouldn't have left in the first place. Tyler surprised herself. She'd never been that brusque with Alex, but it had to be done.

Alex stared into Tyler's eyes. Tyler tightened her lips to send the right message—she was angry and fed up. In return, Alex's eyes sent a note of remorse. She rubbed Tyler's arms. "How can I make it up to you?"

Tyler finally summoned up her courage to tell Alex what needed saying for nearly a year, "It's not just me you have to make things up to. It's everyone in this room."

Alex slumped and her mouth closed in humble submission. Perhaps she too missed spending not just quality time but any uninterrupted time with her partner. At least that was what Tyler hoped.

Alex stared into Tyler's eyes for several more silent moments, making clear how deep her regret ran. Alex's eyes moistened. "I'm so sorry, T. I know I've been the worst partner and friend lately." She ran a thumb across Tyler's cheek when a single tear trickled down it. "We need to get back on track."

Tyler nodded in painful agreement. "Yes, we do."

After the tension had passed, Harley came up beside Alex, holding a glass of wine and grinning between sips. She whispered so only Alex could hear, "Are we all set for tonight?"

Alex nodded with a sly grin. "We leave after dark."

CHAPTER FOUR

Yale University, New Haven, Connecticut

The sun had gone to bed hours ago, and the historic Ivy League campus was awash with artificial light. At nearly midnight on graduation night, the campus was still buzzing with activity, but mostly inside the dorms. The conditions were perfect for traditional senior pranks. And two alumni stood ready to help two seniors carry on the long Yale tradition of Morse Residential College residents.

Four slim figures, all dressed in dark clothing, weaved their way on foot through the streets, careful to stay as much as possible out of the reach of the bright white lights that lit up the roads and pathways in the newer and remodeled sections of campus, and the warm amber ones that illuminated buildings in the older area—their destination.

The youngest of the four had strapped on her a small backpack filled with the items that had been carefully crafted for tonight's mischief. Once the covert group passed the corner of College and Chapel Streets, it peeled off to a dimly lit walkway bisecting Bingham Hall and Welch Hall. At that corner, their target came into view, out in the open and not fifteen feet away.

They paused.

Connor removed the pack from her back, unzipped the middle compartment, and handed an item to each of the older cohorts.

"Connor, you lift me up on your shoulders so I can get the top," directed Erin. Connor was by far the strongest of the four. Years on the Yale crew team had left her incredibly fit and able to lift any of the other women. "Alex, you cover the middle. Harley, you get the base."

All three checked off with "Got it." Erin was in charge of this little caper; that much was clear. She had planned it well, down to learning the customary timing of campus security guards.

The campus police were out in full force, on the lookout for the inevitable senior pranks. The mischievous foursome would have to be quick and work as a well-trained team, each completing her task in less than a minute.

Erin waited for a police officer on foot patrol to stroll past Connecticut Hall, where the target sat a few yards off its corner. When the coast was clear, she ordered, "Let's go."

With laser-like precision, the four women sprang into action. Within seconds they were at the foot of Yale's most treasured monument, the statue of Nathan Hale, Revolutionary War hero and beloved graduate of the university.

Connor crouched down to allow Erin to climb onto her shoulders. When she used her arms to secure Erin's legs tight against her chest, Connor suggested in a low husky tone, "We should try this position in reverse."

Erin giggled.

"Try it against a wall," Harley said. "You'll love it."

Alex, ever the taskmaster, said, "Ladies, there's no time for that now. Focus."

After Connor snorted her "sorry," Alex, the tallest, took charge of installing the custom-made running shorts, which were cut down the side seams with Velcro attached to enable it to be fastened around the statue. Her task took seconds, freeing her up to monitor the others.

Connor carefully plodded toward the statue, giving Erin access to its top. Erin clumsily draped a men's navy blue track team tank top with the traditional white "Y" on the front and the number eleven blazoned on the back over Hale's head. She then shimmied the fabric down to cover the statue's torso. For her final task, she placed a dark blue and white headband over Hale's brow to complete the look.

Simultaneously, Harley installed a pair of running sneakers, stripped of their soles, with ankle straps added to the back.

A loud, melodic tone sounded from Alex's jacket pocket just as everyone had completed their covert tasks. It was the familiar custom ringtone she had assigned to Castle Resorts in Hong Kong. "Shit!" Alex stabbed her hand into her pocket to fish out her phone.

Connor jerked at the sudden noise, and Erin rocked atop her shoulders. Erin cried out, "Whoa!"

"For heaven's sake, Alex," Harley fussed. "Shut that damn thing off."

As Alex silenced her phone, the security officer who had passed by moments earlier had doubled back, appearing from the corner of Connecticut Hall at top speed. He shined his flashlight toward the statue, spotlighting the four accomplices. He'd caught them red-handed. The Morsel tradition of dressing up Nathan Hale in Yale apparel would not be successful this year.

"Stop right there," he ordered.

"Fuck." Harley raised her hands in the air to surrender.

Alex and Erin followed suit, while Connor had no choice but to hold on to Erin's legs. Alex glanced at the two youngest ladies. Both had panicked expressions. Conversely, Harley, who had gotten herself out of worse brushes with the law in her youth, didn't appear the least bit concerned. Alex was angry at herself. *How could I have forgotten to mute my phone?*

The officer approached, shining his light on them one at a time. He pointed to Erin and Connor first. "You two I get." He then shined the light at Alex and Harley. "But you two. Aren't you a little old for this stuff?"

Harley couldn't hold it in and laughed. Erin and Connor followed up with snickers.

They'd offended Alex. Well, sort of. She wasn't forty yet and had kept in great shape. "I am not that old." The others snickered again.

The officer looked Alex up and down again. "You're certainly acting like you're not." Everyone but Alex laughed. He shifted the beam toward Erin. "Get down, young lady. You're all coming with me."

Two hours later, all four women were lined up along a wall in the Yale Police Station lobby, sitting in uncomfortable plastic chairs. Occasionally, a police officer walked past, but none gave a hint of how much longer they'd have to wait.

The phone call Alex had made after their detention kept her and Harley relaxed. Experienced at situations like this from their youth, they were familiar with how the Ivy League dealt with infractions of this ilk. Connor and Erin were a different story. As far as Alex knew, neither had previous encounters with campus police. And their nonstop nervous twitching and knee bouncing meant they had assumed the worst—Yale wouldn't let them into grad school and they would have a police record for the rest of their lives.

Erin finally broke the silence. "What are we going to tell Mom, Alex? She's going to kill me."

Alex narrowed an eye and replied, "We tell her nothing."

"Nothing?"

Alex leaned back in her chair, crossed her arms behind her head, and closed her eyes before answering, "Trust me. We say nothing."

Harley grinned, leaned back in her chair, and joined Alex in a catnap.

Another hour had passed when the police station's tempered glass doors swung open to a familiar voice. "Where might I find your lieutenant?"

Alex cracked an eye open and snickered.

The desk sergeant replied, "Who are you, ma'am?"

"Abigail Spencer. I believe President Nevil called ahead."

"I'll get my lieutenant."

The moment the desk sergeant disappeared into a back office, Abby shot Alex and Harley the patented glare that had left countless Manhattan elite quaking in their oxfords. Alex simply grinned, though faintly.

Minutes later, the sergeant returned with his superior. The lieutenant rested his hands atop his gear belt and addressed Abby. "Good morning, Mrs. Spencer. I'm sorry to make you come all this way in the middle of the night, but President Nevil was specific as to how we released them into your custody."

"I understand. I assume everything is in order."

"Yes, ma'am. We won't file a report so long as Miss Falling and Miss Edwards keep their noses clean next academic year."

"I assure you they will." Abby looked over her shoulder at the gang of miscreants, prompting Alex to glance down the line as well. While Harley matched Alex's smile, the younger two appeared sheepish. Alex couldn't blame them. This marked the first time Abby Spencer had had to come to a police station at the middle of the night to get them out of a jam. Unfortunately, Alex couldn't say the same for her and Harley.

On their way out, Alex first shook the sergeant's hand, followed by the lieutenant's. "Call my office anytime and let me know when you want to book those reservations. Dinner is on me."

"You got it, Alex." The lieutenant winked. "Stay out of trouble."

"You got it, Dave."

All the women filed out to the parking lot and into Abby's town car. Once Richard drove off, navigating the streets of New Haven in search of Alex's car, Alex asked Abby, "How much?"

Abby replied, "Ten thousand—from each of you." That was the personal donation amount she'd apparently negotiated with Yale President Nevil to expunge all record of the night's misguided escapade. Alex and Harley laughed. Two simple donations to the university would take care of the harmless matter.

Erin and Connor still appeared nervous. Alex patted Erin on the knee. "Don't worry. It's all taken care of."

Erin, along with Connor, let out a long sigh. "Thank God. I thought they might not let us start grad school in the fall."

"You just stay out of trouble next year, and it's like this never happened," Alex said.

Erin mouthed "thank you" before turning her attention to the woman who bailed them out of trouble. "I'm sorry about all of this, Abby. It won't happen again."

"I'm sure it won't, my dear," Abby said in a firm tone. Clearly, she wasn't happy. "Though, you owe me for my troubles tonight." Erin and Connor gulped hard. "You will muck out the stalls at our Greenwich stables this weekend." Abby paused when Alex and Harley chuckled. "Along with your two other cohorts in crime. I'll expect all of you first thing Saturday morning."

Erin and Connor humbly replied, "Yes, ma'am."

Harley slapped Alex on the arm when she laughed at Abby's way of getting her loved ones together at the estate while appearing to be stern. "What are you laughing at?" she asked playfully. "It's your fault the campus bumpkins caught us. It's called a mute button, Alex."

Alex sheepishly glanced over to Erin and Connor. "I'm sorry, girls. I completely forgot to silence my phone."

"Business, I take it." Abby shook her head at Alex's forgetful misstep. If *she* had noticed how Alex had been working too many hours and not spending enough time with family and friends, then Alex definitely had to change her ways. It was only a matter of time before her workaholic pattern would irrevocably damage her family life.

Alex nodded in the affirmative.

"My dear Alex," Abby said. "Please learn from an old woman who made that same mistake. No job is worth sacrificing your family."

Alex recalled the charged discussion she and Tyler had earlier in the evening. It was along the same lines. "I'm realizing that, Abby. I know I've taken on way too much and have already put some thought into cutting back. But if I want to avoid chaos, it's going to take some time to extricate myself."

"Don't take too long," Abby replied.

CHAPTER FIVE

Queens, New York

Today marked the last time Andrew Castle would trek down the spotless stairwell of Queensboro Correctional Facility to the fourth-floor counselor's office. It was two flights down from the residential floor, his transitional home for the last five weeks, pending parole. The barracks-style housing unit to which the staff had assigned him was a dream compared to the crowded two-man cell he'd lived in for the previous four years. Fishkill, a medium-security prison one hour north of Manhattan, was nothing like Attica or Sing Sing, but it was packed with career criminals, gangbangers, and drug addicts with several soft, white-collar first-timers, like Andrew, thrown into the mix. Here and at Fishkill, he'd had to learn, and in a hurry, the lay of the land, especially the practices related to protection and earning special privileges.

His stints at both prisons were both humbling and transformational. Many prisoners walked away from prison hardened; it was only a matter of time before they returned. Andrew fell into another category. That was the assessment at least of his counselors at both facilities.

* * *

Fishkill Correctional Facility, New York, July 2007

Weekends at Fishkill meant that the friends and families of dozens, and sometimes hundreds, of prisoners would soon fill the visitors' room. This Saturday afternoon Andrew Castle was meeting with the first visitor he'd received since his incarceration six weeks ago.

The guard's baton knock against his cell door surprised him. "Castle, you have a visitor." Andrew had no real friends to speak of, especially none who would go out of their way to visit him in prison. And his only family, sisters Syd and Alex, were still angry at him for what he had done to earn himself five years behind bars, fewer if he kept his nose clean.

"Who is it?" Andrew asked.

"What do I look like, an information booth? Are you taking the visit or not?" Smarting off, Andrew knew, could not only cost him the visit but also earn him a week in isolation. So he swallowed his opinion and replied, "Sure."

The visitors' room was filled mostly with men, some of them inmates and some of them visitors, a few women, and a dozen or so children. The chatter droned, making every conversation indistinguishable. As he walked down the center aisle, his eyes scanned each table, looking for someone he recognized. Finally, in the far corner, he spotted Syd, not with a smile on her face but a stern look of displeasure. He closed the distance between them, stood at the table's edge for a few beats to stare her in the eye. Her expression changed little. If anything, it got harder. He took a seat directly across before saying his first words to her since his arrest. "It's good to see you, Syd."

Syd shook her head in overwhelming disapproval, appearing to choke back one emotion after another. She opened her mouth, but words didn't come out.

Andrew remained quiet. The only thing waiting for him was a cold cell with a not-so-friendly cellmate. Suffice it to say, he was in no hurry to end this unexpected and, to his surprise, welcome visit.

Syd had searched his eyes. What was she looking for? Remorse? Shame? She was wasting her time because he had none. Andrew was still angry at ending up in prison. He was sure his father had had a great deal to do with his embezzlement coming to light, but he also suspected Alex might have tipped off the police to save her hide during the murder investigation.

"Do you have any regrets?" Syd finally asked.

"I regret being born into a fucked-up family."

Syd shook her head in trademark Castle disapproval, only more definitive this time. "Typical. Blame someone else for your shortcomings. Will you ever take responsibility for your own actions?"

"I did when I signed the plea agreement."

"Not even close. You saved your ass from a longer sentence, plain and simple."

"Look, if you came here to rip me a new one, give it your best shot. Take as long as you want. You got me out of working the laundry today." He leaned back in his chair, lifted his arms behind his head, interlacing his fingers. He was arrogant, but to survive in this place, he had to be. If Syd came here looking for him to make amends, she'd leave empty-handed.

"Put your damn arms down and knock that smug look off your face," she ordered.

And there it was. Andrew prepared for Syd to give it to him with both barrels. "Andrew, you're a disappointment." "Andrew, you should be ashamed of yourself." "Andrew, you'll never be good enough." His father had hammered all those things into him the night he died. He slowly lowered his arms and sat upright in his chair, though, to avoid attracting the guards' attention.

Syd's expression softened. "I love you, and I always will, but you're better than this. Yes, we had a father who had evolved into a controlling, manipulative hypocrite, but that is not a license to be reckless and cavalier with those who love you. If you hold the hope of having a relationship with Alex and me, you better start making some significant life changes because we won't put up with your crap forever. For starters, no more gambling.

Second, while you're not a classic alcoholic, you abuse alcohol. That must change. Prison can be a lonely place. If you want me to come back, you'll get counseling while you're here. I'll only visit again if a counselor tells me you're making progress."

Andrew wasn't expecting Syd's softer side and didn't know how to react or think. Finally, following a long silence, he asked, "Are you done?"

"I guess so," she replied.

Without another word, Andrew stood and walked away.

* * *

January 2008

The Fishkill infirmary was small, with only six beds for sick or injured inmates. Andrew had learned from the intake nurse that January had drawn its fair share of flu victims, the result of the traditional influx of visitors over the holidays. Indeed, five beds of the six held flu patients. Andrew was occupying the sixth one while being treated for injuries sustained during a beating he had taken while working in the laundry facility. Two cracked ribs, a broken nose, and a concussion had earned him a three-day stay.

While the medical staff tended to the sick patients with broth and crackers for dinner, a trustee set up a food tray for Andrew that contained a sandwich and vegetables from the prison cafeteria. The trustee whispered so as to not attract attention from the staff, "I got a message from the Dealer: Pay up."

This was the second time the Dealer had sent his not-so-subtle message. Andrew was into the prison game-maker for several thousand, and his payment was overdue. His ten-million-dollar trust fund and the four-hundred million dollars he'd banked after Alex bought his shares of Castle Resorts were sitting safely in an investment account, so he had the money. That wasn't the problem. It would take only one phone call to make good on his debt, but he couldn't get to it for a week. He cursed himself for getting into a prison yard fight before

Christmas, something that had earned him four weeks without privileges, including making phone calls.

Andrew was in over his head and, for the first time since his imprisonment, scared for his life. He flinched, imagining too easily a shiv piercing between his ribs. "Ow," he groaned, pressing a hand to his injured side to ease the pain. "He'll get the money. I get my phone privileges back next week."

"One week," the trustee said and walked out.

Andrew winced again when he shifted to inspect his food. He couldn't be too careful at this point. The absence of gravel or human shit hidden between the slices of bread was a good sign that he had yet to burn every bridge in prison. He nibbled a corner.

"Andrew Castle, right?" He looked up at the sound of his name.

Whoever the guy standing there was, he was prison staff, dressed in business casual. Andrew replied, "Yeah."

"I'm Gary Roman. I'm a counselor here." The tattoos on his arms and neck, though, made him look more like an inmate than a counselor. He sat on the corner of the bed and continued, "Do you mind if we talk for a minute?"

"As if I have a choice in the matter." Andrew threw him his best stone-cold stare, telling Gary he would not be cooperative.

"We always have a choice. How about I talk, and you listen?"

Andrew shrugged. The less he said, the sooner this would be over.

"Guys like you find themselves in prison for many reasons, but the one thing all of you have in common is that you're not here by accident. And sadly, a lot of you, yourself included, could have avoided being sent here with the right intervention. I know you're back to gambling again." Andrew shifted in his bed, wincing when Gary pointed at his bandages. "Those broken ribs tell me so. I've helped many guys just like you, and I think I can help you too. When you're ready to make a change, real change, come see me."

With that, Gary patted Andrew on the knee and walked out.

The Dealer had Andrew scared, but mostly, he was angry. Angry at his father, angry at Alex, angry at Kelly, angry at Victor, and, yes, he could finally admit it, angry at himself. Unable to choke back the idea that he'd put himself here, he felt a lump form in his throat. *I'm so fucked up*, he thought. Something had to change. If it didn't, he'd have to do the next five years in fear.

Within a week, Andrew arranged for the Dealer to receive his money. A week after that, he broke his routine of joining the rest of his cell block in the rec room for TV and knocked on the office door of Gary Roman. He was curious about the man who had recognized during a two-minute, one-sided talk in the infirmary that he was at a crossroads following the severe beating.

Gary looked up. His unchanged expression suggested Andrew hadn't surprised him by showing up at his door. He walked around his desk, invited Andrew to take a seat, and closed the door. As he returned to his desk, he said, "I'm glad you came."

* * *

May 2009

During her Christmas Eve visit five months ago, Syd's beaming smile had shouted her pleasure with the changes Andrew had made. Genuinely interested in what his family was up to, he'd asked a lot of questions about Syd and John and Alex and Tyler, dropping the reference to his sister's dyke, as he'd called her previously. Maybe it was Gary's influence, but he'd realized that without friends, Syd and Alex were the only ones with a remote chance of caring whether he lived or died.

Today's visit would help him gauge if Syd's belief in him had stuck. Sadly, the first twenty minutes didn't give him much hope that it had. He'd talked about his prison life in unvarnished terms, but she sat silently. He couldn't tell if he'd failed to impress her or if she was still evaluating him. A course correction was in order.

"I appreciate the new books, Syd." Andrew scanned the two thick fiction novels Syd had brought this trip. "When I finished the last ones you brought at Christmas, I passed them on to my cellmate and then across the block. They're a big hit."

Syd chuckled. "Who would have thought a bunch of prisoners would be Harry Potter fans."

"I wouldn't have bet on it." He paused when Syd raised a questioning eyebrow at his poor choice of words. He threw her a lighthearted wink. "The best thing to come of your books was that I learned one of my neighbors couldn't read very well. To make a long story short, I worked with him every day for three months, and now he's reading novels all by himself," Andrew recited the final part of the story with a hint of pride. But just a hint. According to Gary, he should be careful to only partake of self-pride in small spoonfuls. Otherwise, it could become another addiction.

"That's great, Andrew. It's good to hear that you're making a difference in here."

He shrugged, downplaying his accomplishment. "Yeah, it was nothing."

"Nothing? I think it's something. You've likely changed that man's life forever. You should be proud of yourself."

He took in a deep breath, recalling another of Gary's lessons: failing to help when it was in your power to do so was something to be ashamed of. "I would have disappointed myself if I didn't help him."

"You're about to turn thirty-five, Andrew, and in all those years, I never heard you talk like this. You only did something if it benefited you. I can see that you've changed."

"I *have* changed, and I'm glad that you can see it. But I won't lie. I still have work to do and I understand that nothing I do now will excuse how I was before."

"Let me ask you, Andrew. When you get out of here, what do you expect from Alex and me?"

Andrew thought carefully, reflecting on what he had learned in counseling. "I expect nothing from you, but I do hope to earn your trust one day and that we can be a real family again."

"We'll see when you have access to your millions." He deserved the skepticism in Syd's voice.

* * *

2011, two months ago

The dozen inmates filtered out of the group counseling room, and Andrew and Gary began to restack the chairs and clean up the half-empty water cups left behind. After three and a half years of working together, they had a system down.

Gary went around the room with a large trash bag. "You were quiet tonight in group. Is something on your mind?"

Andrew continued to stack the hard plastic chairs. "Yeah, my parole."

"It's only two months away; I thought you'd be thrilled."

Andrew stacked the last chair and turned to Gary, his only real friend since he entered prison. "Don't get me wrong, I *am* thrilled to be leaving this place. It's just that the actual hard work will begin once I'm out. I'm going to be tested on day one."

One of the first things Andrew learned in counseling was to avoid triggers that would tempt him to gamble. For him, that had meant giving up access to his money while in prison. He had turned control of his inheritance over to his lawyer. But once he was out on parole, he would have access to millions again.

"You know as well as I do that your money won't be your biggest issue. Avoiding those things that might throw you back into a depression will be."

"I know, I know. It's all about controlling my need to feel accepted. I can't fall into the trap that my self-worth depends on my family forgiving and accepting me for who I am."

Gary patted Andrew on the back. "You're going to do fine, Andrew. Just focus on settling into your new life free of gambling and alcohol. You'll have to build their trust."

"And what if it never comes?"

"Then that's on them. The important thing is that you live up to being worthy of their trust. Just keep going to meetings and never give up hope."

Andrew looked up at his friend. "I'm going to miss you, Gary."

* * *

Back to Queens, New York, 2011

Andrew stood at the open door and knocked three times on the doorframe, waiting for permission to enter. After four years behind bars, he was well-versed in the rules of the institution. One fundamental rule in the minimum-security facility was to never enter a staff area without permission, even if you had an appointment, so he waited patiently for a response. The counselor looked up. Wrapping up his phone call, he politely waved in Andrew, who complied and stood silently at the foot of his desk.

"Yes. Thursday night at seven…You'll have room three-twelve…Check in with the guard first…See you then." Returning the handset to the desktop phone cradle, Dennis invited Andrew to take a seat. "Sorry about that. Our regular Narcotics Anonymous counselor can't make it this week, so I had to get a fill-in."

Andrew nodded his acknowledgment before sitting on the hard metal guest chair at the side of the desk. Per the rules, he never spoke to the staff outside of group setting unless asked to do so. If he did, though, he didn't expect recrimination from this man. Dennis differed from most of the staff who got off on wielding power over the incarcerated. He'd come across as someone who loved his job and wanted to help the inmates who rotated in and out at a high frequency. In fact, in Andrew's short experience at the Queens facility, Dennis was the only one who showed that he cared.

Dennis swiveled his chair to look directly at him. "It's good to see you one last time, Andrew. Let's go over the final phase of your parole discharge plan. Are you anxious about tomorrow?"

"Thanks, Dennis. Yes, I am."

"You're not my typical client, so I have to ask. What makes you the most anxious?"

With the last name of Castle in New York, it was hard to hide the fact that Andrew came from a wealthy family and had inherited much of his father's estate. So, finding a job to stay out of trouble was not an issue for him as it was for the bulk of Dennis's clients.

Andrew carefully thought about Dennis's question. The time he'd spent in prison, especially the counseling sessions at Fishkill, had changed him. "I thought I'd be anxious about the gambling, which was a big reason I ended up in prison. But now that I know why I felt the need to gamble, that doesn't worry me much anymore."

"So, you don't think you'll fall back into that trap again?"

"I don't believe so. I now know I suffered from depression, a direct result of the dysfunctional relationship with my father. That depression led me to drink and gamble. He's dead, but…" Andrew trailed off.

"But…" Dennis took an accurate stab at finishing his thought, "his death doesn't mean you're cured."

"No, it doesn't." Still, despite Dennis's doubts, Andrew was confident that his years of counseling had provided him a solid foundation to move forward and make a new life for himself without drinking and gambling. "His death and the way he disowned me before he died freed me and put me on the path to recovery before I set foot in prison. I can see that now."

Dennis smiled. "I believe you're on the right path, but this will be a lifetime struggle. If you can recognize your triggers and face them head-on, I'm confident you won't be back here anytime soon. So, if not the gambling, what worries you the most?"

Andrew sighed. "My family. I'll have my work cut out for me when I try to make amends with my sisters." His biggest challenge would be reconnecting with Alex. Syd was a different story. She'd visited him several times each year, and they'd already laid the groundwork for reconciling. Alex, though, never came. He couldn't blame her. He had been a lousy twin for as far back as he could remember.

Dennis reassured him. "Remember that you'll have to earn their trust. It may take a long time, or it may never come at all. Just remain worthy of it and never give up trying." The same parting advice Gary had given him.

"I'll do my best. I hope I can earn their trust in time to make a difference."

"You're talking about the company, right?" Dennis asked.

Andrew had followed news reports about Castle Resorts from prison the last few years. It was no secret that the company was struggling in the wake of the great recession, as were most of its competitors. And if it was in as bad a shape as he suspected, he might have the means enough to save it. "Yes, but I have a sinking feeling Alex won't accept the help."

"All you can do is offer. Then the ball will be in her court."

Andrew sighed again. If conditions were as bad as he feared, he might have to move things along much more quickly and not have the time to earn Alex's trust. "We'll see."

Dennis pursed his lips in clear skepticism. "I don't like how that sounds, Andrew. Tread lightly when you're on parole." He tapped the paper in front of him. "Speaking of which, let's talk about your parole officer. He's classified you as low risk."

Andrew was already formulating a plan. He would tread as lightly as he could to save his family's legacy, but tread he would.

CHAPTER SIX

Palmer, Massachusetts

Destiny's only clue to begin the search for her birth parents was a birth certificate that told her she was born on May 8, 1972, in the town of Palmer, Massachusetts, to an unknown father and a mother named Sarah Scott, a waitress also born in Palmer. Her research began with finding out everything she could about the hometown she had no memory of.

Between the Internet and the library, she'd discovered that Palmer, known as the "Town of Seven Railroads," had been a railroad town as early as 1830. Being centrally located between Boston and Albany and Boston and Hartford had made it the ideal waypoint for those traveling between those state capitals. When the demand for rail service fell off in the mid-twentieth century, businesses in Palmer began to close their doors. The last passenger train made its final stop there in the summer of 1971, and the next few years saw a slow exodus of lifelong residents searching for employment in major cities.

For Sarah Scott, a single mother of a five-year-old daughter, she likely held on for as long as she could before making the decision to leave the railroad town she grew up in and take her chances in New York City. As far as she could recall, that was 1977, the last time Destiny had set foot in Palmer until today.

"I don't remember any of this." Destiny stared out the passenger window of Ethan Falling's SUV as they rolled down North Main Street.

"You were a kindergartner," Ethan said, keeping his eyes focused on the road and his hands on the steering wheel. The quaint main part of town featured an old-timey breakfast diner and many shops displaying memorabilia of its rich railroad history in their storefronts.

"I'm trying to imagine what it was like here before we moved to Brooklyn, but I can't."

"Hopefully, we can find someone who can shed some light on your adoption."

"It's been thirty-nine years. I won't hold my breath."

"Don't fold your hand just yet," Ethan said. "In smaller towns like Palmer, we're bound to find someone who was around back then."

Destiny wished she shared Ethan's optimism. The entire drive to Palmer, he'd made her search seem like a treasure hunt that could open a world of possibilities. "Where do we start looking?"

"You said your mother was a waitress, so we start with the cafés."

"Adopted mother." Destiny intentionally laced her reply with an edge. She was angry at her mother for hiding her parentage until she was on her deathbed. Truth be told, she would have preferred it if her mother had taken that secret to the grave. She felt like her whole life had been a lie. What she needed now was answers, not a buried treasure.

"This may be none of my business." Ethan pulled into the parking lot of the first restaurant they came across. "But she raised you. That makes her your mother."

"Intellectually, I understand that, but I have birth parents out there who abandoned me. I want to know why."

"Just keep an open mind. You never know why a parent might hide an adoption. Trust they made the best choice for you." There was something behind Ethan's visible swallow and poignant comment, Destiny sensed. She acknowledged it with a polite nod as he pulled into a slot and put the car into park.

An hour later, Destiny and Ethan walked into their fourth restaurant, having struck out at the first three. The Steaming Stack occupied the once-bustling Union Station and was chock-full of railroad memorabilia. The interior appeared refurbished, down to the Civil War-era brick archways separating sections of the dining room.

Ethan's stomach growled for the third time today, prompting Destiny to scan the menu displayed at the hostess station. While he'd impressed her by remaining focused on the job, she needed him focused on finding answers, not on his stomach. She suggested, "Let's grab a bite to eat first. We can ask questions after lunch."

"I thought you'd never ask." Ethan rubbed his belly, confirming that her suggestion was long overdue.

Once seated, Destiny studied the menu more closely, amused that every dish had a railroad-themed title. "I'm thinking about the Pullman Car Club."

Ethan closed his menu, announcing, "I'm going with the Trainmaster's Burger."

Soon, a server came to take their orders. Ruth, according to her name tag, was a memorable little thing with a thick New England accent. She had to be at least seventy years old but was as spry on her feet as anyone half her age. She'd perfectly coiffed her short brown hair and had immaculately pressed her pink and white uniform. Destiny could tell just by looking at Ruth that she took pride in her appearance, and when she saw her in action, it was apparent she took equal pride in her work.

While they waited for their food, Ethan scanned the room. "What are you looking for?" Destiny asked.

"For any patrons or employees who might be of help."

Destiny joined his examination. The dining room contained a teenage busboy, two businessmen in their forties, several families, two servers who appeared in their twenties, and a couple in the corner who appeared to be in their sixties. So far, their best bets were Ruth and the elderly couple.

When Ruth dropped off their drinks, Destiny retrieved two sugar packets from a container on the table, vigorously shaking them before pouring them in her iced tea. As she stirred her drink, she recalled their frustrating, unfinished business at the Hampden County Recorder's Office in Springfield earlier today. The cogs of government were never slower.

"I hate dealing with bureaucrats. I can't believe the only two people capable of making a copy of a birth certificate are out sick."

"Patience, Destiny. We can pick it up tomorrow on our way back to the city." Ethan sipped on his Coke. "We're lucky Massachusetts state law changed and allows this. Most states don't."

"I'll have to take Jesse out to lunch for researching this over the weekend and preparing the right request forms for me," Destiny said. "When she told me that the state law changed a few years ago, allowing an adoptee born before 1974 to get an uncertified copy of their original birth certificate, it gave me hope I'd find answers."

"She's pretty amazing, isn't she?" Ethan puffed his chest out in pride at the mention of his wife. "She's sorry she couldn't come with us to Springfield today. You wouldn't believe how much is on her plate right now."

"She's gone above and beyond, Ethan." In a few short days, Destiny had discovered Jesse was a remarkable lawyer and Ethan an equally astonishing investigator who was working tirelessly to help her for no other reason other than she was important to Alex. She considered herself lucky to have fallen into such an incredible group.

Minutes later, Ruth returned with their meals, laying the plates down. "Here you go, kiddos. Anything else I can getcha?"

"I think we're good, Ruth, but I have a question." Ethan reached into his shirt breast pocket and showed her a photograph. It was a picture of Destiny's mother from about twenty years ago. It wasn't precisely from the year Destiny and her mother had moved away from Palmer, but perhaps close enough for someone to recognize her. "We're looking for someone who may have known Sarah Scott. She grew up here and moved away around 1977."

Ruth gently took the photograph and examined it, shifting her head from right to left as if digging deep into her memory. "Oh hun, that was a long time ago. The name sounds familiar."

Destiny thought if anyone in this small town could help her, it would be Ruth. Pressing her was worth a shot. "She was my mom. She passed away a few weeks ago, and I'm trying to find out more about her."

A look of sympathy enveloped Ruth's face. "I'm so sorry for your loss, hun." She looked at the photo again and returned it to Ethan. "My memory isn't so good these days. You might ask Dorothy Dowell. She's been around these parts almost as long as me." She pointed to a table in the corner where the elderly couple Destiny had spotted earlier were dining. "She's having dinner with her husband, Clarence."

"Do you know if they'll be leaving soon?" Ethan asked.

Ruth laughed as if the question was absurd. "Those two? They're the slowest eaters in town. Take your time."

"Thanks, Ruth. You're a gem." Ethan gave her a friendly wink.

After they finished their meals, Ethan left cash on the table, enough to cover the bill, plus a tip big enough to buy Ruth the daily special for a week. He and Destiny navigated the crowded dining room to the corner table where Dorothy and Clarence were still working away on their dinners, with no sign of finishing anytime soon.

Steps away from the table, Ethan whispered to Destiny, "I hope you don't take this the wrong way, but this is small-town New England. You better let me do the introductions."

Destiny wasn't surprised by this. Her skin always looked lightly tanned, and whenever she spent any time in the sun, it got pretty dark. Her mother had never said anything about her father, which made sense now that she knew she was adopted. But from the time that people and official forms of various sorts asked her about such things, she'd always assumed she was of mixed race, neither entirely white nor whatever. She was no stranger to prejudice, whether about her ethnicity or what people assumed about her work as a dancer. She was okay with Ethan taking the lead here. Almost everyone they had come across today in Palmer was white. While times had changed for the better over recent decades, there was no guarantee that someone from the Dowells' generation would respond positively to Destiny. She'd love to confront their bias if it existed, but the goal was to discover more about her origins.

"I get it, Ethan. I'll follow your lead."

Ethan nodded and completed the last few steps to the corner table while Destiny remained several feet behind. He pulled out his leather-bound credentials. "Excuse me, folks. My name is Ethan Falling. I'm a private detective. Our server, Ruth, suggested we speak with you."

Several skepticism-filled moments passed after Ethan explained about Destiny's mother passing away and that she was now searching for her birth mother. But when Ethan showed Dorothy the photograph, she gave an animated look of recognition that was also filled with disdain. She then glanced over to Destiny and said in a faint accent, "Every child deserves a father. Sarah Scott had no business taking that baby in without a husband."

"So, you knew her adoptive mother. Can you tell me anything about the birth parents?" Ethan asked.

"Mind you the times"—Dorothy returned the photo to Ethan—"but it was all very sordid back then. All the whispering." Clarence glared at his wife. Apparently, he didn't appreciate his wife's eagerness to spread gossip at the drop of a hat. But that didn't slow her. "That cousin of hers showing up pregnant like that. I bet the father was glad to be rid of her."

Clarence tossed his napkin in the middle of his nearly empty plate. "Enough, woman. Mind your business. Talking about this will come to no good. Best we be leaving now, Mr. Falling." He grabbed his wife by the hand and walked toward the main entrance in a huff.

Dorothy looked over her shoulder and apologized as she passed Destiny, "Sorry, girl. Perhaps another time."

Destiny called out, "Can you just give me a name?"

Dorothy opened her mouth to reply, but Clarence interrupted, "No, she can't," and pulled her out the front door.

Destiny closed her eyes in crushing disappointment. "Dammit." They were close to getting answers, but given this small-town close-mindedness, she might never find them.

"I have an idea." Ethan scanned the restaurant again and spotted Ruth clearing the table he and Destiny had vacated minutes earlier. He took Destiny by the hand. "Come with me." Once at the table, Ethan got Ruth's attention. "I hate to bother you again, Ruth, but I need your help one more time."

Ruth winked, stuffing Ethan's generous tip into her apron pocket. "Anything for my favorite new customer. What do you need, hun?"

"First, thank you for suggesting Dorothy. She might be able to help us, but Clarence—"

Before he could complete the thought, Ruth laughed, "Shut down the old busybody, did he?"

Ethan chuckled, "He sure did. Do you know where I can speak to her without Clarence there to shut her down?"

"Oh, sure. Tomorrow is discount day at Lena's. She goes every other week."

"Lena's?"

"It's the hair salon just off Main. I suspect she'd be arriving after ten or so. Half the women in town do."

"You're a gem, Ruth." Ethan leaned down and kissed Ruth on the cheek, provoking a blush bright enough to match the red carnation pinned to her uniform collar.

Ethan and Destiny walked out of the Steaming Stack with the plan to catch up with Dorothy Dowell tomorrow when she was in her element and away from her cross husband. When they hopped into Ethan's SUV, Destiny fluffed the bottom of her hair in the rearview mirror. "It looks like I might get my hair done tomorrow."

CHAPTER SEVEN

Manhattan, New York

Months before the economic downturn, the corporate offices of Castle Resorts, under Alex's leadership, had dramatically changed in terms of appearance, culture, and mood—a transformation that made her proud. The brighter contemporary furnishings and decorations matched the upbeat mission-driven environment she'd set, one that embraced transparency, career growth, and generous compensation. Even through the lean years of the current financial crisis, Alex had focused on maintaining the highest quality of service for her customers by avoiding dramatic staff cuts. That strategy preserved Castle Resorts' reputation in the industry but came at a price. She floated much of the operational costs by taking on more debt and leveraging her own personal wealth. In recent years, profits were rising but not fast enough to whittle down the principal on the debt. Something had to give soon.

According to Gretchen, Alex's personal assistant, the headquarters had never looked better and the staff was never more enthused to be there. However, Gretchen had said she attributed the latter part to Alex's refreshing leadership, not the new decor. When Alex finally safely steered the company through the storm, rewarding Gretchen for her years of loyalty was first on her list.

Syd was in for quite a surprise when she arrived; it had been four years since she had last walked the halls of the corporate offices. Alex waited patiently at the elevator doors, excited to escort her sister through the suite to experience the makeover. The door swooshed open, Alex greeting Syd with the eagerness of a child on Christmas morning.

"You're making me feel like a VIP, meeting me at the elevator like this." Syd adjusted the purse she'd slung over her shoulder before giving Alex a hug.

"Don't let it go to your head. I wanted to see your reaction when you walked in. It's really changed since you were last here."

Syd linked arms with Alex, stifling a laugh. "All right, baby sis, lead the way."

Alex opened the main doors to the bright and modern refurbished waiting room, a stark contrast to their father's stately, time-honored taste.

"Oh, my." Syd brought a hand to her chest, her mouth remaining agape. "This is incredible."

"I wanted the headquarters to reflect the new look and feel of the resorts."

"I've only visited San Francisco and Times Square since the remodeling projects, but I'd say you captured it."

The hallway changes weren't as dramatic as those in the waiting room, but Syd eyed them as they walked, marveling at them as if they were. "It's so much brighter, Alex. I love it."

"Wait until you see my office."

When Alex took over the company after William Castle's death and Syd temporarily filled in, both sisters had refused to occupy the space where their father had lived and died. Renovating it was the first change Alex had made. She had removed the massive wood door that once guarded William's old office and had perfectly reflected his personality—intense, traditional, and finely detailed but not overly ornate. In its place, she installed an opaque sleek glass door with brushed stainless-steel fixtures to reflect her leadership's transparency and modern direction.

Alex opened the door, exposing a modern office, highlighted with light and dark woods, several pops of green, and loads of personal and feminine touches. It fit Alex to a T.

"Father would hate it," Syd said before a grin slowly formed on her lips. "But I love it. You done good, baby sis. Real good."

"Thanks, Syd. I wanted to change things up and set a new tone." Alex took a seat on the plush white leather couch now anchoring the conversation area.

"You've definitely accomplished that. It looks nothing like it did when Father was alive. And from what I hear, neither does the rest of the company." Syd joined her on the couch.

"I've made a lot of changes, but I hope I haven't overextended in the process."

"I was wondering about the urgency for the loan at lunch the other day."

The company's financial footing had been questionable for the last two quarters, and the time had come for Alex to be honest about it. She began with a sigh. "Syd, we've been in the red for quite some time now. We need the cash infusion now."

"How bad is it?"

"If you recall, 2008 and 2009 were the leanest years. I've done my best to avoid layoffs, but I can't stop the bleeding. Projections show if we can hold on through the next two quarters, we should be okay. The loan should be enough to carry us through. If we don't get it, though, I'm afraid we'll have to start massive layoffs and consider restructuring."

Syd listened, her long expression revealing sadness. "I wish circumstances were different, Alex. John and I have dedicated our cash reserves to keep the winery afloat. And with a possible debacle in the offing with the '08 vintage, we might need every penny."

"I know, Syd. That's why I haven't mentioned it before now. By the way, we've pulled every bottle at every resort. How do you plan to get to the bottom of this?"

"I started calling the hotel restaurants around the world and asked the managers to sample the wine. So far, it looks as if the bad wine is limited to resorts in the eastern United States. I'm having several bad bottles couriered over. Ethan said he'll save me some time and detour to the Boston resort tomorrow and bring back the supply personally. John is looking into the shipping company from his end. I plan to do the same thing here."

Before Alex could respond, Gretchen buzzed on the intercom. "Ms. Castle, your next appointment is here."

"When Destiny gets back from her personal time, I'll have her work with you." Alex walked to her desk and engaged the intercom. "Thanks, Gretchen. We're just finishing up here. Send him in." She glanced at Syd, thinking an apology was in order. "I'm sorry, Syd. It's a reporter from the *Daily News* whom I normally wouldn't give the time of day to, but Public Relations insisted. He's doing a piece on how the luxury hotel industry has fared in the recession."

"A little positive PR might be a good thing right now," Syd said.

"We'll see." Alex gave herself a silent pep talk. *Put on your game face, Alex.*

The glass doors opened, and seasoned New York reporter Matt Crown walked through. Two-day stubble, a wrinkled off-the-shelf brown suit, and a black tie wrapped loosely around the collar of a well-worn white button-down shirt were how Alex remembered him—unlike the slicked-up appearance he'd presented at William's retirement party and announcement of Alex's coronation as his successor.

Alex walked toward her guest, keeping her guard up. She'd learned a long time ago to never give the media an opening, especially a member of it who had an axe to grind. And Matt Crown did, considering the lashing he took after his paper had forced a retraction from him of his one-sided coverage of William's death following Kelly's confession.

He met her halfway, extending his hand. "Thanks for meeting with me, Ms. Castle."

"Pleased to see you again, Mr. Crown. I appreciate your paper doing a piece on the industry. We've taken several hard blows the last few years." She glanced toward Syd and added, "This is my sister, Sydney Barnette."

Crown extended his hand to Syd. "It's a pleasure, Mrs. Barnette. If you don't mind staying, I might have some background questions since you used to work here."

Syd agreed.

"Why don't we sit?" Alex gestured toward the leather couch and matching chairs.

Crown started off with simple questions about Castle Resorts and its struggles during the great recession. Alex provided well-thought-out, unguarded responses that were both truthful and optimistic about the company's and industry's future.

Crown then pivoted. "I understand Castle Resorts carries several of the Barnette wines. It's pretty high-end stuff."

"As a luxury resort, we cater to a high-end clientele. Each resort also offers mid-priced selections from local and regional wineries," Alex replied.

Crown turned to Syd. "Is it true that last week you pulled some of your wines from the resorts because of poor quality?"

How did an interview about Castle Resorts turn to the troubles of Syd's winery? One of the first lessons Alex's father had taught her after she earned her MBA from Yale was that it was best to get ahead of a problem and control its narrative. She hoped Syd remembered that vital lesson and carefully considered how to answer Crown's question.

Syd shifted in her seat, mirroring Alex's uneasiness, before speaking. "We've had some issues with shipments of a particular vintage and are currently investigating possible breakdowns in the transportation pipeline."

"So, you're ruling out problems during the winemaking or bottling process? Meaning you're pointing the finger at someone else, not you?"

Alex didn't like where this was going. Screw controlling the narrative. She'd had enough of his tangents. "That sounds like an accusation, Mr. Crown."

He handed Alex a file, directing his next question to her. "In 2007, before you took over as chief executive officer, I understand you temporarily hired Kelly Thatcher at the Times Square Resort months before she confessed to killing your father. Is she the same Kelly you reference in this letter?"

Alex pulled out the document, a copy of a handwritten letter. It only took reading the first few sentences to realize what it was. It had been seventeen years since she'd written those words, but they had the same gut-wrenching effect on her as the day she penned them. Her eyes darted back and forth at the deep secret that was about to raise its ugly head.

Syd rested a comforting hand on Alex's thigh. "Alex?"

Alex finally gathered herself together. "Where did you get this?"

"I never reveal a source. Is this a letter you wrote to Kelly Thatcher in 1994 following an apparent suicide attempt with sleeping pills?"

"Suicide?" Syd rightly sounded as if Crown's question had thrown her for a loop. Alex had never told her about the scariest and dumbest thing she'd ever done.

Alex looked at her sister with pleading eyes. "Please, believe me, Syd. I didn't try to kill myself. It was an accident."

"So, the letter is real." Crown then began peppering her with questions like a Gatling gun at full speed. "Is it true that while you were having an affair with Kelly Thatcher at Yale, you used cocaine, helped her cheat on final exams, and after an emotional breakup, overdosed on sleeping pills?"

Before Alex could respond, Syd raised her hand at her in a stopping motion. "Don't answer that." She then glared at the man who had quickly become public enemy number one. "I don't know what you're trying to pull here, Mr. Crown, but you've worn out your welcome."

Crown threw down a set of photographs on the table—the blackmail photos of Alex and Kelly with the most salacious ones on top.

"Jesus." Syd covered her eyes.

Alex shot daggers at Crown. The heat of a volcano spiked in her chest, her contempt for him surpassing what she had felt for her father on his final night alive. She had thought that all this ugly business was behind her with Kelly in prison, but now she could see it never would be. So she asked one question. "What do you want?"

"To get your side of the story. How you conduct your personal life greatly impacts your ability to serve as CEO of an international multibillion-dollar company. How can your customers and employees trust someone who might be mentally unstable with a history of drug use who posed for pornography? Not to mention that your brother, who has a well-documented gambling addiction, is about to be paroled after embezzling from the same company. The same embezzlement that you covered up for months. And you continue to cover up for your sister's poor-quality wine. Are you helping to keep its value artificially high?"

Once Crown finished his diatribe, Alex glanced to her left. She and Syd were fuming at the same stack-blowing level.

"Are you done?" Alex asked, suppressing her well-deserved hatred for this man. She then calmly stood, walked to her desk, and picked up the desk phone when he didn't respond. "Gretchen, please call security and have Mr. Crown escorted off our floor. I'm banning him from all Castle Resorts properties."

"No need for that. I'll leave. Just so you know, I'm running an exposé on your family in tomorrow's edition. If you want your side of the story told, this is your chance."

"I won't dignify your type of journalism with a response. Twisted facts is all you and your paper are good for. If you print the contents of that letter, I'll slap you with a defamation suit so fast your head will spin." Alex pointed at the door. "Now, get off my property before I call the police."

Crown left without as much as a nod.

Once Alex returned to the couch, she and Syd both slumped backward. After several awkward silent moments, Syd asked, "What the hell just happened here?"

"Kelly just happened, and after I call Jesse to get the *Daily News* to squash the article, I plan to give her a piece of my mind." Alex calmly gathered up the photos and letter, formulating in her head the things she'd like to say to the biggest mistake in her life. They all ended with, *"If you think your life is miserable now, think again."*

"Don't you dare, Alex. Leave well enough alone."

"It burns me that she's still wreaking havoc from behind bars." Alex clenched her fists, grinding her teeth so hard she'd have to check for damage. "When will I be done with that woman?"

"I don't think it's just Kelly stirring the pot, Alex. How else would Matt Crown know to ask about the wine?"

Alex picked up the letter and scanned it again. "Well, he definitely got this letter from Kelly. I sent it to her a couple of months after she dumped me."

Syd leaned forward, her expression softening. "Alex, talk to me about the sleeping pills."

"It's not what you think, Syd. Yes, Kelly dumped me and I was upset. I got drunk with Harley at the beach house, and when I went to the bathroom to take some aspirin, I mistakenly grabbed a sleeping pill bottle. Long story short, Harley found me in time and called 911."

Moisture pooled at the bottom of Syd's eyes. She covered her mouth with a hand to muffle a gasp. "Dear God, Alex. Who knew about it?"

"Just Harley back then. I told Tyler, of course." A memory from the night she met with Kelly and got her to confess to killing William rushed back. "Dammit. I told Kelly about it the night she was arrested, too, so it's on video."

"What were you thinking?"

"That I needed to get her to trust me so I could get a confession out of her, and it worked."

"Well, soon, the entire world is going to know about it."

Alex rubbed her temples. "You're not helping, Syd."

CHAPTER EIGHT

The front door of the Castle mansion on the Upper East Side swung open, teenage laughter instantly filling the entry hall. Since the day she moved in, Bree had liked how sounds echoed off the white marble floor there. She especially enjoyed the nearly musical scrape of Callie's nails against the tiles as she fought frantically for footing when her mom dangled the leash in front of her.

Bree and her best friend, Kaitlyn, continued their chatter to the kitchen for their traditional after-school snack.

"I don't get why you're so excited about driving. Driving and parking in Manhattan is a nightmare and we can go anywhere on the subway. Plus, Uber just started up here." Kaitlyn was a New Yorker. She hadn't grown up in a sprawling suburban city where cars were the primary way of getting around. A driver's license represented freedom to Bree.

"I guess it's a California thing," Bree said. "Everyone there couldn't wait to turn sixteen and get their license."

"Whatevs. I'm hungry." Kaitlyn opened the refrigerator door. They grabbed snacks and drinks before heading upstairs to Bree's bedroom to study for finals.

Once settled in, Bree spread several textbooks and notebooks across her bed though she had no desire to actually study. Her mind kept drifting to her after-school appointment on Thursday at the DMV to take the written test for her driver's permit. She pulled out the application and reviewed everything the DMV website said she needed to bring. "Shoot. I forgot to ask Mom for my birth certificate. I'll be right back."

"Hurry," Kaitlyn said. "If I don't pass chemistry, my dad says I'll have to go to summer school."

Bree pushed herself off the bed and looked over her shoulder before she left the room. "Don't worry, Kaitlyn. You'll pass." Her statement was more certainty than conjecture. Now that a certain cute boy was no longer in her chemistry class, the conditions were ripe for Kaitlyn to pay more attention to the teacher.

Bree sprinted downstairs and to the home office where her mother should be working. The office, a colorful cozy space with a daybed designed for maximum function and comfort, mirrored her mother's persona—warm, tasteful, and functional. Two top-of-the-line computer workstations, multiple monitors, and a professional-level color laser printer made it a graphic designer's dream. Her mother had added a second desk in the oversized room to accommodate Erin when she started the internship with her and Maddie's company, Creative Juices, later that summer.

Bree walked in. Her mother was at her desk, talking on the phone, a flustered look on her face and a hand messing up her hair. Those were not good signs. Her mom only did the hair thing when she was extra anxious about something. Bree patiently waited for her to finish her call.

"You're talking Greek to me again, Maddie." Tyler continued to run a hand through her long blond hair. "I just need to know if you're going to meet the deadline for the changes…You're kidding." Following a long breathy sigh, she said, "All right.

You'll have it in the morning, but I'm not working all night on it."

When her mother hung up the phone, Bree leaned against the doorframe. "Got a second?"

Her mom's smile told Bree her mood had changed on a dime. No matter how much was on her plate, her mother always put aside business when Bree needed her.

"Hey, you. How was school today?"

"We got our finals schedule, and Kaitlyn is freaking out over chemistry."

Her mother snickered. "When is she not freaking out over chemistry these days?"

"Uh, never. Hey, Mom. I need my birth certificate for Thursday."

Tyler swung herself around in the desk chair, taking Bree in for a few moments. "It seems like it was only yesterday that I was walking you to the first day of kindergarten. Where did the time go? You've grown up to be such a beautiful, smart, articulate, and independent young woman."

With role models such as her parents, of course, Bree had become some of those things. Nevertheless, she had no response to the compliment, sensing the blush in her cheeks spoke for her.

Her mom glanced at her computer when it beeped to another incoming email. "I think I have a copy in my personal files in the master bedroom, but I don't have time to look for it right now. Maddie just dumped a butt-load of work on me that I have to get done tonight."

"I need it, Mom. Can I look for it myself?"

"No need, Bree. I'll make sure you have it before Thursday," her mom said, already half-focused on the email staring her in the face.

"Fine." Bree returned upstairs, disgruntled by her mother's answer. What if they both forgot, and Bree had to show up at the DMV without her birth certificate? It would be months before she'd get another appointment. Figuring she'd save her mom some time, she veered toward the master bedroom. She placed her hands on her hips, contemplating the stack of boxes in her mom's closet. The box marked "Family" seemed like the best starting point. Of course, it would be on the bottom.

Unstacking one box after another, she thumbed through folder after folder inside until she came across one labeled "Birth Certificates." She opened it. On top was her dad's. Doing the math in her head, she snickered at the thought he was closer to fifty than forty. Next was her mom's. She was three years younger. *You two are old*, she thought.

Bree flipped past Erin's and came to hers. "There you are." She pulled out the copy. To her surprise, she found a second copy of her birth certificate with it, but this one appeared older. She looked at it carefully and saw that it listed the father as "Unknown."

"What the hell?"

Bree then looked at the copy in her hand and saw it listed the father as Ethan Falling. She looked back and forth between the two documents ten or twenty times as she tried to grasp what she was reading. She looked more closely at both certificates. The one with her father's name had a date stamp of 2007, and the other had a 1995 date, the year she was born.

Her breathing shallowed.

She pawed through more folders in the box until she found one labeled "Adoption." She was afraid of what she might find, but she had to open it. The court filing language was full of legalese, a language she hoped to master one day, but today it was alien to her. She flipped through the papers until she came across the name of a respondent: Paul Stevens.

She grabbed both certificate copies and the paper with the man's name and ran down the hallway, her heart pounding so loudly it drowned out Kaitlyn's voice until she felt a hand on her arm. She looked at her friend but said nothing.

"Are you all right?" Concern laced Kaitlyn's question.

Bree didn't answer. She didn't know what she was feeling. Her universe had flipped on its head in that closet. She grabbed her iPhone and dialed. "Come on, come on. Answer, dammit!"

"Bree, what's wrong?"

She still ignored her friend. When her call went to voice mail, she looked at Kaitlyn. "I have to find my sister." She frantically gathered a few things into a backpack and darted toward the door, gesturing for Kaitlyn to join her. "Hurry. Let's go."

Though Erin didn't answer Bree's desperate calls, Bree knew precisely where to find her—at Connor's. That meant a short subway ride with one change of trains to Chelsea.

A gradual underground turn rattled the subway car along the decades' old rail, the sound of metal scraping metal enveloping the cabin. Bree huddled with Kaitlyn on the plastic seat after showing her the two birth certificates and the adoption papers. "I have to talk to Erin about this."

"What do you think this means?" Kaitlyn asked.

"I don't know, but it might explain a few things." For years, Bree wondered why she was a redhead with a brunette father and a blonde mother. When she asked her mother about it when she was ten, her mom had attributed it to a recessive gene on her father's side, but Bree didn't understand what that meant.

Once off the subway, Bree and Kaitlyn walked the two blocks to West Nineteenth Street at a fast clip. This part of Chelsea wasn't the trendiest, but it was centrally located between the offices of Connor's parents, who worked long crazy hours. Whenever Connor was home from Yale, like she was now, she had the run of the apartment. That made Bree one hundred percent sure her sister was there.

Bree opened the street access door, sandwiched inconspicuously between a wine bar and a jewelry store, and trekked up the two flights to Connor's place with Kaitlyn trailing steps behind. She pounded impatiently on the apartment door, waited thirty seconds for an answer, and pounded again.

"Maybe she's not here," Kaitlyn said.

"Trust me, she's here." Bree continued to pound.

Finally, Connor answered the door. She appeared to be hastily dressed, clad in running shorts and a tank top, both askew. Adjusting her top, she said, "What the hell, Bree? We were a little busy."

"I need to talk to my sister." Bree pushed her way through the door. "Erin!"

Erin emerged from the hallway, also adjusting a tank top. The "What the fuck?" look she lasered at Bree could have bored a hole in her skull. Bree ignored it. She pulled the copies of her birth certificate and adoption paperwork from her backpack and handed them to her sister. Erin scanned them. Her lack of surprise threw Bree for another loop. She understood now that her sister already knew what the papers were and what they meant.

"You knew?"

"They told me during sophomore year."

"Why did they tell you and not me?"

"It's not my story to tell."

"What does that mean?"

"It means you're going to have to ask Mom and Dad about it." Erin's response was infuriatingly vague, which in the Falling world meant she knew more than what she was saying.

"This is bullshit. Who is Paul Stevens? How did Mom know him?"

"Again, you'll have to ask Mom and Dad."

"So, Dad knows about him, and he's okay with it?"

Erin pulled Bree toward the couch and said in a comforting voice, "Let's sit down."

Bree shook off her sister's hand, anger building by the minute. "Just tell me what you know."

Erin's pained stare told Bree that this secret ran deep and affected more than just her. Was Erin involved too? Before Bree could figure it out, Erin gently took Bree's elbows into her hands. "I can tell you that Dad knew from the very beginning, and he considers you his daughter in every way that counts."

That was confirmation she was adopted, but this was going nowhere for any real answers. Her voice seethed from the anger boiling inside. "If you won't tell me, I'll have to get answers from the source." She stormed toward the door with Kaitlyn trailing behind.

Erin yelled out, "Talk to Mom first. It's her story to tell."

Bree slammed the door on her way out and mumbled, "As if she's ever going to tell me anything."

CHAPTER NINE

The sun was down, but Alex had made it home at a relatively decent hour compared to her track record of the last two months. She leaned against the doorframe of Tyler's home office, soaking in the breathtaking creature who had captured her interest at first sight and her heart at the first kiss. Tyler had become her North Star the day they moved into this house. Everything Alex did, she did for her. Or had done. When the economic crash came six months later, the eleven thousand employees who depended on her for their livelihoods had taken a front seat. She couldn't say that she'd squandered her time with Tyler, but she could have done better. Should have.

Watching Tyler, deep in thought and running her hand through her hair, Alex realized she'd laid too much responsibility on her. With her being gone from sunrise to past bedtime most days, Tyler had taken over many of the household tasks, refusing all but a weekly maid cleaning service that included stocking the fridge and pantry. On top of her own demanding work and parenting Bree, Tyler also cared for energetic Callie, who needed daily walking. Without a doubt, everything on Tyler's plate had stretched her to the limit.

Her back to the door, Tyler pushed herself from the desk, letting out a long, frustrated breath. She then rubbed the back of her neck and rocked her head in a circular motion, her signal that she'd been at her workstation far too long and stiffness had taken over. "Where is Alex when I need her?"

"I'm right here." Alex laid her hands atop Tyler's shoulders, instantly sensing a melting shudder. Tyler reacted in the same fashion every time Alex touched her when they were alone. Sadly, Alex couldn't remember the last time she felt Tyler surrender to her touch like this, and she missed it more than she realized. She began kneading Tyler's tight muscles, which were too taut for a woman who deserved daily pampering for her steadfast devotion.

"Perfect timing," Tyler moaned.

"I missed you last night." Alex's words held needless longing. She'd spent countless nights on only her side of the bed, under the conviction that she needed not to disturb Tyler's precious sleep after arriving home well after bedtime. Tyler had never complained about her virtual absence, but last night's absence had been about graduation shenanigans, not saving jobs.

"Mmmmm." Tyler's muscles relaxed when Alex pressed her thumbs firmly into the base of her neck. "I'll give you exactly fifteen minutes to stop that."

Alex whispered in Tyler's ear, "Am I out of the doghouse yet?"

"That depends."

"On what?" Alex loved Tyler's playfulness, especially when she didn't deserve it—a state Alex hoped to rectify, starting tonight.

"Are you going to tell me what you were doing with my daughter at Yale until six o'clock this morning?"

"I've been sworn to secrecy, but I will say she was upholding a long-standing Morsel tradition. You would have been proud of her."

"You know I'll find out, eventually."

"I have no doubt you will, but we plan on making you work for it this time."

Following a few quiet moments of dissolving into Alex's expert touch, Tyler asked, "Did you let Callie out?"

"Done, including her bedtime treat." Alex continued to knead Tyler's tired shoulders, considering what she didn't find after walking through the front door tonight. "I thought it was our night for Bree."

"She texted me before dinnertime." Tyler rolled her neck twice. "She said she wanted to track down Erin and would then stay with her dad until her driver's license test."

A lump formed in Alex's throat when she realized she'd become more like her father than she cared to admit. She'd put business above family. Until Tyler had briefed her on Bree's dissertation at Erin's graduation party, Alex had had no inkling the young woman living under her roof, albeit every other week, was interested in getting her driver's license.

Alex stopped her ministrations and slowly spun Tyler around in her chair. "I'm sorry I missed Bree's grand argument yesterday."

"You've been missing a lot lately." An involuntary tear rolled down each of Tyler's cheeks, breaking Alex's heart even more if it were possible.

Alex knelt and gently wiped the tears away with her thumbs. "Abby is right. No job is worth sacrificing my family. I'm tired of falling asleep without you in my arms."

"Abby Spencer is a very wise woman." Tyler gave Alex a nose-scrunching smile as if a long wait had finally come to an end.

And the saddest part, Alex thought, was that missing all those meals and nights holding Tyler may have been for nothing.

"Indeed." Alex managed to return her smile. "It may take me some time to unravel myself from so much responsibility at the company, but I promise I will. I just hope people don't start jumping ship before I can make the change."

"Why would you think that?"

Alex stood and took Tyler by the hands. "Let's sit on the daybed. I need to talk to you about something."

A queasy feeling settled into Alex's stomach in the few strides it took to cross the room in silence. She'd hoped tonight would mark the beginning of some necessary changes but worried she was too late, considering the events of this afternoon.

They sat on the plush cushion of the daybed built into the bay window. A feeling of foreboding hung in the air; this business with Matt Crown had come at the worst possible time. Castle Resorts was on the cusp of financial ruin, a cash infusion hanging in the balance. And at the very time when Alex had concluded that divesting herself of responsibility was necessary, she was no longer sure if the people in key positions would still be there when the dust settled.

Alex took Tyler's hand into hers and let out a deep calming breath. "Syd and I had an unusual visitor today at the office."

"Okay." Tyler drew out her response, the brittleness in her voice signaling a concern beyond mere curiosity. Alex ran her thumb across the top of the hand that she couldn't bear living without. It was strong, distinctive, and capable of expressing so much love and affection. She hoped that despite her missteps of the past few years she'd still have a chance to ask for that hand in marriage.

"A reporter from the *Daily News* by the name of Matt Crown interviewed us today. He arranged for the interview through our public relations office, claiming to be writing a story on how the luxury hotel business was faring through the bad economy. He started the conversation innocently. Then he asked Syd questions about her wine and her recalling the 2008 cabernet sold at the hotels."

"But she just started that on Friday and only at Castle Resorts, right?"

"Which makes me think he has some inside information. It became apparent he wasn't there to write about Castle Resorts. He was there to write a hit piece on my family...because he also asked me questions about Kelly."

"You're kidding." Tyler's pursed lips weren't a good sign. The last time she and Alex had dealt with that woman was at her allocution, when the judge questioned her before sentencing her to up to twenty years for manslaughter. Among other things, the way Kelly had exaggerated the events leading up to her arrest had made it sound like Alex had taken things a lot further than she had to to get a confession.

"I wish I were." Alex squeezed Tyler's hand, drawing from her the strength to finish what needed saying. "T, he had a copy of the letter I wrote to Kelly."

Tyler gasped, covering her mouth with her free hand. She knew how deeply personal that letter was and what it contained. "He also had a copy of the photographs Kelly used to blackmail me."

"That woman is like a bad penny."

"That's not the worst of it. Crown is publishing an exposé in tomorrow's paper about me and Kelly, Syd and the wine, and Andrew and the embezzlement."

"Can we do anything about it? Can your lawyers squash it?"

"Castle Resorts counsel said it's too late to stop it, but as my personal lawyer, Jesse will be on it tomorrow to see if I have a case for libel. In the meantime, she recommended not commenting on it. Making matters worse, I'm supposed to close on the corporate loan tomorrow afternoon. If the bank backs out, I'll have no choice but to implement the downsizing plan in order to cover expenses."

Tyler shifted her hands and squeezed both of Alex's. "Babe, I'm so sorry. I know you've been doing everything possible to avoid laying off staff."

They weren't merely staff. They were family. When Alex formally took the reins of Castle Resorts, she'd made a promise to the eleven-thousand-strong cadre that she would treat them like that, not as nameless faces as her father had done. Turning her back on Andrew had left an irreplaceable hole in her heart. Now, she faced having to break the promise she'd made and let thousands go based on a complicated financial formula, not loyalty or hard work.

Tyler kicked off her shoes, leaned back behind Alex, and lay down flat. She patted a hand on the daybed several times. "Come here. Let me hold you."

Alex faced chaos upon chaos, yet Tyler knew exactly what she needed—to know something in her life was going right. To feel loved. Alex removed her shoes and laid her tired body on the cushion beside her. She slid an arm underneath a small pillow and scooted herself back until she felt her backside touch Tyler. "You feel so good. How do you always know what I need?"

"Because you're part of me." Tyler wrapped her arms around Alex.

Thoughts of the thousands of men and women of Castle Resorts who depended on her and the thousands upon thousands of spouses and children who depended on them swirled in Alex's head. If circumstances forced her to downsize, how many would miss paying the mortgage? How many would lose their homes? And how many wouldn't be able to afford college for their kids?

Her mind drifted to the things she'd written seventeen years ago to purge the pain Kelly had heaped upon her. Things that were deeply personal and meant only for Kelly. She wished she'd never sent the letter, that she had burned it as her therapist had suggested as an option.

"Stupid, stupid, stupid," she whispered.

"What's stupid?"

"Me. I can take the heat for my actions, but tomorrow the bank manager will read that letter and see those pictures. I'm afraid the people who work for me will pay the price."

"We don't know that for sure. I have faith you'll find a way out of this."

Alex rolled her body over to face the woman who always gave her hope. She whispered, "I've missed you." Without fail, Tyler made her feel loved. She searched the beautiful gray eyes she'd taken for granted for too many months before shifting her gaze to Tyler's pink lips. The lips that could stop her in her tracks with a single smile. And there it was—a faint wrinkle of those lips. Tyler wanted to be kissed.

Hungry for this for months, Alex stole her kiss. She couldn't remember the last time they'd made love, let alone just fucked. Was it in March to celebrate four years since their first meeting? Yes, it was. *Damn, that was months ago.*

That realization made her even hungrier. Her lips drifted to Tyler's neck in search of a particular little patch of tender skin behind her ear. She drank in the faint scent of lavender that had come to represent Tyler and the one place she wanted to be. She was home.

Hands explored gentle curves while legs entwined. *Thank God*, Alex thought. The soft fabric of Tyler's trousers was thin enough to feel every soft swell of her muscles. Sheer enough to feel each ripple of toned flesh earned through hour upon hour of walking the winding trails of Central Park with Callie. Sadly, Tyler largely had spent those hours alone when Alex was at work.

God, I've missed this. Why she'd let months pass without luxuriating in this feeling, she didn't know, but she swore to never go that long without it again.

Tyler's voice was thick when she whispered into Alex's ear, "You feel so good." She exposed her neck even more, signaling she wanted to be taken. "Babe…" was all she got out before her voice faded off, subjugated by the pleasure Alex was doling out.

That was all the encouragement Alex needed. Clothing quickly made its way to the floor, and the moment their bodies touched skin to skin intimacy ceased being a memory. It was real, it was good, and it was long overdue. Each movement was a reminder of the unbreakable connection they shared.

It had been months since Alex's mind had dwelt on anything besides business, but tonight was different. She *was* different. She wanted nothing more than to stay in the moment with Tyler as she relished her body. She never wanted to stop. Each lick and squeeze of flesh electrified her. And after each of them had tumbled over the edge, Alex crawled to the back of the daybed and lay down again, pulling Tyler against her. She wrapped her arms around Tyler, nuzzling her chin into the crook of her neck until Tyler's breathing calmed.

"Promise me we'll never go this long without sex again."

Tyler tightened an arm around Alex's back. "I was going to say the same thing."

Alex lay on the daybed with her arms wrapped tightly around Tyler, savoring the sensation of touching skin to skin. With her body sated and exhausted, Alex's mind settled into a peaceful calm. She had only one thought, *marry me, T,* but she didn't voice it. This wasn't the time. When she finally proposed, it would be memorable, with the diamond ring she'd designed to last a lifetime.

After their breathing synced into a slow, deep rhythm, Tyler broke the silence. "I love you, Alex. We'll find a way out of this mess."

Alex felt stronger and more confident with Tyler in her arms. T always had that effect on her. "With you, I know we will."

CHAPTER TEN

Palmer, Massachusetts

Destiny opened the door to leave her room at Palmer's newest bed-and-breakfast, The Brakeman's Berth, with her repacked overnight bag and purse draped over a shoulder. Like the Steaming Stack restaurant, the B&B had been designed to transport its visitors back to the late nineteenth century at the height of Palmer's rich railroad history. Even the photographs and paintings by local artists lining the second-floor hallway walls depicted life in the railroad town throughout the last century and a half.

Walking down the corridor, she stopped to inspect several photos, trying to imagine the town as it was when she lived there as a small child. She finally came across a picture of Main Street from the 1950s, showing dozens of pedestrians and cars lining the street in front of the Five Star Theater, which was the town's only cinema, according to her research. Memories began flashing in Destiny's head. Lasers. Spaceships. Princess. Vader. She ran her fingers across the marquee sign in the photo and whispered, "Star Wars."

The memories were fragmented, but Destiny remembered sitting in the dark theater while fantastic laser fights unfolded on the screen. Another memory flashed. She'd been walking across the street, holding a woman's hand, and then looked over her shoulder to watch a group of young boys reenacting the laser fights that had played out on the giant screen minutes earlier. She'd looked back at the woman whose hand she was holding and asked, "Can we see it again?" The woman had answered, "I'm sorry, but we can't afford it." The woman was the mother who raised her.

Destiny recalled her mother telling her stories about how life was simpler before moving to New York City and how she'd regretted moving to Brooklyn for a job, any job to make ends meet. She wished she could remember what her mother was like before they moved. She imagined she must have been happy and loving, but sadly, Destiny only knew her as a bitter woman who preferred the company of a bottle over that of her child. It all made sense now. Destiny wasn't hers.

Making her way downstairs to the entry room, she placed her bags on the floor against the wall near the door. Ethan was sitting at the tiny dining table near the entryway, sipping on a cup of coffee. As she approached, he raised his cup and asked, "Nescafé?"

Destiny laughed. In New York City, a gourmet coffee shop occupied virtually every corner, yet here in Palmer, the B&B offered guests the freeze-dried staple of decades past. "They certainly have this vintage thing down."

"That they do." Ethan raised his cup again. "I really like the old ticket taker's booth by the front door."

"Me too." Destiny padded to the other side of the room, filled a cup with Nescafé and a plate with fruit and pastries, and returned to the table. "When did you get back from Boston?"

"About ten minutes ago. The bottles of cabernet are in the trunk."

"That was nice of you to wake up before dawn to help Syd."

"Just part of the service." He checked his watch. "Dorothy should be at Lena's by now. Have you checked out yet?"

"Yep. Just let me nibble on this and drink my yummy cup of Nescafé," she said with a grin, "and I'll be ready to go."

Minutes later, she and Ethan began the short walk to Lena's Hair Salon, a few blocks down from the B&B. They passed several quaint, freshly remodeled storefronts, a clear sign the town was experiencing rejuvenation. A boutique wine store was one of them.

Lena's was a small shop at the far end of a well-trafficked strip mall. At first blush, it seemed like any other salon with its reception counter, shampoo area, and six haircutting stations. But what set Lena's apart were two back-to-back rows of guest chairs sitting in the middle of a black-and-white checkered linoleum floor. According to the innkeeper, those chairs were the heartbeat of the salon. Every socially connected woman in Palmer sat in one of those chairs several times a month to catch up on and spread local town gossip.

Ethan and Destiny walked into the shop, setting off the bell anchored above the door. All heads turned, and voices silenced. A blind person could recognize that the newcomers were out-of-towners.

At one of the haircutting stations, Dorothy was well into her cut and style. She looked into the mirror, her eyes widening in recognition. She appeared happy the visitors had tracked her down. That meant two things: Ethan had made an impression at the restaurant, and she had some unfinished gossip to share.

"Good morning, Mrs. Dowell," Ethan said. "We didn't get to finish our conversation last night."

The hairstylist, busily working away on Dorothy's mop, chimed in with a thick New England accent, "Oh, darlin', she's always up for a conversation."

Dorothy tossed her stylist a stern look.

Destiny stepped behind Dorothy, looking at her in the mirror. "Please, Mrs. Dowell. I've come a long way to find out about my birth mother." Those words earned head turns from everyone in the salon. Destiny was sure they wondered who this woman was and who in town had given birth to her and then gave her up. "You mentioned something about a cousin," Destiny pressed.

"You must be asking 'bout Sarah Scott," the hairstylist said.

"Hush now, Lena. This is my story to tell," Dorothy chided before turning her attention to Destiny. "Mind you, child, this was the biggest scandal in Palmer back then. Sarah Scott lived in Palmer all her life. Then one day, that cousin of hers shows up, belly swollen with a baby. You, I presume."

"What was her name?"

Dorothy paused, tapping her temple with an index finger. "Sarah only mentioned her name once."

"Wasn't she a southern gal?" Lena asked.

"Will you keep quiet, woman?" Dorothy said. "If memory serves me, I believe she was from New York, the city."

Destiny became anxious at the thought that her birth mother could be living in the same city as her. She was more determined than ever to learn more. "Can you tell me anything about her?"

"I saw her just a few times shopping," Dorothy said. "She seemed pleasant enough."

"What did she look like?"

"She was a tall gal if I recall. Dark hair, I think."

"Do you know why she left me with Sarah?"

"Rumor had it the father was rich and famous, and it all had to be hush-hush. I remember her coming to town, getting bigger, and then she was gone. Sarah then showed up around town with that light brown baby."

Destiny squinted, irritated at Dorothy's racial dig.

"Sorry, child. Times were different then." Dorothy's sorrow-filled expression made her apology seem genuine. Almost. "I remember Sarah saying once that her cousin had put you up for adoption when she left, but Sarah couldn't bear seeing her kin raised by a stranger, so she took you in."

"Thank you, Mrs. Dowell. This is the most I've learned about my birth mother. Can you tell me anything about Sarah before she moved to New York City?"

"She was a sweet young lady and a damn good waitress before her cousin came to town, but she wasn't capable of raising a child all by herself."

Destiny knew where this was going. "You're saying she needed a husband."

"Yes. I'm saying a child should be raised by a mother and a father. You never had a chance, you poor thing."

"Marriage does not guarantee a child is raised right," Ethan said. "As you can see, Mrs. Dowell, that child turned out just fine and is doing quite well for herself."

Destiny appreciated Ethan for coming to her defense and not letting a comment like that slide. She had it rough growing up, but she didn't let that slow her down. Destiny turned her head toward Ethan so Dorothy couldn't see her mouth the words, "*Thank you.*"

Dorothy stiffened her posture underneath the black drape. Her reply came out sharp, "Yes, well, unless you two plan on having your hair done, I suspect you best be going now."

"Thank you for your time, Mrs. Dowell." Ethan left a business card on Lena's workstation and turned to the rest of the customers. "If any of you can think of more information regarding Sarah Scott or her cousin, please give my office a call. Good day, ladies."

Ethan and Destiny exited the salon and retraced their steps toward the B&B where Ethan had left his car.

Excited about the few nuggets she'd learned, Destiny walked with an extra pep in her stride. She now knew her birth mother was her mother's cousin, tall, dark-haired, single, and from New York City. That meant there was a good chance her father was too. "Let's get going to Springfield. Hopefully, they'll have my original birth certificate ready by the time we get there."

As they walked past the shops on Main Street, Ethan placed his hand on Destiny's forearm to bring her to a halt. "I need to make one quick stop." He entered the boutique wine shop they'd passed earlier and perused the shelves. For a store in a relatively small town, it carried some very exclusive wines, implying that tourism was alive and well in Palmer.

Ethan approached the store clerk and asked, "By chance do you carry Barnette wines from Napa?"

Apparently well acquainted with the stock, the clerk replied without hesitation, "I'm sorry, sir, but we don't. However, I can recommend other comparable wines."

Destiny guessed what Ethan was up to—he was hunting for the cabernet that had Syd worried, but she didn't know why.

"That won't do. I'm looking for a specific wine and vintage. I need a 2008 Barnette cabernet sauvignon. Can you help me locate one in the area? We're heading to Springfield and then to New York City."

The clerk rubbed his chin before flexing an index finger in the air. "I know of a shop in Hartford. Let me call." After disappearing into a back room, he returned minutes later. "That's quite an expensive bottle of wine. I found one." The clerk passed on the address of the store in Hartford and told Ethan, "They'll hold it for you until tomorrow."

Ethan thanked and tipped the clerk for his troubles. He and Destiny returned to the car and began the half-hour drive to Springfield. "What was that about?" Destiny asked.

"I have a hunch. I need to compare the wine to the ones I picked up from the resort."

"Your mind is always working overtime."

"A downside of the job. I'm always working."

Destiny remained quiet for the rest of the trip. She was a bundle of nerves, thinking about what she might discover once she saw her original birth certificate. Would she finally know who she was? She wondered what other family might be out there besides a mother and father. Did she have brothers, sisters, aunts, uncles, cousins, nieces, or nephews? The possibilities were endless.

When they arrived at the Hampden County offices in Springfield, Destiny asked Ethan to wait in the lobby while she went inside the clerk's office. She couldn't have explained it if he asked, but she wanted to take this final step herself.

The building looked like several Jenga blocks stacked precariously on top of one another, giving the building a haphazard yet fresh and modern feel. The interior appeared the same, with jagged hallways and matching modern architecture. The Clerk's Office staff, however, was a contradiction. They were old and worked methodically. In other words, slowly.

After twenty minutes in line, Destiny heard the magic word, "Next," and stepped up to the clerk. After explaining the purpose of her visit and providing her ID and the appropriate governmental form Jesse had completed for her, the clerk nodded and disappeared behind an intricate labyrinth of file cabinets. Minutes later, the clerk reappeared with some papers in hand.

"You're lucky. Somebody pulled it this morning. Otherwise, you'd have to wait an hour or so."

Destiny smiled, ignoring the predictable institutional bottleneck, and retrieved the document from the counter. All told, she had had to wait almost twenty-four hours because the only two people in the world capable of photocopying her birth certificate were home sick yesterday. She folded the document in half, and before she walked away, offered a polite, "Thank you."

Tossing and turning in her bed at the B&B last night, Destiny had spent hours considering this moment, weighing her options. Should she look at the document right away or wait until she was in the car with Ethan? Who did she want to share it with? Sadly, the answer was no one. She had no living family that she knew of, and her only friends were those at work. She decided on opening it alone, but not in a sterile office.

She dashed toward the exit and, as she passed Ethan, said, "Let's go outside." She led him out of the county office building's main doors to the fountain courtyard guarding its entrance. She turned to Ethan. "If you don't mind, I'd like to take this last step alone. I'll meet you back at the car."

"Take your time." Ethan placed a hand on the large part of her back before returning to the car.

Destiny sat on the cement bench surrounding the fountain, carefully placing her purse beside her. She unfolded the documents and stared at the attached cover letter. Below the official county seal was the standard bureaucratic language, explaining various rules and regulations. Behind the letter was a single stapled sheet of paper—her birth certificate.

Her palms dampened with sweat. Her hands shook. Her heart thumped so hard it could have drowned out her old high school marching band. This was it. She turned the cover letter and exposed a document titled, Certificate of Live Birth. When she read the names listed there, her heart raced even more. She couldn't believe what she was reading. This must be some cruel cosmic joke. Though, considering how her life had turned out, somehow it made sense. There was a reason she had landed in *that* jail cell on *that* Friday night four years ago. She wasn't sure how long it took her to come to that conclusion, but when she finally absorbed the words on the paper, finally accepted them, she whispered, "Holy shit."

CHAPTER ELEVEN

Manhattan, New York

For midweek, an unusually large number of joggers were crowding the southern spur of the bridle path. She preferred the softer surface of the firmly packed dirt trail over the wide asphalt pathways elsewhere in the park. Besides it being more forgiving on her knees, there was something more natural about running on dirt rather than pavement.

This was Alex's time to connect with nature in the middle of an unforgiving concrete jungle. She weaved her way around slower joggers, trying not to break her steady nine-minute mile pace. The words of Lady Gaga blared through her headphones, muffling the sounds of the outside world and helping her set the fast pace of her morning jog. The lyrics of not hiding in regret and being born this way repeated and fueled her resolve. She panted heavily and pushed herself beyond the burn in her lungs and legs to expel the pent-up anger that had returned the moment she woke this morning.

Twice now she had dreaded the release of the blackmail pictures, but for two very different reasons. Four years ago, she'd feared her father's repercussions and leveraged every resource to ensure the photos remained buried. Today, though, the repercussions would be felt by thousands, and that was, sadly, out of her hands.

Alex increased her stride. No matter what happened today, she wouldn't hide in regret. She wouldn't deny who she was. She was born this way.

When a distinct ringtone came through the headphones, Alex slowed her pace to compensate for her heavy breathing. Following a press of the mic on the headphone cord, an insistent smile grew on her lips. "Hey, T."

"I love hearing you breathing hard." Tyler's reply had a husky tone and had Alex conjuring up memories of last night. Alex's mind drifted to the two of them on the daybed in Tyler's office. They'd rushed their lovemaking, and it was sexy as hell, but she couldn't help herself. She had needed—correction: they *both* had needed—to reconnect after such a long, self-imposed dry spell. She slowed her pace even more and finally came to a halt.

"I loved last night. I've really missed being with you like that."

"I loved it, too." Tyler's words had lost their playfulness as she let out a breathy sigh. Both concerned Alex.

"What is it, T?"

"The Matt Crown piece hit the online edition. It's not good. I called Jesse. She said she'd meet you at your office."

"I don't need this right now." Alex rubbed her temple with her free hand, feeling her back muscles tense. She had her work cut out for her, she knew, to minimize the damage as Hurricane Kelly roared through her life again, showing up as usual at the worst possible time. *The loan*, she thought. "All right, I'll head back to the office. And T?" Alex trailed off.

"Yes, babe?"

No matter how things unfolded today, Alex wouldn't go back to the way things were. She was lucky to have Tyler in her life and would never take that for granted again. "I love you."

"I love you, too, Alex."

Alex disconnected the call and retraced her route on the bridle loop heading back toward the Castle Resorts corporate offices. Once outside the park, she weaved her way along the city streets until she returned to the Madison Avenue building. At the entrance, a group of reporters surrounded her like a pack of wild dogs. A cacophony of voices and clicking cameras exploded. Flashing camera lights from every direction disoriented her. Reporters blocked her way into the building and pelted her with one question after another as she tried to push her way through the gauntlet. Her initial worry centered on looking more like a disheveled, sweaty jogger than the CEO of a multi-billion-dollar company, not on answering preposterous questions.

"Alex, is it true that you covered up your brother's embezzlement?"

"Were you involved?"

"Are you propping up your sister's failing winery by covering up tainted wines?"

"Is it true that you had an affair with Kelly Thatcher?"

"Were you having an affair with her when she killed your father?"

"Did you also cheat on your college exams?"

"Are you still using drugs?"

"Is it true the overdose wasn't accidental?"

"Were you in on the plan to kill your father?"

The last question earned Alex's ire. She fired back, "What? Of course not. That's a preposterous lie. I had nothing to do with that."

The wall of reporters parted, and Jesse pushed her way through. Aside from the time Jesse met her for her arraignment following an awful night in The Tombs, Alex had never been so happy to see a lawyer in her life. Jesse shielded Alex with an arm carefully placed around her back and shouted, "My client is not taking questions." She continued to push through the sea of reporters.

"Alex. Alex. What do you mean it's a lie? Which part?" Several reporters shouted over each other.

Jesse pushed her way to the front entrance and shoved Alex past the threshold. She turned around and warned the reporters, "This is private property. Unless you have business in this building, we will consider you a trespasser and will call the police."

Jesse stepped inside. The sliding glass doors closed behind her, reducing the reporters' shouting to indistinguishable noises. She guided Alex to the bank of elevators, punched the up button, and within moments a car arrived. She boarded with Alex, holding her hand up to stop two other passengers from boarding. "Take the next car, please."

Alex turned the instant the doors closed. "What the hell was that?"

"That was a feeding frenzy. Until this story dies down, you're going to have to avoid going out in public."

Alex closed her eyes, effectively accepting her near-term fate of isolation. She leaned against the back wall of the elevator with a loud thump. "What are our options of countering this mess?"

"There's not much I can do about the photos. The ones published don't violate current New York state pornography laws, as far as I can tell. We can look at filing a defamation suit, but that's a pretty high bar since you're a public figure."

Alex slowly ran her hands down her face, ending at her mouth. "You're saying we can't do anything about it."

"Those photos were consensual, so no. In the exposé, Crown walked a fine line by raising questions and not outright accusing you of being involved in the embezzlement, fraud, or your father's death, so again no. We could try to tie them up in court for months, but for what purpose?"

"What do I do about it?" Alex's hopes deflated in another breathy exhale. She felt like she had a big red target painted on her back, and every reporter in the city had her in their sights.

"You let it go. Do you really want to drag this out in the media for months? Can your business sustain such negative attention?"

Jesse was right. As maddening as this was, there wasn't much Alex could do other than ride it out and wait for the fallout.

The elevator finally reached the twenty-third floor, and Alex led the way toward her office, with Jesse trailing behind. Inside the office suite, every eye in the room followed her as if expecting more spectacle. *Great*, Alex thought, *everyone has already seen it.* She held her head high and walked with confidence, looking each person in the eye as she passed until she reached her personal suite.

"Good morning, Gretchen. Can you get me the daily reports and then set up a meeting with the board members this afternoon?"

"Of course, Ms. Castle," Gretchen replied. Before Alex walked past her, she added, "Mr. Ward is waiting in your office."

"Thank you." Alex paused when she placed a hand on the handle of the frosted glass door guarding her office. It couldn't be good if her CFO was waiting for her. She composed herself and then pushed the door open, waiting for Jesse to take a seat on the couch.

"Good morning, Blake." Alex extended her hand when he rose from the guest chair in front of her desk. The deep worry lines along his brow were not a good sign and explained why he didn't accept her hand. She withdrew it. "Please excuse the attire; I was just on my morning run."

Blake ignored Alex's pleasantries. "Your family's exposé couldn't have come at a worse time. We lost the loan."

Alex feared this would happen, but she kept her composure. She calmly walked around her desk, removing her iPhone arm pouch as she sat down. "What's our next move?"

"We put the downsizing plan in motion. That should buy us a few quarters."

"What's the last possible date for implementation?" she asked.

"The layoffs need to take effect by the end of the third quarter," Blake said. "Keep in mind, we're dealing with multiple layers of laws in multiple countries. But to cover us legally in all jurisdictions, we need to send out notifications by June first."

Wow. In six days, Alex thought. She pushed back the sick feeling sweeping through her and collected herself. "All right then, prep everything for a June first rollout." Her decision was the prudent course of action, but she still held hope that she wouldn't have to pull the trigger.

After Blake left to begin the unpleasant task of laying off thousands of employees worldwide, Alex walked to the floor-to-ceiling wall of windows and stared out at the lush panorama below.

Jesse finally broke her silence. "It's not your fault, Alex."

Alex shook her head, trying to keep herself from drowning in a rising sea of self-loathing. "But it is. I once stood in this very office and smugly told Father that the way I live my personal life had no bearing on my professional one. I could not have been more wrong. So many people are now going to pay the price for my arrogance."

CHAPTER TWELVE

Queens, New York

Terminal B at LaGuardia was bustling with midweek sky-bound passengers. Hundreds were sitting in hard plastic chairs designed for anything but comfort. Some were in line to purchase last-minute snacks and drinks at the concession stands. And one teenager, no rookie to air travel, was huddled up at one of the few available power sources, looking to juice up her cell phone before takeoff.

After plugging her iPhone into the wall socket, Bree propped her carry-on suitcase close to it and sat on the not-so-clean carpet, using her bag as a makeshift cushion. The charging cable was long enough to use her phone, so Bree checked her unread text messages. She had two.

She opened the first from her hometown friend, Derrick, and began a conversation.

sure. u cn crash on floor
How long u stayin
2 or 3 nights. dont tell ur mom
can u pick me up

yep. text when u land
see ya Bree
see ya D

Bree opened the second unread text from her sister and began a heated back and forth.

sorry i never told u
when u plan 2 talk 2 mom & dad
when I'm good and ready
what does that mean
means im tired of being lied 2

Bree put her phone down, still fuming. Erin had known the truth yet had said nothing for years. She certainly couldn't trust her with her plans. The only person she trusted was Derrick. He'd never let her down. When she took a deep, calming breath, an announcement came over the loudspeaker. "Attention. We will start boarding for United Flight 1312 with nonstop service to Sacramento at Gate B-7 in just a few minutes…"

After boarding and stowing her carry-on, Bree settled into her seat for the six-hour flight. She put her headphones on and tried listening to some music to pass the time, but her mind kept drifting to what she might find when she came face-to-face with her real father, Paul Stevens. Would he accept her with open arms? Or would he push her away? Would he lie to her like the rest of her family had her entire life? Either way, she hoped to get answers.

CHAPTER THIRTEEN

Today was the first day of the rest of Andrew Castle's life. He would walk through the main door of Queensboro Correctional Facility in a few minutes and begin his life as an ex-con on parole. The staff had provided him and his fellow soon-to-be parolees with their final briefing, a warning really, that one brush with the law could put them back behind bars before the ink dried on their parole forms.

One by one, ex-cons exited the facility, each carrying a blue folder with the New York State Department of Corrections emblem emblazoned on the front and forty-five dollars in their pocket, courtesy of the state. When it was Andrew's turn, he paused at the threshold, swearing to put his old life behind him and to work at being worthy of Syd and Alex's trust. On his first step outside, the chains of the past fell to the wayside. He set his sights firmly on the future.

Before he reached the corner, a man's voice called out from behind him, "Andrew Castle, right?"

Andrew stopped and turned around, not recognizing the two-day stubble and wrinkled, poorly fitting off-the-rack brown suit. *Who is this guy? Columbo?* "Yeah, who wants to know?"

"I'm Matt Crown, *Daily News*. I have some questions about Kelly Thatcher."

"She killed my father. What else do you have to know?"

"You worked at Castle Resorts when your sister hired her, isn't that right?"

"Yeah?"

"Can you tell me why she hired her?"

"Why do you want to know?" A master of subterfuge in his former life, Andrew didn't know where this was going, but he smelled a dirty ploy.

"It seemed strange, considering Miss Thatcher's poor track record in business, that your sister would hire her. Did it have anything to do with the sex photos they took together when they were at Yale?"

"What the fuck? How the hell—?" Andrew stopped before he confirmed the existence of the photos. "Look, man, I don't know what you're after, but—"

"Can you tell me why Alex covered your tracks after you embezzled a quarter-million dollars from Castle Resorts?"

"Why don't you ask her?"

"I did. Now I'm asking you."

"Well, I have nothing to say to you."

"Do you believe the rumor that Alex was in on the plan to kill your father?"

Andrew laughed. Before all hell broke loose that night, Alex was the favorite child and adored their father, a blind loyalty he never understood back then. What this Crown clown was suggesting was absurd. "You're kidding, right?"

"No, I'm not, but rumor has it that Alex and Kelly had rekindled their relationship around the time Kelly killed your father. Considering your father's views on homosexuality, it's reasonable to question if Alex wanted him out of the way."

"No way. She was already with Tyler."

"So, you can confirm that Alex was in a lesbian relationship the night Kelly Thatcher killed your father."

"I'm not confirming a damn thing. We're done here." Andrew walked away, pissed at himself for putting the bloodhound onto the scent. Whatever this Matt Crown character had in mind, he was sure it wasn't good for his twin.

After catching a cab, his first stop was the offices of Wexler and Associates, one of Manhattan's most exclusive law firms. For the last twenty years, they had been the best at representing Manhattan's wealthy, specializing in criminal, tax, estate, business, and real estate law. They had also been in control of his inheritance since his first meeting with Gary Roman in prison. They'd hired an excellent portfolio manager, who had seen to it that his assets had recovered from the crash and then some, making him a high-value client.

"Thanks for meeting with me, Barry," Andrew said.

"Of course, Mr. Castle. Please have a seat. We have everything prepared for you." Barry Wexler, the law firm's senior partner, reached into his desk and handed Andrew a set of keys. "Your new Tribeca condo is all set. It's completely furnished and stocked with food, clothing, and necessities."

"Great, I was wondering where I was going to sleep tonight," Andrew replied.

Barry handed Andrew a second set of keys. "I had your BMW motorcycle stored in your condo building parking space. It's registered and fueled."

"I guess I'll have to renew my license this week," Andrew joked.

"That would be prudent, Mr. Castle. We scheduled an appointment for you at the DMV on Monday. You'll find the completed application form and a study guide in your client packet." Barry slid a leather-bound portfolio across his desk and handed Andrew a new cell phone. "Your iPhone, sir."

Andrew inspected his new gadget, perplexed by its complexity. During his four years behind bars, he'd missed the entire smartphone revolution. "It appears I have a steep learning curve ahead of me."

"We prepared a tutorial and loaded it onto your new laptop, which is at your condo."

"I appreciate that. It's been a while since I've even handled a cell phone. Can you show me how to make a call?"

"Of course." Barry instructed Andrew on the essential phone functions, returned to his chair, and reviewed several papers on his desk. "If you open your client packet, the top report reflects the current balance, positions, and performance of your investment portfolio." Andrew opened his folder and followed along. This was his wheelhouse, as Alex had pointed out with great frequency.

Barry continued, "As you can see, your financial counselor has managed your portfolio well." He then handed Andrew his passport, several bank cards, a stack of cash, and a new wallet. "Your ATM and credit cards, along with five thousand in cash as you requested."

Andrew opened the passport, noting it would expire before the travel restrictions of his parole would end next year. At least the state had categorized him as a low-risk parolee, which would allow him to travel to neighboring states. Not that he had any plans for doing so.

After Andrew set up his wallet, Barry asked him to turn to the last section in his client packet. "We set up the LLC per your instructions and filed the necessary paperwork on your behalf. We've also set up a corporate account and funded it with an initial two hundred million dollars."

"Are the funds available now?"

"Yes. The wire transfer cleared yesterday."

"Thank you. It looks like you thought of everything." Andrew silently laughed at the final mandatory lecture before Queensboro released him today. The counselors outlined the traditional difficulties parolees first encounter when released from prison, including securing housing and employment. *Done and done*, he thought.

"It's been a pleasure doing business with you, Barry." Andrew offered him a firm, respectful handshake.

"We remain at your disposal, Mr. Castle."

Andrew returned to the busy, humid streets of Manhattan. He pulled out his new phone, swiped the screen as Barry had taught him, and opened the web browser. He Googled Alex's name. The first thing that popped up was a link to *The Daily News* and an article titled, "Lies, Lust, and Larceny: How the Mighty Have Fallen."

He clicked on the link.

The article started off by recounting William's murder and Kelly's involvement. It detailed the affair she had with Alex while at Yale and the sex photos documenting it. He clicked on another link and brought up the images. There they were. The very pictures, albeit now redacted to stay within pornography laws, that he had tried desperately to get his hands on in order to turn the tables on his twin. The very things for which he had sold his soul. Those photos. Those fucking photos. *Two million*, he thought. That was the price he had been willing to pay to get his hands on those damn pictures, the amount he had borrowed from Victor Padula and the amount he had planned to repay using funds stolen from the company. He loathed his former self. "I was such an arrogant asshole."

Also on the website was a photo of a scanned letter. Andrew zoomed in on it and realized it was in Alex's handwriting. Below the image was another link, which he clicked. A pop-up window contained a typed transcript of the letter. Reading the things Alex had recounted in her private, soul-baring letter to Kelly made his heart sink. Now he understood Alex's strange behavior during junior year, quitting the track team and isolating herself from everyone but Harley. She'd almost killed herself. Even if it was an accident, that must have shaken her to the core. "My God, Alex. How could I have not known this?"

He clicked to return to the main article and read the account of his own foibles—drinking, gambling, and embezzlement. He was ashamed. How could he ever make it up to Alex and Syd? It was a tall order, but he was up to the task, he hoped. He'd redeem himself no matter how long it took.

He continued to read.

The article detailed the businesses the Castle sisters ran, Castle Resorts and Barnette Winery. Crown weaved the tale as if Alex and Syd had run both companies into the ground, and

Alex was helping prop up Barnette Wines' reputation despite a growing scandal of a tainted, substandard vintage. Crown speculated at the end that it was only a matter of months before both companies would be bankrupt, and the Castle family would be to blame for their demise.

"Holy shit." He hoped his release from prison was in time for him to save not only Castle Resorts but now Syd's business as well.

He dialed an old number, hoping it was still in service. After several rings, the call connected. A mix of regret, shame, and love swelled in his throat at the familiar "Hello."

"Hi, Alex, it's Andrew."

CHAPTER FOURTEEN

Danbury, Connecticut

Ethan slowly weaved his way through the streets of Danbury, following the voice commands of his onboard navigation system. He glanced at Destiny in the passenger seat. She'd had the same "deer in the headlights" look since hopping in the car in Springfield. The information in that birth certificate had clearly thrown her for a massive loop. Other than a quick, "Let's go," she had yet to offer anything more than "sure" or "fine" when Ethan asked if she'd mind if he made a few detours on his way back to New York.

"Hey, how about after I drop off this wine, we stop for a beer?" Ethan asked.

"Sure." Destiny's delayed response was flat and monotone.

"All right then." Ethan pulled into a parking space in front of a small industrial-looking building marked New England Wine Labs. "I'll be right back."

He retrieved two bottles of wine from the trunk, one he'd picked up from the Castle Resort in Baltimore and another he'd purchased at a high-end wine shop in Hartford an hour ago. The building's reception area was sterile, with a buffed concrete floor and nothing beyond a single company logo painted on the far wall for decoration. Leaning over the unmanned reception desk, he scanned the two open doors leading to the back, but no one was in sight. Finally, his gaze drifted to the call bell on the counter and the handwritten sign taped to it that read, "Ring for Service."

He pounded on the bell several times.

Seconds later, a woman appeared through a door leading to the back, removing her safety glasses. Her white lab coat was a giant giveaway that she was a lab tech or chemist. She wiped back her short graying brown hair. "How can I help you?"

Ethan placed two identical bottles of wine on the counter. "I need you to test these two bottles of wine and tell me if they're different."

She cocked her head to examine each bottle, both of which were labeled as 2008 Barnette cabernet sauvignon. "Interesting. Do you suspect spoilage?"

"I'm not sure what to suspect. It could be spoilage during transport, or it could be something else."

The woman rubbed her chin once. "Then I suggest running a full chemistry and juice analysis. Those panels will compare every aspect of the samples."

"Great. Be sure to label this one Hartford." Ethan pointed to the bottle he picked up on the way here. "I need the results as soon as possible."

They agreed on a price and to rush the results within a few days. Ethan returned to his car and asked with a smile, "Miss me?" Destiny nodded with what he would describe as a forced smile. "How about that beer?"

"Sure," she said, her voice still flat.

Soon Ethan came across an Applebee's and pulled in. "I'm in the mood for nachos. How about you?"

"I'm starved." Destiny straightened in her seat, and for the first time since leaving Springfield, she made eye contact with him.

"Finally." Ethan had been waiting all afternoon for Destiny to shake off whatever had her in shock. "More than a one-word response."

"I'm sorry. I've been distracted." She climbed out of the car.

Ethan also stepped out and closed the car door. "You think?" he said in a playful tone.

After they received the large platter of beef nachos and pitcher of beer they ordered, Ethan paced himself with the beer but heartily dug into the nachos. "I appreciate you being patient with my detours this afternoon. I have a hunch about my cousin's wines."

"I was with Syd on Friday when she first discovered the problem. I hope it's an isolated issue."

"I find it strange that the spoiled wine only appears at the Northeast resorts and only for a vintage expected to be their best yet. I suspect foul play."

"When I get back to work tomorrow, I can research the deliveries to those resorts for the past few years and see if anything stands out," Destiny offered.

"That reminds me." Ethan pulled out his cell phone. "I need to call my cousin. Do you mind?"

"No, go right ahead."

Ethan dialed, and after a few rings, John answered with, "Hey, cuz."

"Hey, John. You busy?…Good…I was near Boston today and picked up the 2008 cabs from the resort for Syd, and it got me thinking. Have you checked out the transportation pipeline from your end?"

"Ethan, I don't think you have to get involved in this. It's probably an issue with the trucks or warehouse."

"Listen to me, John. I have a hunch about this. What did you find out about the trucks?"

"Nothing changed since last year."

Ethan was a thorough, detail-orientated investigator, and a cursory review of the transportation arrangements didn't satisfy him. Based on Jesse's text message an hour ago detailing Alex's new woes and reporting on the wine issue, his gut told him to go back further in time and dive deep into the transportation pipeline. "Do me a favor, cuz. Pull all contracts for all Castle Resorts since the beginning of 2007 and email them to me."

"Why go that far back?" John asked.

"It might be nothing, but that's when Alex's life started going haywire. It's going haywire again, so I want to know if it's connected to the wine problem."

"I think you're wasting your time, but all right. I'll get the contracts to you tomorrow."

Ethan finished his call and returned his attention to Destiny. "I'm sorry about the interruption. So, where were we?" He dug in and grabbed a nacho filled with beef, sour cream, jalapeno, and a heavenly portion of melted cheese.

Destiny's second glass of beer clearly already had had its intended effect. She seemed more relaxed and focused. "I overheard what you said to your cousin. I'll get with Syd tomorrow, research the shipments, and send you everything we find."

"Thanks, I appreciate it."

Destiny squeezed her bottom lip with a hand. Undoubtedly, something had her worried. Her breathy sigh confirmed she was focused on troubling matters again. Looking Ethan directly in the eyes, she asked, "What would you do if you knew something that would completely toss someone's world upside down and might irrevocably harm your relationship with them? Would you tell them?"

Ethan carefully considered her question, wondering whose life she was about to turn upside down. "That's hard to say."

He thought of his own situation with Bree. DNA or not, she was his daughter. She was getting older and was evolving into a mature, responsible young woman, which was making him wrestle with the idea of when, if ever, he and Tyler should tell her that he wasn't her birth father. A more significant decision was whether to tell her she was the product of rape.

"If it involves a child," he said, "you have to consider if they're old enough to understand and process whatever emotional damage it might cause. On the other hand, if it involves an adult, if you love them and they love you, I guess it would depend on whether you can see any good coming out of it."

"Even if it might irrevocably harm your relationship with them?" Destiny asked again.

"All I can say is that if only bad could come of it, then maybe that secret is meant to be kept. Only you can assess whether any good could come from telling the truth."

"That's good advice, but I'm not sure it helps. Thanks anyway, Ethan."

CHAPTER FIFTEEN

Manhattan, New York

Tyler had finished her work in her home office some time ago and had gone looking for Alex. She found her on the patio, lit by the moon and the lights along its perimeter. She paused inside the French door to observe her for a few moments. Alex had sunk into her favorite double-wide lounge chair and was sipping a glass of red wine while watching Callie romp through the planter boxes and tear up the pansies she'd taken pride in planting last month. Alex wasn't trying to stop her, a worrisome sign.

Beyond a short text message exchange about losing the corporate loan and having to approve the downsizing plan, they hadn't communicated since the exposé hit the wires. She could tell the pressure was getting to Alex. It hurt seeing how deeply the company's impending failure was impacting her. That ache drew Tyler toward her.

She grabbed a second wineglass and opened the sliding glass door, drawing Callie's attention but not enough to stop her from chomping colorful petals. "Stop that, girl. You know better." Tyler regularly spoke to Callie like she was one of her children. Sometimes, she believed the dog half-understood every conversation. Callie's tucked-in tail and cowering swooped-back pointy ears lent credence to her suspicion.

This once-thin refugee, who had captured Tyler's heart the first time she jumped into her lap, had grown into a majestic adult German shepherd. That instant connection took Tyler by surprise, considering the devastation she'd felt years earlier after losing Shadow, the Falling family shepherd. That perfect, loving, and lovable dog had left a hole Tyler had thought no other dog could fill. But she was wrong. Callie did, and she'd become her dog as much as Alex's. And with Alex's long hours, Callie relied on Tyler for most of her needs, including discipline.

Callie approached and sat patiently beside Tyler near her feet. Tyler rubbed her now erect ears. "Good girl. Now, go get a toy." Callie dutifully darted across the patio to her doghouse. She reemerged with a furry chew toy clutched in her jaws. As Tyler neared Alex's lounge chair, Callie assumed a position at its foot. "Good girl."

Alex patted the empty spot next to her. "Sit with me, T." Her voice sounded as drained as she appeared.

Before Tyler sat, she poured herself a serving of wine, inspecting the bottle as she returned it to the nearby end table. It was the 2008 vintage Syd had concerns about. A sip confirmed the taste was impeccable. She placed her glass next to the bottle and curled up next to Alex, drawing in tight the arm Alex had wrapped around her. "It's not your fault."

"I can't help but believe it is. We lost our loan because of that exposé." The pain in Alex's voice sounded as if she'd taken on the weight of the world. "Castle Resorts could fail because of the poor choices I made when I was twenty. So many families ruined and lives destroyed because of my youthful arrogance."

Tyler pressed the side of her face more firmly against the top of Alex's breast. If it were possible to hear a heart break, Tyler just did. She lifted her head to stare into Alex's sad, tear-filled eyes. "If anyone can save the company, it's you."

Alex pressed their lips together, but this kiss lacked the heat of passion. It was cold with sadness. Alex wept without pulling away. With each tremble of her lips, Tyler's heart ached for her more and more. How could Tyler convince her that she hadn't failed? That she couldn't control what others around her did? That sometimes she could do everything right and still not get the results she desperately needed? The answer was that she couldn't. Alex had to believe it for herself.

When the tears subsided, Alex pulled away and wrapped Tyler in her arms again. They lay there for minutes or hours, Tyler couldn't be sure, but when Alex finally broke the silence, she said, "I talked to Andrew today."

"How did it go?"

"He wants to meet with Syd and me tomorrow."

"And?" Tyler asked.

"We're meeting at Lara's for lunch."

Tyler didn't know what to make of Andrew's return. Since long before his incarceration, he'd been a sore spot for Alex, as evidenced by her refusal to talk about him except in general terms. Would he come back and make trouble for a sister who already had too much on her plate? Tyler hoped prison had changed him for the better and that her reservations about him were for nothing.

"I'm glad Syd will be there too." Tyler squeezed a little tighter.

"I've been thinking about making some changes, T. More than just cutting back on time spent away from you, I mean."

"What kind of changes?"

"I'm not sure yet. I just know I need to do things differently."

CHAPTER SIXTEEN

Headquarters of the *Daily News* was buzzing with all hands on deck this morning. It was nearly moving day. In two days the entire news operation was going to relocate four and a half miles away to Manhattan's lower tip. Boxes filled every office and workstation, and technicians had already prepared and staged most electronics for transport. Most employees had prepped their offices for the weekend movers, except for a few holdouts. Matt Crown was the worst offender. True to his history of procrastination, he had yet to consider packing. He'd focused his attention on his computer screen, reading the online morning edition of the *New York Times* and the statement Alex Castle's lawyer had released exclusively to them last night in response to his exposé.

"Nothing to do with her, my ass," Crown barked to himself, not caring if his voice had carried into the hallway until he saw his grumpy, overworked boss turn on his heel near his office door.

The editor poked his head inside. "Crown, get off your ass and pack up your stuff by the end of the day. Our division is first up. Movers will relocate us tomorrow morning."

"Yeah, I know. I'll be ready." Crown returned his attention to his computer screen, incensed over the laziness at the *Times*. They were always a day late and a dollar short in their brand of journalism. Their understated piece summarizing his Castle family exposé and account of Alex's response when the press's equivalent of a mob had cornered her in front of her office building was downright embarrassing in his opinion.

"Can you believe this pile of BS from the *Times*? Alex Castle says, and I quote: 'What? Of course not. That's a preposterous lie. I had nothing to do with that.'"

"Can you prove she's lying?" his boss asked.

Crown remembered the anonymous package he'd received, containing the titillating photos and Alex's tell-all letter. It also had included a note hinting that the police had a video that proved Alex and Kelly were intimately involved when Kelly killed William Castle. The only catch: it was evidence in her manslaughter case and in police custody.

"I think I can."

"Well, then get to it."

"As much as I enjoy packing—" Crown started.

"Go." His boss looked around at Crown's office, which was in its natural state of disarray. "But you better be back in time to pack up all this stuff."

"You got it."

After his boss left, Crown rummaged through his desk drawer, locating the gift he'd given him for last year's award-winning series on local government corruption—an unopened box of Johnny Walker Blue with the gold ribbon and bow still attached. He'd held off breaking into it, waiting for a special occasion. The prospect of bringing down one of Manhattan's most elite families couldn't get more special.

"This should do it." He grabbed the bottle, checked the time on his cell phone, and dialed the one person he knew could get the evidence he needed to prove Alex Castle lied. The call connected. "Hey, Tommy. I've got a bottle of Johnny Walker Blue with your name on it."

Half an hour later, Crown was staring at a menu at a Lower Manhattan diner close to Tommy's office. He pulled his gaze away when the server returned. "I'll take the ham and cheese omelet with hash browns."

A voice sounded behind the cute redhead, "Make that two, with a cup of joe."

Crown looked past her. "Tommy, I'm glad you could make it." The server wrote their orders on her notepad before scurrying off.

"Well, you did mention scotch." Tommy limped over and sat in the booth. Other than putting on a few extra pounds on his doughy white body, he hadn't changed much since the last time Crown had wangled a favor out of him. The knee injury that he'd incurred on the job, buying him a position in the police property room versus walking a beat, however, appeared to be giving him more problems.

"That I did." Crown placed a paper sack containing the ribbon-clad blue and gold box on the table.

Tommy inspected the bag and whistled appreciatively before narrowing an eye at Crown. "I've known you long enough to know this means you want something big."

"You know me well, my friend. I want something from a 2007 case involving Kelly Thatcher—a copy of the undercover video that has her initial confession." Crown understood the risk he was asking his old high school buddy to take. His previous requests had amounted to Tommy photographing evidence from unusual cases using his cell phone. This request would entail making a copy of actual evidence.

"That's pretty dicey, Matt."

"Tommy, it's the same as you taking pictures for me. Only this time, you make a copy of the digital file. It's not like I'm asking you to steal it."

Tommy rubbed his clean-shaven face, his tell that Crown had yet to convince him, so he pushed.

"Look, you've been a clerk at the property office for eight years, and I know for a fact that you know how to cover your tracks. The case was a plea agreement, so there's no chance of appeal. There's no way this can come back to you."

"I don't know, man."

As well as Tommy knew Crown, Crown knew Tommy. They'd been friends for nearly a quarter-century, from chasing girls in high school to drunken weekends at the neighborhood pub. That deep-rooted comradery meant that anytime Crown called, Tommy provided him information about a case that no other reporter in town had access to in exchange for a little something. All Tommy needed was one final push.

"Let me sweeten the pot," Crown offered. "Why don't you join me in the Yankees' locker room with the rest of the press after a game this week?"

"You're kidding?"

Crown nervously spun a spoon on the table, hoping the prospect of making an up-close and personal contact with Jeter, A-Rod, and Rivera would be enough to tip the scale with Tommy. "Totally legit. I can have the paper issue you press creds for a day. With those, I can get you into the press area for the entire game."

When Tommy grinned from ear to ear, Crown knew he had him. Over breakfast, they discussed the specifics of the tape and which game Tommy wanted to attend as a temporary member of the press. After Crown settled the check, he walked Tommy to the street.

"So, when do you think I can get my hands on that video?" Crown asked.

"Tonight. I'll have to wait until the other guys take their meal break to copy the file. How about we meet at The Ale House around seven?"

"That works for me."

Crown and Tommy parted ways on the corner, each heading back to their offices, Tommy to stretch the boundary of NYPD ethics and Crown to pack up his stuff for the big move.

Fifteen minutes later, Crown had a seat on the northbound subway train. When the doors closed and he settled into a commuter's trance, his mind focused on the Castle exposé. He was confident the video would blow the lid off Alex's denials and earn him another award.

He laced his fingers, placing his linked hands behind his head. *This should score me another bottle of Johnny Walker Blue.*

CHAPTER SEVENTEEN

As he walked into the Castle Resorts headquarters, Ethan pondered the things Destiny had said to him yesterday over their late lunch in Connecticut. Reading the contents of her original birth certificate had visibly shaken her, enough to ask him, "What would you do if you knew something that would completely toss someone's world upside down if it might irrevocably harm your relationship with them?" What that birth certificate had disclosed seemed likely to affect someone close to her, maybe even someone close to him. Whatever the truth was about her birth, he had a hunch it would come out soon. When it did, she might need someone to lean on.

Armed with two large gourmet coffees, he popped his head into Destiny's workstation. "Hey, you. It's not Nescafé, but I thought you could use a little java this morning."

"Nescafé was surprisingly good for instant." Destiny eagerly accepted Ethan's steaming liquid offering and took a sip. "But *this* is coffee. What brings you here?"

"I thought I'd save some time and help you and Syd research the wine deliveries. Mind if I sit for a bit?"

Destiny gestured her hand toward a small guest chair. "Knock yourself out. I was just printing out the Barnette files for the last several years."

"Perfect timing. I received my cousin's email about the wine orders from his end. I want to match them up with Castle Resorts records." He pulled out his cell phone and forwarded the email to Destiny. "Can you print these out as well?"

"Sure thing."

While she printed and organized the Barnette files, Ethan thought again about her reaction to reading her birth certificate yesterday. "Have you decided what to do about your birth parents?"

"I think so, but first, I need to have a conversation with my birth mother."

"Do you need any help finding her?"

"No. I have that covered."

"All right then." *Interesting.* If Destiny didn't need help finding her, her birth mother must be someone already in her life. But who? "If you need anything or just want to talk, give me a call."

Syd appeared at Destiny's workstation. "Good morning, girl. Oh, hey, Ethan. I appreciated your detour to Boston yesterday. You saved me a lot of trouble."

"I hope you didn't mind me dropping off those samples at the testing lab," Ethan said.

"Of course not. I'm glad you did. Once I tasted the wine from the bottles you picked up at the resort, I knew something wasn't right."

"I put a rush on the testing. We should get the results back tomorrow," Ethan said.

"Good, I'm anxious to sort this out." Syd pivoted toward Destiny, who was staring vacantly at her cubicle wall with the same strange look on her face as she had in the car with him yesterday during the drive from Springfield. "Are we ready to review the files?" she asked.

Destiny didn't answer at first. Ethan gently placed his hand on hers. "Destiny, are we ready to review the files?"

Destiny shook off whatever had had her distracted. "Yeah. I reserved the conference room for us."

They spent the next hour reviewing and comparing John's records to those from Castle Resorts. Similar to when he built "murder boards" during his days on the Sacramento police force, Ethan used a white dry erase board to outline the relevant information. When they finished, they stood in a row, arms crossed, studying their handiwork. They'd uncovered an intriguing change.

"So, nothing changed from our end," Syd said, referring to the Barnette Winery. "We've shipped every order of cabernet to the same warehouse in Philly, using the same transporter and same procedures, for as far back as our search went."

"The only change is from our end." Destiny pointed to a handwritten line on the board, referring to Castle Resorts. "This year, our carrier made the pickups, each destined to be transported to the four Northeastern resorts three days after delivery to Philly Cold Storage versus the next business day. The storage company, however, did not charge us for the extended storage time."

Ethan was curious about the delay and why the warehouse didn't charge to store expensive cases of wine requiring special refrigeration. He examined the warehouse documents again. "I'll be damned." He highlighted sets of numbers on several transport orders. "I can't believe I almost missed this."

"Missed what?" Syd asked.

He pointed to the highlighted numbers with delivery dates from 2007 through 2010 for the two vintages Barnette Winery had shipped to Castle Resorts—cabernet and merlot. "Note the warehouse dock numbers for each order."

Syd examined the numbers. "Okay, they're the same."

He then pointed to the delivery and pickup sheets for 2011. "Now, look at the dock numbers."

Syd and Destiny studied the sheets before glancing at each other. The numbers were different in one instance—the cabernet shipment. Drivers had delivered Syd's cabernet to one dock and picked it up at another.

Ethan continued, "Why the change in docks this year? Why did the warehouse move only your cabernet between arrival and pickup? I'm suspecting foul play, Syd."

Syd appeared puzzled. "Couldn't the warehouse have just moved the wine to a different cooler while waiting for pickup?"

"That could be the case, but we need to check out the warehouse in Philly."

"We should go tomorrow," Syd said. "The second shipment of cabernet is scheduled to arrive at the warehouse Saturday evening. I'd like to get to the bottom of this before another shipment is spoiled."

"Tomorrow works for me. I'm taking Bree to the DMV after school today so she can get her learner's permit."

Syd laughed. "That's right. The budding lawyer made a persuasive argument, didn't she?"

"That she did." Ethan grinned with a sense of pride over Bree's maturity and Jesse's influence. The perfectly crafted rationale Bree had presented for getting her driver's license— devised as if she were speaking in front of a jury—had his wife's fingerprints all over it.

CHAPTER EIGHTEEN

Customers streamed steadily in and out of Lara's at Times Square—a good sign the new eatery was thriving. However, it wouldn't be enough for Alex to reverse the company-wide downsizing plan she'd approved for implementation yesterday. Despair about that aside, Alex considered the busy public setting, taking place on her turf, was an ideal location for what would likely be an uncomfortable, even contentious, meeting.

In minutes, she would come face-to-face with the one person in the world, other than Tyler, with whom she should have an unshakable or at least undeniable connection. She had neither of those with her twin, however, and that was heartbreaking. She blamed him and their father equally for that sad truth. William had manipulated her and Andrew like chess pieces, pitting one against the other in a long-term strategy to win...what? Love? Absolutely not. William Castle used love as a tool, something to leverage as a means to an end. All their father had cared about was power and influence, which inevitably broke the connection between the twins.

As she walked through the glass doors and past the hostess station toward their reserved table, Alex weighed the dilemmas facing the Castle family. Andrew's release from prison was the least of them. Despite Matt Crown's slanted journalism, he was right about one thing—both Castle Resorts and Barnette Winery were on the verge of collapse.

When she and Syd reached Alex's customary table next to the kitchen entrance, Alex asked, "Do you think someone tampered with the wine?"

"I don't know what to think yet, but Ethan thinks something funny is going on."

"I'm glad he's on this," Alex said. "He'll get to the bottom of it."

"I'm glad too. I don't know if the winery can survive a scandal right now."

"I feel the same way about Castle Resorts." Alex sighed deeply. Her world was coming apart along with Syd's; they were both bailing water from their sinking ships at a furious pace and new leaks were appearing every time they turned around. "How did our businesses get so fucked up, Syd?"

"I don't know, baby sis."

Alex and Syd looked up when someone stopped at their table. Emotion swelled in Alex's throat when she locked gazes with her twin for the first time in four years. The last time she'd seen him outside of a courtroom, just before his sentencing, was when she and Ethan had suspected him of killing her father, the same day she learned he'd swiped her mother's prized camera from her in exchange for getting a car from their manipulative father. Living on the edge, addicted to gambling and alcohol and with an unquenchable thirst for control of Castle Resorts, had taken its toll back then. Today he appeared different. Gone was his cold, hollow appearance, replaced by traces of the young man he'd been right out of Yale, when he was full of optimism.

"Alex. Syd. Thanks for meeting me today." He'd exchanged his trademark arrogance for contriteness, but Alex wasn't buying it. Not yet.

Anger, regret, and sorrow all ran through her. Every argument, every tear, and every harsh word that had passed between the two of them flashed through her mind. He had been an ass to her and to most people around him in his quest for money and power. That was something she couldn't readily forgive or forget. Everything to him had been a competition, from grades to running on the track team to courting their father's love. She regretted not caring enough to figure out why he'd been that way because, as his twin, she should have tried. They should have been inseparable. They should have been best friends. Much needed saying, but no words came to her lips. All she could do was stare at the one person she wanted to connect with but never could as an adult.

Syd broke the awkward silence and rose to give their brother a hug. "It's good to see you, Andrew. Let's sit."

Andrew ran a hand through his hair, signaling he welcomed the meager beginning. "Thanks, Syd."

Silence settled again between the siblings, with Andrew and Alex staring at each other, neither attempting to start things off. Alex searched her brother's eyes, trying to read what was in his heart. Was he still the same self-centered ass who would do anything to get what he wanted? Do anything to get under her skin? Or had he changed as Syd had tried to convince her last week?

Syd squeezed Andrew's hand. "Do you have a place to stay?"

Andrew broke his stare at Alex to answer Syd. "Don't worry about me. I have a place in Tribeca with all the basics."

"Until it belongs to your bookie." Alex wasn't sure why she was striking out at him like this. Was it to let him know she didn't trust him? Or to return the hurt he'd inflicted on her for so many years? Either way, it wasn't like her, and it wasn't called for. Before she could say so, Syd spoke.

"There's no need for hostility."

"No, Syd. It's all right." Andrew looked Alex in the eye again. He appeared neither hurt nor angered but resolved. "I deserved that."

Alex leaned back in her chair, folding her arms across her chest. She hadn't finished unloading on him apparently. "On the phone, you said that we should meet. Not 'can we meet' or

'I'd like to meet.' That was presumptuous. What do you want, Andrew?"

"You're right, Alex. It was presumptuous. I'm sorry. I want us to be a family, but I'll settle for anything I can get."

Andrew had said the right words, but did he genuinely mean them? Years ago, Alex would have given anything to hear those things from him, but she wasn't ready to listen to them now. Forgiveness wasn't within reach. Not yet. "That is a long way off."

"Fair enough," Andrew said. "You should know that Matt Crown ambushed me in Queensboro yesterday."

"Don't tell me you've been feeding dirt to that prick!" Alex snapped.

"Alex, I'm sure—" Syd stopped her defense of Andrew when he raised a hand in a stopping motion.

Andrew calmly answered, "Of course not. He asked me about Kelly and the photos and my embezzlement and you covering it up. I told him to fuck off when he tried to link you to Kelly and to Father's murder."

"That snake hit us up the other day about the same thing, including some trouble with Barnette wine," Syd said.

"The timing of this is pretty bad, isn't it?" Andrew asked. "I've been following the *Financial Times*, and I saw the quarterly reports online. I know Castle Resorts is struggling. I'd like to help."

Without thinking, Alex fired back, "We don't need your help. You certainly didn't care about the company when you stole from it."

"I deserve that too, but I'm in a position to help. I'm prepared to float the company any amount to keep it in the black."

Alex had exhausted every option for a cash infusion, including leveraging her personal wealth. Even if he had good intentions, which she seriously doubted, she couldn't bring herself to accept Andrew's offer. She'd rather green-light the downsizing plan than allow him to sink his money-grubbing hands into the company she'd nursed for years.

"No."

She knew that with that one word she was sealing the fate of eleven thousand families, and it drove a knife through her heart. This was insane. If it were anyone else in the world, she would have jumped at the money. She was pissed at herself for not accepting it and pissed at Andrew for making her feel that way. She couldn't bring herself to reverse her decision, though.

When Andrew slumped in his chair, Alex stormed out of the restaurant onto the streets of Times Square, her temples throbbing. She'd walked into that meeting feeling anger, regret, and sadness, and she had walked out the same way, only for different reasons. She'd ruined the lives of every employee who expected better of her. She pulled out her cell phone. After the third ring, the call connected, and she heard the one voice in the world that could calm her with a single word. "Alex," she heard.

She responded with a single choked syllable, "T."

CHAPTER NINETEEN

The Midtown Manhattan branch of the DMV was a sea of humanity, teeming with men, women, and teens of every ethnic group. Conversations in English, Spanish, Chinese, French Creole, and Russian filled the room.

Ethan had arrived twenty minutes ago and was growing impatient. He paced back and forth near the exit and redialed his phone. When the call went to voice mail for the fifth time, he hung up, holding his temper the best he could. "Where the hell are you?"

Bree was already ten minutes late for her appointment. Considering her eagerness to schedule it, her tardiness perplexed him. School had let out an hour ago, and even with her usual slow, distracted walking pace, she was at most a twenty-five-minute subway ride away. He waited another ten minutes before walking outside to make another call.

"Hey, Ethan. How did it go?" Tyler asked.

"She never showed," he replied. Just saying those words made the hairs on the back of his neck tingle, but he didn't want to alarm Tyler unnecessarily, so he kept emotion out of his voice as much as he could.

"What do you mean she never showed? Did you call her?"

"Several times, but my calls go to voice mail. Did she say anything this morning about having to stay after school?"

"This morning? Wasn't she with you last night?" Tyler asked.

"I'm confused. I haven't seen her since the graduation party," Ethan said.

"Wait. Didn't Bree spend the night at your house?"

"When did you see her last?" A sinking feeling took hold as Ethan pieced it together. Bree had pulled a fast one, but why? What would drive his daughter to lie to him and Tyler? He tried to not jump to conclusions, but serving so many years as a cop steered him toward worst-case scenarios.

"Tuesday afternoon, I think. Oh damn, she asked for her birth certificate for the DMV. I completely forgot to pull it out." She put the call on speaker. "She texted me that night, saying she was visiting with Erin and then would stay with you until today."

"Son of a bitch." Ethan increased his pace down West Thirty-First Street. Injured, kidnapped, or dead were his worst nightmare, but her finding out about the adoption was a close second. "So, we haven't seen her in almost two days."

"How could this happen?" Worry cut through Tyler's voice.

"Let's just concentrate on finding her. I'll call Erin."

"I'll call Kaitlyn. She was with Bree on Tuesday," Tyler said. "Can you come over after you reach Erin?"

Ethan agreed to touch base later and ended the call, taking a moment to gather himself. He might not carry a badge any longer, but he still had a cop's instinct. His gut told him something was desperately wrong and that their family would never be the same. Making it worse, he didn't know whether he'd find Bree at some friend's house or the morgue.

* * *

Tyler's call to Kaitlyn, Bree's best friend, proved fruitless. Those two had a code of silence stronger than the one Alex had with Erin about what had happened on graduation night. An hour passed as Tyler anxiously awaited an update from Ethan. Finally, the doorbell rang. Flying to the door, she opened it to find Ethan and Erin on the stoop, both looking pale and long-faced. She teetered on frantic, assuming the worst. "What happened to her?"

"Let's sit down, Tyler."

This had to be disastrous. The last time Ethan asked her to sit down before a conversation he had broken the news that a passing car had killed the family dog. This was going to be about Bree, though. It had to be something so much worse. Every inch of her went numb as she led the way through the entrance hall to the living room, each step seeming to require double the effort of the previous one. Too afraid to ask, she perched silently on the couch, quivering on the edge of terror.

Ethan and Erin sat on the sofa, flanking Tyler. Ethan brought her hand into his. He visibly swallowed. "Bree knows about Paul."

Tyler slumped. Present tense. "Knows." So she wasn't dead. Her relief that Bree wasn't in the morgue was short-lived, replaced by a different kind of dread. Paul was the one truth Tyler had never wanted to be surfaced. She'd spent sixteen years keeping this secret from Bree, and now that had blown up on her. Every fear she'd ever had about Bree swirled in her head. *She'll never look at Ethan the same way again. She'll want to know how she was conceived. She'll want to meet her birth father. She'll hate me.*

"How did she find out?"

Ethan turned to Erin, giving her a go-ahead nod.

"Her birth certificate." Erin paused when Tyler looked confused. "She found both along with the adoption papers."

Tyler felt the blood rush from her face. This was her fault. She had been so wrapped up in a work deadline that Bree had discovered the secret she wanted to be hidden forever. Why hadn't she made sure all those records were under lock and key?

Erin continued, "She tracked me down at Connor's Tuesday night and wanted to know who Paul Stevens was and if I knew about it. She was so angry, Mom."

"And you're just now telling us?" Tyler gave her an incredulous look.

"She said she was going to get answers from the source." Erin lowered her head, resting her forehead against both palms. "I should have listened to Conner and come to you right away. I thought she was going to talk to you. I was giving her time."

Tyler buried her face in her hands, dreading what was ahead for Bree, for all of them. "It's all my fault."

"What exactly did you tell her?" Ethan asked Erin.

"I told her she'd have to talk to you two." Erin glanced between Tyler and Ethan before settling on her father. "She asked if you knew, Dad. I told her you did from the beginning and that you were her father in every way that counted. She was so mad that she was the only one who didn't know she was adopted. I think she hates me now."

Tyler seized Erin's hand. Her heart was breaking for her. "Did you explain why I told you?"

Erin shook her head, her eyes watering like Tyler's, in keeping with the deep pain they had each endured. "No, there was no reason for her to know."

Tyler shifted on the couch, kicking herself for being so careless. She looked Erin in the eye, sensing her anguish. "I should have never asked you to keep this from Bree. I'm sorry I put you in that position."

"It's all right, Mom. Like I said when you told me, it was your story to tell, no one else's."

"Thank you, honey. Why didn't you call me?"

"Show her the text messages," Ethan said.

Erin pulled up the text messages she'd exchanged with Bree yesterday and let Tyler read them. "I'm so sorry I didn't tell you sooner. I thought Bree meant she was just going to talk to you after she calmed down."

Tyler looked to Ethan, fearing the answer to her next question. "Where is she?"

"I checked her prepaid card. She bought a plane ticket to Sacramento," he said.

Images of the bastard who lived there flashed in her head, dredging up the paralyzing fear she'd felt on that hideous night. "We need to go after her."

Bree was searching for him. Everything Tyler had done to keep the truth buried had been for nothing. Her breathing became shallow. Her heart thumped so hard she became lightheaded. She recognized the signs—she'd triggered another tachycardia episode, something she hadn't done in years.

Ethan knelt in front of Tyler. "Where are your pills?"

Tyler's upper body swayed, but Ethan caught her. "My purse in the entry hall."

Minutes later, Ethan returned with Tyler's purse and medication. Once the pills took effect and her breathing and heart rate returned to normal, he said, "I'll let Maddie know what's going on and book us a flight for the first thing tomorrow morning."

Tyler shook her head, trying but failing to remain calm. "That's not soon enough. We need to leave tonight." She pulled out her cell phone and dialed. Not an hour earlier, she'd buoyed Alex after an emotional reunion with her brother. Now she needed Alex to do the same for her. The call connected on two rings. "Alex, I need your help."

* * *

Alex sat on the foot of the bed, trying to soak in the additional bombshell Tyler had dropped moments ago. When she had called an hour earlier, explaining about Bree and asking her help to borrow the Spencer Foundation jet, she had buried the lede as far as Alex was concerned—the fact that this crisis had triggered another heart episode. It had been years since Tyler had gotten so worked up that her arrhythmia presented itself, let alone put her on the verge of fainting.

"You should have told me when it happened, T." Alex suppressed her concern that Tyler may have reverted to her old ways, burying painful feelings and ignoring troubling events instead of coming to terms with them. Piling on at this point wouldn't help.

Tyler stopped packing her suitcase, shoved it aside to sit next to Alex on the bed. She interlaced her fingers of her left hand with Alex's right. "I wanted to tell you in person so you could see for yourself that I was fine. Ethan was here, and it passed quickly."

"I'm worried about you. All this stress can't be good for your heart. I wish you'd rethink letting me come with you."

"I always want you with me, but this is something Ethan and I have to do alone as parents. We decided years ago as a couple to keep the truth from her, and now it's up to us to find her and fix it. Besides, you have your hands full. Castle Resorts and Syd's business are both in chaos. You need to be here."

Damn her logic. Tyler was right. She was always right. "Promise me that you won't overdo it. I don't think *my* heart could take it if anything happened to yours."

"You have no idea how much I love you." Tyler gently pushed Alex's torso flat on the bed, atop the blouses, slacks, and underwear she had yet to place in the suitcase. She rolled her body on top of Alex, pressing their lips together in a long, passionate kiss.

Alex needed this connection. The day had left her feeling hollow. Human Resources would send out notices to a quarter of her worldwide workforce in a few days, telling thousands they would lose their jobs in ninety days. She felt powerless to help them and very much wanted, needed, to feel in control.

Alex rolled Tyler over, crumpling the unpacked clothing. She latched her lips onto Tyler's neck, kissing the lightly lavender-scented area behind her ear. Tyler's faint moan and subtle writhe encouraged her to move down to the soft skin below her clavicle and glide a hand up to massage a breast.

Tyler nudged Alex until they were face-to-face, nose-to-nose, inhaling the other's breath. "Don't get me started. We have to leave in fifteen minutes." Her words said one thing, but their tone said another. The breathy release behind them said she wanted this as much as Alex did.

Alex formed a devilish grin, having every intention of getting her started. "That's plenty of time." She kissed Tyler on the lips again before returning to her neck. They rocked to a slow, passionate rhythm.

"Whoa, whoa, whoa. Sorry, ladies. I let myself in." Ethan's voice, peppered with embarrassment, sounded from the doorway. Alex rolled to the side, freeing Tyler to sit up.

"Sorry, I'm not quite ready," Tyler said.

Ethan snickered, "From the look of things, I'd say you were well on your way."

Alex snickered, too.

"You two are incorrigible." Tyler swatted Ethan on the arm as she passed him. "I need to get some things from the bathroom."

"I'll finish packing your clothes." Alex began folding the crumpled items. Once she and Ethan were alone, she turned to him. "I'm depending on you to make sure she doesn't have another episode like the one she had today."

"I'll do my best to keep her calm, but we're both pretty upset about Bree taking off like this." Ethan put his hands on his hips in apparent frustration. "I can't believe she left without talking to us first about her birth father."

"She's hurt. She just found out you've lied to her for her entire life. I'm sure Bree feels she doesn't know who she can trust. She needs the truth right now, and she thinks she's going to find it in Paul."

"I hope she's ready for the truth." Ethan lowered his head, his worry evident.

"She's a strong young woman just like her sister, just like her mother. You and Tyler are great parents. I'm sure you two will get her through learning the ugly truth."

"I hope so."

Tyler reentered the room with her travel toiletries and placed them in her suitcase. "Are we sure the jet is ready to go, babe?"

"Harley said it's ready when you are," Alex said. "You should arrive in Sacramento before breakfast."

"Good, I'm all set," Tyler said.

Ethan kissed Alex on the cheek and grabbed the suitcase before turning to Tyler. "I'll meet you downstairs."

Tyler stepped up close to Alex and threw her arms around her neck when Ethan left. Alex wrapped her arms tight around Tyler's waist until their bodies became one. The unyielding embrace gave Alex comfort that the journeys they were both on would end well and strengthen their family. She whispered into Tyler's ear, hoping the words she was about to say would help prevent her from letting herself get worked up again. "Remember your promise."

"I will," Tyler said. She released her grasp and gave Alex a final, sweet kiss goodbye.

CHAPTER TWENTY

Brooklyn, New York

Only six miles separated the densely populated neighborhoods of Flatbush and Greenpoint in Brooklyn. Despite their proximity, though, two people, one living in each community, could go an entire lifetime without running into the other. Such was the case with Destiny and her birth mother. A thirty-minute drive would change that circumstance today and possibly alter her life forever.

After parking along Franklin Street, Destiny ascended the few stairs to one of Greenpoint's older single-family homes. Her nerves pulsated, many, too many, questions swirling in her head. She didn't know where to start. Hell, she wasn't even sure how to introduce herself. She paused at the front door, straightened her suit jacket, and told herself, "You got this."

She knocked.

Soon she heard the distinct sound of locks disengaging. The door swung open, revealing a tall, black- and gray-haired woman in her sixties. She looked exactly like she did in the photo Destiny had printed yesterday.

The woman looked on curiously when Destiny said nothing. "May I help you?"

Destiny cleared her nervousness from her throat. "I believe you knew my mother, Sarah Scott."

The woman's face went pale, a sure sign Destiny had found her birth mother. She stood silent for several moments. Had she wondered what her daughter looked like? If she'd married and had children? If she was happy and healthy? If she was still alive? Or did she give up her daughter for adoption and never look back?

"May I come in?" Destiny asked.

"Of course, of course," the woman said as she opened the door wider to let Destiny pass. She guided her to the couch. "Please, sit down. May I get you anything?"

"No, thank you."

The woman sat on a well-worn chair that was at right angles to the mismatched, older couch. Destiny wondered what she was thinking. Was she filled with excitement or regret? Then again, only a woman who cared about the daughter she abandoned would have those emotions. The woman shifted nervously against the frayed fabric, crossing and uncrossing her legs. "You're my cousin's daughter, and I don't even know your name."

"My name is Destiny."

"That's a beautiful name."

"My mother." Destiny paused, struggling over what to call the woman who raised her and the woman sitting before her. She could call both her mother, but this woman hadn't earned that coveted title yet. "My mom said the first time she held me, she knew I was destined for good things. I never understood why until a few weeks ago."

"And what happened a few weeks ago?"

"She died."

"I'm so sorry, dear. Sarah was a good woman." She paused when Destiny harrumphed.

"The night before my mother passed away, she told me I was adopted. The other day, with the help of a good lawyer and private detective, I discovered that it was you who put me up for adoption but that Sarah took me in after you left."

"It's you." The woman gasped, clutching her chest. She appeared thrown by the news and looked at Destiny more intently. "When you said Sarah was your mother, I'd assumed she'd also had a child. I had no idea she'd raised you. All these years, I've thought you were being raised by a family the county adoption agency found."

She shifted taller in her chair. "Let me look at you." She studied Destiny up and down for several beats. "It appears my cousin raised you well."

"She did the best she could, but at times I felt like I raised myself."

The woman furrowed her brow in curiosity but didn't question Destiny's statement. Instead, she settled her gaze on her eyes. Finally, she said, "You have your father's eyes. I assume you have a lot of questions. I know I do."

Her birth mother was correct. Destiny had many questions, but it all boiled down to one. "I guess all I want to know is why did you give me up?"

"That is a complicated story. Let's just say I loved your father, but he didn't love me. He was very good at using people and throwing them away."

"Like you threw me away?" Destiny intentionally sharpened her words. She needed to signal that this would not be a loving family reunion.

"I can see why you would think that."

"Are you suggesting it wasn't your choice to give me away? Did my birth father even know about me?"

The woman laughed and slapped her hands on her thighs. "Oh, sweetie. He knew about you. He didn't want you. You didn't fit into his picture-perfect life."

"Did you know he was like that before you began the affair with him?"

"I can assure you I didn't. At the start, he was kind and attentive and was already a father."

"Tell me, Georgia. Was it worth sleeping with the boss? In your thirty-seven years at Castle Resorts, you never made it out of Accounting."

"I can see you've done your homework."

"It wasn't that hard. I've been working for Alex Castle for the last four years. In fact, I have your old job."

Georgia's eyebrows rose in surprise. "Ironic. William never wanted you, yet here you are, working at the same company he gave birth to." She laughed.

The irony hadn't impressed Destiny. She wanted to know why her birth parents gave her up and needed to press harder. She stood as if readying to leave. "Look, if you won't give me any answers—"

Georgia extended her hand in a stopping motion. "Please, stay. I'll tell you whatever you want to know."

"Tell me why you and William gave me up."

Georgia shifted uncomfortably in her chair. "All right. It was 1971…"

* * *

Manhattan, New York, Fall 1971

It was Tuesday evening, which meant at six p.m. sharp Georgia Cushing meticulously tidied her desk, packed up her purse, and double-checked to make sure she'd tucked her special keys safely inside it. Once she checked her lipstick in the ladies' room, she entered a private elevator off the lobby, inserted the first key in the wall panel, and selected the penthouse floor as she had done every Tuesday night for the past two years. The top floor of Castle Resorts Times Square was home to two suites— the Presidential and the Owner's. They were reserved for only William Castle and his special guests. Georgia was one such guest, at least on Tuesdays. This night was special, however. She had important news to share but was unsure how he'd react. Debating how to tell him occupied her mind during the ride up.

At the door to the Owner's suite, she used her second key, walked in, and placed her purse on a small table near the entrance. A single desk lamp illuminated the room and highlighted

William, looking ever so handsome, sitting in his executive chair, thumbing through a stack of documents. Georgia took a position behind him and began kneading his neck and muscular shoulders with her long, slender hands.

William showed his approval by rocking his head from side to side. "Ummm. That feels good."

She continued to dig into his muscles, alternating between her fingers and thumbs. "You feel tight. Did you have a rough day?"

He nodded, slinging his head forward. "Construction in Boston is falling behind. We may have to push back the grand opening, so I'm heading up there tomorrow to oversee things myself."

She leaned down and kissed the base of his neck. "I have faith you'll get things back on track."

He swung his chair around and wrapped his arms around her waist, pulling her toward him. "You seem to be the only one who has faith in me these days. My wife thinks my expansion plans will bankrupt us."

The mention that he was still married to that silly woman who underappreciated him and failed to satisfy him gave Georgia the shivers. She lifted his chin and looked into his eyes, hoping one day he'd see she could do both for him every day of the week, not just on Tuesdays. "She doesn't know you as I do. She's never seen how determined you get when you're challenged."

He buried his face against the dress fabric covering her abdomen. "She doesn't know how much I love this company."

"Why do you stay married to her then?"

William pushed her away, walked the few steps to the wet bar, and poured two glasses of scotch. "I told you. I need access to her money for another year or two until I expand in DC and Baltimore." He offered a glass to Georgia.

The way to tell him her news suddenly became apparent. Georgia waved him off, declining the drink. "No. Let's sit. I need to tell you why I can't drink tonight."

William downed his shot of smooth amber liquid and returned both glasses to the counter. He turned around and pulled Georgia to his body, kissing her on her neck. She'd give anything to continue this, but she'd waited too many weeks to tell him the truth.

"I don't want to talk." He reached around to unzip her dress, but she pushed him back.

"We need to talk, William."

His tight expression revealed his impatience. By this time every Tuesday, he usually was nearing release, but Georgia needed to break the life-changing news. Before she could, he marched back to the wet bar and poured another drink. "Is this about the promotion? I told you, people are already talking about us. I can't chance word getting back to my wife because of petty competitiveness."

Though her lack of upward mobility in Castle Resorts for the sake of discretion bothered her, this was not the time to discuss it. "No, this isn't about that. I saw my doctor last week. I'm pregnant."

He stopped dead in his tracks and swigged the scotch in one gulp. "Is it mine?"

The insult took her aback, hurting more than she thought possible. "Of course, it's yours. I love you. You're the only one I've been with in two years."

"Humph," he snorted and shook his head. "Yes, well, the timing couldn't be worse." He reached into his hip pocket, pulling out his wallet. "Can you take care of it?"

Georgia recoiled at the suggestion. "Take care of it? Do you mean an abortion?"

"Of course, I mean an abortion. It's the practical thing to do." He fished through his wallet. "Should two hundred cover it?"

She snapped her hand up. "I don't want your money. This is our child. Doesn't that mean anything to you?"

"Be reasonable, Georgia. I'm married, I already have a child, and I'm not about to leave her until I can afford to."

"Please, William. This is my child. I can't abort it." She buried her face in her hands, soaking her palms quickly with the tears prompted by the heartless thing he expected of her.

He grabbed her by the shoulders and shook her slightly. "Get a grip, woman. You need to think about the future. If I'm out on the street because of this, you will be too. I trust you'll do the right thing."

Get a grip? Georgia's self-pity turned to anger on a dime. "Did you ever love me?"

He lowered his hands and retraced his steps to the wet bar. "This is an affair, Georgia. Nothing more."

"I've been such a fool. If you want me to take care of things your way, it will cost you a lot more than two hundred dollars to keep my silence."

By the time she stormed out, she had extracted a lifetime of security from him in the form of a rent-free house. She would take care of "things" her way, though, not his.

Five months later

"He'll see you now," William's secretary said, scrutinizing Georgia's growing belly.

Georgia had publicly blamed it on overindulging in holiday sweets, but she got the impression the explanation was no longer enough of a cover story. Already she had noticed several hushed conversations among coworkers coming to a halt when she walked by. The weather would soon change, too, and wearing bulky winter clothing would no longer be an option for hiding her condition, especially from the man who had put her in it. The next five minutes would make that issue moot, she hoped.

Once she was inside, William gestured toward the guest chairs. "Miss Cushing, come in. Please, have a seat." Since she broke the news of her pregnancy, he had stopped asking her up to his suite and kept their interactions professional. She had rightly expected better of him, but now that she'd seen his true colors, she wanted nothing to do with him. She'd have his baby, but that was as far as she could go for her child. If he discovered that she had defied him, he'd have her head and the child's too. Someone else would have to raise it.

"No, thank you. I'll stand, Mr. Castle. I just need you to approve my leave of absence," she said, adjusting her oversized winter coat.

"Leave of absence?" he asked.

"Yes. My cousin was in an accident, and I'm the only family she has. She'll need my help for three months or so while she's recuperating."

"Three months? That's quite a long time to be away from work."

"It can't be helped." She threw him a dirty look and added, "I trust you'll do the right thing."

William swallowed hard at the harsh implication of her last words. "Of course. Your job will be waiting for you when you return."

* * *

Back to Brooklyn, New York, 2011

"I stayed with Sarah until you were born. Then I dropped you off at the county adoption agency and never saw Sarah again," Georgia said.

Georgia's story wasn't entirely unexpected. Alex had rarely talked about her father, but when she did, she'd given Destiny the impression he was a heartless man. This confirmed it. The surprising aspect was that though Georgia had never looked back she had benefited from her part ever since.

"And why didn't you? Was it because you used her to get what you needed and then no longer had any use for her? No wonder she never mentioned you whenever I asked about her extended family. And all these years, you sat in a free house while the two of us struggled to put a roof over our heads and food on the table. I'm glad I told Alex to sell it. You've profited enough from my birth."

"You're responsible? You're the reason I won't have a home next month?" Georgia rose to her feet, hands formed into fists. "You'd kick out your own mother?"

"You are not my mother." Destiny walked out, and like Georgia, she didn't look back.

CHAPTER TWENTY-ONE

Sacramento, California

Tyler was exhausted, drained during their overnight cross-country flight by hours of guilt and worry. Guilt over keeping secrets and worry about Bree discovering the truth without the two of them there to explain. The catnap she managed on the plane wasn't enough, nor were the short nap and shower she took at her and Ethan's hotel suite after landing.

Ethan poured two cups of coffee when Tyler emerged from one of the bedrooms. "I had breakfast brought up. Coffee?" he offered.

"God, yes." Tyler struggled to shake off her fatigue and gladly accepted the cup before firing up her laptop. "Have you thought about what we're going to tell her?"

"It's time to tell her everything." Ethan checked his laptop, too. "Good news. Marco came through with Paul's new work and home addresses. This will save hours of research." He jotted down the information from his old partner, who still worked for the Sacramento PD. "We should start at his home. Anything new from Maddie?"

Tyler logged on and scanned through her emails. The top one was from her friend and business partner, Maddie. "Hold on, she just sent me something." She mumbled as she read. "No one's heard from Bree. She'll keep us posted. She wants to know if I'm okay since Alex's video hit the news." Maddie's note confused Tyler. She looked up. "Do you know what video she's talking about?"

Ethan shrugged. "I have no idea. Let me check this email from the lab that's testing Syd's wine, then we should get going if we want to find Paul before Bree does and remind him of the restraining order."

Tyler waved him off. "Give me a minute." Maddie had her worried that there was more terrible news involving Alex. She Googled Alex's name. The top search results displayed a news article titled, "Lies, Lust, and Larceny: Linked Lovers." She clicked on the first link. Multiple news outlets had picked up Matt Crown's follow-up article in the *New York Daily News* that contained more of the same carefully couched speculation and misinformation about Alex's involvement in her father's death.

"Counterfeit?" Ethan's outburst drew Tyler's attention and a demand for him to explain it. "I dropped off two bottles of Barnette wine at a lab Wednesday. The tests concluded that the wines were *not* the same and had an entirely different chemical composition. That means the one from the resort is counterfeit."

"That's both good and bad news. Syd and John can salvage the Barnette reputation, but now they have to figure out who is stealing their wine."

"Or intentionally sabotaging them." Ethan's comment contained an ominous tone, indicating that he felt he'd only scratched the surface of this mystery—and that he was determined to get to the bottom of it.

Tyler turned her attention back to the news article on her laptop and clicked on the accompanying video. She couldn't tear her eyes from the screen. Alex had told her she had to do some things to get Kelly to trust her the night the police arrested Kelly and that she wasn't proud of the lengths she had to go to seduce a confession from her. Tyler hadn't wanted to know the specifics back then, but this tape provided them in perfect high-definition, playing out every nauseating touch, kiss, and dirty word they shared.

The video started with Alex saying, *"I missed your gentle touch. The pillow-soft feel of your lips and how turned on I felt every time I wrapped myself against your body. That woman reminded me of you—blonde, runner's body, attractive, and smart. I tried it with her, but it wasn't the same. She wasn't you."* It ended with Alex playfully reaching to fondle Kelly after she had removed her blouse and Alex saying, *"The last time you stripped for me, I took pictures of you…fuck."*

Tyler couldn't move. She could barely breathe. Her heart beat faster than it ever had at something she should have never seen. The room spun, whirling her around the drain. She tried calling for Ethan but could only grunt before the surrounding light dimmed. She fell off the chair, hitting the floor with a thud.

The room was a blur. Ethan called her name, but she hadn't the energy to respond. She felt him touch her wrist and chest. He spoke again, his words calm, giving her the sense she'd be okay. Before the room went black, she heard him say, "Ten fifty-two. Unresponsive woman."

CHAPTER TWENTY-TWO

Her stomach in knots, Bree focused on the reason she had come to Sacramento—to meet her birth father. She'd passed on breakfast when Derrick hit the drive-thru, and now the pungent smell of greasy breakfast sandwiches filling his hand-me-down Toyota was making her nauseous. She looked on as he stuffed the last bite of McMuffin into his mouth, followed by another swig of Coke. After wiping his hands with a napkin, he tossed it in the back seat to join the rest of the fast-food litter cluttering the rear bench.

"What time does he leave for work?" Derrick asked Bree.

"Yesterday, he came out of his house at eight thirty, so he should be awake by now." The irony of how she had been able to track down Paul Stevens didn't escape her. Her dad… Scratch that. She needed to stop thinking of Ethan in those terms. Years ago, *Ethan* had proudly showed her how he did parts of his job, including conducting Internet searches on suspects and staking them out to learn their patterns before confronting them. *Ironic*, she thought. She'd used knowledge gained from her fake father to find her real one.

Armed with a home address, Bree had taken a bus and spent yesterday morning camped out on a quiet cul-de-sac, not unlike the middle-income neighborhood of Sacramento she'd grown up in. She'd waited for someone to leave the older-looking home. When a man finally pulled out of the garage in a beat-up car, she'd hid in the bushes to watch. His wavy red hair was virtually the mirror image of hers in color, she knew he had to be Paul. She'd resisted the urge to confront him alone and returned to Derrick's home.

"What's your plan?" Derrick asked. "Walk up there, knock on the door, and ask him if he's your father?"

"Something like that." Bree bounced her knee up and down, chewing a fingernail down to its nub. She'd planned little past knocking on his door, including what to call him. "Thanks for coming with me today."

"Well, I wasn't about to let you go into some guy's house alone when you're not sure if he's your father. I'm relieved you didn't talk to him yesterday."

"My dad taught me…I mean Ethan…I mean…I don't know what I mean."

"Look, Bree. Your dad is still your dad. You even said that he raised you since the day you were born. That makes him your dad in my book. This other guy was just the sperm donor."

Sure, Ethan was her dad in every way that counted, as Erin said, but until she knew why they never told her about her biological father, Bree didn't know what to think about Paul. Did he know about her? If he did, why didn't he want her? Was he just a fling for Mom, or was he something more? She had so many questions, and he was the only one who might give her honest answers.

"I don't even know if this guy knows about me. Maybe he would have been more than just a sperm donor if he knew." Her face heated at the possibility that her mother had lied to him too. She pounded a fist on her thigh and grunted. "I can't believe they kept this from me, especially Erin. She should have told me."

"She probably had a good reason," Derrick said. When Bree relaxed her fists, he asked, "Are you ready?"

Bree opened the passenger door. "Let's go."

Her stomach flip-flopped with each step she took up the walkway, but she refused to turn back; answers lay behind that front door. She stood on the porch with Derrick right behind her, raising and lowering her hand several times before mustering the courage to knock three times. Within seconds, the door was opened by the redheaded man she'd seen yesterday. He had to be Paul. He had to be her father.

"Yeah?" the man said in a gruff tone, still grasping the doorknob with one hand and holding a coffee mug in the other. The janitor coveralls were an unexpected curveball. She didn't know what she had expected him to be, but a janitor wasn't it.

Bree stood motionless, slack-jawed. For two days now she had not known who she was and she had sworn to herself that she would find out. But now that she was face-to-face with the person who could provide the answers to her questions, words escaped her. Courage did too.

The man appeared to grow impatient and started to close the door. She said, "Wait," but said nothing more.

His gaze inspected her from toe to head, settling on her long, wavy red locks. Though his hair was cropped in a traditional business style, its color and texture were virtually identical to hers. His brow furrowed. "Bree?"

Her heart thudded so fiercely at the mention of her name that it drowned out the rest of the world. She repeated in her head, *he had to be Paul.* "Yeah."

Paul shifted his gaze to Derrick standing behind her. He poked his head out the door, looking left and then right. "Do your parents know you're here?"

"They probably know by now." Bree handed Paul a copy of the adoption papers with his name on them. "That's you, right?"

Paul glanced at the papers and then back at Bree. His eyes had misted over with years of unmistakable regret. "Yeah, that's me." He returned the documents to Bree and lowered his head. "You have to go."

"What do you mean I have to go? I have a lot of questions, like, why didn't you want me?"

"Look, I'd like nothing more than to answer your questions and get to know you, but I'm not allowed to, so you have to leave. Now." His words conveyed a disappointing sense of finality.

He started to close the door again, but Bree slapped her hand on the flaking wood, stopping it. "Wait. Why can't you talk to me? I never knew you existed until a few days ago. I flew all the way across the country to find you. Were you just a one-night stand with my mom or something?"

"Or something." He lowered his head again, stoking Bree's curiosity. "Your parents will have to answer the rest of your questions." He slammed the door closed, crushing her hope of getting to the truth.

She stormed toward the car, Derrick lagging a few steps behind. The pavement below her feet was barely visible through the tears pouring down her face. She couldn't believe it. Every adult in her life didn't want her to know the truth. Screw Paul. Screw Ethan. Screw Mom. Screw Erin.

Stepping off the curb, she continued to walk into the street. Screeching brakes sounded to her left. She glanced in its direction. A dark bumper. A dark car hood. A windshield. All came into sharp focus and got larger and larger with every passing millisecond. Her breathing stopped. Her heart felt as if it did too. Then something yanked her from the car's path.

Derrick had wrapped her into his strong arms and pulled her to safety as the sedan came to an abrupt stop, inches past where she had just stood. If not for his quick thinking, the car would've crushed her.

"Fuck, Bree." Derrick held on to her until the car passed by, its horn blasting. "What were you thinking?"

Her heart restarted, beating wildly out of control. "Take me…back…to…your house," she said between sobs.

Bree returned to Derrick's room, where she'd secretly been camping out for the last two nights. She sat on the floor with her back against the long side of his bed, hugging her knees and rocking herself back and forth while processing her confusing encounter with Paul.

Derrick walked in with a glass of water. He knelt in front of her, offering her two Tylenol tablets. His words were soft. "Here, take these. They'll help with your headache."

Bree swallowed the pills and handed back the glass. "I don't get it. He knew about me. He even knew my name, but he won't talk to me."

Derrick placed the glass on the nightstand and sat beside her on the floor. "He said he wasn't allowed to speak to you. It could be some legal thing."

"So, he just gave me up without a fight? What a loser."

"We don't know what happened."

"Yeah, and the only ones who do are my parents. As if they're ever going to tell me the truth."

"I think you need to give them a chance, Bree."

A light knock on the bedroom door drew her attention. It slowly opened, and Maddie's head peered around it. "Hey, kiddo," she said gently.

Shit, Bree thought. Of course, Derrick had told his mother that she was there after this morning's fiasco. Everyone was turning on her.

Derrick glanced at Bree and placed his hand on her knee. "It's all right. I called her." He pushed himself off the floor and walked toward the door. As he passed his mother, he said, "Thanks, Mom. I didn't know what else to do."

Maddie patted him on the shoulder. "You did the right thing, sweetheart." After closing the door behind him, she sat on the bed close to Bree. "I'd sit down with you, but I'm not sure I could get back up. Getting old sucks." She patted the mattress beside her, inviting Bree to join her.

Bree pushed herself up with both hands and plopped down on the bed, unable to hold back her sniffling. Her head throbbed. Her life made no sense, and this cross-country trip to figure out why was a bust.

Maddie put an arm around Bree's shoulder and, in a calm voice, said, "Your parents are worried sick about you."

Bree shifted her eyes toward Maddie. "Do they know I'm here?"

"They flew out early this morning."

"Crap. Are they coming to get me?"

"Not yet, sweetie. I called your mom and dad after Derrick told me you were here, but neither picked up. I left messages."

"They must be so mad at me."

Maddie rubbed Bree's back. "I don't think they're mad. They just want to know you're safe and to sit down and explain things to you."

Bree snapped her head toward Maddie. "You knew?" She flailed her arms. "Of course, you did. Everyone knows the truth but me."

"Sweetie, your mom and I have been friends for a very long time as well as business partners. Yes, she confided in me, and I hope you understand why I couldn't break that trust."

"I do, but I don't understand why they never told me that Dad wasn't my real father."

Maddie placed both hands on Bree's shoulders and turned her to look her in the eyes. "Young lady, your dad is your real father. Who stayed up all night cradling you in a steamy bathroom when you had croup? Who held your hand all the way to the school bus on your first day of kindergarten? Who checked under the bed for monsters every night before you fell asleep? Who sat in the stands for every one of your softball games and cheered you on? Your dad did. All those things make him your father, not DNA."

"But…" Bree trailed off, crying again. Maddie was right. Whoever Paul was, Ethan was the one who was always there for her.

"No buts about it. Now, when they get here, I hope you'll give them a chance to explain everything."

"Do you know why they never told me?"

Tears pooled in Maddie's eyes when she nodded her head, yes. "I do. Just listen to them, all right."

"All right." Bree wiped her nose with the back of her hand, resolved to listen and finally get some answers.

CHAPTER TWENTY-THREE

Manhattan, New York

A somberness hung over Castle Resorts headquarters. The emergency meeting Alex had called broke up moments ago, with executives and department heads filing out of the conference room one by one, each with a blank expression, Alex among them. Drawdown was the order. Unless a miracle happened, many employees, all of whom Alex considered family, would have to be let go in ninety days. The notifications would roll out early next week.

Alex walked past Gretchen's desk, the weight of thousands of shattered lives making her legs heavy. Without as much as a glance at the assistant who had served as her right hand and proved her loyalty daily for four years, she said, "No calls or visitors. I need a few minutes alone."

"Of course, Ms. Castle." Gretchen's position was safe. Alex saw to it. But many others, would have to pack up their things, dust off their résumés, and hope for the best in the most challenging economy since the Great Depression.

Alex closed the door to her office. Her instinct was to call Tyler for shoring up, but she was on the other side of the country, dealing with an issue just as grave, if not more so. She considered reaching out to Harley or Abby, but they couldn't give her what she really needed—an embrace with their words rather than reassurance that she'd done the right thing. Only Tyler knew how to do that for her.

She slogged through piles of self-reproach to reach the window. Once there, she took in the magnificent view of Central Park, the same one her father had gazed at for decades as if he were king of the mountain. As much as she despised him for manipulating her and her siblings like chess pieces and for convincing her that denying her own needs was better than denying his, he had been a masterful businessman. How would he have kept the empire afloat? Would he have leveraged most of his personal wealth just to delay the inevitable as she had done? She'd painted herself into a corner. If the company failed, not only would eleven thousand be out of work, she would be broke. And unemployable to boot.

The recognizable sound of her frosted glass door swooshing open drew her attention. "I said no—" Gretchen scurried inside, locked the door, and turned her ashen face toward Alex. "Gretchen? Is everything all right?"

"It's Mr. Ward, he's in your outer office, and I've never seen him this upset before. He has a box full of his things and is demanding to see you. Do you want me to get security in here just in case?"

"Don't be silly. I just saw him fifteen minutes ago in the executive meeting. The drawdown news upset everyone, but he seemed fine with how it was rolling out. I'm sure it's just some grumbling from the troops that has him upset. Show him in. I'll be fine," Alex reassured her.

"All right, but if I hear any screaming or crashing sounds, I'm calling security."

Alex shooed Gretchen out the door. "Go, crazy woman. Let the man in."

Gretchen opened the door, watching Blake closely as he walked through. On her way out, she made sure he heard her offer a final caution. "Buzz me if you need the calvary, Ms. Castle. I'll be right outside."

At first, Alex was confident Gretchen was overreacting, but the disdain etched on Blake's face when he marched in made her think otherwise. Cautious, she circled her desk to greet him. "Please have a seat, Blake. You have Gretchen thinking you might chop my head off." She sat in a leather chair in the seating area, crossing her legs at the ankles. "Sit, please. What has you upset?"

"No, thank you. I'll stand." He reached into his breast pocket, pulled out an envelope, and handed it to Alex. "My resignation."

Alex recoiled, refusing to accept his letter. Blake was the one who insisted on the drawdown to keep the company solvent. Neither his anger nor his resignation made sense. "Blake? I don't understand."

He tossed the letter on the glass and metal coffee table, placing his hands on his hips, ready for an argument. "You've run this company into the ground, starting the day your father died."

Alex snapped to her feet, closed the distance between her and this blowhard until she invaded his personal space and could smell the coffee on his breath. He presented an intimidating figure at nearly six feet, but thankfully in heels, Alex stood roughly eye-to-eye with him. She expected a volatile conversation and wasn't about to show any weakness. Matching his posture, she placed her fists on her hips. "Killed, you mean. My father was killed."

He raised his chin, amplifying his contempt for her. "The entire city was reminded of that this morning and has been every day for the last four years. Between you and your brother, it's no wonder Castle Resorts is in horrible shape. Just when I'd thought your family's dirty laundry was behind us, the exposé killed our last-ditch loan. That video will now kill any hope of coming back from the drawdown. I'm done. I won't go down with the sinking ship. You made this mess. Now you have to live with it."

"What are you talking about? What video?"

Blake taunted her with a laugh. "It figures you're the last to know. Check out the *Daily News* website. You'll get an eyeful, just as the rest of the world has."

"I'll do that, Blake. Resignation accepted." Alex grabbed his letter, turned on her Jimmy Choos, and returned to her desk. "I expect you to run through HR and turn in your credentials. You realize that by resigning without board approval you forfeit your stock options. Castle Resorts thanks you for your contribution."

The veins on Blake's neck popped an inch above his collar. He marched out with Alex following steps behind.

Gretchen looked wide-eyed when Blake huffed and snatched up his box of belongings.

"Be sure to stop by HR, Blake," Alex shouted as he stormed down the hallway before redirecting her attention to Gretchen. "He's out. Please follow up and ensure he *finds* his way out. Then send up the next senior person in Accounting right away."

"Yes, Ms. Castle." Gretchen picked up her desk phone, mumbling, "It's never dull around here."

"What's that, Gretchen?" Alex asked with an edge. She was in no mood for sarcasm.

"Nothing, Ms. Castle. I'll get someone in Accounting."

Alex thanked Gretchen with a pat on the hand, signaling her apology for acting brusque, and then returned to her desk. She wondered what could be in this video that gave "the world an eyeful." Whatever it was, she was sure Matt Crown was behind it.

She clicked the computer mouse and keyboard, pulling up the *Daily News* website. Three extra clicks brought up the article "Lies, Lust, and Larceny: Linked Lovers." Crown's exaggerations and bloated innuendos weaved a barely believable tale that she and Kelly were involved and may have planned her father's murder together. She pressed the video link. Within seconds Alex recognized the scene playing out on her computer screen, and dread flooded her pores.

"How in the hell did he get this?" Alex let the entire video play in stunned silence. Once it ended, she jumped from her chair, yelling at the screen, "Where's the rest of it?"

The video stopped short of Kelly's confession and Alex's crystal clear surprise at her revelation. Hell, it didn't even show Alex stuffing a bra down Kelly's mouth when the police detectives stormed in. Crown had edited the video to make it appear Alex wanted to have sex with Kelly, which couldn't be further from the truth.

Her anger boomed, a volcano on the verge of blowing. One after another, these attacks kept coming and at the worst possible time for her, Syd, and Castle Resorts. Clenched teeth weren't nearly enough of a release. She threw her large mug at the wall, spraying coffee along the way and causing it to shatter with a loud crack.

Gretchen burst through the door, looked at Alex, and then to the wall on which Alex had locked her stare. Brown liquid dripped down the wall and mixed with dozens of white ceramic shards in a spreading stain on the carpet. Gretchen grabbed a trash can and began the tedious job of picking up the pieces. "Are you okay, Alex?"

Alex knelt beside her repentantly, helping clean up the mess she'd made. She'd like to think her outburst helped, but it hadn't come close to making her feel better.

"No, I'm not. We announced our downsizing, my CFO resigned, and my life is tabloid fodder."

Gretchen finished the cleanup and stood. "I take it you saw the video?"

Alex returned to her desk, absorbing what Gretchen had just said. "You knew about it? Why didn't you warn me?"

"I heard about it when Mr. Ward was in your office. Bad news travels fast."

"It always does." Alex picked up her cell phone, which Gretchen apparently took as her cue to leave.

On her way out, Gretchen said, "I'll hold your calls and Accounting for a while. Buzz me when you're ready. Oh, and I'll get someone to clean the carpet over the weekend."

Alex gave Gretchen a grateful smile. "You don't know how much I appreciate you hanging in there with me."

Gretchen returned Alex's smile. "I've known you since you were fifteen, and even then, I could tell you loved this company as much as your father did. It couldn't be in better hands. I'll hang in there with you for as long as you'll have me." She walked out, clutching the trash can and closing the door behind her.

Alex rubbed her temple to stave off a pounding headache. She needed to get ahead of the fallout. Her first call was to Jesse.

"I'm already on it," Jesse said, answering Alex's call.

"Geez, bad news travels fast."

"It's my job to stay on top of this, Alex."

"How in the hell did Crown get his hands on that video?"

"Whoever leaked it most likely left a digital footprint," Jesse said. "The NYPD installed a new evidence inventory system last year, and it's virtually impossible for anyone to cover their tracks. But I'm just as interested in knowing how Crown found out about the video. Somebody involved in the case must have told him about it."

Alex didn't have to guess. The one person in the world who wanted to see her ruined had to be behind it. "First the letter. Now the video. It has to be Kelly Thatcher."

"That's my guess, too, but why now?"

Alex rocked back in her chair, wiping the tension from her face with her free hand. She couldn't decide which would help more—screaming or crying. "Kelly has created the perfect storm. Maybe I should pay her a visit."

"You will do no such thing. You'd just be throwing gasoline on the fire. Ethan's out of town, so I'll have Jimmy go with me to Bedford Hills. Hopefully, I can get some answers."

"Good, because I want to know who to sue this time."

"You let me worry about that. How is Tyler taking it?"

God, the thought of Tyler seeing that video... She was already under tremendous stress, and this would only add to it.

"I don't know. I haven't called her yet."

"I rarely get involved in other people's relationships, but she should have been your first call, Alex."

"I know, I know. Tyler's already on edge with Bree, so I needed to calm down first."

Once Alex finished the call with Jesse, she dialed Tyler, but it went to voice mail. She tried to not read anything into that, choosing to believe she was busy tracking down Bree. She left a short message, "T, we need to talk. Please call me when you get this. I love you." She hung up and called Ethan, but that call went to voice mail too. Were they both avoiding her? "Dammit, Kelly. If you cost me Tyler, you're a dead woman."

Alex sat alone in her office for an hour following an emotional call to Syd, waiting to hear from Tyler. Hoping to. The isolation and unresolved anticipation were crushing. The only sound in the room was generated by Alex repeatedly tapping a pen against the top of her desk. She didn't know whether Tyler hadn't received her message or if she had and was shunning her. Not knowing was the worst. She wouldn't wish this kind of limbo on anyone but her worst enemy. Kelly Thatcher deserved to experience this type of torture for eternity.

Her cell phone finally rang, raising her hope that Tyler had taken her time to think and was now calling to say all was forgiven. The ring tone told her it wasn't Tyler, though. The screen lit up, displaying the name "Ethan." She swiped. "Ethan. Please don't tell me she doesn't want to talk to me."

"Alex, Tyler is okay, but she's in the hospital." His voice was calm but lacked his usual spirit, meaning Tyler's condition was likely serious.

"What happened? Is it her heart?"

"I won't sugarcoat this, Alex. She saw the sting video of you and Kelly. Her heart rate went out of control, and she passed out. I had to call 911. Doctors put her on medication to keep her calm and her heart rate steady. It makes her sleep a lot. They want to run a battery of tests to make sure nothing else is wrong with her."

"I did this." Whatever the worst feeling in the world was, Alex had found it. The woman she loved more than life itself was in the hospital with wires and tubing attached to her and doctors poking and prodding her to find…what? Alex already knew what they'd find—a broken heart. And all because she insisted on participating in clearing her name of the bogus charge that she'd killed her father. Why couldn't she have just trusted Ethan and Jesse to find the evidence to clear her instead of being so arrogant to think that entrapping Kelly was the only way?

Alex told Ethan she'd be on the next flight out, immediately asking Gretchen to make a reservation. Before she finished packing her satchel to return home, Gretchen buzzed her on the intercom.

"Ms. Castle, commercial flights wouldn't get you to Sacramento until nearly midnight, so I booked you a charter flight. It leaves out of Teterboro in two hours."

Alex pressed the intercom button on her desk phone. "Thank you, Gretchen. You're a lifesaver."

CHAPTER TWENTY-FOUR

Sacramento, California

A distinctive antiseptic smell permeated the wide hospital hallway Maddie was leading Bree down. Every step she took toward her mother's cardiac care room was torture. If not for her running away across the country, her mother would not be here. She'd never forgive herself if something terrible happened and her mother never left this place.

Bree passed open doors, getting glimpses of gray-haired, wrinkled patients lying motionless in their beds hooked up to all kinds of equipment. The beeping sounds of heart and other monitors, the only signs of life, made her cringe. *Mom's too young for this.*

Bree's stomach clenched, knowing she was about to face the consequences of her selfishness. She squeezed Maddie's hand. "This is all my fault."

Maddie didn't answer. Instead, she returned Bree's squeeze and continued her march toward Tyler's room, stopping between doors. "Do you want me to go in first?"

Bree shook her head. "No, I want to see her."

"Okay." Maddie gave her hand one more squeeze and led the way into her mother's hospital room.

Bree's stomach convulsed the moment she stepped inside. Short gasps for air did little to alleviate the swelling guilt gripping her. She blamed herself for everything in this room. Her dad, as she had decided to think of Ethan again, was leaned forward in a chair next to the bed, staring at the floor, his elbows on his knees. That was his worried stance. Her mother was sleeping partially reclined in the hospital bed and had the same scary tubes and wires attached to her body as the other patients. A nearby monitor beeped continuously, reading her mother's heart rate, blood pressure, and oxygen level according to the writing on the screen. Bree tried to make sense of the numbers but couldn't tell if they were good signs or bad ones.

Bree remained silent, but Maddie stepped further in and whispered to her dad, "Hey, you."

He looked toward the voice. His face relaxed in palpable relief. He got up and wrapped his arms around Bree, the embrace lasting longer than any of their hugs ever had. Each tightening of his arms emphasized his love for her. Erin, Derrick, and Maddie were right. He was her dad in every way that mattered. Bree trembled, regretting that she ever thought of him as anything less.

When he loosened his hold, she asked in a hushed tone, "How's Mom?"

"She'll be fine," he said in his textbook reassuring fashion. "They changed her meds and are keeping her overnight for more tests."

Her dad approached the bed and placed his hand on her mom's shoulder. She stirred, fluttering her eyes. He said softly, "Bree and Maddie are here."

Her mom opened her eyes and pushed herself up in bed, her expression turning into sadness. "Baby." She held out her arms, inviting Bree for a hug.

When Bree wrapped her arms around her mother, the floodgates of emotion and tears opened. "I'm so sorry, Mom." The feel of the cold wires reminded her how serious her mother's condition was and that her selfishness and stupidity put her there. "This is all my fault."

Her mom sniffled back her tears. "It's not your fault, honey. I let myself get all worked up about things, but I'm going to be all right. The doctors just want to run a bunch of tests to make sure I'm on the right medicine and see to it that I get some rest."

"I love you, Mom."

Her mom rubbed Bree's back, exhaling slowly. "I love you, too." She raised Bree's head by the chin. "We have a lot to talk about."

Bree wiped her face with the back of her hand and nodded. Her mom reached for the side rail and pressed a button. The head of the bed rose, shifting her to a more upright sitting position.

Maddie cleared her throat. "I'm going to take off." She pointed at her mom's messy hair and grinned. "You might want to fix that bird's nest you have going there."

Her dad snickered while her mom flattened her hair with both hands. She shot back at him, "You're one to talk. I've seen you in the morning before you've hit the shower."

Maddie chuckled. "All right, you guys. Call me if you need anything."

Her mom mouthed, "Thank you," while her dad gave Maddie a brief hug and said, "Tell Derrick thanks for taking care of Bree and for letting us know she was here."

"Will do. I'm just glad she's safe." Maddie rubbed Bree's back and walked out the door.

Bree moved to a chair, and her dad took a seat next to her. He leaned forward and rested his elbows on his knees, a signal he was still worried. He turned his head to look Bree in the eyes. "First off, I love you very much, and I'm relieved you're safe. I know you feel bad about running away and what you've put your mother and me through, and you should. I know why you did it, but that doesn't excuse your actions." He straightened up, a sign his worry was over but his lecture wasn't. "Never run away again, Bree. If we have problems with one another, we work them out as a family."

Bree nodded. Most of his words had come out sharp but without the anger she had expected. She accepted the fact, though, that she deserved it.

Her dad continued, "You must have a lot of questions." He softened his tone. "What do you want to ask us?"

Bree swallowed through the lump in her throat. She wasn't mad anymore, merely anxious to get the answers she'd been looking for. Bree turned to her mother, assuming she had an affair. "How did you meet him?"

Tyler sighed. "He was in my grad school class and offered to tutor me on a new software program."

"Then?" Bree asked, assuming where this was going.

"Then, one night, we went out after class to celebrate our good grades. He had too much to drink, so I drove him home. When I helped him inside, he—" Her mother paused, emotion clearly overtaking her. An alarm on the monitor sounded.

A panic washed over Bree. "Mom?"

Within seconds, a nurse in blue scrubs rushed into the room. She read the numbers on the monitor before turning off the alarm. "How are you feeling? Any shortness of breath or dizziness?" The nurse lowered the head of the bed to a more reclined position.

"No. I'm just a little flushed," her mom said.

"You should be resting, young lady."

"And I will. We just need to talk to our daughter first."

The nurse shot her mom a stern look. "Don't make me come back in here, or I'll send a note home to your parents."

Her mom smiled, holding up her hands in surrender. "I promise."

"I'm holding you to it." The nurse adjusted the monitor and left.

Bree calmed but remained concerned. "Are you okay, Mom?"

Her mom shifted in the bed, bending her knees at a slight angle. "I'm good, honey."

Her dad interrupted, "Tyler, are you sure you don't want to rest? We can come back after dinner."

"I'm sure. Bree's been through a lot in the last few days. I owe her this much. I owe her the truth."

"All right, but if you get upset, I'm shutting this down." Her dad was firm, leaving no room for negotiation.

"I'll be fine." Her mom turned toward Bree, searching her eyes. "Paul was drunk, and when I helped him inside, he made a pass at me. I told him I wasn't interested, but he pushed me down on the bed and kissed me. I tried to fight him off and even hit him in the nose, but he overpowered me." Her mother paused, her lips trembling. "He beat me severely and raped me."

Bree gasped at the brutal revelation. She had never imagined her mother had suffered an unspeakable attack, only that she'd had an affair. She couldn't imagine the horror her mother had gone through and what that man did to her.

Then it hit her. She had resulted from that horrible act. A wave of nausea rippled through her, hitting her like a tidal wave. She darted to the attached bathroom, retching into the toilet.

Ethan followed Bree into the bathroom, holding her hair back until she finished heaving. He then filled a plastic cup with water and handed it to her. "Here, honey. Rinse and spit." After she cleared the awful taste from her mouth, he said, "I know this is hard. Now you know why we never told you."

Bree gathered her strength, but her stomach was still in knots when she stepped out of the bathroom. She couldn't process the fact that she came out of such a vile, brutal act. "I wish I never knew."

Her dad placed a comforting hand on her shoulder. "That bell can't be unrung. What you choose to do next will forever change the rest of our lives. You can either hate us for shielding you from the truth, or you can put yourself in our shoes and try to understand that we did what we thought was best for you. We made sure you grew up knowing you were always loved, believing you were conceived in love because, in my mind, you were. I have loved you since the day I found out Mom was pregnant with you. To me, that was the day you were conceived. I have never considered you to be anything other than my daughter."

Bree wrapped her arms around her dad's midsection and squeezed tight. How could she hate him? He knew the awful truth, but it didn't matter. He loved her simply because she existed. "I love you, Dad. I want nothing to do with that guy."

He wrapped his arms around Bree, his embrace alone telling her what she'd known since she was old enough to understand what the word meant. "I love you, Bree."

Bree loosened her hold, carefully crawled into bed, and snuggled with her mother. How could she hold a grudge knowing what this incredibly strong woman had been through? For days, Bree had believed her life would never be the same when she discovered the truth, but she hadn't expected a revelation of this magnitude. Nor could she have imagined that something like this might change her life for the better, but it did. She loved her parents more for it. "I love you, Mom. I'm so sorry for what happened to you."

Tyler accepted the hug and craned her neck to look Bree in the eyes. They still contained too much regret. "Honey, what happened to me was horrible and affected me for years. You were the only good thing to come of it, and my life and the world are so much better because you're in it."

Soon, the nurse returned, looking overly officious and carrying a small clear plastic cup of pills. "It's time for your medication, young lady." After scanning Tyler's wristband and logging something in the computer workstation in the corner of the room, she passed the pills to Tyler, who swigged them down with a cup of water. "If you have any hope of the doctor releasing you soon, you better get more rest."

"We should let you sleep, Tyler," Ethan said.

"I will," Tyler replied to the nurse. More rest sounded appropriate, but she needed some time alone with Ethan before he and Bree left. After the nurse exited, Tyler turned to Bree. "Honey, would you mind waiting for Dad in the hallway? I need to talk to him for a minute."

The moment Bree left the room, relief and sadness hit Tyler in a powerful double punch. She struggled to hold back the tears and not set off that damn alarm again. "Do you think Bree will change her mind about not wanting to see Paul again?"

"I doubt it. Learning about the rape rattled her. But just in case, after I drop her off at the hotel, I'll pay him a visit and gently remind him about the court order."

Tyler shook her head no, envisioning Ethan in handcuffs. When it came to Paul, Ethan was never gentle. "Please don't do anything that would—"

Ethan clenched his jaw and interrupted, "He fucked with my family, Tyler." He paused when Tyler sighed her disappointment. "But, you're right. I'll ask Marco to come with me."

"Thank you," Tyler said softly. Ethan's old partner would provide the buffer necessary to keep Ethan out of jail.

"By the way, I talked to Alex while you were sleeping. I thought she should know."

Tyler rubbed her temples, concentrating on calming herself before she set off the alarms again. She had yet to process the shock that had put her in this hospital bed. "I don't know what to think about that video. It's still upsetting."

"I looked at that farce while I was in the Emergency waiting room," Ethan said. "It doesn't tell the entire story, Tyler. That Crown guy left out the best part. The image of Alex straddling Kelly, stuffing a bra down her throat. That scene will forever be etched on my brain."

Tyler's jaw dropped. "She did what?"

Ethan laughed at the memory. "Yep, a 34C right down her throat. We had to pull Alex off before Kelly choked on pink lace."

Tyler laughed at the image. "She never told me."

Ethan's face turned serious. "That's because she wasn't proud of the rest of it, and she didn't want to hurt you. Trust me, Tyler. I was with her minutes before and after the police recorded that video. She did what she had to do to get a confession and nothing more. She handled herself like a pro, except for that whole choking Kelly with a bra thing."

Tyler chuckled with the man who had been making her laugh for more than a quarter-century. When Ethan stood to leave, her mood sobered. "I believe you, but it was hard seeing her with another woman like that. I need to tell her that much."

"You'll get a chance to do it in person tonight. She's flying out and should be here by dinnertime." He kissed her on the forehead and left.

Tyler hadn't intended to pull Alex from work when both Castle Resorts and Barnette Winery were facing economic disaster, but having her at her bedside was the best medicine she could have asked for.

CHAPTER TWENTY-FIVE

Ethan sat quietly in the passenger seat while Marco Banuelos coasted his unmarked sedan to a stop one house down from Paul Stevens' childhood home. The moment Marco put the car into park, Ethan's jaw muscles twitched, seething anger building in the back of his throat. This was the place where his family had been changed forever. The place from which Tyler ran for her life, bloody and barefoot, and was never the same.

Ethan loathed this loser. He'd raped his wife, spent an inadequate five years in jail, and for the last four had bounced from one low-paying job to another. Yet he owned a mortgage-free house in a charming part of Sacramento that was nicer than Ethan's when he had lived there, thanks to the death last year of his mother, something Ethan had learned about yesterday. Knowing the little prick no longer had to worry about paying the rent stuck in Ethan's craw. So deep-rooted was his anger that he had asked his former partner to come with him today—he didn't trust himself not to do something that could get him arrested.

Staring out the windshield, Marco broke the silence. "Remember that time back in 2003 when Dancing Dan helped us take down Santiago? I loved that guy. I could tell time by him. He'd hit the same street corner at the same time every day, twirling a sign for minimum wage for…." He rubbed his chin. "What place was it?"

After a decade of sitting stakeouts and working cases with Marco, Ethan appreciated what he was doing, but a walk down memory lane wasn't going to put a dent in his hatred for Paul Stevens. "The Buggy Whip Café," Ethan answered in a flat tone.

"That's right, the Buggy Whip. After Santiago made me and took off running, you yelled at Dancing Dan, and he took him down with one swing. Dan deserved a medal."

"And a new sign." Ethan glanced at Marco, forcing a smile. He was grateful for their years of mutual trust and respect because, in a few minutes, he would do what had to be done as a father. Hopefully, Marco would keep him from blurring the line and ending up in jail. "Thanks for coming with me today."

"I'll always have your back, Falling." The garage door opened, and an old sedan slowly turned into the driveway and pulled into the cluttered garage. "We're up," Marco said.

He pulled his sedan forward, blocking the end of Paul's driveway. He and Ethan exited, with Ethan making a beeline for the driver's door of Paul's car, his rage building with each step. Seconds later, he ripped the door open with the force of a tornado and snatched Paul out by his shirt sleeve. Resisting, barely, the urge to end Paul's miserable life right there, Ethan studied the bastard's face for a moment. The red eyes, hollow cheeks, pale complexion, and deep crevasses he saw were unmistakable signs of drug abuse, if not addiction.

Ethan pointed a finger an inch from his nose. "You talked to Bree." Anger dripped from each word.

Paul recoiled as if expecting to dodge a punch. "Wasn't my idea. She just showed up. I reported the contact to the police."

Ethan positioned a forearm across Paul's throat, backing him into the rear passenger door. "That doesn't excuse a damn thing. What did you say to her?"

"To talk to you and Tyler." The beads of sweat building on Paul's weaselly forehead gave Ethan hope that he might piss his pants before this was over. "That's all, I swear."

Marco placed a calming hand on Ethan's shoulder, the touch giving Ethan's anger the chance to recede enough for him to say his piece.

"I'm here to make sure that you understand the cold hard facts." Ethan decided on how to carefully refer to Bree to drive his searing point home. "I told *my* daughter the whole truth. She threw up and cried for hours, trying to cope with the reality that she was a product of rape. I've never seen her in so much pain." Ethan jabbed a finger into Paul's chest. "You did that. She'll have to carry that with her for the rest of her life. She wants nothing to do with you. Ever."

Paul dropped his head in what Ethan hoped was shame, but he doubted Paul's sense of morality ran that deep. Ethan took a step back and a deep breath. "A real father should never cause his child that kind of pain. You're nothing more than a knife in her heart. After she turns eighteen, I expect you to do the right thing and stay away."

The muscles in Paul's jaw rippled. "She'll never hear from me."

"I recommend you get a new zip code." Ethan walked away, a jumble of emotions. He hadn't been able to protect Tyler from being assaulted, and just as importantly, he hadn't protected Bree from discovering the awful truth. But this was one pain from which he could spare her, though. He took solace in knowing he had finally done his job as a father.

As Marco drove Ethan to where his rental was parked, he glanced at him. "I'm proud of you, Falling. I would have put the guy in the hospital."

"The thought crossed my mind. I'm glad you were there to keep me out of jail."

CHAPTER TWENTY-SIX

Alex had made no other arrangements beyond getting herself to the charter flight and reserving a rental car in Sacramento. She couldn't fathom sleeping in a hotel room while Tyler was hooked up to monitors in a hospital room. She'd buy the damn hospital if necessary in order to spend the night in the same room as her.

Suitcase in tow, Alex stood near the entrance of Tyler's hospital room, gathering herself and wondering if Tyler wanted her there. If she wanted anything to do with her after seeing that damn videotape. She might not. If so, Alex planned to fight for her, to regain her trust. She took in a deep, resolute breath and stepped inside.

Seeing Tyler asleep on the bed, surrounded by monitors, wires, and tubes, was even more disturbing than Alex had expected. She had done this. She'd put Tyler in that bed, and that was something for which she'd never forgive herself.

She lowered the handle on her overnight bag and carried it to a corner of the room so the sound of the wheels scraping across the linoleum wouldn't wake Tyler. The monitor softly beeped, displaying updated numbers. Tyler's vitals—heart rate, blood pressure, and oxygen level—all appeared good, confirming Ethan hadn't understated her condition. Alex sat on the guest chair next to her, deciding to wait quietly for Tyler to wake.

Alex studied Tyler as she slept. After four years of sharing a bed with her, she was intimately familiar with her sleeping habits. She'd toss and turn every half hour or so, clutching and taking the blanket with her when she did. Tonight, though, Tyler was uncharacteristically still, likely a byproduct of the medication Ethan had mentioned during their earlier phone call.

According to the clock next to the wall-mounted TV, nearly an hour passed before Tyler stirred. Alex still waited, unsure whether Tyler would welcome the visit. Tyler finally opened her eyes. When she locked gazes with Alex, a smile slowly formed on her lips, as did moisture at the lower rims of her eyes. Tyler reached for her, stretching the IV tube attached to her hand and removing a great weight from Alex's shoulders.

Alex sat on the edge of the bed, taking Tyler's hand and being careful to not disturb the myriad tubes and wires. "I'm so sorry, T. You have every right to be mad at me."

Tyler rose to a sitting position and wrapped her arms around Alex. Alex had promised herself to not cry, no matter Tyler's reception. She didn't want to add to an already emotional moment. Alex melted, though, tears in both eyes, when Tyler nuzzled her neck and whispered, "There's no need to be sorry."

Alex loosened her hold and pulled back. She looked Tyler in the eyes when she said, "Please, believe me when I say that what I did that night made me sick."

"I believe you," Tyler said, barely above a whisper. Following Alex's breathy sigh of relief, she continued stronger, "Ethan reassured me the video was heavily edited."

"It was."

Alex moved further up the bed to hold Tyler in her arms. They would need to talk more, but she wanted to give Tyler the chance to share what she'd been dealing with. Wanted to hear what had happened with Bree. Slowly, tearfully, in the course of the next hour, Tyler told her of the morning's events, describing first her heartbreaking talk with Bree and then the visceral reaction Tyler had had to the video. It was a difficult conversation, but she and Tyler concluded it by promising to never hold back and always share the good and especially the bad. To serve as each other's rocks and not shield the other from perceived harm.

Alex struck an agreement with the nurse—she could stay the night if she didn't disturb Tyler's sleep. A condition she readily accepted. While the monitor made it impossible for her to show Tyler exactly how much she regretted putting her in this bed, holding Tyler's hand while she was in a deep, medication-assisted sleep was enough to keep Alex content throughout the night. The resulting painfully stiff arm was a small price to pay for staying.

Alex's phone buzzed from atop the rolling bed table a few feet away. She cringed, not only at the early hour but also at the cramp that developed in her bicep when she removed it from around Tyler. The caller ID read "Destiny." Her chief accountant would only call at this hour on a Saturday—three o'clock in the morning West Coast time—if it were important. Alex tiptoed to Tyler's private bathroom and swiped the iPhone screen, keeping her voice low. "Hi, Destiny. Is everything okay?"

"I'm sorry to disturb your visit with Tyler, but this couldn't wait. First, how is she?"

"Tyler will be fine, but she has to stay in the hospital another day for more tests."

"That's good to hear. Now for better news. Right before the close of business yesterday, we received an offer for an initial two hundred-million-dollar line of credit, extendable to five hundred million."

"What?" Alex checked her voice level. Tyler, she saw, was still sleeping, thank God. "From who?"

"M-Three Investments. It's a newly incorporated LLC set up through Barry Wexler and Associates. There's only one officer, Ignis Opus. Wexler is one of the top law firms in the city, so the LLC has to be legit."

"Has Legal looked this over?"

"Yes, every which way. We spent the entire night looking at every angle. We can't find a single downside. The offer is a simple fifteen-year note with a fixed rate of prime plus a half-point and no collateral requirements."

Alex jerked her head back at the generous offer. The terms were incredibly favorable. Too good, but she was out of options. "This couldn't have come at a better time. We must have a fairy godmother somewhere. What do you recommend?"

"Legal recommends accepting, and so do I."

Alex rubbed her chin for a moment. Accepting it would enable them to quash the downsizing plan and would carry them through the downturn. She'd save thousands of jobs. "I concur. Make it happen. I'll sign it when I return on Monday."

"I'm sorry to have to tell you this, but the offer expires at five o'clock tonight, and we need your original signature, not a facsimile."

Alex's gaze returned to Tyler. Leaving her right now seemed unfathomable, but eleven thousand people were depending on her to do the right thing. This would be the last time work took priority over Tyler, though. The. Very. Last. Time. "All right. I'll arrange to be back in New York in the early afternoon."

Destiny's audible sigh meant Alex had made the right choice. "I'll prep everything and have a new budget ready for your review by the time you land."

"I can't thank you enough for stepping up, Destiny." Alex considered Destiny's performance since she came to work at Castle Resorts four years ago. She had far exceeded every expectation. As the ranking member of her accounting team, she would make an excellent interim CFO. "Blake left me shorthanded, when he and his deputy resigned. Frankly, I was relieved you were the next senior person on that side of the house. I've come to trust you implicitly. I'd like you to move up as interim CFO."

"Wow. CFO? Do you really think I'm up for the job?" Destiny sounded uncharacteristically unsure of herself. In Alex's opinion she was more qualified for the position than Andrew was when William had wanted to crown him king of the company coffers.

"You're ready for this, Destiny. I wouldn't have asked otherwise."

Destiny let out a sputtering breath. "Then I'd be honored, Alex. I've come to love this company as much as you do. I consider you family and will always have your back."

Family, Alex thought. She, Syd, and Destiny were alike in their drive for excellence. As for the rest…after ending the call she asked herself if she loved Castle Resorts as much as Destiny appeared to. The answer eluded her, solidifying her determination to make the bold changes she'd started considering the minute she hopped on the plane to get here. She called the charter company, arranging for her return flight in two hours, then returned to Tyler's bedside and nudged her shoulder. "T." It required one more attempt before Tyler finally woke.

"Babe?" Her voice was groggy.

"I have great news." Alex explained about Castle Resorts' mysterious benefactor and how the company had dodged a gut-wrenching bullet. She briefly considered that her brother might be behind it, but the "no strings attached" terms weren't his style, so she dismissed the idea.

"That's wonderful. Why aren't you bouncing off the ceiling?"

"Because I need to sign the papers in person before five tonight, in New York, or we lose the offer."

Tyler stroked an index finger along the length of Alex's jawline. Her eyes spoke of deep love and understanding. "Go. Save the company. Thousands need you more than I do right now."

"I hate leaving you."

"And that's why I love you."

CHAPTER TWENTY-SEVEN

Manhattan, New York

The moment Alex crossed the "t" in her last name, doing so with an extra flair, she was flooded with the same relief she'd felt when Tyler first hugged her in her hospital bed last night. It washed over her like a cleansing rain. She knew in her gut that Castle Resorts' financial woes were behind them, making this a time to celebrate. "Done. Champagne?"

Before Destiny could answer, Syd appeared at Alex's office door. "Hey, Alex." She looked Alex up and down. Clearly, she was still riding the buzz she got from the miraculous turn of events. "You look much happier than when you left the house yesterday." She shifted her attention to Destiny. "Hi, Destiny. It's good seeing you again. So...what's up?"

Alex shifted her attention to Destiny and gestured for her to tell the story. "Go ahead. My new interim CFO will tell you the good news?"

Syd cocked her head in surprise. "Wonderful choice after that coward jumped ship following yesterday's viral video. I say good riddance. He always had a chip on his shoulder."

She turned to Destiny, smiling. "Congratulations. It's a well-deserved promotion. Now, what is this good news?"

"We just secured a half-billion-dollar line of credit."

"Which means?" Syd grinned, leading Alex to finish that thought.

"No downsizing."

"That's wonderful." Syd gave her and then Destiny a giant bear hug. "Congratulations, you two, well done. We'll have to celebrate after I get back from Philly. Ethan called. He said the lab results confirm the wine delivered to the resorts is counterfeit. Any chance you can come with me?"

"Don't you think you should wait for Ethan? He should be back tomorrow."

"I can't wait that long. The final shipment is scheduled to arrive tonight. I want to be there to supervise the delivery and have the warehouse manager research what happened to the first shipment." Syd pleaded with both hands. "So how about it? A sister road trip?"

"I wish I could. I have a lot to undo now that funding has come through. Termination notices are supposed to go out on Monday." This was one instance when Alex was happy to work overtime. She wanted to tell every executive and hotel manager personally that she'd put the downsizing plan on hold.

Syd pursed her lips. "I'll just have to go it alone, then."

"Do you think it's a good idea to go by yourself?" Destiny asked. "You never know what you might run into in that part of town."

"Are you familiar with Philly?" Syd asked.

"Oh yes," Destiny said. "The warehouses can have some shady elements. You're going to want someone with you who's street smart."

"That's definitely not me," Alex said. The twenty-four hours she'd spent in a holding cell in no way had made her a streetwise badass. "How about you, Destiny? The first time we met, seems like you had some very useful insights on the shadier elements of street life." She smiled. "I'd feel much better if you went with her."

"Alex," Syd chastised.

Destiny waved Syd off. "It's fine, Syd. She's right. I did have some hard-earned insights to share with Alex. I'm not ashamed of that part of my life. On the contrary, I'm proud of it because it made me who I am. I'd be happy to go with you. We can drop off this paperwork at Wexler and Associates on the way out of town."

"Deal," Syd said. She turned to Alex. "I'm not sure what time we'll be back, so don't wait up."

CHAPTER TWENTY-EIGHT

Philadelphia, Pennsylvania

Living at the Barnette Winery, buffered by the rolling hills of Napa for a decade, had heightened Syd's wariness of big city life. She saw danger lurking on every corner here in one of the seedier parts of Philly, but the woman sitting in the driver's seat appeared calm and confident, maneuvering her small sedan into a long line of freight trucks that virtually swallowed it. Rumbling down the parkway in the industrial outskirts of Philly, the trucks peeled off to their destinations one by one, dropping off or picking up cargo. Soon, Destiny's GPS alerted them that their destination was five hundred feet ahead. *Just in time*, Syd thought. The office closed at five on Saturdays, and the shipment was due at six.

Destiny pulled into the parking lot of Philly Cold Storage, and Syd scanned the area. To the right, a good-sized area was full of beat-up pickups and sedans, likely employee parking for the warehouse workers. She spotted a sign tacked to the side of a building and pointed left. "There. Visitors' parking is by the main office."

Destiny turned and parked. "Be prepared to be talked down to and given the runaround. The union guys in this town don't take kindly to people asking questions."

Syd cocked up one corner of her lips, recalling the union strong-arm tactics that had accompanied the construction and remodeling of several hotels she oversaw when she was Castle Resorts Chief of Operations. "This isn't my first rodeo."

Destiny turned off the car, opened the driver's door, and slid out of her seat into the warm late-afternoon air. "Let's get us some answers."

Syd was glad she hadn't come alone. Destiny shared many of her and Alex's more robust features, which was comforting right now. Both of them being toned and tall and having nervy demeanors would serve them well when dealing with the intimidating union types.

They strode into the warehouse office, confident and professional. Syd plopped her folio onto the counter and bellowed at the young, lanky clerk, who had his feet propped on the countertop. "Are you in charge?"

He flinched, pulling his stare from the small television at the end of the counter. Once he stopped sneering, he lowered his feet to the floor. "Who's asking?"

"A very pissed-off customer, that's who's asking. I pay you guys a lot of money to stage my product here for distribution, but my last shipment was spoiled." Blaming things on faulty facilities was a much safer cover story than saying she suspected theft. That would only put whoever ran this place on the defensive. Syd saw no sense in showing all her cards yet. "Now, get someone who can provide me with some answers and quit wasting my time."

The clerk pulled a well-worn toothpick from his mouth and pushed his roller office chair back. "I'll be right back."

A grin formed on Destiny's lips the moment he disappeared into a back room. "Damn, girl, I'm impressed. It appears I'm nothing but a straphanger today."

"You're my wing-woman. I know better than to come to the warehouse district alone." Syd winked.

Minutes later, the clerk returned, followed by a forty-something man, cursing under his breath and adjusting his loose-fitting slacks around his potbelly. When the older man saw Syd and Destiny, he stopped to straighten a mustard-stained necktie. A wasted preening effort in Syd's book.

"I got this, Billy. You head back to the docks." The young clerk left and the other man turned his attention to Syd and Destiny. "Good evening, ladies. I'm Sal. Now, what seems to be the trouble?"

"I represent Barnette Winery." Syd briefly paused when the supervisor arched an eyebrow. "Last month's shipment may have spoiled in transit. We've traced the problem, and your warehouse staged the impacted batch."

Sal cleared his throat and adjusted his tie again, nervously this time. "I can assure you that our climate-controlled warehouses are well-maintained and kept at the appropriate temperature."

Syd sensed something odd about his response. Sal didn't ask specific questions about when the wine was shipped or how big a shipment it was. Instead, he went right into defending his operations.

"Your assurances are worth nothing to me right now. I have another shipment coming in tonight. I want to see your records for our shipments for the last six months and inspect the holding areas where you stage and store our wine."

Sal rubbed the back of his neck before wiping several newly formed sweat beads from his brow. "Let me see what I can dig up." He disappeared into the back office, closing the door behind him.

Syd and Destiny turned toward each other simultaneously, locking gazes. "He's not going to dig up a damn thing," Destiny said.

"My thought exactly. But why is he stalling?"

"Likely to get his ducks in a row."

Sal returned ten painfully long minutes later. His delaying tactics could best be described as a runaround. "Policy this" and "procedure that" comprised his explanations for why he couldn't provide Syd the records of her shipments.

Following Syd's long, piercing, fuming stare, Sal said, "Look, Miss—"

"That's Mrs. Barnette. I own the company, and if I don't get some answers, I may very well end up owning this company, too."

"Look, Mrs. Barnette, we have certain procedures for releasing information about our customers. You'll need to—" He paused when static and voices came over the portable two-way radio.

A voice garbled over the crackle. "Sal…problem…truck hit dock eight."

Sal snatched the radio from the charging station, yelling into it. "Who the hell's supervising there? On my way." He snapped at Syd, "I gotta go. Send us a letter on your company stationery, and we'll send you everything we have." He then disappeared into the bowels of the warehouse.

Syd tossed her hands in the air. She and Destiny didn't drive a hundred miles, only for some paper-pusher to blow them off. "What the hell?"

Destiny scanned the empty visitor area and tilted her head toward the back office. "How about we do a little snooping on our own?"

Clearly good old Sal had no intention of helping them. The question was why? That unanswered question made up Syd's mind. She wasn't about to leave Philly empty-handed. She went into stealth mode, scanning the area left and right. She confirmed they were the only two people around. "I like your style, Destiny. I don't trust these guys."

"Ready to do a little Cagney and Lacey?"

Destiny led the way to the back office with Syd a few steps behind. The room was pure chaos. Old 1960s-era file cabinets topped with papers of various sorts. An adjacent wall teemed with old calendars filled with scantily clad women, sticky notes, and photos. The only evidence of modern technology was the clunky computer monitor sitting on top of a battered metal desk.

"I'll take the computer," Destiny said. "You check out the file cabinets."

"On it." Syd rifled through several drawers, looking for any file associated with Barnette Winery.

Destiny snorted. "Nothing like making this easy. He didn't password protect a thing." The sound of fingers clicking a coffee-stained keyboard filled the room. "I'm in their company tracking system." Several more clicks. "I found the Barnette work orders, but I'm not seeing anything that would tell us if something was wrong with the storage unit."

Syd stopped her search and hovered over Destiny's shoulder. "Maybe we should search for records on the cold storage units instead."

Destiny tapped her lips several times. "Didn't Ethan say that the wine was delivered to one dock and picked up at another?"

"Yeah, why?"

"We should look at dock records." Destiny first scrolled to the Barnette files. "Okay, so last month, the trucking company delivered your wine to dock six but picked it up on dock three." She clicked in a flurry, bringing up another set of records. "There. See?"

"What am I looking at?" Syd asked, scanning the screen.

"These are the pickups from every dock the day after the trucks delivered your wine to the warehouse at dock six last month." She pointed to a particular record on the screen. "See? The next day, the same number of cases were picked up at the same dock, but someone logged them out as liquor. The day after that, the same number of cases were delivered to dock three, also logged as liquor. Later that day, your load with the same number of cases was picked up for delivery to their final destination. This can't be a coincidence."

Syd strained to examine the records, the pattern becoming apparent now that Destiny pointed it out. "Son of a bitch. This proves someone here helped to steal my wine."

Destiny craned her neck to look at Syd. "Not just stole, but substituted."

This all puzzled Syd. Sure, her wine was pricier than most typical hotel wines, but it wasn't a vintage that would typically attract organized thieves. "Who would want to steal Barnette wines?"

Destiny and Syd turned their heads toward the door when the office door swung fully open, bouncing off the metal file cabinet. Sal stepped in, pointing a gun at them, followed by a second man who said, "That would be me."

CHAPTER TWENTY-NINE

Manhattan, New York

Yesterday's revelation that she had caused Tyler's cardiac episode brought into clarity Alex's need to make dramatic life changes not soon but now. She had formulated a rough plan during the flight back, and now, having signed the loan paperwork, she was determined to set those changes in motion. A crucial part of her plan, however, rested on how Harley would take it.

With the downsizing plan put on hold, all the managers notified, and the infusion of funds expected Monday morning, Castle Resorts would be on a sound footing for at least the next year or two. Translation—Alex could begin extricating herself from the business sooner than expected. With that weight no longer on her shoulders, she could implement her first significant change—doing absolutely no work on weekends after today. Her second change—putting Tyler and family and Callie in the center of her life.

Alex had just settled into her favorite chair on her back patio and was sipping a glass of Barnette wine when the French door leading to the house opened. "You and Tyler certainly have gone to great lengths to delay you having to serve out Mother's punishment for our brush with the law on graduation night," Harley said.

Alex smirked. "What's with the Lands' End outfit?"

"I thought I'd give you a preview of the wardrobe I've chosen for mucking out the stalls." Harley twirled around, displaying herself like a proud four-year-old showing off her long-awaited ballerina outfit for the big recital.

Harley had attempted to dress appropriately. Jeans were an obvious choice, but the five-hundred-dollar calf-high boots she was wearing were going to take a beating. "The long-sleeved flannel shirt is a nice lesbian touch."

"I thought so, too." Harley poured herself a glass of wine and joined Alex, sitting in the neighboring patio chair.

As they watched Callie sniff the bushes along the fence line for several minutes, sipping their drinks, Alex's mind drifted to the changes she needed to make for Tyler's sake as well as her own.

"Worried about Tyler?" Harley asked.

"Very much. I'm the reason she's in the hospital. I can't be the cause of that again, so I plan to make several dramatic changes. For starters, I've decided to sell my shares in Castle Resorts and resign."

The moment she said those words, her plan became real. She was giving up her life's work. Surprisingly, leaving didn't bother her, but the idea of a Castle not being at the helm did. Despite the bitterness she still held for her father, Castle Resorts belonged to her family, and handing it over to someone else felt wrong. It hurt, but she still didn't trust Andrew enough to consider him a possible successor. But leaving was the only way to give her and Tyler what they both needed—peace of mind.

Harley jerked in surprise. "Wow."

Alex continued, "I also want to sell the mansion."

"Wow," Harley repeated.

"Can you say anything more than wow?" Alex gave Callie a scratch behind the ears when she returned from her romp in the planter beds, tongue wagging as fast as her tail.

Harley repeated, "Wow."

Alex gave Harley an exaggerated eye roll. "You're as bad as Syd." She returned to petting Callie.

Harley dropped her mischievous grin, turning soft eyes on her. "I'm very proud of you, Alex. It's about time you let go of your father's legacy."

"Tyler, her girls, and this lovable dog are my legacy now."

"Have you thought about where you want to live?"

"I have, which is why I asked you here. I'd like to ask Abby about buying the beach house. But since it was your father's, I know she intended it for you. If you have your eye on it, I can check what's on the market."

A smile as wide as Central Park grew on Harley's lips. "I think it's a wonderful idea. You and Tyler have been the only ones using it for years. It's a perfect fit. I'm sure you can work out something with Mother."

"Thank you, Harley. The beach house has been special to us."

"Would you continue to work?" Harley asked.

Alex rubbed her chin a few times, wondering if her plan was too far-fetched. "I have something in mind."

"Care to share?"

"Not yet. I need to do a little research first." Alex's plan was taking shape. She and Tyler would live at the beach with Callie and with room for Bree and several guests, would share in a new business venture she still had to work out, and get married the moment same-sex marriage became legal in New York.

Alex's phone rang, the custom ringtone bringing a smile to her face. "Hi, T. I was just thinking about you."

"You're sounding rather chipper," Tyler said.

"You and a certain furry dog have that effect on me."

"Good to know I can still brighten your evening."

"You have since we first crossed paths on that Napa riverfront." Alex's breath caught in her chest, remembering the instant connection she felt that day. "Please tell me you're coming home tomorrow."

"I am. The doctor just gave me a clean bill of health. If my heart rate remains steady overnight, we can leave first thing in the morning and should be back in Manhattan by dinnertime."

"Good, because Callie and I miss you. We'll pick you up."

"John is catching a ride with us. He wants to sort out this wine fiasco with Syd and Ethan. Can you let Syd know he's coming? She didn't answer John's call."

"Sure thing. I'll let Syd know when she comes home."

CHAPTER THIRTY

Alex woke for the second time this morning and ran a hand across the cold sheets. Tyler should have been there with three-quarters of the blanket bunched up on her side of the bed. She let a smile emerge. Tyler would be back in their bed tonight, and Alex would be back to fighting for a corner of the covers again. "So worth the wait."

The jingle of Callie's collar signaled that Alex's day was about to begin for real this time. A five a.m. canine call of nature had had Alex up way too early for a Sunday and back in bed for another few hours. Once her lovable shepherd finished her morning scratching ritual, she nosed up to Alex's side of the bed, signaling she needed to go outside again. "All right, girl. Let's start the day in earnest and see what Auntie Syd is up to."

Throwing on jeans, a casual T-shirt, and a pair of Chucks, Alex went to the main floor, Callie in the lead down the sweeping staircase. Surprisingly, the smell of freshly brewed coffee was absent. Syd always rose with the sun, no matter her location, and started every morning with two cups of her favorite blend.

Then again, Alex had overslept. The aroma had likely faded hours ago.

Once Callie finished outside, Alex rubbed her behind the ears. "Let's go find Auntie Syd, shall we?"

Alex called out for her sister, searching for her in the kitchen and then on the back patio when she didn't respond. She found no sign of Syd in the guest room or private bathroom either. The bed was made, and the shower showed no sign of recent use. Her earlier curiosity morphed into concern. She called out, going from room to room on both floors. She even checked the garage; both cars were still there, and the engines were cold. Finally, she checked the playhouse in the back garden, the site of many hours of fun for the Castle children, but it too was unoccupied.

Syd hadn't come home. Now she was seriously concerned. She dialed Syd's cell phone, but the call went to voice mail and Alex's concern changed instantly into worry. The last time she saw her sister, Syd and Destiny were about to take off for the warehouse in Philly to research the wine deliveries. When she dialed Destiny's number, that call too went to voice mail. She then tried Castle Resorts headquarters, eventually reaching a lower-level, hard-working executive who had come in on Sunday to get a jump on new budget needs now that Alex had secured the loan. He said he hadn't seen Syd or Destiny since yesterday and, after checking her office, confirmed Destiny wasn't there.

Alex conjured up one gut-wrenching scenario after another, starting with a horrible traffic accident and ending with a terrifying encounter with thugs, all of which ended with her identifying Syd's and Destiny's bodies at the morgue. She called the state troopers in New York, New Jersey, and Pennsylvania, but they reported no overnight traffic accidents on Syd's route that would have required hospitalization or worse.

They were missing and had been since last night.

Unsure what to do, she called the one person she relied on whenever trouble had engulfed her. That call also went to voice mail. She then remembered the Spencer Foundation jet had likely already taken off. She dialed the in-flight phone and waited for the pilot to connect her. "Ethan, Syd is missing."

"What do you mean missing?"

"She and Destiny went to Philadelphia yesterday afternoon to track down information about the counterfeit wine and supervise the delivery of the next shipment. No one has seen them since. I checked with the police, and she wasn't in an accident. I'm worried something may have happened to her."

"Why in the hell did you let them go?"

"They went just to ask questions and watch the load arrive. You had enough on your plate."

"This is a mess, Alex. I'll let John know what's going on and have the pilot reroute us to Philly. I'll text you an ETA, but I'm guessing we'll land in about four hours."

"I don't know if I can wait that long. My sister is missing, dammit."

"Wait for me, Alex. Counterfeiting means planning and organization, which means trouble if you poke your head where it doesn't belong."

"I'll meet you there." Alex hung up without committing to wait for Ethan to land. Philly was two hours away by car. She could at least look for Destiny's car if she left now.

Alex grabbed her purse and car keys. She hadn't driven in months, and the idea of navigating a congested turnpike at highway speed made her anxious. She was just steps away from the garage when the doorbell rang. Escaping in her Audi wasn't an option; whoever was at the door would see her when she pulled out of the garage.

"It's always something." She retraced her steps to the front door, hoping to get rid of whoever it was quickly. The door opened to the last person she expected to see. "Andrew."

"I'm sorry to bother you, but I'm here to see Syd." He carried himself differently than he did before going to prison, she noted. His posture no longer gave off that air of superiority that once was his signature look. In its place was a humility, making Alex think, or at least hope, that prison had changed him for the better.

"She's not here."

"That's strange. I must have misunderstood. We'd planned to meet for Sunday brunch this morning, but Syd never showed."

"I hate to cut this short, but I was just on my way out."

"I'm sorry. I'll leave, but do you know where she is?"

Alex twisted the doorknob, debating what to tell him. Regardless of the bad blood between them, he didn't deserve to be told that their sister was missing under questionable circumstances while standing on her front stoop. She opened the door further and gestured into the entry hall. "Come inside."

His expression scrunched in textbook Castle skepticism. At least Alex could still read a few of his cues. They settled into the main room, with Andrew walking directly to the room's main feature, a cozy floor-to-ceiling, stone-faced, wood-burning fireplace that had replaced the dramatic black marble gas fireplace that had perfectly mirrored her father's cold, dark personality. She and Tyler had transformed this room from a rarely used, oversized showroom to impress the Manhattan elite into the warm and inviting heart of the home.

Andrew lifted a wood picture frame from the mantel that contained a photo of him and Alex at the beach when they were five years old.

"I remember that day," he said.

Alex stood shoulder to shoulder with him, sensing the rebirth of a long-absent vibe between them. Was the connection they once shared as twins returning? The one they had before Kelly came into their lives? Before their father had pitted them against one another? Before Andrew betrayed her with those damn photos of her and Kelly? She once had hoped for its return, but too much hurt had passed between them. She doubted they could ever be that close again, but the idea of forging a new connection was a promising one.

Andrew studied the photo. "We built sandcastles, right?"

"Until you kicked them down."

Andrew returned the frame to the mantel, turning toward her. "I was such a jerk to you."

"Look, Andrew, I'm in a hurry. Syd didn't come home last night, and she's not answering her cell. I'm worried about her."

"Where did she go?"

"To Philadelphia to check on some wine shipments that someone may have tampered with. I was heading there now to find out if anyone has seen her."

"Have you called the police?"

"Just to see if she was in an accident. I wanted to go to the warehouse before I involve the authorities."

Andrew started toward the door. "Come on, let's go."

Alex couldn't remember the last time Andrew volunteered to help, particularly when it didn't benefit himself. She tilted her head to one side to figure him out. "Are you allowed to travel out of New York?"

Andrew stopped and pivoted on his heel toward her. "To neighboring states, yes. Do you want me to drive? Unless you've changed, I tend to drive faster."

Alex thought maybe Syd was right—he *had* changed. She tossed him the keys to her new Audi sedan. "If you put a scratch on it, you're paying for it."

CHAPTER THIRTY-ONE

Philadelphia, Pennsylvania

Without windows or a clock to help them mark the passage of time, Syd had no sense of how long those thugs had had her and Destiny tied up back-to-back on chairs in Sal's stuffy office. Sal had released them only once, one at a time, to use the bathroom and sip on a warm bottle of water. She'd managed a few catnaps. The only other measure was how tired and sore her limbs were from constantly pushing and pulling against the sharp edges of the plastic strips around her wrists and ankles. She'd gotten nowhere and had sliced sections of her flesh in the process.

Destiny grunted, presumably still tugging at her own restraints. "What do you think they're going to do with us?"

Syd rolled her neck to relieve the stiffness that had set in like her arthritis during a rainstorm—sharp and persistent. She flexed her toes and legs and then her fingers and arms to keep the circulation flowing in her extremities. "I don't think *they* know what they're going to do with us. They can't agree on much of anything."

The loud, partially overheard conversations between Sal and the mystery man on the other side of the flimsy door and shaded glass window had been entertaining, if not informational or reassuring. They revealed that Sal was the only experienced criminal between them and that the other guy was in way over his head.

"I heard them say that they were waiting for someone. A woman, maybe," Destiny said.

Since Syd had first seen the other man last night, something had been gnawing at her. She'd seen him before, she thought, though she couldn't remember where or when. She had the vague feeling that somehow, he was associated with Alex. "I still can't figure out where I know that other guy. How about you?"

Destiny said no, adding, "But I've seen his type before. Always out for a quick buck, tough when things are going good, but the first one to roll over when the shit hits the fan. If we have any hope of getting out of this alive, we gotta work on him. I don't trust Sal. He has a short fuse."

"I think you're right about both men." Syd may have worked with Destiny for only a few weeks when she had the reins of Castle Resorts, but that was long enough for her determine that the woman knew how to read people.

An hour passed. The other man returned, this time with the gun and bologna sandwiches and water. He untied one hand for each of the women and held the gun on them while they ate.

This might be their only opportunity to soften up the weak link, Syd thought, and hoped Destiny did too. "A lot of people knew we came here last night. I'm sure they've reported us missing by now. It's only a matter of time before the police come looking for us."

"And when they do, it's only a matter of time before someone starts talking," Destiny added. "I know from experience that the police will only cut a deal with the first one to flip on the others, but only if no one gets hurt."

"It's not too late to let us go and cut a deal," Syd said.

"Shut up and eat, or I'll tape your traps shut," the man ordered, tying up Destiny and Syd again. He left, mumbling to himself with the only discernible words as "myself into."

Minutes later, the two men argued again outside the office door. Syd made out bits and pieces. "How much longer?" "...attracting attention..." "...my other business partners..." "...any minute..." "...we'll figure this out..." and "...better be soon..."

Those fragments convinced Syd that dissension had permeated the ranks, which was the best thing she could have hoped for. She had them paying more attention to themselves than to her and Destiny. She hoped that would give her time to find a way to get them out of there.

CHAPTER THIRTY-TWO

Somewhere over the Midwest

Inspired by a faint floral scent, Tyler glided her lips down the angles of Alex's arched neck. Desire that had been smoldering below the surface ignited at the carnal hum of Alex's moans. Tyler pressed her body against Alex's, pinning her against the bedroom wall.

"T..." Alex groaned in a husky tone. So much hunger was behind that sexy growl. It was as if she hadn't devoured Tyler for months.

Tyler ripped Alex's blouse open, raking her mouth across the sheer black lace of her bra and down the soft skin of her abdomen. She licked the flesh above the waistband of Alex's trousers while loosening the button. The scent of arousal wafted upward, hastening Tyler's effort to touch its source. Tyler rose and captured Alex's lips as she drove her hand down past the light fabric of Alex's lace thong, her breath hitching.

"Alex," she moaned. A tug on Tyler's shoulder distracted her.

"Tyler. Tyler," the male voice gently beckoned.

Tyler opened her eyes, shaking off the fog of sleep. "What?" The haze slowly lifted. She recognized the jet engines' hypnotic hum, remembering that she was on the Spencer jet. Ethan came into focus, hovering above her.

"I'm sorry to wake you, but Alex is on the sat phone again." Ethan handed her the handset. "She wants to talk to you this time."

"Thanks, Ethan." Tyler righted her seat, her cheeks heating with embarrassment at the thought that her sexy dream may have had her inappropriately animated. She put the phone to her ear. "Hey, babe. I was just thinking about you."

"Ethan said you were sleeping. I hope you were dreaming something…umm, nice."

"I was." Tyler couldn't have stopped her grin from forming even if she wanted to.

"Good to know I still have that effect on you," Alex said.

"Would you like to know a little secret?"

"Why, Tyler Falling. I didn't know you kept secrets from me."

"I think you'll like this one. I started having dreams about you right after we ran into each other on the riverfront."

"My, my. You were a married woman back then."

"That should tell you the kind of hold you have had over me since day one." Tyler enjoyed their sexy banter, but Alex must have called for something more substantial. "Have you heard anything about Syd?"

"Still no word. I just miss you, T."

"So, is that why you called? To tell me that you miss me?"

"That, too, but I needed to tell Ethan that an accident on the turnpike has slowed traffic. We should still get to the warehouse before they close up shop, but it might affect your route from the airport."

"I wish you would wait until we land at Northeast Philly. We shouldn't be too far behind you."

"I can't chance waiting too long. We don't know if Syd even made it to the warehouse. If I don't make it there before five, we'll have to wait until tomorrow. Besides, Andrew is with me, so I won't be alone," Alex said.

"How is that going?"

"Jury's still out. At least we agree on the choice of music."

"Classic Motown?" Tyler asked.

"Nothing but."

Ethan motioned to Tyler, mouthing, "We'll meet her at the warehouse."

Tyler nodded. "Ethan said he and John will meet you two there. Please don't take any chances." She wrapped up her call, returning the handset to Ethan. "She's stubborn. We'll need to hurry."

"I figured as much. The pilot has received clearance to bump up the speed. She should shave some time off. I also arranged for rental cars. They'll be waiting for us on the ramp." Ethan returned the handset to its cradle.

"You think of everything," Tyler replied.

"If I did, we wouldn't be on this plane right now," Ethan said softly as he sat in the chair facing Tyler.

Tyler leaned forward so only Ethan could hear. "Stop that right now, Ethan Falling. Stop blaming yourself for things out of your control. You were a good husband to me, and you are an even better father to our girls. If anyone's to blame for Bree finding out the truth, it's me. I should have stored those documents separately."

Ethan glanced toward Bree, two seats away, engrossed in a movie playing on the flat screen. "It was hard seeing her go through all of this."

"And that's what makes you a good father."

Bree tore her attention from the screen and removed her headphones. "Can I ask you guys something?"

Tyler swiveled her chair toward the aisle, as did Ethan. She replied, "Sure, honey."

Bree bounced a knee up and down. "Why did you tell Erin?"

Tyler had expected this question. It was only natural. She and Ethan had already agreed on how to respond. Ethan sat back in his seat, letting Tyler take the lead because this was between mother and daughter. Tyler leaned forward. The mood in the cabin cooled. "Tell me. What did Erin say to you when you asked her why she knew about your adoption?"

"She said it was your story to tell."

Tyler reached out for Bree's hand and, in a calm voice, said, "Well, this is Erin's story, but she's given me permission to tell you."

Bree's eyes widened. Tyler wasn't sure if Bree was ready to hear it, but it was time every family secret saw daylight. "One night, I received a call from Erin's roommate…"

* * *

Yale Campus, New Haven, Connecticut, February 2008

The late-night call Tyler received from Carol, Erin's roommate, was strangely vague. "She's not hurt or anything, but she's really upset, and I can't get her to stop crying. She only wants to talk to you. Can you come up tonight?"

The drive to New Haven was tense, with Ethan and Tyler barely exchanging a word. Tyler's fears had gone into overdrive, wondering what had happened to her baby girl.

Inside Morse Hall, Ethan and Tyler quickened their pace, each cursing aloud that Erin's room was at the farthest end of the corridor. They reached her room and knocked. Carol opened the door, worry etched on her face. "She's calmed down some, but she still won't tell me what happened." Carol grabbed her backpack. "I'll leave you guys alone." She left, closing the door behind her.

Erin was curled up in a ball on the far corner of her bed, sniffling, with her head buried in a pillow. While Ethan remained near the door, Tyler sat on the edge of the bed, dreading what she might find when her daughter finally looked up. Tyler raised her chin with a hand. Erin's eyes were red and swollen, and she had a blank and distant look on her face. That look was unmistakable to Tyler. She had lived behind that same look for a decade and knew the pain associated with it. Her heart split in two.

Tyler scooted closer and gently caressed her daughter's cheek before looking her in the eyes. She softly said, "I know you're terrified, baby. What did he do to you?"

When Erin didn't immediately respond, Tyler glanced over her shoulder at Ethan. Tears rolled down his face as he realized the unthinkable connection Tyler and Erin now shared. Heartbroken too, Tyler returned her attention to her shattered daughter. "If you ever hope to get past this, you need to face it head-on. That starts with telling me what he did to you."

"Mom," Erin said, but sobs choked back the rest of her words. That was more than Tyler had managed after being raped, making her hopeful that Erin would be strong enough to get through this. So Tyler remained patient and waited. Finally, Erin continued, "He... he forced me."

Tyler understood Erin's pain and fear all too well. A vital lesson she learned from her therapist was that her healing could only begin once she faced what happened. That started by saying it out loud. "I know this is hard, but you need to say it."

"Phillip raped me." Erin buried her face in her pillow again, her body quaking.

Tyler took her into her arms. Experience told her that nothing she said or did, other than providing a comforting touch, would help at this point. She glanced at Ethan, who had clenched his fists. She could tell he was digging deep to find every ounce of restraint and not storm out of that dorm room, find Phillip Mattos, and beat him to a pulp.

"I fail every woman in my life," Ethan said, still and blank.

Manhattan, New York, a week later

Tyler adjusted the pillow behind her head again, unsuccessfully reading the same paragraph for the fifth time. She looked up when she heard Alex's footsteps. Alex placed her leather satchel on the dresser before approaching the bed and giving Tyler a sweet, loving kiss. "Love you."

"Love you, too."

"How is she today?" Alex asked.

"The same." Erin had spent the week in their home, cocooned in her bedroom. She barely came out, hardly ate, and spent most of the day sleeping.

"I think she needs help, T."

"I know she does. I've tried talking to her, but she's not ready to open up yet." Tyler already knew what she had to do next. "I need to tell her."

Alex slid atop the covers next to Tyler and held her hand. "Are you going to tell her everything?"

"I have to. Erin has to know she's not alone in this."

Tyler walked down the hallway and knocked on Erin's door. She didn't expect an answer, so after waiting a polite thirty seconds, she walked in and closed the door behind her. Erin was lying in bed, watching television, locked in a trance. Tyler turned on the lights and then turned off the television. Erin objected, but Tyler was firm. "We need to talk."

Erin turned over to face the wall, away from her mother. "I don't feel like talking, Mom."

Tyler sat on the edge of the bed. She knew precisely how Erin felt. Talking about what happened would only put the horrific event on a rewind loop, forcing her to relive it when all she wanted was to bury it deep and forget. But if Erin had any hope of healing, that had to stop.

"I didn't feel like talking for years. You and I have experienced things no woman ever should."

Erin rolled over, wrapped her arms around her mother, and wept and wept and wept.

Tyler cradled her, soaking up every ounce of her pain, disgust, shame, fear, and anger. Once her own weeping stopped, she began, "I relived it every time I had to recount what happened. Each time, I felt powerless, like a trapped animal. I felt disgusted by how he touched me and ashamed that I somehow encouraged him. So, I stopped talking about it. I stopped thinking about it. I buried it so deep I pretended it never happened. I figured I was okay, but I was anything but fine. I became too good at ignoring the parts that might bring me pain, and I lived a lie for the longest time. And the worst part was that I wasn't fair to your father, the one person who supported and loved me the most. That, I regret. I don't want you to live your life lying to yourself and regretting your choices."

Erin pulled back, searching her mother's eyes. "What do I do, Mom?"

"You need help to make sense of what you went through and everything you're feeling. I wish I'd done it sooner. I didn't get help and start seeing a therapist until thirteen years later."

"What pushed you to want to get help?"

"Seeing him again and…" Tyler paused. Erin deserved to hear the entire truth, but the next part would forever change how Erin viewed their family. "And him realizing that Bree was his daughter."

Erin's breath hitched. She covered her mouth with a hand to hold back shock from the awful truth.

"I'm so glad you're on the pill." Tyler loved Bree with every ounce of her heart, but she was a daily living reminder of how she came into this world. Thankfully, Erin had dodged that gut-wrenching bullet.

Erin wept again, but only for a moment. "Dad knows?"

Tyler nodded. "He's known from the beginning. When that bastard wanted to see Bree, we took him to court, and Dad formally adopted her. I hope you understand why we don't want her to know."

Erin nodded her understanding. They shared a bond that no mother and daughter ever should. "It's your story to tell, no one else's."

* * *

Back to 2011

Recalling that night stirred a mixed bag of emotion for Tyler. No mother should ever have to console her daughter for experiencing such a horrible act. Nor should Tyler have asked Erin to keep the truth from her sister.

"Phillip confessed, Yale expelled him, and he served two-and-a-half years of a three-year sentence. Do you remember when Erin moved back with us for a few months?"

Bree offered a tentative, affirmative nod, tears staining her cheeks. "All Erin said was that she was going to fail a class, so she needed a break from school."

"She went into therapy to deal with it. It's an awful but unbreakable bond we share, and she understood when I asked her not to say anything to you. I hope you can find it in your heart to forgive us."

Bree unbuckled her seat belt and collapsed into her mother's arms, shedding tears. Soon Tyler pulled back, searching Bree's eyes, and for the first time since this all began, she saw clear understanding in them.

CHAPTER THIRTY-THREE

Philadelphia, Pennsylvania

Ethan unbuckled before the Spencer jet coasted to a stop on the parking ramp in Philadelphia. Looking out the small window of the plane, he confirmed that two rental cars were waiting for them. He turned to Tyler. "You and Bree head to the hotel. John and I will head to the warehouse. I'll text you when I get there."

Tyler started collecting her things. "If you think I'm waiting this out in some hotel, you're crazy. We're going with you."

"We don't have time to argue about this, Tyler."

"Then don't. We're going."

Ethan placed his hands on his hips, resigned he would not win this one. He blew out a long, frustrated breath. "All right, but we take both cars." He pointed his index finger toward Tyler and then Bree. "You two stay back. I mean it."

"Deal," Tyler said. "Bree, get your bag."

* * *

The classic sound of The Temptations filled the cabin of Alex's Audi. Alex and Andrew bobbed their heads to the beat and softly sang along, their eyes fixed on the oncoming traffic. She couldn't remember the last time she and her brother had connected like this. The closest was at the funeral when they'd recalled long, dormant memories of their father dancing with them when they were little. Though they didn't exchange words today in the car, none needed saying for her to feel again the intimacy of their shared experience. It was only a few hours, but it felt like a lifetime connection.

Andrew followed the GPS voice instructions, pulling onto a busy parkway in Philadelphia's north-end industrial area. When the song ended, he said, "You're lucky, Alex."

"How is that?"

"Based on what I heard earlier when you were on the phone, it sounds like you and Tyler are doing good."

I am lucky, Alex thought. Though until she had Tyler in her arms again following the media pummeling this week, a sliver of doubt would continue to pick at her. "I think so."

"Just think so? That doesn't sound good."

Red flags went off in Alex's head. When Andrew last took an interest in her love life, he had tried to get his hands on Kelly's blackmail photos. "What's it to you, brother?"

Andrew pulled off the road and into a parking lot. He stopped the car and turned off the radio. He shifted in the driver's seat to look Alex straight in the eyes. "I know you have no reason to believe a word I say, but I hope to earn your trust one day. I spent a lot of time in prison figuring out why I was always a jerk to you and everyone around me."

"And what did you figure out?"

"I won't throw out excuses. It was my fault. I constantly felt that I had to prove myself to Father. Even then, I wasn't proud of much of what I did. It took me years, but I've learned that the only approval I need is my own. I know I can never wipe the slate clean with you or with myself for that matter, but would you like to know what else I learned in prison?" He continued after Alex offered a genuine, affirmative nod. "I learned that I shouldn't clean the slate. Who I was and how I treated you should serve as a constant reminder of what I'm capable of when I lose my way. I never want to go back there again. I've never been so sure of myself when I say my gambling and drinking are in the past. I hope to prove to you that my being a jerk is also history."

Alex's throat tightened. She'd never grasped why her relationship with Andrew was so fractured. Now, she was beginning to understand. Growing up, she had clamored for their father's praise, which she regularly received. But no matter how hard he tried, Andrew only earned their father's criticism. She never realized how deeply it affected him.

"What's it to me? You ask," Andrew continued. "I just want to know that you're happy. Syd kept me up-to-date on her and John and you and Tyler. Every time she visited, she showed me pictures. In every one of you and Tyler, you always looked happy. I could tell by the way you looked at her that she was the reason behind that smile. After our sophomore year at Yale, you always looked so sad." Andrew reached out a hand and placed it on Alex's. "I never knew how much Kelly hurt you. I feel like such an ass for getting mixed up with her."

Andrew wiped back a tear, setting Alex aback. She'd seen him cry only once as an adult, and it took their father dying to make it happen. "I'm sorry, Alex. Especially knowing that we almost lost you because of her." Andrew choked out his last words. He'd laid all his cards on the table, and now the ball was in Alex's court.

Alex's lips quivered. It didn't matter that it was an accidental overdose. If Harley hadn't found her in time, she would have died and never known true love with Tyler. She joined her brother in shedding several emotion-filled tears.

Andrew put the transmission in drive. "Let's go find our sister."

Minutes later, he navigated into the warehouse parking lot, triggering an adrenaline spike in Alex. She sensed danger. Checking the time on her phone, she calculated they had a half hour before the office would close. "Let's troll the lot and see if we can find Destiny's car," Alex said.

"Good idea. What is she driving?" Andrew asked.

"A new dark gray Camry, I think."

"I'll look left. You look right," Andrew suggested.

The visitor area was empty, so he proceeded to the employee lot. Most vehicles were pickup trucks, SUVs, or beat-up clunkers, so a new Toyota with New York plates would likely stand out. Andrew slowly navigated up and down each aisle, eventually reaching the end of the lot.

"Nothing," Alex said. When an eighteen-wheeler rolled into the lot. Andrew pulled Alex's sedan behind it and followed it into the dock area. "What are you doing?" Alex asked after looking at the signs, spelling out, "Restricted Area."

Andrew shrugged his shoulders. "What? There's no one around controlling access. If anyone stops us, we just play dumb."

Alex reluctantly nodded her concurrence.

Once the truck proceeded toward the back of the industrial lot, no other moving vehicles were in sight. Andrew peeled off between two buildings and drove to the end. He looked left while Alex searched right. Nothing. He turned to the next set of buildings and repeated.

"There." Alex pointed out her side window.

Andrew threw the car into park.

"It looks like her car," Alex said.

She and Andrew approached the car on foot. She tried opening the passenger door, but it was locked. Glancing into the front seat, she saw nothing that would hint at Syd and Destiny's location. She examined the back seat. "That's Syd's jacket."

"Are you sure?" Andrew asked as he peered through the back window.

"I gave it to her for Christmas, and she had it on when I picked her up at the airport. It's hers, all right."

Alex froze, feeling the cold steel of something hard pressing against the back of her head. It had the unmistakable feel of a gun.

A deep voice behind her said, "Hold it right there."

Andrew turned his head and froze. "Fuck."

Minutes later, the gun-wielding thug herded Alex and Andrew into the main office building, shoving the weapon periodically into each of their backs to ensure their cooperation. Alex's mind raced to make sense of the harrowing turn of events. They'd discovered Destiny's car, so it was clear Destiny and Syd had made it to the warehouse. Were they still alive? Something made her think her worst fear was accurate.

Once inside the main office building, the gunman locked the door behind them and yelled, "We have another problem."

The man who emerged from a back office looked vaguely familiar. Alex tilted her head from side to side trying to jog her memory. "I know you," she said.

"This just keeps getting better and better," the gunman grumbled.

Alex snapped her fingers. All the craziness swirling around Alex and Syd made more sense now. "Nick Castor. Kelly's boy toy."

"What in the hell does Kelly have to do with this?" Andrew's tight tenor reflected the tension in the room.

The other man tossed Nick a roll of pallet strapping, telling him to tie Alex's and Andrew's hands behind their backs. "Toss them in the back with the others. Then we all gotta talk."

We all, Alex thought. That equaled more people, which meant more trouble. But he also said, "the others," which implied that Syd and Destiny were alive. The pit in her stomach that had formed the moment she felt cold steel against her skull eased up a bit at the possibility of a morsel of good news.

Nick led them to a smaller office, opened the door, and pushed them in. Alex stumbled, but caught herself before she fell. Recovering her balance, she spotted Syd and Destiny behind her, alive and in one piece, but strapped to office chairs. "Thank God. Are you two all right?"

Nick continued to shove Alex toward the back wall. "Both of you, sit on the floor and shut up." He tied their ankles together with the plastic strapping, making it impossible for them to stand up. He left, slamming the door shut on his way out. The moment he was gone, hushed exchanges began to flow.

Andrew lowered his voice. "What the hell is going on here?" Destiny, who was seated closest to him, facing the wall, answered in a low, soft tone. "The warehouse manager, Sal, caught us rummaging through his files and pulled a gun on us."

"So did the guy who caught us. Destiny, right? I'm Andrew. We found your car around back."

"We found evidence that someone has been substituting counterfeit wine for the wine we shipped here," Syd said, twisting to speak over her shoulder. "That meshes with the lab results Ethan received that proved that the resort wines differed from one he picked up at a store."

Alex paused her struggle to free her restraints when the sharp plastic edges cut into the skin around her wrists. "Well, Nick Castor is helping him."

"Castor?" Syd's shocked expression hinted that a memory had bumped loose, clearing up a mystery. "Now, I remember him. Indra Kapoor fired him from PopCo for insider trading when he was doing the nasty with Kelly Thatcher. It can't be a coincidence that he's part of the counterfeiting scheme." She shook her head. "Kelly has to be behind this. But why would she hate me that much? And how could she orchestrate this from prison? It doesn't make sense."

"I'm to blame." Alex couldn't shake the weight of her combined dread and guilt. She had set all of this in motion years ago when she began her ill-fated affair with Kelly at Yale. If not for her rampaging hormones, Kelly wouldn't have embarked on this elaborate path of revenge. "I brought Kelly into our lives because I was a stupid, horny teenager."

Syd tilted her head in unmistakable sympathy. "Don't put any of this on yourself, Alex. There's a reason Kelly is in prison."

"But—" Alex started.

"No buts," Syd continued. "Anyone who would do this is unstable, plain and simple. You did nothing wrong."

They quieted, hearing a third muffled voice joining the conversation of the men outside the door. Its tone was lighter, more feminine, and seemed to calm the other two. After a moment the door swung open, and the two men walked in, followed by someone wearing pumps.

When the men stepped to the side, revealing the newcomer, Alex's jaw dropped. "What the hell are you doing here?" The last time either Castle dealt with Georgia Cushing was when Syd fired her and had security perp-walk her out the front door. Why in the hell would she be mixed up with a bunch of wine counterfeiters? Did she hate Syd that much?

Sal turned toward her, waving his arms in the air, a gun still in his hand. "Fucking great. She knows you too. How did I let myself get involved with two amateurs?"

"It was a sound plan," Georgia retorted. "All you had to do was substitute the Barnette shipments with Mr. Castor's swill and snag half of the profit after he sold the original wine. Not hold people at gunpoint."

"This is all your fault, Georgia. I should have never agreed to get involved." Nick Castor looked as if he was on the brink of making a dash for it. "They've been missing for too long. I bet the police are already on their way."

"Such a gutless wonder," Sal said.

Alex watched as Destiny twisted in her chair, apparently trying to see who was talking. When she managed finally to turn until her knees bumped against Syd's thigh, getting a good look at them and giving them a good look at her, Alex heard a gasp and saw the color drain from Georgia's face. She looked even more shocked than Kelly had when the police broke down her door and arrested her for William's murder.

Her eyes blinking rapidly, Georgia turned toward Sal and Nick. "Let me have the room. I know these people. I'll find out what they know and if the police are really on to us."

Sal waved the gun at Georgia. "Five minutes. My other business partners don't take kindly to the police poking around the warehouse."

Once Sal and Nick left, Georgia stepped toward Destiny. "What are you doing here, child?"

Why on earth would Georgia call Destiny that? Alex thought.

Destiny raised her chin defiantly. "I'm helping my sisters, the ones you're trying to destroy."

Syd snapped her head toward Destiny. "Did you just say sisters?"

"Half sisters, actually. I found out two days ago." Without skipping a beat, Destiny said to Georgia, "My instincts were right when I walked out on you the other day. You are a vindictive shrew. I can't believe you gave birth to me."

Destiny's bombshell had Alex's head spinning. She had a million questions, but asking them would only inflame the situation. Calm was needed. "Georgia, you're clearly upset about how you left the company, but this isn't like you at all. You need to get us out of here."

"I'm not lifting a finger to help you." Each word came out sharp as a knife, cutting to shreds the hope Alex had held to appeal to Georgia's humanity. Her face was flushed and fiery—more furious than anything Alex had ever seen. Years of cordiality, working side by side, had disappeared as if they never happened.

"I can't believe you hate us so much that you'd wish to see us dead." Alex had difficulty reconciling the professional woman she'd worked with for a decade with the callous one standing before her.

"The Castle family destroyed my life." Georgia sneered. "First, William makes me give up my daughter. Then Sydney takes away my job. And now you're taking away my home."

"What are you talking about?" Syd asked.

"William Castle is my birth father," Destiny explained. "And that house in Brooklyn we're closing on next month? Georgia has been living there rent-free since giving birth to me, courtesy of a deal she made with him."

"This is too much," Syd said, shaking her head.

Georgia turned soft eyes on Destiny. "You're still my child. I don't want you hurt. I'll try to get you out of here."

"If you hope to see me again"—Destiny narrowed her eyes convincingly—"you'll help all of us."

"Even if I wanted to, I can't. The Castles are rich and powerful. And they know who we are. There's no way I can convince those two to let them go. But I can say you're just a driver and would take money for your silence."

"Well, you better try to help us all because I'll tell them that you panicked when you were in here and called the police."

Georgia appeared hurt by what she viewed as Destiny's betrayal. "I'll try to stall for time."

The office door flew open. Sal stormed in, looking ten times angrier than when he left. "Well?"

"It's Sunday. I doubt anyone's going to miss any of them until tomorrow."

"If there's a chance the cops are on to us, we have to clean up loose ends." Sal pointed his gun at Destiny's head. "And these four are loose ends."

Georgia rushed forward, placing a hand on Sal's arm. "Not here, you fool."

Nick wiped the sweat from his brow. "Let's think this through."

"The only thing to think through is when and where," Sal said, lowering his weapon. "They know too much, and they know who we are. If we don't take care of them, my other business associates will."

Georgia raised and lowered her hands in a calming fashion. "Let's step outside and come up with a proper plan."

Sal stormed out with Georgia and Nick on his heels. Alex had the impression Georgia was looking for a way to avoid bloodshed, but... Sal was the wild card. Sal and his other "associates," whoever they might be. No matter how she looked at it, she thought the chances of her, Andrew, Syd, and Destiny surviving the day weren't good.

CHAPTER THIRTY-FOUR

When their rental cars pulled into the warehouse parking lot a few feet past the roadside entrance, Ethan positioned his car side by side with the one Tyler was driving. He asked John to roll down his window so he could talk to Tyler. "Park it back here and wait. And I mean *wait*. John and I will check things out."

Tyler complied, parking her car at a safe distance from the main office but with a good view of the building. Too close for Ethan's comfort. The other side of town would be much safer, but trying to get Tyler to leave at this point would be like trying to convince him that bacon was a bad thing. It would never happen.

Ethan coasted his car to the empty visitor lot and parked in a spot not visible from the main entrance. Something wasn't right. Alex should have arrived over an hour ago, but where was her car? Why hadn't she called or texted?

He and John exited the car and approached the door. The hairs on the back of Ethan's neck tingled. The place was unnaturally quiet. Warehouses of this size were usually bustling all hours of the day and night. He reached inside his loosely zipped jacket and pulled out his Beretta automatic pistol, switching off the safety. Ever since leaving the police department, he had spent hours at the firing range, practicing for moments like this. He knew every operational facet of his weapon and was ready.

Ethan raised his free hand waist-high. "I'll go through first, John. Come in only after I give you the all-clear."

John nodded.

Inside

Alex continued to work on loosening the straps at her wrists and ankles, trying to ignore what the sharp edges were doing to her skin. "Damn. I'm not strong enough to break these things."

"Good thing I went to prison and did all that weight lifting," Andrew said. "I've stretched these—" His ankle straps snapped with a sharp crack. "A few more minutes and I should have my wrists free."

The office door swung open, slamming against the wall. Sal stomped through, waving his gun, his eyes glaring with rage, followed reluctantly by Nick and Georgia. He'd apparently decided on a course of action, though it wasn't clear that it was one they approved of.

"Which one gets it first?" Sal pointed the muzzle at Syd, who recoiled in fear.

"No!" Alex yelled. Both she and Andrew squirmed frantically, trying to escape from their remaining restraints, but they were too tight and too thick, at least for her.

Sal shifted and pointed the gun toward Destiny. "Her then?"

Georgia threw herself in front of Destiny. "No. Not my daughter!"

"Daughter?" Sal hissed, waving his arms. "You all are fucking nuts."

Georgia's revelation seemed to have pushed him to the limit. Thinking it was only a matter of seconds before he erupted, Alex decided to do what she did best—stall. She'd successfully held off the need to downsize at Castle Resorts for years. Hopefully, she could hold off Sal long enough for Andrew to break free.

"Wait!" Alex shouted to get his attention. "How much would it take to get you to let us go? A million? Two million?"

Sal turned toward Alex, aiming the pistol between her eyes. On second thought, maybe getting Sal's attention wasn't a smart move. "No amount of money is going to get me out of this jam," he said, snarling.

"Then how about a private jet to take you anywhere you want?" she asked, not giving him time to think. "I have access to one. It can take you anywhere in the world."

"There's nowhere I can hide. They'll find me." Deciding apparently that he had nothing to lose, he shoved Georgia and wheeled to fire at Destiny.

Georgia righted herself in time to fling her body in front of her daughter a second before a shot rang out. Blood sprayed in every direction, and Georgia fell to the floor.

Sal turned then and pointed the gun toward Syd. Before he could pull the trigger again, Andrew lurched to his feet and lunged, throwing himself between Syd and the gun. A second earsplitting shot rang out. Andrew fell to the floor, blood pooling on the floor next to him.

Alex's heart stopped. "Andrew! No!"

The distinctive crack of gunfire, muffled though it was, penetrated the wooden door at the entrance to the building. Ethan had heard that sound too many times while policing the streets of Sacramento. There was no time to call for backup. He didn't hesitate. People he loved were likely in that room and in the line of fire. He raised his right leg and kicked the front door open, sending splinters from the frame flying into the office. "Wait here. Call 911," he yelled to John as he prepared to enter.

Ethan stepped through the half-broken door, his pulse pounding. The office was dimly lit, and danger could lurk around any corner. He swung his pistol first left and then right, scanning the room for targets. Nothing. He heard voices, but from where? Brighter, more concentrated light was coming from a back office behind a counter. He shifted direction and headed straight for it.

A second shot rang out. Ethan heard someone yell, "Andrew! No!"

Ethan rounded the counter at a fast clip. He pushed through the open door, assuming a Weaver stance, a two-handed grip around his pistol. He held it so hard his fingertips pulsated against the metal and rubber.

Two targets were standing. One with a gun pointed at Alex. High threat. Ethan fired. Double-tap to the chest. Two hits, center mass. The gunman stumbled backward at the first bullet and to the floor with the second, spitting blood while he lay there.

Ethan pivoted his upper body like a turret, training his weapon on the second, less threatening target—a man with empty hands. "Give me a reason." The man froze.

Alex screamed, "Andrew!"

"Hands up," Ethan ordered the man, lowering his weapon after he complied.

Ethan scanned the room in every direction with his weapon at the ready. Alex… Syd… Destiny… The miserable excuse for a brother, the gunman, and some woman were down in a sea of blood. "Syd, any others?"

Syd trembled. "No."

John appeared in the doorway, spotting blood and bodies lying everywhere. "My God." He started toward Syd.

Ethan understood his cousin's urge to reach his wife, but he needed his help. "John, get something to tie up this dirtbag." Giving Syd a desolate look, John turned on his heels and headed back toward the outer office.

Struggling still to reach her brother despite her restraints, Alex cried out, "Help him, Ethan. Help Andrew!"

Ethan rushed to Andrew, kneeling beside him. Keeping his gun aimed at the last standing target, he checked with his other hand for a pulse. One was present, but it was faint. He checked his breathing. It was shallow, a sure sign Ethan needed to stem his bleeding. He looked over the barrel of his gun at his shaking captive and gave him an unnecessary perhaps, but unambiguous, warning. "You move, you die."

Securing his gun in his waistband, he peeled off his jacket and pressed it against the oozing wound on Andrew's abdomen. With his other hand, he pulled out and dialed his cell phone.

"Nine-one-one, what's your emergency?"

"Ten-fifty-two. Three GSWs. Warehouse at three-eight-zero Coral Street."

"Units already en route. Dispatching buses."

As Ethan completed the emergency call, John returned with a roll of strapping from the outer office, pulled down the prisoner's quivering hands and lashed them behind his back. He rushed then to Syd and worked futilely on loosening her bindings. "Are you all right? Did they hurt you?"

Syd shook her head no. "I'm all right." Her hands visibly shook. "Help Alex. She needs…" She shook her head again, words failing her.

The scene mostly secure, Ethan pressed his jacket more tightly against Andrew's chest, took a breath, and tried to process what he was seeing. He'd never heard such fright and despair in the voices of his cousin and Syd. And Alex… She was frantic, nearly hysterical, as she tried to work her way to Andrew, who lay bleeding out on the floor. Strangely, Destiny had managed to work her way over to the woman lying lifeless on the floor, and she was crying over her body.

How the hell had a wine counterfeiting effort resulted in a bloodbath? He shuddered at the thought of how things might have turned out if he'd arrived five minutes later. None of them might have survived.

Tyler burst through the door, flinching as she discovered the carnage on the floor…and Alex, covered in blood and crying, thrashing around on the floor. "Alex! No!"

Frantic, Tyler sprinted over bodies and blood to get Alex, only to hear Alex yell out, "I'm fine, T. Help Andrew. Help him!"

Ethan motioned Tyler over. "Press here," he instructed, guiding her hands to the jacket above Andrew's wound. "Hard." Giving her a glum look, he rose, walked over to the last perp and dragged him out of the room. Throwing him on the outer office floor, he started scouring the countertop and drawers for anything to cut Alex's restraints with. Hearing the man behind him rustle on the floor, he whipped out his pistol and trained it on him. "One reason, asshole. Just give me one reason to blow you away."

The man cringed as he shifted his wrists and the straps binding them. "Don't shoot."

Ethan finally took a good look at the man and cocked his head. "I know you. You're that slug, Nick Castor." If Nick was involved, Ethan would bet his last dollar Kelly Thatcher somehow was too. "Figures."

Ethan returned the weapon to his waistband. He rifled through drawers until he located a pair of scissors. He pointed to Nick with an index finger and ordered, "Stay." Popping his head into the inner office, he handed John the scissors. "Cut them loose. Tyler, where's Bree?"

"She's in the car near the street," Tyler answered, focused on tending to Andrew's wound. She appeared rattled, but not to the point that the stress might trigger another heart episode. "He's still losing blood. What do I do?"

"Constant pressure. Don't let up," Ethan said. He took up a position where he could keep an eye on Nick and await the police.

John freed Syd and Destiny before stepping over the bodies to Alex. When he cut her straps, Alex quick-crawled to Andrew and Tyler. Andrew's wrists were still bound. "Cut those damn things off."

John cut off the last of Andrew's bindings, allowing Alex to move Andrew's arms to a more comfortable position. Alex wept at his side. "Don't you die on me, Andrew. Don't you fucking dare."

Syd and Destiny cried too as they watched Andrew's lifeblood continue to drain from his body. John wrapped an arm around Syd, offering her a sliver of comfort in the middle of this bloody horror.

The faint sound of sirens grew louder outside the warehouse. If the first responders had been trained similarly to Ethan, they would treat this scene as having an active shooter. Their first task would be to eliminate any threats. Knowing that multiple victims were already down, going into a semi-lit room would have them on edge. Ethan knew he and the others needed to present no threat. He took a few steps toward the front door, threw his weapon toward it, and flung himself flat on the floor with his hands interlaced behind his head.

Red and blue lights flashed through the front windows. Ethan turned his head and yelled, "Police are here. Everyone, stay down." He then turned his head toward Nick. "If you don't want to die in the next thirty seconds, I suggest you lie flat."

"Fuck," Nick said as he took one last deep breath and positioned himself as flat as he could.

Two, no three, patrol cars skidded to a stop outside. "Stay down. Stay down," Ethan yelled one last time. He fixed an eye on the door but kept himself low.

The first two officers rushed the door, one swinging his weapon left and the other toward the right. The next two officers stormed in, guns drawn, ready to fire.

The second set of officers lasered their weapons on Ethan. One jammed a knee into Ethan's back and secured his hands to keep him down. Ethan coughed. "Falling. Credentials in my hip pocket. Perp behind me. Vics in the back. All secure."

The officer ordered, "Stay down," as he pulled out Ethan's private security identification and badge.

His partner approached Nick near the far wall. She ordered, "Stay down."

The officer holding Ethan down released his pressure, allowing him to rise. "Stay here."

The other set of officers passed and approached the back office with guns drawn. John's voice rang out, "Don't shoot."

"Hands. Show me your hands," an officer yelled.

"He'll bleed out if I do," he heard Tyler say, her voice unsteady. "I'm not leaving him." Ethan hoped the officers had trained well and knew how to discern friendlies from foes.

An officer in the bloody, body-filled room keyed his radio. "All clear. Send in the bus." Following a squelch, he added, "If you can walk, clear the room for the EMTs."

That was Ethan's cue that it was safe to move in. He stood near the doorway, letting Destiny pass by, followed by John with his arm wrapped around Syd's shoulder. Each had a blank expression.

Tyler had remained at Andrew's side, kneeling with both hands pressed against his wound. Andrew was motionless, his face was pale. Alex grabbed his limp hand. She looked up at Tyler, tears streaming down her cheeks. "He can't die."

Ethan's heart went out to Alex and to Tyler. Alex had been through the wringer more times than any one person should have to endure. He had a difficult time admitting this to himself after all the trouble Alex's twin caused, but he hoped Andrew survived, for both their sakes.

An officer grabbed Alex by the elbow, but she resisted. Tyler begged, "Please go with him, Alex. I got this."

The officer pulled harder, dragging Alex toward the door. When she reached the threshold, she yelled. "Don't let him die, Tyler. Don't let him die."

CHAPTER THIRTY-FIVE

The glass doors of the Philadelphia Memorial Hospital Emergency Room swooshed open, admitting again the sounds of blaring horns and revving bus engines struggling to get up to speed. The additional noise, however, paled in comparison to the chaos inside. People filled every seat, with dozens more standing or sitting overflow along the walls and aisles. Crying babies, arguing women, arguing men, and loud, anxious conversations were creating a mind-numbing ruckus.

Tyler had been banished to this chaos some time ago, kicked out of the exam room when the ER doctor arrived to assess Alex's injuries. Frankly, having already determined on her own that Alex's wounds were limited to the cuts on her wrists, she welcomed the break from keeping Alex from falling apart from her emotional injuries. It gave her time finally to process what had happened. She'd never before held someone's life in her hands. The prospect that her efforts might have fallen short, that she might have failed Alex as well as Andrew, weighed heavy.

She looked up again as the outer doors opened, looking for Erin, who had texted that she and Connor were on their way. This time, Erin and Connor walked through. After acknowledging Tyler with a jut of her chin, Erin tugged on Connor's sleeve and pointed in Tyler's direction. Seeing the friendly face of someone who wasn't involved in last night's horrendous events provided more of a relief than Tyler had expected. It suggested that at some point the horrible nightmare she was in would end.

Erin approached, her eyes growing wider each step. She stopped near Tyler's feet, staring her mother's blood-stained shirt. "Geez, Mom. That's not your blood, is it? You're okay?"

Tyler slowly shook her head no, mentally recounting the number of times she'd wiped her hands on her blouse to remove the blood from them. "No, honey. It's mostly Andrew's, I think."

"You think?" Erin bent at the knees until she was at eye level with Tyler.

"There was blood everywhere." Tyler inspected her hands, still streaked with lines of dark red. Strangely, she thought about getting a manicure. She'd rather have someone else scrape the blood from beneath her nails.

Erin scanned the waiting area. "Where are Dad and Bree?"

"In the cafeteria, I think. We didn't want Bree seeing me caked in blood."

"And Alex?"

"A doctor is examining her and the others."

Erin lowered the backpack that had been slung over her shoulder. "I picked up a change of clothes for you, Alex, Syd, and their friend. How about we get you cleaned up and into some fresh clothes?" Tyler lacked the energy to do more than nod her response. Erin turned to Connor. "Why don't you catch up with Bree and my dad? I'll take care of Mom."

"Sure thing, Erin." Connor kissed Erin on the cheek before following the signage down the hallway. The brief and tender kiss brought a smile to Tyler. She was happy that her daughter hadn't made the same mistakes she had. She was proud that Erin had not only faced her trauma head-on but also figured out her sexuality at a young age without wasting decades of her life. If nothing else, Tyler had gotten motherhood right the first time around.

Erin led Tyler to the ladies' restroom off the waiting area. The quiet in there was a welcome respite from the general chaos they'd just escaped. Erin's voice echoed as she counted off the items she'd brought for her mother. "It was warm outside, so I brought you jeans and a tank top. Then I remembered how cold hospitals can get, so I brought Alex's Yale sweatshirt. I know it's your favorite." Erin's talkativeness was a sign that whatever Ethan had told her about the events of tonight, they had rattled her, too.

Tyler placed a hand on Erin's arm, reassuring her. "I'm fine, honey."

"You were released from the hospital twelve hours ago, Mom. I'm nervous that you might have another episode because of Alex." Erin's tone contained more than concern. It was full of bitterness.

There were plenty of people to blame for what happened in that warehouse, and most of them were dead. Erin had misplaced her blame, but it was somewhat understandable. "None of what happened is Alex's fault."

"Oh, pah-lease. That woman's past is going to put you in the grave. First, Dad was shot in her hotel. Then the half-naked video with Kelly Thatcher pops up for the entire world to see. And now, she's involved with a kidnapping and another deadly shooting. Alex Castle attracts trouble."

Tyler hoped Erin's protective nature was at the root of her new animosity toward Alex, not a personal grudge. While she appreciated her daughter's Mama Bear response, Tyler needed to nip it in the bud before it blossomed into something more. "Alex has her faults, but being a trouble magnet is not one of them. We can't control what the people around us do. Blaming her for what Kelly and Georgia did would be like blaming you and me for what Phillip and Paul did to us."

Erin lowered her head, wiping away her sniffles. "I'm sorry, Mom. It's not that I blame her. It's just that she's surrounded by crazy, and I don't want you to be collateral damage."

Tyler raised Erin's chin with a hand. "We're all stressed about what's happened the last few days with Bree, my episode, and the events here in Philly. I appreciate that you're worried about me, but the doctor in Sacramento adjusted my meds. I can already tell that they're working better."

"I'm still going to worry."

"You wouldn't be my daughter if you didn't."

Tyler washed her face, head, arms, and hands the best she could before slipping into a stall to change clothes. As she balled up the bloodied shirt she'd been wearing, her mind drifted to the terrified look she'd seen on Alex's face when the police officer dragged her out of that horrific warehouse scene. *"Don't let him die, Tyler. Don't let him die."* Tyler was sure Alex didn't intend it, but those words had laid a heavy responsibility at Tyler's feet. Too heavy. She ran her fingers through her damp, stringy hair and whispered to herself, "I hope I didn't let you down, Alex."

A light rap on the stall door returned Tyler to the present. "Mom? Are you okay in there?"

Tyler straightened her back, putting on her most robust "mom" game face, and opened the door. "I'm fine." She walked to the sink and pulled on Alex's sweatshirt.

"You don't look fine," Erin said.

Tyler inspected herself in the mirror. The long last few days, and even longer last few hours, had manifested themselves on her face. The dark circles under her bloodshot eyes and a puffy red nose made her look as if she'd been up for days cramming for finals while enduring the cold from hell. "Geez, I look worse than when I wake up in the morning."

"Which is why I'm worried."

"I just need a shower and a long night's sleep next to Alex."

"I know what you mean. I feel the same way about Connor."

"I'm so happy for you two and so very proud of you." Tyler pulled Erin into a tight, loving hug. It had taken Tyler thirteen years to begin to come to grips with her trauma; Erin had done so in less than one. "You've worked your way back in a way I wish I had."

Erin pulled back. Her eyes reflected a unique understanding only survivors truly appreciated. "But you made it through. I'm happy that you found someone." The fact that she hadn't said

Alex's name was troublesome, Tyler thought, and a sign perhaps that she was holding a grudge.

"I am, too." Tyler swiped a tear off her cheek. "The doctors should be done examining Alex and the others by now. I should get back there. Catch up with your father and Bree, and I'll text one of you updates."

Minutes later, Tyler passed the nurses station in the heart of the emergency room, carrying the backpack of extra clothes Erin had brought. Destiny was occupying a chair outside the examination room where Tyler had last left Alex and where a police officer was standing watch from a comfortable distance away. She appeared lost in thought. If Tyler had to characterize her expression, she would say it was conflicted.

"Hey." Tyler sat in the chair next to her, looking to help in some small measure. "Did the doctor give you a clean bill of health?"

"Yeah. Just a few cuts." Destiny displayed her bandaged wrists and resumed bouncing her left leg up and down.

"How are you holding up?"

"Holding up?" Destiny rubbed her temples in the same fashion Alex and Syd did when their heads pounded like a kettle drum. She was definitely a Castle. Tyler couldn't believe she hadn't seen it before. "In the last three days, I've discovered a family I never knew I had, was kidnapped, held at gunpoint, nearly killed, and watched my birth mother die while taking a bullet meant for me."

"Just another day at the office for a Castle."

Destiny snorted. "I'm getting that impression."

"Have the three of you talked yet?" Tyler asked.

Destiny shook her head, no. "They were upset about Andrew, so I wanted to give them some space."

"I know this is none of my business, but even though you never met before, he's your brother, too. You, Alex, and Syd need each other at a time like this."

"This isn't the time to push things," Destiny said with a sense of certainty. "Alex and Syd only learned about me last night. They need time to process it."

"You're just like Alex. Stubborn as all hell." Tyler fished through Erin's backpack and pulled out a T-shirt and leggings. "A fresh change of clothes might help."

"You're a lifesaver."

"I hope so." Tyler handed her the fresh clothes. "There's a restroom down the hallway. You'll feel a lot better."

After Destiny went to clean up, Tyler stood, ready to knock on the examination room door, but paused to listen when she heard muffled voices inside.

"I don't trust her, Alex," Syd said. "She knew about her birth parents days ago and said nothing."

"Well, I do trust her," Alex said. "She's pulled my ass out of the fire more times than I can count. I'm sure she had her reasons."

"We need to tread lightly," Syd said.

"We just need to talk to her."

Tyler was proud of Alex. She was refusing to let this earth-shattering revelation alter the close-knit relationship she and Destiny had built over the past four years. Tyler knocked, cautiously pushed the door open, and peeked in. Alex and Syd stopped talking when she entered. "Babe?"

Alex looked up from her seated position on the examination table, wiping her nose with a well-used tissue. The moment she locked her swollen eyes with Tyler's, her lips trembled, making Tyler's heart ache for her. She was clearly close to the breaking point. She barely uttered, "T."

Had the unthinkable happened? Tyler thought back to the minutes she'd held Andrew's life in her hands, applying pressure to his wound and refusing to let up until the paramedics arrived. During those harrowing moments, the one thing that went through her mind was that if she slipped, even once, he would die and Alex would lose a part of herself. Hours later, as doctors rushed Andrew into surgery, the only prognosis they had been given to go on was, "It doesn't look good." Had he died?

Tyler was afraid to ask if news had come. She stepped between Alex's legs and wrapped her arms around her neck. It took two seconds for Alex to begin to quake and for tears to soak Tyler's neck.

Soon, Alex pulled back, gently stroking Tyler's cheek. "I'm sorry."

Tyler searched Alex's eyes, trying to understand what she meant. "Sorry about what?"

"I had no right saying what I did, telling you to not let Andrew die. I should have never put that responsibility on you. I could have lost both of you."

Tyler would never say it, but she agreed. The last few hours had been excruciating, waiting on word. If Andrew died, she would feel responsible and forever wonder what else she could have done. "It's all right." She cupped Alex's cheeks.

"No, it's not. I put you under too much stress. If anything happened to you—"

"But nothing did. The new meds are working much better."

Alex lowered Tyler's hand to her lips and kissed her fingers. "I can't lose you."

"You won't. I'll be kicking you in your sleep for many, many years."

Alex cracked a faint grin. "And hogging the covers."

Tyler rolled her eyes. "I'll work on that."

Alex tapped Tyler on the tip of her nose. "Don't you dare. I love your clutch and roll. Every time you pull the covers, you force me to search for warmth against you. Sometimes I think you do it on purpose." When Tyler let a naughty grin form, Alex's mouth fell open. "You little devil." She pulled Tyler closer for a long, passionate kiss.

The door swung open, forcing them to pull apart. A woman in scrubs appeared, weary from hours of surgery. "I'm sorry…"

Tyler had learned through unfortunate experience that the hours before dawn in a hospital were typically quiet. Visitor hours were over, patients were sleeping, and doctors and technicians had yet to make their morning rounds. The emergency room, however, was a universal exception. Those looking for respite from the chaos there generally ended up retreating to a deserted hallway nearby. That's where Tyler found Destiny after they heard the surgeon's news.

"You are a hard one to track down," Tyler said, catching up to her near the security doors leading to the MRI rooms.

Destiny stopped her mechanical pacing and turned. "I'm sorry. I needed to walk off some nervous energy."

"I get it. Waiting is the worst part. The doctors have news."

"And?"

"He survived the surgery but will need to be in the intensive care unit for a few days. The doctor said the next twenty-four hours will be crucial."

Destiny slumped against the wall with the same relief Alex and Syd shared minutes ago. When her eyes teared up, she asked, "Why am I crying over a brother I've never even met?"

"Because that's what families do. They care. They also support each other, especially during times like this. This is silly, Destiny. You need to be with your sisters. C'mon, let's go find Alex and Syd. I'm not taking no for an answer."

Once Destiny pushed herself off the wall, Tyler led her to the ICU, where nurses and machines were closely monitoring Andrew's condition. Destiny stopped three steps shy of the door leading to his room, reluctance swirling in her eyes. Remembering perhaps the grilling Syd and Alex had given her on the ride to the hospital, during which she had confirmed that she discovered Georgia and William were her birth parents during her trip to Massachusetts with Ethan, but nothing beyond those basic facts. Clearly, there was still much more they needed to discuss.

Fidgeting by the door, Destiny said, "I'll be right in. Just need a moment to…you know."

"Sure." Tyler rubbed Destiny's arm for reassurance before going inside. She walked to Alex, who was sitting at Andrew's bedside. She slid her hands along Alex's shoulders, hoping the touch would relieve a fraction of the worry overwhelming her. Being without siblings herself, much less a twin, Tyler could only imagine the anguish Alex was going through. She was glad that Alex and Syd had each other, but they were leaving out one crucial family member—Destiny.

"Oh no. You don't belong in here," Syd said, spotting Destiny when she quietly slipped into the room and leaned against the nearest wall.

Destiny turned to leave, but Alex reached out and stopped her. "Destiny, stay."

"For all we know, she could've been part of Georgia's plan. She could be responsible for this." Syd pointed to Andrew lying in the hospital bed, looking terrifyingly pale.

"Syd!" Alex barked.

Tyler had enough. Emotions were high, and everyone was on edge. With Andrew's life hanging in the balance, a family squabble was not what everyone needed right then. She clenched her fists and kept her tone a smidge below a shout. "Enough!" She had all three sisters' attention. "This is ridiculous."

Syd sprang from her chair. The anger on her face told Tyler she needed to get this situation under control quickly. She pointed at Syd and ordered, "Sit." When Syd hesitated, she repeated firmly, "Sit."

Tyler pivoted and pointed to Destiny and then to the empty chair next to Syd. "You too. Sit."

Destiny sat to the left of Syd and glanced at her. Syd sneered at her and harrumphed. Tyler shook her finger. "Behave." She turned her attention to Alex. "Babe, scoot your chair over here. We're having a family meeting."

Tyler was typically a calming influence during family moments, but on rare occasions like this one, where a swift kick in the pants was needed, she took on a commanding persona. She winked at Alex, who had told her the last time she displayed her bossy side that she was sexy as hell. Tyler hoped to not disappoint this time.

Alex repositioned her chair next to Destiny and said with a naughty smile, "Yes, ma'am."

Tyler shook her finger at Alex, winking again. "Behave."

Tyler then looked at Syd. "You need to get over this shit right now." Syd opened her mouth to object, but Tyler wagged her index finger in the air. "Unh-unh." Syd closed her mouth. "Yes, Destiny knew Georgia was her mother, but only for a few days. So, she didn't come forward with the information immediately? Big deal."

Tyler paced in front of the three sisters like a lawyer giving a jury her closing argument. "Her head was spinning. She needed time to figure things out. I would have too. She wasn't trying to hide anything or to conspire with Georgia. You don't know Destiny like we do. For the last four years, she's not only been a trusted employee but a good friend to Alex and me. I know her. This woman would rather cut off her right arm than betray Alex or anyone she cares about."

Tyler stopped pacing and focused on Destiny. "Do you have anything else to add?"

Destiny vigorously shook her head no.

"Good, because you shouldn't have to defend yourself." Tyler sidestepped in front of Syd and said, "Don't transfer your anger at Georgia onto Destiny. That would be like me blaming you for something your father did to Alex."

Syd dropped her head. "You're right, Tyler." She took a deep breath. "I'm sorry, Destiny. This has been hard on all of us. What did Georgia tell you about our father?"

"She told me that William pressured her to get an abortion. Instead, she took a leave of absence, gave birth, and then gave me up for adoption. I got the impression she held a grudge against William and his other children. Frankly, nothing she said told me she was a good person, so I wanted nothing to do with her."

Alex placed a hand on Destiny's knee. "I know this is difficult for you. It comes as a shock to all of us, but I couldn't be happier knowing the truth. You're an incredible woman, Destiny. You pulled yourself out of poverty, put yourself through college, and proved yourself a financial genius. I'm very proud to have a woman like you as my sister."

Destiny placed a hand over Alex's and squeezed. "Thank you, Alex. This is all very surreal." She glanced at Andrew when a machine beeped oddly and then stopped. "How is he? What did the doctors say?"

Alex's eyes welled with tears. She cleared her throat and replied, "The bullet hit a kidney, and they had to remove it. He lost a lot of blood, so the next twenty-four hours are critical."

Destiny squeezed Alex's hand again. "Can I do anything to help? Donate blood? Pick up anything for you?"

"You're not going anywhere. We're family," Alex said.

Syd reached across and grabbed Destiny's other hand. "We need to stick together."

Seeing the three sisters sitting in a row, holding hands and giving each other strength, warmed Tyler's heart. They needed each other more than ever. "We have plenty of people who love us who can pick up anything we need. You three just concentrate on Andrew."

Alex grabbed Tyler's hand. "Family meeting over?"

"Yes, babe. Family meeting over."

CHAPTER THIRTY-SIX

Greenwich, Connecticut, one week later

Alex clutched the coffee mug Indra had ensured was waiting for Abby's compulsory cleanup crew, absorbing its warmth as she leaned her forearms on the top horse-fence rail. A light fog hung low in the exercise pasture, leaving a thin sheen of morning dew blanketing the grass. Rhythmic snorting from Firelight broke into the soothing chirping of sparrows and robins waking in the distant tree line as Indra pushed the Morgan horse through her morning paces. It was a bit early for Indra's standing date with Firelight, but Alex assumed she didn't want the crew disturbing her prized possession until she'd been properly exercised. Alex had heard the story only once, how Indra had named her the day she and Abby reconnected after thirty-four years of living the life expected of them, but once was enough to understand the importance to her of this graceful animal.

Tyler snaked her arms around Alex's waist from behind, pressing their bodies together. If Alex had to choose a single source of warmth for the rest of her life, Tyler would be it. Nothing else compared. The coffee she was drinking was temporary at best. The clothing she had on and blankets she was beneath not two hours ago each were longer-lasting than the beverage, but they too were impermanent and required replacing. Tyler's warm embrace, however, was eternal. Each time Tyler's arms enveloped her, the love Alex felt warmed every nook and cranny of her skin and every muscle and tendon down to her bones.

"Indra looks content." The sweet sound of Tyler's voice vibrated in Alex's ear, warming that too.

"She always looks at home atop a steed." Alex released one hand from her mug long enough to bring one of Tyler's hands to her mouth and kiss the back of it.

Indra neared Alex and Tyler's position at the fence and gently pulled back on the reins, slowing Firelight to a trot and then to a walk. She reached down and patted Firelight's neck on the side of her mane. "That's my girl. Nothing like stretching your legs in the morning." Firelight responded with several loud, healthy snorts. They came to a stop between Alex and Tyler and Harley and Lara a yard farther down the fence line, and Indra peered from beneath her riding helmet at Alex. "Ready to serve out Abby's punishment?"

"And willing." Alex raised her mug, toasting to the bond she'd thought she had firmly cemented between her and Erin during their covert graduation night shenanigans. The cold shoulder she'd been receiving from Erin since that awful night in Philadelphia, however, suggested that bond was sinking in quicksand.

"It's your fault we're here." Harley's ribbing contained a hint of resentment, early morning exercises like this being a rarity in her life.

Tyler pivoted toward Harley, her interest clearly piqued. "And why is Alex to blame? It's high time I learned what you two were doing with my daughter to earn a weekend mucking out Abby and Indra's stalls."

Harley opened her mouth, likely to give Tyler a truthful answer to the closely held mystery, but shut it quickly when Alex gave her a stern look and said, "Morsels never spill the beans."

The cadence of gravel crunching beneath footsteps coming from behind Alex meant the last of Abby's internees had arrived. Despite the fact that the work would be, literally, crappy, Alex hoped the hour or two she was about to spend with Erin and Connor shoveling hay and horse droppings would go a long way to mend the fissure that had formed between her and Erin.

Once the crew assembled at the fence, Indra smiled and tightened her grip on the reins. "Now that everyone is here, we'll go. Shouldn't be gone more than an hour." She patted Firelight's muscular neck. "All right, young lady. Let's finish your workout so I can get you back for breakfast."

Indra trotted off deep into the pasture, her departure cueing Tyler and Lara to kiss their women goodbye and retreat to the main house—but not before Alex gave Tyler a playful swat on the bottom and said, "Tell Abby the stable will be ready for inspection before brunch." The suggestion-filled wink Tyler shot her from over her shoulder made Alex shudder. Discovering what Tyler had in mind behind that wink would be her reward for spurring this motley crew into completing their task quickly.

Inside the barn, the crew broke out into teams—the young and the not so young. While others rolled up their sleeves and dove right in, Harley adopted an air of resignation. She refused to use her hands directly, opting to gingerly operate the shavings fork. It wasn't long before she paused—for the tenth time in less than an hour—to wipe smudges from her pricey boots with a red bandana that was so new the fold creases were still prominent.

"It's a lost cause, Harley." Alex stopped sweeping the remaining manure, resting both hands atop the handle and leaning her weight onto one leg. "Expensive boots and stall mucking don't mix."

Harley wiped harder, appearing wholly flummoxed. "They're ruined, completely ruined."

Alex placed an arm around Harley's shoulders. She knew that the cleaners could make them look like new, but convincing Harley of that was out of the question right then. Alex chose the easiest route to console her. "Since this is all my fault, as you put it, I'll buy you another pair."

"Something is always your fault," Erin mumbled from the neighboring stall.

Alex ignored the jab, deciding keeping the peace was more important than correcting Erin's manners. Resuming her sweeping, she backed up to add the remnants to the pile in the center aisle, stopping abruptly when she bumped against someone. "Sorry," she said before looking over her shoulder.

"You're always saying you're sorry about something. At least no one got shot this time."

"Erin." Connor's chiding tone left no doubt she was as disappointed in Erin's pointed comment as Alex was hurt by it. Two people had died that night in Philly, and her twin brother was still in the hospital, waiting for the green light from his doctor to begin recuperating at home. Alex knew intellectually that Georgia was the one who was responsible for what happened that night, but in her heart, she felt she shared the blame. She'd brought Kelly Thatcher into their lives, and without that conniving bottomfeeder's help, Georgia might not have been able to take things to such extremes.

The distinct sound of a wooden tool handle hitting concrete echoed throughout the stable. Harley stomped over in her soiled Rhinestone Cowgirl boots, positioning herself between Alex and Erin. "I've had enough of you, young lady. You need to stop this tantrum of yours and see things how they are. The person to blame for what happened is dead."

Harley hadn't defended Alex's honor like this since they were in grade school. Not since Alex had had a growth spurt that made her almost a head taller. "Please, Harley. She has every right to be upset. She's just worried about her mother."

Erin leaned to one side to laser holes in Alex's head with her eyes. "Not just Mom. You're toxic. You attract crazy and put all of us in danger."

Rather than face the cold, hard truth, Alex trudged out of the stable, her legs as heavy as her heart. She shut out the bickering at her back and slumped on the nearby six-foot-long oak log that had been halved and lacquered and fashioned into a rustic bench.

The word "toxic" swirled in her head like a tornado, leaving damage a mile wide in its path. She *was* toxic to the Falling family. Ethan had been shot because of those damn blackmail photos, and then Tyler had ended up in the hospital last week because of that damn undercover video.

Moments later, Indra rode through the pasture gate leading to the stable yard. She dismounted, loosening the girth a notch. "Better, girl?" Indra patted Firelight on her side. "Nothing worse than a skirt tight around the waist." She laughed when Firelight snorted again. "I see you agree."

Indra guided Firelight toward the stable but paused before she passed Alex, her gaze narrowing. Alex gave her a bleak smile and waved her on. She led Firelight toward the bench instead, lashed her reins to the hitching post, and sat beside Alex. She removed her riding gloves and placed a reassuring hand on her thigh, saying nothing. That was Indra's way with loved ones— support, comfort, and above all, patience.

Alex dropped her head. "I'm toxic, Indra. I endanger everyone around me."

"Who gave you that idea?"

"It doesn't matter who said it. It's true."

"It sounds as if someone needs her eyes opened." Indra bounced to her feet, turned toward the stable, and in a firm voice shouted, "Girls, come out here, please. Now."

Harley was the first to march out. If fuming had a picture by it in the dictionary, it would have borne Harley's portrait. Erin and Connor followed, Connor with her head down and hands buried in her back pockets. "Dammit, Erin," she muttered. "Now Indra's pissed."

"I'm right, and you know it." Erin stomped to a halt, several yards away yet from the older women, but not far enough, unfortunately, for her words to be muffled. Alex winced.

"No, you're being unreasonable. I love you anyway, but we need to get over there before Indra kicks us out."

Erin grudgingly walked the remaining few steps to where the others were gathered. She held her chin high. "Yes, ma'am."

Indra shot Erin a look scary enough to stop a hungry pack of wolves in its tracks. Mama Bear was about to defend her cub. "Young lady."

"Indra, please," Alex pleaded. "This is between Erin and me."

Indra kept her eyes trained on Erin but raised her hand toward Alex. "No, Alex. I know you won't defend yourself, so I will."

Indra returned her attention to Erin. "You have no idea how much Alex has done for you and your family. I can understand why you would be upset after your family's close calls over the years. But that is no reason to place blame at Alex's feet. There's no accounting for psychopaths. Since the day she met your mother, Alex has done nothing but love and protect her, and by extension, you and your sister. Did you know that if it wasn't for her, you might not have gone to Yale?"

"Indra, please. Don't," Alex pleaded again. Harley stepped beside Alex and caressed her back between the shoulder blades when Alex lowered her head briefly. The touch from her dearest friend was well-timed and very needed.

Erin looked confused. "What do you mean?"

"No, Alex. This young lady needs to hear the truth about you." Indra turned back to Erin. "How do you think PopCo's Friends of Yale Scholarships get funded each year?"

"I just assumed they're funded by your company."

"PopCo funds only part of it. A good portion of the money comes from donors. And who do you think specifically funded your scholarship in its entirety?"

Erin turned and looked at Alex, eyes narrowed in suspicion.

"That's right, Alex did, and that was before she knew that she and your mother were going to end up together. She had never met you, yet she believed in you enough to bankroll your entire education."

"Did Mom ask you to do it?" Erin turned toward Alex, her stare losing none of its bite or its intensity. She sneered. "Or did you think money would buy her affection?"

Alex didn't answer. Couldn't. That accusation hurt more than anything Erin had slung at her today.

Indra continued, "I'm disappointed in you, Erin, for even asking. You know very well your mother would never tolerate such a thing. She and your father would have mortgaged their own future to put you through college. But thanks to the scholarship, they didn't have to. Alex came to Abby and me with explicit instructions that no one was to know where the money came from, especially your mother. She knows the truth now, so keeping it secret is no longer pertinent." She looked at Erin sternly. "As a result of her anonymous generosity, you have a degree from one of the most prestigious universities in the country. Your dream school. And a promising future you might not have had otherwise. I wouldn't call that kind of selflessness 'toxic,' Erin. Would you?"

"No." Erin's eyes filled with obvious regret. Her lips trembled. "May I be excused for the rest of the day? I...I need to..." She didn't finish her thought. At Indra's nod, she added, "Please give Abby my apology."

"Of course."

Erin grabbed Connor by a shirt sleeve and dragged her at a fast clip around the main house and toward the parking area.

Alex bowed her head and ran her fingers through her hair. Erin's one-word response to Indra's question gave Alex some hope that this broad chasm between them could one day be repaired. It was a start anyway. That didn't change the fact that Erin was partially right. Alex attracted crazy. Giving up Castle Resorts and life in the city wasn't enough. She needed a complete reset. Now. Not months or years from now.

"It appears I may have cracked her icy facade. Just give her time." Indra offered her arm to Alex. "Let's rejoin our better halves."

After Indra arranged for the groom to stable and brush out Firelight, the women entered the main living room. Indra and Harley reunited with Abby and Lara, kissing them on the lips before joining them on a couch in front of a roaring fireplace. Alex, still numb from the painful confrontation, stopped short of the group, as if glued to the marble floor.

She gazed at Tyler's face, captivated by its gentle curves, reflecting on how beautiful and rosy it was when the ocean breeze chapped her cheeks and nose. She loved Tyler's imperfections. For the way she faced her flaws without fear or reservation. She wanted to be reminded every day to live up to her sterling example. Kelly, Georgia, and crazy were in the past. Only love and contentment were in her future, she vowed—mixed with a bit of fun.

"You smell like a barn," Lara said, scooting inches away from Harley and toward fresher air.

"Blame Alex." Harley swiped at her boots again with her now crumpled bandana.

"A censure worth bearing," Alex declared. Despite the recent exchange at the stable, she would always remember fondly the evening spent with Harley, Erin, and Connor, she decided, especially the hours detained in the police station. They were hours well spent because they were dedicated to family. She silently vowed to find ways to spend more days and nights like that, though hopefully without attracting a police escort.

Alex joined Tyler on a love seat, kissing her as if it were their first kiss, full of wonder and the promise of a future. A kiss that lingered beyond the limits of social graces. Her hand grazed the exposed skin above the trim of the scooped neckline of Tyler's shirt. And might have ventured further, if not for the loud clearing of someone's throat. If Tyler—and propriety—would've allowed, she would've pushed her prone and kissed every inch of her body. Alex pulled back, unashamed of testing the boundary. Tyler deserved such attentiveness each day.

As Tyler settled her head onto Alex's outstretched arm atop the back of the couch, Harley recrossed her legs. "Is it me, or is it hot in here?"

"Those two definitely raised the temperature of the room," her mother said, an uncharacteristic blush in her cheeks.

A cell phone rang. Not Alex's for a change, but the distinctive ringtone signaled that Ethan was calling Tyler. Just in time. Nothing could douse a blazing fire quicker than the injection of an ex. Tyler fished her phone from her sweater pocket, looking toward Abby and Indra for permission. "Sorry. It's Ethan. I should take this." Both nodded their tacit approval. Tyler's smile faded during their short exchange on the phone, replaced by a familiar look of concern. "Of course, Ethan. Come out to the estate. We can discuss it when you get here with Bree and Jesse."

Tyler's face was pale when she ended the call. Alex took Tyler's hand in hers. "T? What is it?"

Tyler took in a sharp breath, rubbing her chest. Alex's worry turned into a near panic. Only a week had passed since Tyler had been released from the hospital after having a cardiac episode, and it appeared she was on the cusp of another.

Alex knelt in front of her partner at the love seat. "T?"

Following several silent, tense moments of gripping Alex's arm, Tyler finally caught her breath. "Can you get my pills?"

"I'll get them," Indra said.

"Thank you, Indra. She keeps them in her purse. It's—"

Indra cut Alex off. "I saw it when we came in."

Of the five episodes Tyler had over the years, this was the first time Alex was front and center for one. She'd done her homework years ago, though, just in case—learning the signs of tachycardia and how to care for someone during an episode. She calmly walked to the wet bar, filled a glass of water, and wet a bar towel. Returning to the couch, she offered Tyler the cup. "Sip on this."

Alex placed the glass on the coffee table after Tyler took several sips. "Lay back." Alex leaned her back further, fluffing a decorative pillow for a headrest and placing the cold compress on her forehead. Tyler's breathing didn't improve, so Alex applied gentle pressure to her abdomen and waited patiently, forcing the corners of her mouth upward in a calming fashion. "Try to take deeper breaths."

The minute required for Indra to dash through the house and return with Tyler's purse felt like an eternity, but Alex made an effort to not let it show. "Thank you, Indra." Alex fumbled through Tyler's bag, located the right pill, and offered it and the water. "Here, T."

She maintained her vigil, kneeling in front of Tyler until her breathing returned to normal. The relief in the room was palpable. Tyler rose to a sitting position and gently stroked Alex's cheek with her fingertips. "I should have eaten this morning and not waited until you were done serving Abby's punishment. I'm fine now."

"You gave us all a fright, my dear." The worry in Abby's tone reflected everyone's concern. "Alex, I'm curious. Why did you press on her stomach?"

"It's called a Vagal maneuver. Stimulating the vagus nerve helps to slow the heart rate." Alex returned to the couch, wrapping an arm around Tyler. "Are you sure you're okay?" When Tyler gave her a vigorous affirmative nod, Alex asked, "What did Ethan say?"

"Marco called." She turned to the others. "Marco is Ethan's old partner in Sacramento. He said that the police found Paul Stevens dead in his home from an overdose."

"Suicide?" Indra asked. Alex thought the same, expecting nothing less from that bastard. Suicide wasn't a sufficient death for that wretched man. Alex didn't wish ill will upon people, but Paul Stevens was the exception. She hoped he suffered in the end.

"They don't know," Tyler said. "There wasn't a note."

"I'm glad he's dead," Alex said.

"I think it's safe to say that we all are," Abby said.

Tyler gave Abby a small pat on the hand. "I couldn't agree more." She returned her attention to Alex. "It seems he listed Bree as his only heir and me as executor."

"What the hell? How is Bree taking it?" Alex asked. The others' headshakes suggested they were as shocked as she.

"The news has thrown her for a loop. It throws me too. We thought we'd heard the last of him." Tyler took a long, drawn-out breath. "Apparently, he inherited his mother's house after she passed away last year, so now it belongs to Bree."

"Not *the* house?" Alex asked. The silent nod and tears flooding Tyler's eyes confirmed Alex's fear. Bree had just inherited the house in which her mother was raped. The house in which she was conceived. This was the worst possible freaking emotional nightmare.

CHAPTER THIRTY-SEVEN

Sacramento, California, five days later

Tyler had been living in Alex's one-percent world for four years and had flown three times on a private jet—once after Kelly Thatcher killed Alex's father, last week after Bree ran away to find her birth father, and now. Despite their luxury, complete with plump leather seats and everything a traveler might need at her fingertips, she had come to associate private jets with bad things.

She'd spent hours lost in thought, recalling the man who had changed her life so irrevocably. The friendly, kind Paul who helped her in grad school. If it weren't for him, she wouldn't have gotten a passing grade on their shared project. Then the monstrous Paul, who betrayed her trust in the worst possible way. Yet, despite the ordeal he'd put her through, two good things had come of it—Bree and Alex.

She glanced at Bree sleeping across from her. In less than two weeks, her daughter's life had been turned upside down four times—learning she was adopted, learning she was a product of rape, learning about Erin's rape, and learning her mother's rapist was dead and she was heir to his estate. Tyler didn't regret withholding the truth all those years—because no child should ever have to deal with such harsh realities. But Bree's reaction after learning the truth had surprised her. Bree's respect for Ethan had deepened, and, if anything, Ethan had become more of a father in her eyes.

Tyler glanced at Ethan, brooding next to his sleeping wife, likely not finding a silver lining in anything having to do with Paul Stevens. She leaned forward, tapping him on the knee. "Why so glum? You should be on cloud nine about Jesse's legislation. It looks like it will pass the state senate next week."

He leaned closer, matching Tyler's posture. "I am. It's just that I thought I'd forgiven myself for everything."

Tyler gently rubbed his leg. "You're too hard on yourself." Over the years, she'd gathered from snippets of conversation that he'd always blamed himself for failing to protect his family. Trying to convince him otherwise had been impossible.

He gazed at Jesse, visibly swallowing. "At least I haven't failed her. Not yet." He said those words as if he assumed something horrible would happen to Jesse, something he'd fail to prevent, and that broke Tyler's heart.

Hours later, following a contentious meeting with the lawyer for the estate, Ethan parked their rental car in front of the Stevens' house. Tyler stared at the front door, wishing she hadn't convinced Alex to stay behind and help settle her brother into their downstairs guestroom to complete his recuperation and begin physical therapy. Having Alex by her side now would make it easier to walk inside this house.

As she stepped to the curb, Tyler felt a paralyzing dread engulf her. This was where it had happened. Where her life forever changed. Memories of running from this house, naked, bleeding, in the dark, nearly choked her.

Ethan propped her up, gripping her by the elbow when she froze. "You don't have to go inside, Tyler."

"I need to do this, for Bree," she said, glancing at her daughter. Bree's posture was strong but her face didn't lie. Her pale, blank expression said she was afraid to discover what waited for her inside. The part Tyler and Ethan had kept secret for years for all their sakes.

Tyler may have said going in was for her daughter, but she needed to walk into that house for herself too. She needed to prove that memories of that night no longer had the hold on her they once did. She shook off unexpected chills, willing herself to be strong enough to push through this.

Ethan threw a supportive arm over her shoulder. "I'll be with you every step of the way."

Tyler struggled to remember how the house appeared seventeen years ago but couldn't recall details. It had been painted not too many years ago, and assorted signs of renovations made the well-maintained home stand out in its middle-income neighborhood. Paint and updating couldn't hide the horrible thing that had happened inside, though. Not from her eyes.

"How long had the Stevens' owned the home?" Jesse asked the estate lawyer.

"Thirty-three years," the lawyer replied, inserting the key into the lock. He pushed the front door open. "They bought it when it was built in 1978. They remodeled a few times and refaced the front two years ago."

Tyler threw off the bone-chilling sensation caused by being in this house again. She whispered into Ethan's ear, "I'm fine. I'll walk around with Bree."

Mother and daughter meandered from room to room. Bree refused to touch a thing, merely surveying the home that was now hers. The house was strangely void of personal photographs other than a handful of framed pictures on the fireplace mantel and nightstands. Every wall was adorned with framed works of art of various sizes and styles, from abstracts to landscapes to surrealist images, oils and acrylics and watercolors. They were all quite beautiful in their own way.

Tyler paced past the island in the freshly renovated contemporary kitchen to peek inside the walk-in pantry. The small room also looked to have been redone. The inside door trim was the only thing untouched by fresh paint. She inspected the frame more closely, spotting pencil markings at different heights with dates etched to the side of each line. Suddenly, she realized what she was looking at. Her parents had made similar scribbles on the laundry room door every year on her birthday when she was growing up. Paul Stevens had been an only child, so those lines had to be for him, she thought, a chill running through her. Each rough pencil line signified the passage of time, of innocence. Moments in a carefree childhood likely filled with hopes and dreams of a full life to come.

Tyler covered her mouth with a hand. She had expected to feel strange walking through the home where Paul Stevens had raped her. She had not expected to feel sorry for the parents who would later discover they'd raised a rapist.

Tyler flinched when Bree touched her shoulder. "Mom, are you okay?"

Needing to focus on something other than her recent insight, she cleared her head and dropped her hand. "I'm fine, honey. Let's take another look at those paintings."

A few pieces seemed familiar, but Tyler couldn't recall why. Was she remembering them from before? Or more recently? In the course of remodeling the mansion, they'd visited a number of galleries to pick out the perfect paintings for each room. Tyler hadn't taken the time to acquaint herself with that field as well as Alex had, but she couldn't help but pick up on the work of several contemporary artists while thumbing through the myriad art journals and magazines Harley had asked them to look at.

Tyler returned to the hallway with Bree. She studied several paintings and settled on one that had a familiar feel to it. Still not able to place it, she snapped a picture of it with her cell phone and sent it with a short text message to Alex.

A minute later, Tyler's phone rang. "Hi, babe. You got my text?"

"I did," Alex replied. "Since you texted to say you were going to the house, I've been on pins and needles, waiting to hear from you. How are you doing?"

"It's been awkward, but I'm doing better than…Scratch that." After her episode at Abby and Indra's, Tyler had promised herself and Alex to not hold anything back. "Walking inside made me feel trapped, but having a bunch of people I love around me has helped. I didn't feel suffocated." She wrapped an arm around Bree's shoulder and gave it a brief squeeze.

"I'm glad you have family with you. I feel much better about not being there with you."

"I am too. Andrew needed you today. Now, about those paintings."

"It's a little hard to tell with the lighting, but I think that's a Sally Putnam. Is it a print?" Alex asked.

"No, it's on canvas." The silence from Alex told Tyler she was on to something. "Do you think it's worth something?"

"Quite a bit. Are there more?"

"Dozens. Let's switch this to FaceTime. I'll walk you through the house." Once they reconnected, she slowly walked through each room, showing Alex each painting.

The estate lawyer approached Tyler. "I was just out in the garage. I saw more there, stacked on racks. Mrs. Stevens once mentioned she collected at least two pieces each year since she married. It was a hobby of hers to find a young artist and buy a painting directly from them. A lot of them have Putnam's name on them."

Tyler followed him into the garage while Bree went with Ethan and Jesse to another part of the house. Between the pieces inside the house and the stacks in the garage, she calculated that there must have been over a hundred paintings. While the lawyer flipped through them, Tyler held up her phone so Alex could catch a glimpse.

After they worked their way through a good portion of them, Alex said, "I've seen enough, T. I'll call you right back so we can talk privately." Seconds later, Alex rang Tyler's line. "If these pieces are what I think they are, Bree could be sitting on a small fortune."

Tyler was at a loss for words. The quality and size of the art collection didn't fit with the meager home housing them. "Are you sure?"

"Without seeing them in person, I can't be absolutely sure. But, if memory serves me, several of those pieces haven't been seen since their original sale, sold before the artist became famous. There's no telling what some of them could fetch at auction."

Tyler's first thought was that Alex really had missed her calling. She had such an excellent eye for art. "I think I'm in over my head here. Can you recommend someone who can appraise the collection?"

"I'll do one better. I'll ask Harley to send out the appraiser the Spencer Foundation uses for its annual art auction. It might be some time before she can get him out there, though. In the meantime, I recommend hiring a security firm to pack and store each piece in a guarded facility."

"Do you really think they're worth that much?" Tyler asked.

"If my instincts are correct, we could be looking at eight figures."

"What?" Tyler briefly goggled at the estimate, prompting Ethan to grab her by the elbow again as he came to see what she was up to.

"Whoa, Tyler. Are you okay?" he said.

"Just a little dizzy."

"T. Are you all right?" Worry coated Alex's voice.

"I'm fine, babe. Your estimate just threw me for a loop."

"That's it. I'm catching the first flight out there."

Tyler ended her call, unable to persuade Alex into not coming to California. Though, a part of her was relieved. Alex was the medicine she needed to get through this nauseating trip. She refocused on Paul Stevens. He'd been sitting on a small fortune, likely without realizing it. Harley and her appraiser would be in the best position to advise Bree about that. She returned inside, finding Bree crying on the living room couch, with Ethan and Jesse on either side consoling her.

Bree had surprised Tyler by lasting this long before breaking down. She'd been on the verge of doing so herself several times since their plane landed. Kneeling in front of the girl, she pulled her into her arms and let tears roll down her cheeks.

Moments later, Bree pulled back with watery eyes. "I don't want it. I don't want anything from him."

Tyler placed a hand on her daughter's cheeks, seeing the pain in her eyes. She felt the same way, wanting no more from Paul Stevens than the child before her. "You don't have to do anything you don't want to do. Nothing needs deciding today. Let's go back to the hotel."

CHAPTER THIRTY-EIGHT

Sleep was eluding Tyler. She'd lost count of the number of times she'd adjusted her pillow, tugged on the covers, and flipped from one side to the other. She couldn't switch off her brain, couldn't push back the memories of that awful night. She couldn't shake the horror she'd felt when he'd trapped her on the bed, crushing her body with his. The feeling of having no control, no way of defending herself, no way of escaping had terrified her. When he'd punched her face again and again, she'd thought she wouldn't survive. And when it was all over, she'd wished she hadn't.

A clicking at the door of her hotel room triggered some panic, until she found the dim red numbers on the alarm clock on the nearby nightstand. It was a few minutes after ten o'clock. Reassured, she sat up. The timing was right. Having Alex here would be such a relief. The tension in her shoulders eased as the door swung open and light from the hallway spilled into the darkened room. "Alex?"

"It's me, T," Alex replied. The sound of her wheeling in her carry-on bag was followed by the sound of the door closing and the safety latch being secured.

Tyler turned on the bedside light as Alex emerged around the wall separating the bathroom from the rest of the room. *She's tired.* The last few weeks had taken a toll on all of them.

Tyler's eyes followed Alex as she dropped her bags near the foot of the bed and made her way to her side. Neither uttering a word, they wrapped their arms around one another, each melting into the warm comfort of the embrace. Shortly, though, Tyler found herself sobbing lightly, recalling the images that had kept her awake now that Alex was there to comfort her.

Alex pulled back, inspecting Tyler's face with concern. "I'm worried about you. This can't be easy."

Tyler pushed a few words through her constricted throat, barely holding back a whimper. "I thought I was past all this."

Alex caressed Tyler's cheek. "Tell me what you need."

Tyler's thoughts returned to the first time they made love. Before their first touch, Alex had questioned Tyler for nearly an hour, learning her fears and trigger points so she could avoid them during intimacy. She'd then put Tyler in complete control of what they did and didn't do that night. She needed that again.

Tyler brought Alex's hand to her lips and kissed it, staring into Alex's eyes. "I need to be in control."

Tyler watched breathlessly as Alex stood, kicked off her tennies, and removed a light sweater. Watched as she undid the button on the waistband of her jeans and smoothly removed them and dropped them on a nearby chair. When Alex lifted her shirt over her head and tossed it out of view, heat built in Tyler's cheeks.

Tyler's chest rose as she took in several sharp breaths. The sight of Alex in her matching lace lingerie took her breath away every time. Tyler's baking the last few years had added a slight curve to Alex's hips, but it made her even sexier in Tyler's eyes. The images that had tormented her for hours had disappeared, replaced by that of the beautiful body standing before her.

Alex reached behind her back to unsnap her bra. "Wait," Tyler whispered in a low husky timbre. Alex stopped.

Tyler, dressed in light shorts and a barely there tank top, rose to her feet and stepped toward Alex. She dragged her fingertips along the skin of Alex's thighs, leaving small goose pimples in their wake. Her hands followed the curves of Alex's hips and waist, settling on the toned muscles of her back. She moved closer until their mouths were inches apart and their breaths mingled. Warm, moist air hit the skin above her lips, sending euphoric jolts to the tips of her breasts.

Tyler unsnapped the fasteners holding Alex's bra in place and gently guided it off her torso, revealing the plump flesh she desperately wanted to feel. She splayed her fingers around Alex's breasts, cupping and lifting them before taking a step back to bend at the knees and slip her mouth around one. She sucked and massaged at a fast, unfamiliar pace until blood rushed to her core.

Alex moaned, rocking her head toward the ceiling, mouth agape. "T," she whispered.

Under any other circumstance, Tyler would expect Alex to rip the flimsy cotton top from her torso and begin devouring the soft patches of skin behind her ears. But not tonight. Tyler had asked for control to lock her demons back inside, and Alex was there to make that possible.

Tyler released her breasts. She straightened and pressed her lips against Alex's in a hungry, passion-filled kiss, leaving no doubt that she was in charge of everything that was about to unfold. She felt the freedom and control she desperately needed with every lash of her tongue and every stroke of her hand. She could continue or stop. It was up to her. And when she'd brought Alex up to the edge, she ordered, "Open your eyes, Alex. Look at me."

Gazes locked. Their connection was palpable, deeper and more meaningful than ever. Tyler alone dictated if and when Alex soared. She pressed, pumped, and grazed until every memory of ever feeling trapped had left her. And when her demons were gone, Alex made love to her like it was their first time, gently and passionately, and with a tenderness that came from four years of understanding.

Both bodies were sated, and they laid entangled, skin to skin for hours. Tyler listened to Alex's heart. From the first time they had kissed, she had no doubt its every beat was meant for her. She caressed the skin she had come to need more than air. "I love you, Alex."

"I love you, T." Alex pulled back and craned her head toward her purse where she'd placed on a nearby chair earlier. Several beats passed, and then a few more, giving Tyler the impression Alex was debating something important.

"Wait right here." Alex nudged Tyler to her side and stood. She fished through her purse, pulled out a small red jewelry box, and returned to the bed, her delicious body distracting Tyler. "I wanted for this to be more romantic, over a candlelight dinner, but after everything that has happened, I can't wait a minute longer."

She opened the box, revealing a brilliant diamond ring. "Tyler, since the first time my hand brushed against yours, I have been connected to you. Any day I can't see you, feel you, or hear your voice, I'm lost. You make my day better with a single touch. I want to spend every night with you kicking me and hogging the covers. As your wife. Will you marry me, Tyler?"

Tyler had known from the first time she and Alex made love that they were meant to grow old together. But the idea of marriage had to come from Alex, not the woman who had already failed at it. "Of course, I'll marry you."

Alex slipped the ring onto Tyler's finger, brought it to her mouth, and kissed it. She rubbed Tyler's finger and stared at the engagement ring, giving it a light twist. "It looks so much better on you than in that box."

"How long have you had it?" Tyler asked.

"Two years, but it took me almost a year before that to design the setting and have it made."

Tyler briefly glanced at the stunning ring. "You've wanted to propose for three years?"

"Longer. The last time I spoke with my father, I told him that I was going to ask you to marry me one day."

Tyler brushed some stray hairs from Alex's face, exposing the lines and curves she'd come to cherish. "You did?"

Alex slowly nodded. "That was the last straw for him. I'm glad I said it—because he died knowing how much I loved you."

Tyler leaned in and kissed Alex. "I love you, but what took you so long?"

"I'm a New Yorker. I've been waiting for it to be legal there. And now that it looks like it's going to pass, I want to marry you the first day we can." Alex stroked Tyler's cheek. Her voice was tentative when she said, "Now if you let me, I want to make love to you again."

Tyler kissed her on the lips, happier than she'd ever been. Her demons were slain, and Alex was now her fiancée. She grinned, thinking about that label. It came with a romantic connotation—betrothed, intended, bride-to-be, future wife. Each word made her happier than the next.

She rolled to her back, pulling Alex with her. For the rest of the night, Alex gently teased, touched, and tasted her, taking Tyler over the edge many times and sealing their engagement.

* * *

Thanks to room service, the smell of freshly brewed coffee filled their hotel room. Alex prepared a cup especially to Tyler's liking—one cream and one sugar—before walking it into the bathroom in time to help her finish her morning routine.

Alex handed Tyler the cup and kissed her on the cheek. Images of sweaty bodies, arched backs, and entangled limbs from last night flashed in her head. After four years together, Alex never thought she could love Tyler more than she already did, but proposing to her had proved her wrong. She'd come to believe that her love for this woman was boundless and would grow every day.

Though she anticipated Tyler's response, Alex had to ask. "Did you get enough sleep?"

"Not by a long shot," Tyler replied with a wink and smile. "But I'll survive."

Alex leaned against the bathroom counter, her back to the mirror. Tyler had filled her in about Bree's reluctance to accept her inheritance, and she couldn't blame her one bit. She considered it a bad idea, though. With no other heirs to claim the estate, every asset would revert to the state government.

"I've been thinking, T."

Tyler dropped her hairbrush, positioned herself between Alex's legs, and wrapped her arms around her neck. "I've been thinking, too." She nibbled on Alex's lips before pulling back and forming a naughty grin. "We have time for one more round."

Alex wrapped her arms around Tyler's waist and gave her a deep, luscious kiss before reluctantly pulling back. "They're expecting us in ten minutes. We'll have just enough time for coffee."

Tyler pursed her lips. "Rain check?"

"Always," Alex said. "I was thinking that Bree should reconsider rejecting the inheritance. Even if she doesn't want the money, it could do some good elsewhere. I'd hate to see the state get all of it."

"You're right. I think she might like the idea of turning it over to a charity rather than to the government. We should discuss it with her today." Tyler took one last swig of coffee and rested the mug on the counter. She extended a hand to Alex. "Ready to slay more demons?"

Alex accepted Tyler's hand. "With you? Always."

CHAPTER THIRTY-NINE

Manhattan, New York, one month later...

The day's oppressive heat and humidity had dictated a shortened ceremony in the back garden of Tyler and Alex's Madison Avenue mansion, a change Tyler had reluctantly agreed to. Tyler had had her traditional wedding with Ethan, and she wanted Alex to have that same experience. But Alex had tipped the scale when she whispered into her ear before the ceremony, speaking with a slow seductive cadence, "Of all days, I'd prefer spending more time inside you than outside with our guests."

Since the day Ethan told Tyler he was ready for divorce, a ring hadn't adorned her left hand until Alex proposed. And the moment Alex had slipped Tyler's wedding band on it, it felt as if the world had righted itself. The life she had with Ethan, raising two girls into incredibly strong young women, had been good and rewarding, but what she shared with Alex was fulfilling beyond anything she'd dreamed possible. Whenever she was apart from Ethan, she'd felt as if her role was to hold down the fort. But when she was apart from Alex, even for a minute, she felt as if half of her was missing.

The instant she in turn had slipped the gold band around Alex's left ring finger, she felt whole. Nothing had changed between them, but their place in the world had. To the state of New York, they were now legally married and recognized as next of kin. The entire spectrum of long-fought-for legal benefits that came with being married was now within their reach. Those rights said the one thing Tyler already knew was true: they were partners for life. The kiss they shared during the ceremony, like every kiss since their first, confirmed it.

Hours into the party after the ceremony, Tyler squeezed the hand she knew as well as her own and nodded toward Jesse, who was tucked away in a quiet corner of the main room, away from the crowd in the room's center, her head buried in her phone and smiling from ear to ear. Having checked in on her earlier, Tyler understood why. She'd been on cloud nine all day, reading online accounts of the hundreds of gay and lesbian weddings being performed across New York since the stroke of midnight. That was no reason, though, to miss out on the next delectable offering Lara was going to bring out. Tyler whispered into Alex's ear, "I'm going to drag Jesse back to the party."

"Thank you." Alex returned Tyler's squeeze. "I'd like to share that special drink with her."

Following a brief yet toe-curling kiss, Tyler made her way across the room, her lips tingling all the way, joining Jesse in her corner. She nudged Jesse's shoulder. "You're quite the wallflower today."

"Can you blame me?" Jesse shared her iPhone screen with her, swiping through a score or more of wedding photos. The words she'd penned months ago had finally persuaded state assembly members and senators to pass New York's Marriage Equality Act.

Tyler leaned in to get a closer look. "Oh my. This is a glorious day." She raised her eyes to Jesse's. "You should be so proud. Today would have never come to fruition without your dedication and hard work."

"It was a team effort." Jesse reined in her obvious self-satisfaction, keeping her smile small. "But yes, I am proud to be part of history."

"Nonsense." Tyler waved her off as if she'd equated herself to a cheerleader, not the Super Bowl-winning quarterback that she was. "Everyone in this room knows that, if not for your well-crafted arguments, this day would have never materialized. Have you heard yet how many weddings were performed today?"

"*The Times* estimated it vaguely in the hundreds, but the firm expects four or five hundred."

"This day was long overdue, and to think we were one of those weddings today." Tyler's sharp intake of breath and emotion-filled headshake echoed the exuberance that had followed in their backyard when the retired judge, one of Abby's oldest friends, said, "I now pronounce you married."

"It was beautiful," Jesse said. "You and Alex made stunning brides."

Tyler struggled to follow Jesse's example by keeping her smile small, but she couldn't do so. Alex *was* stunning in her off-white tuxedo. Tyler deflected by scanning the remaining guests, comprised of family and friends. She took Jesse by the elbow. "Come. Join the rest of us so we can all share in the good news."

When they rejoined the group in the room's center, Jesse passed around her cell phone. Each marveled at the dozens of photos that were memorializing gay and lesbian weddings performed at clerks' offices, city halls, and parks throughout the state.

After Abby passed the phone to Indra, she asked, "Has anyone seen my daughter and Lara? It's nearly time for us to present our wedding gift."

If Tyler's suspicions were correct, the last thing Harley would welcome at the moment was her mother's interruption. "I might have an idea."

"If I know my daughter, she's coaxed Lara into a private encounter of a less than judicious nature." She smiled wryly, having come to terms long ago with her daughter's quirks.

"Which is why it's better if I search for her," Tyler's wife suggested.

"Kitchen?" Alex whispered into Tyler's ear, receiving an affirmative nod in reply. "I'll send her out," she told Abby. Before she left the room, she placed a hand on Jesse's forearm. "Don't disappear again. The three of us need to share that drink."

On her previous trip to the kitchen half an hour ago in search of club soda to remove a spill on her blouse, Alex had found Lara lovingly preparing a care package for her and Tyler's wedding night and the next day. Harley was behind her, gliding hands down each hip and whispering something into Lara's ear that had earned her a willpower-melting neck roll. Now that Lara's cooking staff had been sent home, leaving only a two-person cleanup crew, the half-bath off the walk-in pantry was Alex's first and only stop.

As Alex stood outside the closed door, muffled moans and shuffling sounds confirmed she'd guessed correctly. She smirked. Wedding sex was always hot. When someone inside the bathroom dropped a long, drawn-out f-bomb, Alex waited for an appropriate cooldown period and knocked. "Harley? I have orders to drag you back to the party." Following thirty more seconds of silence, she knocked again. "I know you're in there."

Sink water ran for a minute or two before Harley swung the door open, adjusting her dress. She glared, raising her hands like a football referee calling a personal foul. "Clitorference."

Alex laughed under her breath when Harley pushed her aside and stormed toward the hall. She sheepishly turned her attention to Lara. "I'm sorry. Abby's orders."

"She'll get over it." Lara smiled.

As they followed Harley's dust cloud down the hallway, Alex nudged Lara's shoulder. "Any chance of you two walking down the aisle anytime soon?"

Lara nudged her back. "You're such a romantic. I just moved in with her last week. Give us time."

Alex snorted. "I give you six months, tops."

Lara jutted her chin toward Abby and Indra. "My money is on those two going before we do."

Alex envied the subtle intimacy Abby and Indra shared while in public. In the few moments it took for her and Lara to cross the room, Indra gently brushed Abby's hand with hers, and

Abby responded with an uninterrupted desire-filled stare and a private whisper and loving smile. "I think you're right."

Harley sent a second deadly glare in Alex's direction, stopping her in her tracks. "I'm going to stay out of harm's way until your woman cools off a bit."

"Oh, come on. She's harmless," Lara said.

Alex sized up Harley again, appraising the invisible daggers coming in her direction at a fast and furious pace. "I've known her a lot longer than you. No thanks."

While Lara went to douse Harley's fire, Alex retrieved the black walnut box she'd placed hours earlier on a small table near the French doors leading to the patio. She gestured for Tyler and Jesse to join her outside. She was surprised to find Ethan and Andrew there braving the early evening heat and uncomfortable humidity. One of the unexpected outcomes of the mayhem in Philadelphia was the blossoming friendship between the two men. Their family connection, of course, contributed to it, but their rapport went deeper. Alex surmised that Ethan saving Andrew's life had had a significant impact on both of them, not to mention their mutual experience of being shot.

When Alex set the walnut box on their table, it was greeted by Ethan and Jesse with signs of recognition. "Is that what I think it is?" Ethan asked.

"It is." Alex smiled. Having Andrew here would make this toast even more meaningful.

"Wow," Jesse said. "The last time we drank from this bottle, it gave me the liquid courage to shamelessly flirt with this stud." She wagged her thumb in Ethan's direction.

"Wait right here." Alex padded to a nearby refreshment table. Returning with five clean glasses, she placed one in front of each person. She carefully opened the box, exposing a uniquely shaped, nearly quarter-full bottle.

"I can't believe you haven't finished it before now." Ethan leaned back in his chair, clearly looking forward to relishing the treat Alex was about to bestow upon them.

"The day Jesse told me the DA had dropped the charges against me and I knew I was no longer facing twenty years behind bars for a murder I didn't commit, I decided my wedding day would be the perfect day to finish this bottle." Alex accepted Tyler's outreached hand and kissed her palm. "It just took a little longer than expected."

She filled one glass with water from a carafe on the table for Andrew. "I know you're no longer drinking, brother, but I'd like you to join us."

"I'm a little lost here, guys," Andrew said, accepting the glass. "Care to fill me in?"

As Alex poured equal amounts into each glass until the bottle of Gran Patrón Burdeos tequila was empty, she explained, "Father had this bottle sent to me the day he announced his retirement and named me as his successor." She looked at Tyler. "Before I told him I'd found something I wanted more than to follow in his footsteps."

"Ah." Andrew's drawn-out response conveyed a level of understanding that required no further explanation. She and her brother had had ringside seats to their father's manipulations for decades. Andrew, of all people, understood the significance of entwining this day and this bottle. "I hope Father turned in his grave when you and Tyler said, 'I do.'"

Alex carefully inspected her glass, weighing its meaning. William Castle was a relic, a prisoner of antiquated ways and peer pressure. He'd given this gift in true Castle form, with strings attached. Today, she'd married the love of her life in his former home, marking the final shedding of those chains.

Alex raised her glass. Echoing the toast that she, Ethan, and Jesse shared the first time they drank from this bottle, she said, "Here's to kickin' ass."

Jesse raised hers. "And expensive booze."

Ethan raised his. "And beautiful women."

The five downed their drinks simultaneously, Alex relishing the faint burn of the smooth, fine-tasting amber liquid as it descended.

Andrew clutched the bottle and without a second of hesitation hurled it against the exterior limestone wall, shattering it into a hundred pieces. "That felt good."

Alex followed with her glass, its remnants joining those of the dead Castle legacy. "You got that right, brother." She focused on her twin, thinking of his transformation. Unlike the person who entered prison, the Andrew before her was a good man. He proved it by taking a bullet for Syd and by secretly saving the company she loved. Pride filled her heart, but it still ached for the young boy who could finish her thoughts and know what she needed before she did. Their symbiosis was gone, but in its place was a profound, mutual respect.

The others added their glasses to the mix, forever razing their bitter memories of William Castle.

"As long as I have you and Tyler cornered," Jesse said to Alex, "you should know that Nick Castor accepted a plea deal for twenty years, and his sentencing is scheduled for next week. I received a preview of his allocution statement. He'll swear that the counterfeiting scheme and smear campaign were Georgia's ideas and that Kelly Thatcher had given her his name for extra money at the prison commissary."

Alex shook her head, letting a satisfied grin form on her lips. The way Matt Crown had come after her, she'd assumed Kelly was behind everything. She had built up the woman in her head to be some powerful, vengeful witch out to ruin her until either of them took their dying breath. But Kelly was the opposite. She was weak and feckless behind bars, scraping up pennies for shampoo and nail polish. Whatever hold that woman once had over Alex was gone, forever.

"That's in the middle of our honeymoon. Should we reschedule?" Tyler turned to Alex as if deferring to her preference. Her gesture was unnecessary.

"Absolutely not." Alex kissed her hand again. "Jesse can report to us how it went."

Alex glanced through the glass doors, focusing on Abby and Harley engaged in conversation. Harley turned her head, locking eyes with Alex and waving her inside. "We should head back. It appears we're needed."

Ethan pushed himself from the comfortable patio chair and said to Andrew, "Ready to shuffle?"

Andrew slowly rose, gripping the walker waiting a foot to his left. "I'll be glad when I no longer need this thing."

"You're coming along great," Ethan said. "You'll throw that contraption to the curb in no time."

Moments later, Alex was clearing a path for her brother in the living room, pushing a small table out of the way. Despite his protestations, she'd doted over him like this since the day doctors released him from the hospital and she'd brought him to the mansion to recuperate. "There you are. Can I get you anything?"

"I'm good, sis, but can we take this to the couches?"

"I'd love to sit. My feet are killing me. Let me help," Alex offered.

"Let me." Erin stood from the couch, adjusting the pillows for Andrew to take her seat. She nudged Connor, Bree, and Derrick toward the far end.

Alex smiled at Erin's effort at peacemaking. Since that morning outside Indra's stable, she'd bent over backward to make up for her hurtful outburst. *"I'm sorry for the crappy things I said. I can see now that you and Mom were meant to be together,"* she'd said weeks ago. *"Let me design the wedding invitation. It's the least I can do for acting like such an ass."*

Alex adjusted the pillows for added assurance. Andrew had been through enough. With Syd, Destiny, and everyone she loved gathered, this was the perfect time to bring up her little discovery. "By the way, I have a bone to pick with you, brother."

Andrew rolled his eyes. "What did I do now?"

"You thought I'd never put two and two together, did you, Mr. Ignis Opus?"

Andrew mumbled, "Shit."

"That's right, brother. Our sister"—Alex pointed to Destiny—"with Ethan's help, checked out Castle Resorts' benefactor. Very cute calling it M-Three Investments."

John and Syd looked at Alex with outward curiosity. "Your mother's Leica?" Syd asked.

"Exactly. Our dear brother was the one who floated Castle Resorts the loan that saved us." Alex turned to Andrew. "Why didn't you say anything?"

Andrew shrugged as if his generous lending of half a billion with no strings attached was equivalent to lending someone five bucks in the school cafeteria. "When I first offered, you refused."

Alex sighed in regret. Her pigheadedness was another thing she needed to address when she and Tyler embarked on the next phase of their life. Family should always come first without hesitation. "I was a fool."

"I understand. I needed to earn your trust. At the same time, I wasn't ready to stand by and let the company fail. I'm sorry for deceiving you."

"I'm sorry you felt you had to. Tell me, though. Why Ignis Opus?" Alex asked.

"They're Latin words that very loosely translate to fireworks."

Alex cocked an eyebrow, decoding Andrew's alias. "Nature's fireworks, right?"

Andrew smiled. "She told you, too?"

Alex nodded and returned his smile. "Lightning is nature's fireworks."

Andrew continued, "Thunder is part of nature's concerto."

Tyler rubbed Alex's arm. "Care to clue in the rest of us?"

Alex motioned to Andrew with her hand. "Go ahead."

"Our mother died when we were young, so I don't have many memories of her, but this one stuck with me. I think we had just turned five when a strong thunderstorm rolled through. I was terrified when the power flickered, so I jumped in her lap. She held me tight and made the storm seem magical. She told me that lightning was nature's fireworks and that thunder was part of nature's concerto. She explained that a storm was like a symphony. All the instruments—the clouds, lightning, and thunder—combined to make the rain, nature's music."

"That's beautiful," Indra said.

"It stuck with me, too," Alex added. "Father was right about one thing. Mother always saw the beauty in things, even a violent thunderstorm."

Moments later, Harley approached Bree and gave her a light pat on the arm. "I think we're ready." The sixteen-year-old stood. Her nerves were evident, but Harley softly encouraged her, "It'll be fine. You're doing a good thing."

Bree nodded and cleared her throat several times. "Mom. Alex, I have a special gift for you." She waited for the room's undivided attention. "Everyone here knows that last month I inherited an estate from the Stevens family. I'm sure you also understand why I've been reluctant to accept it."

Tyler, Ethan, and Erin each nodded with misty eyes. A constriction formed in Tyler's throat when she thought of how well Bree had eventually accepted the truth about her birth and the compassion she had for what Tyler had gone through.

"With Jesse and Harley's help"—Bree gave each of them a nod—"I came to understand the magnitude of that inheritance." She turned toward Harley. "What's your current estimate on the worth of the art collection?"

Harley took a sip of her wine before answering. "Twenty-five million or more." Voices murmured.

"My response exactly," Bree continued. "Harley convinced me I shouldn't turn that amount of money over to the state of California, so she suggested I talk to Jesse." Harley raised her glass to Bree and then to Jesse in acknowledgment. "To make a long story short, Harley and Jesse have helped me set up a scholarship fund that the Spencer Foundation will manage. With Alex's help, I'd like to hold an auction at Castle Resorts Times Square to sell off the Stevens' art collection. Those funds, along with the money we get for selling the house, will go directly into the scholarship trust."

Tyler's eyes welled with tearful pride. She never dreamed that Bree would find a way to turn something so horrible into something so good.

"Mom. Erin." Bree took a deep breath and continued, "The scholarship will fund the education of survivors of rape and children born out of rape."

Tyler raised a hand to her mouth to mask her weeping. Erin did the same. All eyes in the room turned toward them, knowing now that they were survivors themselves. Alex and Connor did their best to comfort their women, each wrapping an arm around them while the rest in the room murmured their approval.

Tyler stepped forward and took Bree into her arms. Mother and daughter wept. The tears they shed that night would be their last over Paul Stevens and a painful past. Now, only good was on the horizon.

After Tyler broke the embrace, Indra said, "That's a hard act to follow, but I think it's our turn."

Abby nodded and reached into her purse, pulling out a small gift box. She cleared her throat and announced, "Alex. Tyler. A little birdie told me you've been thinking about making some dramatic changes and starting a new chapter in your lives." She handed the box to Alex. "Open it, darling."

Alex handed the box to Tyler, beaming as if she already knew what was inside. Untying the small white bow, Alex nodded to her wife. "You open it, T."

Tyler carefully lifted the lid. In the box were two matching well-worn house keys. It took seconds for her to recognize them. Her jaw dropped before looking to Alex for confirmation. "The beach house?"

Alex smiled and nodded. She brought Tyler into an embrace, whispering, "It's ours."

"I love it." It took a moment for the magnitude of the gift to sink in. Far from the hustle and bustle of the city and busy lives, the beach house had become their quiet refuge. But more importantly, water was Tyler's safe place, the refuge she turned to whenever she didn't feel in control of her world. Now, she and Alex had a place where she could always feel safe.

Indra gently squeezed Abby's hand. "Perfect," she said.

Harley snuck up behind Abby. "Well done, Mother."

CHAPTER FORTY

The last guest had left an hour earlier, and moments ago, Alex had closed the door behind the final member of Lara's cleanup crew. She and Tyler were finally, gloriously, alone on their wedding night. Since the moment Alex had laid eyes on Tyler in her off-the-shoulder cream-colored sheath wedding gown this afternoon, she'd fantasized about slowly lowering its zipper. She wanted to peel it off inch by inch until she'd exposed the surprise beneath it that Tyler said was waiting for her.

Alex secured the deadbolt and turned around. In an instant, her head started spinning at the sight of Tyler still in that dress, standing at the midpoint of the sweeping staircase. Each step she took toward her brought hours of sweet anticipation closer to fruition. She stopped one step below Tyler, bringing their heads to the same level, and kissed her slowly, passionately. Alex pulled their bodies together in a slow seduction without speaking, the heat between them doing all the talking. They had the rest of their lives together.

Tyler stepped backward and upward, pulling Alex along without breaking their kiss. Step by step, kiss by kiss, desire built until they crossed the threshold of the master suite. Alex drew Tyler's zipper down slowly, her chest tingling at the prospect of finally unwrapping her surprise.

Before she could do that, Tyler pulled back. Nudging Alex into a chair positioned in the corner of the room, she pressed PLAY on an iPod resting on the nearby end table. Stepping back several feet, she let the straps of her gown slide down her arms, hooking her thumbs around the gathered material and lowering the dress over her hips. When the garment hit the floor, she kicked it to the side in her two-inch heels.

Oh. My. God. Alex instantly recognized the black lace bra and high-rise thong covering the most luscious parts of Tyler. They were the ones she'd worn the first night they made love in San Francisco. Remembering that night revved Alex's arousal into high gear.

Background music started, a leisurely drum four-beat with an alternating snare and bass. Tyler closed her eyes and gently swayed her hips to the sexy rhythm. Then, at an agonizingly slow pace, she glided her hands up her abdomen, grazing her fingers against her skin. Finally, when her hands reached her breasts, she squeezed them, just the way Alex wanted to do.

When slow but jolting electric guitar chords joined the drums, Tyler abruptly widened her stance, dipped her hips, and swayed to the beat with a grinding force. At the same time, she slid her hands down her breasts, past her abdomen, and lightly cupped her center.

Ho-ly shit. Alex's pulse raced more than it ever had, and her breathing stopped. She wanted...no...needed to run her hands along Tyler's skin and dip her fingers into her hot center. Alex shifted in her seat to ease the ache there that had built to an unbearable level.

Tyler spun sharply on a heel, presenting her backside to Alex, and locked her knees. She slowly bent at the waist, caressing the backs of her legs with both hands all...the...way...down. Once her hair brushed against the floor between her feet, she bent at the knees and slowly pumped her bottom up and down to the music's beat.

Breathe. Dammit. Breathe, Alex reminded herself. Beads of sweat trickled down her brow as the heat inside her boiled over. She was sure a single touch from Tyler would cause her to melt into a pulsating puddle.

The song continued.

Tyler straightened and turned around, still grinding to the beat. The impassioned look on her face was piercing. She was in control, and she was about to push Alex over the edge. She grabbed a chair and slowly corkscrewed her hips toward the floor. Coming back up, she traced an index finger up her abdomen, past her breasts, and devoured it like a popsicle with a long, drawn-out suck.

Lord! Where did T learn to do this?

Alex's body was on fire. Her hunger had become a raging tiger. Tyler was beautiful and sexy, but this was off the chain. "Fuuuuuck" was the only word Alex could form.

When the music changed to soft and romantic, Tyler curled an index finger, gesturing for Alex to join her on the bed. They kissed and made love for hours. They touched and tasted and connected as lovers, as partners, and as wives. Eventually, when exhaustion hit, sleep overcame them, lying nestled in each other's arms.

Alex was the first to wake when morning light hit her face, rousing her out of the best sleep she'd had in months. Her position, still cradling Tyler's naked body, felt heavenly, especially with Tyler's hand resting pleasingly on her breast. *How can I want her again and again with no stop in sight?*

Alex glided her hand to the small of Tyler's back, tracing the length of her spine with a single fingertip up to her neck. Tyler stirred, lightly massaging Alex's breast, her breath bringing to life the smoldering embers that had prompted this wake-up tease. When Alex released a barely audible moan, Tyler lifted her head. "Again?"

"Can you blame me?" Alex smiled down at her.

"You're going to kill me, woman." Tyler's bland tone wasn't the least bit believable.

Alex stroked Tyler's back again. "That incredible dance of yours had me more turned on than I'd been my entire life." She kissed the top of Tyler's head. "Lord knows I'm not complaining, but what brought that on?"

Tyler sighed. "Kelly."

Alex rolled onto her side, propping her head up with one arm. "Ah, the video."

Tyler rolled over, mirroring Alex's position. "I have to admit I was a bit jealous." Alex started to object, but Tyler placed a finger on her lips. "I know you were just putting on a show to get a confession. Her rather dismal performance did, however, inspire me to find a way to give you a proper show."

Alex scooted her body closer and intertwined their legs. "And what a sexy show it was."

"Thanks to your sister."

"Syd?"

Grinning, Tyler shook her head. "Destiny. She gave me private lessons."

"I never thought I'd be grateful to have a former exotic dancer for a sister." Alex rolled on top of Tyler, hovering over her. "I want to make love to you again and again." Alex shifted her lips to work on the soft patch of skin behind Tyler's left ear, the one spot guaranteed to drive her crazy.

"Under one condition," Tyler said, failing to melt into Alex's kisses.

Conditions? That piqued Alex's curiosity. She stopped devouring Tyler's neck and pushed herself up by the elbows. "We've been married less than a day, and you're already using sex as leverage?"

"Yes." Tyler pushed Alex off her, scooted back in the bed, and reclined against the headboard. She grinned, giving away her intentions. "If you want to have your way with me, you'll have to answer one question."

Alex's growing ache made her doubt she would win this battle of wills. Relenting was her best and quickest option. "Okay, what's your question?"

Tyler's lips settled into a sly grin. "What were you and Harley doing with my daughter at Yale on graduation night until six o'clock the next morning?"

Alex narrowed an eye and cocked up one corner of her lips. Her wife had tried prying this tightly held secret from her twice before. Alex liked her tenacity. "You're withholding sex because of a college prank?"

"Yes, now talk," Tyler ordered.

Ah, there it was—bossy Tyler. Alex relished this side of her. Tyler rarely showed it, but when she did, it was sexy as hell. "You realize that my telling you would require breaking a long tradition of secrecy?"

"I do," Tyler replied, grazing a finger across Alex's breasts, first the left and then the right. Alex moaned, her resolve close to breaking. "But I really want to know."

When Tyler circled each erect nipple, Alex groaned, "You drive a hard bargain, T."

Tyler giggled, "Yes, I do."

Alex shot Tyler a stern but short-lived look before letting a smile take over. "All right, but only because I love you so much." Alex sat upright. "Do you know the statue of Nathan Hale on campus?"

Tyler nodded. "Yeah, it's right outside one of the dorms, right?"

Alex tapped Tyler on the tip of her nose with a finger. "The lady is correct. Well, Morse College has a long-standing tradition of seniors dressing up the statue in Yale apparel during graduation week. So when it was Erin and Connor's turn, they planned it all out and asked Harley and me to help pull it off."

"And that took all night?"

"Not exactly. Things were going according to plan. We had successfully dodged campus police and were almost done dressing Nathan in a track uniform when..." Alex paused, turning her eyes downward sheepishly.

"When what?"

"I'd forgotten to mute my cell phone."

Tyler smiled, holding back most of her laugh. "Work?"

"Yep." Alex shook her head at her ill-fated forgetfulness. "A campus cop heard it, doubled back, and caught us red-handed."

Tyler swatted Alex high on the thigh. "You got my baby arrested?"

"Ouch!" Alex thought that swat might leave a mark. "Not exactly."

"Big baby. Tell me my daughter doesn't have a police record."

"She doesn't, I swear. He took us back to the campus police department, but once Abby got there—"

"Wait, Abby was there? I knew she had something to do with the aftermath, but she was there?"

Alex briefly averted her eyes again. "I called her after we were…let's just say detained. She smoothed things over with the university president, and the campus police swept the entire matter under the rug."

"Just like that?"

"Well…"

"Don't tell me. Not exactly."

Alex smiled at Tyler's cheekiness. "Yes, smarty-pants. Not exactly. Harley and I made sizable donations to the campus"—Alex raised both hands, issuing air quotes—"to make it go away." Alex traced Tyler's jawline with a finger. "Don't worry, T. As far as I know, your baby still has a squeaky-clean record."

Tyler shot Alex a skeptical look. "What do you mean, as far as you know?"

Alex raised her hands in surrender. "Hey, I don't know what other trouble she may have gotten herself into. After all, she is your daughter."

Tyler's jaw dropped to a feigned gasp.

Alex gently pushed her wife flat on the bed and, despite Tyler's playful squirms, began devouring her neck. Her faux annoyance didn't last long, though. When Alex reached that spot behind her ear, she melted into the mattress.

Tyler had placed the last of her clothing and toiletries into her travel bag later that morning and was preparing to zip it when Alex stopped her.

"Wait. You forgot these," Alex called out, reopening Tyler's bag. She brought two items to her nose and inhaled deeply, savoring their musky scent. "You can't forget these. I want an encore." She placed the lace bra and thong combo Tyler wore during last night's sexy dance carefully into the bag and zipped it shut.

"You are incorrigible," Tyler laughed, walking away.

Alex gave Tyler a soft slap on the butt before she was out of arm's reach. "When it comes to you? Absolutely."

"We better get going. Richard has been waiting for fifteen minutes to take us to the jet."

They grabbed their bags and made their way to Abby's waiting town car. Richard stowed their luggage and pulled away. "Shall I take the Midtown Tunnel, Ms. Castle?" he asked.

"That's Mrs. Falling-Castle," Alex corrected. Then, she turned to Tyler and asked, "T?"

"No need, Richard. I've gotten used to the bridges. Besides"—Tyler winked at her wife—"Alex is more than capable of distracting me if needed."

Richard grinned, turned up the radio, and drove onto East Fifty-Ninth Street to cross the Queensboro Bridge. Minutes later, they were traveling down Queens Boulevard, the Manhattan skyline well behind them. As they moved steadily along, Alex thought again about the idea she had in mind for leaving Manhattan for good. Considering how Tyler felt about Abby's wedding gift, she suspected she would love the "where" of her idea. She just wasn't so sure if she'd love the "what."

"T?"

Tyler glanced up. "Yeah, babe?"

"Remember a few months ago when I told you I was thinking about making some significant changes but hadn't figured everything out yet?"

Tyler nodded. "You've figured things out now?"

"I think I have, but if you're not up for it, we can—"

"If this is important to you, then it's important to me. Tell me what you have in mind."

Alex gathered her thoughts. Her ideas would dramatically change her, Tyler's, Bree's, and even Callie's lives forever, and she wanted to frame the discussion just right. "I regret spending so much time at work over the last few years, leaving you to pick up the slack with Callie and the house. Even when I was home, I checked out half the time when some work crisis arose." Tyler opened her mouth to object, but Alex continued, "It's true. I'm so sorry for taking you for granted."

Tyler turned her palm over and squeezed Alex's hand. "You were under tremendous stress."

"It doesn't excuse me losing track of what was really important." Alex kissed Tyler's hand. "After everything we've gone through the last few months, I realized I no longer love Castle Resorts like I did before you came into my life. I used to think the company was our family legacy, but I've come to realize that you and your girls are."

Tyler's eyes watered. "I feel the same way about you and my work."

Every tense muscle in Alex relaxed. "Then this might be easier than I thought. I want to sell off all my interests in Castle Resorts and hand it over to Andrew and Destiny."

"Wow," Tyler said. "I knew you were cutting back and might step down from the helm, but not that you were considering wholly divesting yourself of the company you've spent a lifetime nurturing."

"I know this is the right thing to do," Alex said. "I also want to sell the mansion and move us into the beach house. Bree can have her own room, and we'd have the guest house for Erin and Connor when they come to visit. No staff, just us. I liked it better when I was living in my townhouse. I cooked and cleaned and did my own shopping. I want that back, but this time I want it with you. Heck, I even want to get a companion for Callie."

Tyler tapped an index finger on her lips as if thinking about what to say. "Hmmm, I don't know. I like the occasional maid service."

Alex grinned at Tyler's playfulness. "We don't have to go completely crazy, I suppose. How about once-a-month maid service?"

"Deal." Tyler laughed. "So, you want to be a beach bum?"

"Not exactly."

"What is it with you and those two words today?"

"I have overused that phrase," Alex snorted. "While becoming a beach bum sounds appealing after the things we've been through, I was thinking more along the line of becoming an art gallery owner."

"Art gallery?"

"It makes sense. Before my father died, besides telling him that I loved you"—Alex stroked Tyler's cheek—"I told him I wished I would have studied art and made that my life's work. Those weekends we spent with Harley, searching for pieces for our home in out-of-the-way galleries solidified it. I felt alive immersed in the art world."

"It makes perfect sense, babe. Have you thought about where you'd like to open up a gallery?"

"In Southampton. There's a large art community in the Hamptons, and the area needs a good gallery for all mediums, including photography."

"Photography?" Tyler asked, a hint of joy in her voice.

Alex nodded. "You're such an incredible photographer, T. While graphic design is an important profession, I think you're squandering your talent. We can turn part of the gallery space into a studio for you. I want to curate your first show for our grand opening."

"How about you? You're a very impressive photographer yourself. You have a lot of your mother's talent."

"I don't know about that, but I'd like to show the body of her work, too."

Tyler threw her arms around Alex. "It all sounds perfect, Alex. I'd love for us to become beach bums-slash-shutterbugs-slash-gallery owners."

Alex pulled back, holding Tyler at arm's length. "So, you'd sell your share of the company to Maddie?"

"Not exactly," Tyler replied mischievously.

Alex laughed. "All right, all right. I deserved that."

"I couldn't resist." Tyler laughed, too. "Since Erin and Connor are moving in together and staying in the city, I've been thinking about handing over my share of the partnership to Erin. She's ready, and frankly, she's much more talented than I'll ever be."

"Don't let her hear you say that."

"Never."

Alex settled back into her seat, wrapping her arm around Tyler. "I have a good feeling, T. This is going to be perfect for both of us."

CHAPTER FORTY-ONE

Philadelphia, Pennsylvania

A respectful quiet hung in the packed courtroom. Ethan sat patiently in the gallery, observing the other attendees. Local and national reporters filled several rows, ready to get their scoop on the proceedings. He kept his eye on the reporter who particularly grated on his patience—Matt Crown from the *New York Daily News*.

Ethan periodically glanced over his shoulder toward the main doors. He finally leaned to his left, whispering into Jesse's ear, "I wonder what's keeping Syd."

"Me, too," Jesse replied. That moment, Syd appeared, and Jesse waved to her. "There she is."

Syd shimmied through the throng of reporters and took a seat next to Jesse on the long wooden bench. "Phew. There was a long line in the restroom."

Jesse smiled. "Just in time."

A voice bellowed, "All rise."

After the obligatory reading for the official record, Nick Castor gave his public confession. He mentioned that the Kelly

Thatcher police sting video was part of Georgia's plan and that Georgia had conned an unwitting member of the media to surface it. Ethan cocked his head, thinking about the video. *Matt Crown, that dirty son of a bitch. Only a cop would have had access to that video. So how the hell did he get a hold of it?*

Several people murmured in the back of the room when the judge issued Castor his agreed-to twenty-year sentence. The proceeding ended with reporters dashing out of the courtroom in a mad rush, cell phones in hand, to pass the story along to their editors.

Ethan trailed Matt Crown down the hallway. When he caught up, he spun him around by the shoulder. Ethan snarled, "How did you do it?"

Crown flinched, a hint of recognition on his face. "Ethan Falling, right? The private eye at the warehouse. How did I do what?"

"How did you get the sting video? Only the police had access to it."

"I never give up a source." Crown's eyes darted back and forth like the slimy weasel he was. Ethan had dealt with scum like Matt Crown before. However he came into possession of the video, someone had to break the law for him to get his hands on it.

"You've had it in for the Castle family for months with your one-sided reporting. I've seen reporters like you. They run with half-truths and sensational innuendos to grab headlines. You're the worst of the lot."

"Once you read my follow-up story today"—Crown looked at his watch—"which should hit the Internet in two minutes, you may change your mind about me."

Syd had caught up with Ethan halfway through his browbeating of Crown. She rolled her eyes. "Great, another hit piece."

"I may surprise you," Crown replied.

Syd snorted. "That'll be the day."

"Now, if you'll excuse me," Crown said, straightening his wrinkled tie. "I have a story to file."

The moment Crown disappeared out the courthouse doors, Jesse pulled an iPad from her briefcase. Ethan looked over her shoulder as she navigated to the *Daily News* website. She repeatedly hit reload until a breaking headline appeared on the screen: "Lies, Lust, and Larceny: Truth Exposed."

Jesse scanned the article. After reading a few seconds, she mumbled, "I'll be damned."

Syd threw her hands up. "You're killing me. What does he say?"

"Apparently, he interviewed Kelly Thatcher, and she completely dispelled the rumor that Alex had anything to do with William's death." Jesse moved to the next paragraph. "She confirmed that the video in its full unedited version shows that her confession had surprised Alex and that Alex had attacked her afterward."

Ethan chuckled at the memory of Alex straddling Kelly and stuffing a bra down her throat. "Yep, 34C." Jesse slapped Ethan on the arm, shooting him a warning glare. "Sorry." Ethan chuckled again.

"Uh-huh." Jesse squinted one eye to warn Ethan again. She grinned before continuing, "Apparently, Kelly is claiming that Georgia may have had something to do with William's death. Kelly claimed she left the blackmail photos in William's office the night she knocked him down and claims the only way to explain how Georgia had them was if she had been in William's office before staff found his body the next morning."

Syd shook her head. "I wouldn't put it past Georgia."

"Those pictures have bothered me for years." Ethan rubbed his chin, thinking of the ramifications of Kelly's theory. "Could Kelly have her confession vacated because of this?"

"Not likely," Jesse said. "Nothing she claims changes any facts associated with her confession. The coroner's report ruled William's death was due to the head injury he sustained from being pushed. Kelly has an interesting theory but can offer no evidence to support her claim that he may have been alive after she left. This changes nothing. And Georgia's not around to interrogate, so…"

Jesse continued reading. "This figures. Crown writes that Sal Esposito, the guy at the Philadelphia warehouse, was loosely tied to a local crime syndicate, and in the course of their investigation into the wine counterfeiting the FBI discovered a drug-smuggling operation he'd been running out of the warehouse."

"Is that it?" Ethan asked.

Jesse read more, pausing with a stunned expression. "Wow!"

"You're killing me, Jesse." Syd threw her arms up again.

"Crown says: 'I unequivocally believe the evidence shows that Alex Castle was not romantically involved with Kelly Thatcher immediately before or following William Castle's death.' He completely dispels the theory that she was involved with her father's murder."

"I'll be damned." Syd let out a huge breath. "All of this ugliness is finally behind us."

"Maybe for you," Ethan said. Matt Crown may have cleaned the slate with Alex Castle with this article, but he was still sketchy. "I'm still going to find out who gave Crown that video."

EPILOGUE

Southampton, New York, one year later

Six months of remodeling and wooing upcoming artists had paid off. Not only had Nature's Fireworks opened on time and to critical acclaim, but Alex's not-so-little gallery had become a sought-after venue for photographers, painters, and sculptors around the world before she even opened the doors last week. She had already booked showings out for the next two years.

The best decision she had made while prepping the gallery was buying the space next door. Formerly occupied by a confectionery store that had relocated to a renovated shopping area closer to the children's museum in Bridgehampton, it had an eighteen-foot ceiling. The acquisition doubled the wall space she'd first envisioned and added a spacious room to display larger pieces.

Despite all the work the renovation of the building had entailed and the high demand for her keen eye for up-and-coming talent, Alex never worked later than five o'clock, keeping the promise she'd made to herself to never lose sight of what was truly important—family. Life was simple.

Alex checked her leather-banded watch, a gift from Tyler on their first wedding anniversary last month. She smiled whenever she glanced at it, calculating the minutes until she could return to her beautiful wife, curl up on the deck chairs with a glass of Barnette wine, and watch the sunset with her. Tonight, though, she sighed. It was precisely five p.m., her self-imposed quitting time for the last year. But, tonight, with Tyler's concurrence, she'd agreed to keep the gallery open later to accommodate two valued customers who couldn't arrive before its four p.m. closing time.

The door chime sounded, alerting Alex that her guests had arrived. She emerged from her small yet tastefully decorated office off the main showroom, the surprise at the door putting a smile on her face. She closed in on her unexpected visitor, giving her a loving embrace and kiss.

"I didn't know you were coming back to the shop tonight, T."

"I promised Robbie a batch of my cranberry oatmeal cookies." Tyler placed the cloth shopping bag she'd carried in on the sleek wooden table guarding the entryway to Alex's office, which was next door to that of her assistant. Alex had been pleasantly surprised when Robbie, her personal assistant before she became CEO at Castle Resorts, had jumped at the chance to follow his favorite boss to the Hamptons.

Tyler had taken up baking over the holidays, a hobby she shared with Bree twice a month. Alex loved baking weekends. The beach house was often filled with various sweet and alluring aromas, tempting her to taste test each batch of cookies. Her waistline had grown an inch, attesting to her weakness for her wife's baking skills. She was going to have to find a way to put running back on her agenda.

They chatted for the next few minutes about the successful grand opening and the five major sales Alex had made today. Before she could explain how proud that made her, the front door chime sounded. She swung her head around again, this time to greet her expected guests.

"I'm so sorry we're a few minutes late, darling. Traffic was a bear." Abby's elegant voice matched her sophisticated yet casual attire. After stepping down from the Spencer Foundation and handing the reins over to Harley, Abby never had gotten the casual look down as well as Alex had. She would never be caught dead in Alex's now customary Levi's and Chucks.

Distracted by the colorful decal displayed in the street-side glass window, Indra took a little longer to arrive, walking in a few steps behind Abby. Alex couldn't blame her. Every time she entered the gallery, she paused to take in its special meaning. Tyler had hand-painted "Nature's Fireworks" in elegant, flowing letters in a slight arc at the top. Below the letters, she'd placed a striking photo Alex had taken of a recent storm at the beach and drawn the silhouette of a conductor dressed in a floor-length gown, showing her face in profile. The conductor was Alex's mother. The image encapsulated Alex's true inspiration for the gallery and how she wanted to conduct her life—by seeing the beauty in everything and sharing it with others.

Indra gestured toward the window that had mesmerized her moments earlier. "I love the sign out front. It's quite fetching."

Alex nodded, beaming with pride. "Tyler designed it. She's really captured the essence of our little gallery."

"Indeed, she has. But I must say your 'little' gallery has made a huge splash." Abby hugged Alex and Tyler, with Indra doing the same in reverse order.

Alex shrugged off Abby's compliment. "Not so big that I can't make it home for dinner every night as planned," she said with a smile. She turned off the display lights in the street-side windows and locked the door to prevent the odd customer from wandering in. "Let's look at that piece I told you about, so Tyler and I can get home and enjoy the sunset."

She guided the couple to the new showroom as Abby inquired about Erin missing the grand opening. Tyler answered, "She helped set things the week before but had to switch gears when Creative Juices landed another big client. Maddie put her right to work since she's on summer break."

"The samples of her work that you showed us when we visited the beach house last month were stunning," Abby said. "She's quite talented, just like her mother." Tyler smiled her gratitude.

"Very talented." Alex squeezed Tyler's hand and stopped in front of a four-by-six-foot abstract painting filled with blues and greens, resembling a pod of whales swimming toward the ocean surface. It was one of several pieces that a new European artist had prepared for her first show in the United States at Nature's Fireworks.

Indra appeared awestruck by the large canvas. "This is exquisite, Alex."

"I thought this would go well in their living room along the far wall." Alex had looked for months for a piece that would blend with the look and the color palette that Harley's Park Avenue penthouse had taken on since the renovations. What had started as a simple transformation of the kitchen into a chef's dream turned into a full year of remodeling because of Harley's inability to deny her new bride anything. Work had ended this month, marking a total makeover, and Abby and Indra's contribution would complete the look.

Abby smiled with a mother's pride. "It's perfect. Harley and Lara will love it."

A few quiet moments passed before Alex dared to ask the question that had been swirling in her head for twelve months. "I'm curious, you two. Why haven't you tied the knot? It's been legal for a year now."

Indra turned her head, looked lovingly at Abby, and held out a hand to her. Once Abby accepted it, Indra replied, "We don't need rings on these hands to state how much we love one another."

Abby kissed the back of Indra's hand. "Besides, with the tax laws, figuring out inheritance between our two estates would be a mess. So we decided right after you two married to keep things as they are. It's much cleaner this way. We're very happy having found each other again, and at our age, no piece of paper can make our love truer."

Alex and Tyler turned to gaze at one another. No words, just smiles of complete understanding. Five years after their first kiss, they were still in love and happier with each passing year.

* * *

The quiet in the beach house was a welcome change for the longtime city-dwellers, especially Tyler. She had never grown accustomed to the wailing New York sirens that regularly ripped her out of light sleep. This evening typified how she now fell asleep every night. The rhythmic sound of ocean waves hitting the shoreline outside their beach house had created a safe, cozy cocoon in the living room while she waited for Alex so they could commence their nightly ritual.

Tyler patiently sifted through several newspapers scattered on the coffee table where Callie and her little brother, Jack, a matching black and tan German shepherd, lay sentinel nearby, alerting on every stray sound. She picked up a months-old edition of the *New York Times*, which had been flipped to page four. She reread the story headline, "NYPD Evidence Clerk Arrested." She was bitter that this never made it to page one like Matt Crown's sensational exposé on Alex and her family had but was grateful it made the newspaper at all.

It took him months, but with his NYPD friend's help, Ethan had tracked down who gave Crown the police video. The clerk, Thomas Sinclair, or Tommy as Crown referred to him, had confessed to giving Crown a copy of Kelly's sting video recording and access to evidence in other active police investigations over the years. While some might call what Crown did typical investigative reporting, the Manhattan District Attorney thought otherwise and had opened an investigation into possible bribery charges. Tyler hoped Crown would pay a price for cutting corners beyond the *Daily News* letting him go, but the article made it sound doubtful.

Tyler then picked up last week's local *Southampton Press* and admired the front-page headline, "Nature's Fireworks Opens with a Bang." She ran her fingers over the accompanying photograph of her and Alex standing together, hand-in-hand, in front of the doors leading to their new gallery, hours before the grand opening. Their agreed-upon hope for their new venture, they had told the reporter, was that someday someone would walk through those doors and feel moved by their work. That was enough for them both.

A year ago, the gallery was just an idea, a dream of Alex's for her and Tyler to forge a simpler life together, one where they would never lose sight of what was important—family. Last week, that dream became a reality. The opening was a success, and Tyler's, and Rebecca Castle's collections were a hit.

A creak sounded down the hallway, turning Callie's and Jack's ears like battleship turrets toward the moving target. That was Tyler's cue to retrieve two glasses and a bottle of cabernet from the wine fridge. Moments later, Alex appeared from the dark hallway.

"We gotta get the floorboard in front of Bree's door fixed," Alex said, gesturing her thumb over her shoulder.

"Are you kidding? It's like an early warning system for both you and Bree. I know when either of you is coming."

Alex chuckled. "I guess you're right."

Tyler held up the glasses in one hand and the wine bottle in the other. "Shall we?"

Alex smiled, walking across the room. She opened the sliding glass door leading to the oceanfront deck, peeked her head over her shoulder, and patted her hip. "Come on, Callie. Jack. It's our favorite time of the day."

Callie and Jack darted out the door, assuming their traditional position at the deck railing to monitor gulls taking on the breeze on the beach. Since the day Alex rescued Jack from the county shelter on a whim and brought him home, he and Callie had been inseparable. The only downside to having two dogs in the house was not knowing which one to blame when Alex or Tyler discovered evidence of mischief.

Alex and Tyler followed them out the door, taking their customary spot on the double chaise lounge underneath the deck cover, a holdover from when Abby owned the beach house. Tyler poured each of them a glass and placed the bottle on the nearby table. Then, handing Alex her glass, Tyler asked, "You were in there quite a while tonight. Any problems with Bree?"

"Not at all. She was excited about her new camera and showed me the photos she'd taken today."

"I don't get it. She's turned into a mini-Alex." Tyler shook her head in delight, pausing at Alex's snicker. "Bree saw me with a camera for years yet showed not one inkling of interest in photography." Tyler took a sip of wine and gazed out at the ocean and the diminishing sunset. "She sees you with your mother's Leica on one trip, and she's hooked."

"I was so glad Jesse got the police to finally release it from evidence. I had forgotten how much I loved that Leica and how much I missed my mother. Sharing it with Bree made it that much more special."

"Speaking of Jesse," Tyler said, "she called today to confirm she and Ethan will be here on Friday to pick up Bree for their week with her."

"They're staying the night, right?" Alex asked. She sipped her wine and let out a satisfied moan. "I think this 2010 is even better than the 2008."

"Yes, they're staying the night, and I think you're right about the wine." Tyler swirled the wine in her mouth, letting the seductive notes of plum and blackcurrant fruit tickle her taste buds.

"When I talked to Syd this morning, she said this should be their bestseller yet. So much so that she and John are thinking of picking up the twenty acres adjoining their vineyard that came available last week."

"That's wonderful news." Tyler shivered when the breeze picked up and cut through her sweater and light slacks.

"You cold, T? Want the blanket?" Alex placed her wineglass on the neighboring end table after Tyler nodded yes. She retrieved the quilt that had been draped over the high back of the lounger and spread it over them both, covering their legs. "Come here, you." Alex pulled Tyler in close, wrapping her arms around her. "Better?"

"Much." Tyler snuggled closer, drawing in the warmth of Alex's body. "What were the final numbers for the week?"

"I don't know." Alex shrugged. "I'm sure Robbie will let us know on Monday."

Hearing Alex say that business could wait overjoyed Tyler. It drove home her transformation from being workaholic

CEO, who rarely made time for family, to being a laid-back small business owner. Having Castle Resorts in Andrew's and Destiny's capable hands certainly helped. Destiny's transition to CFO had been relatively easy, but Andrew's road to the CEO chair was rocky. It had taken some convincing of the chief operating officer, hotel managers, and other senior executives, but once Alex and Syd had thrown their full support behind Andrew, they accepted his leadership, which surprisingly was styled much like Alex's.

Tyler giggled. "You *have* changed. Do you think Robbie misses Castle Resorts and the old Alex?" The clouds lit up against the darkening sky in the near distance, signaling a lightning storm was minutes away.

Alex squeezed Tyler a little tighter. "Not in the least. I used to be very demanding."

Tyler chuckled. "You think?"

Alex shifted her fingers, tickling Tyler's sides. "Smartass."

The evening sky lit up again with lightning, this time followed by a loud crack of thunder. Callie and Jack scurried back from the railing, taking shelter beneath the deck cover near the sliding door. Tyler laughed and then placed her glass down on the table. "I thought you loved my ass."

Alex turned Tyler around in her arms. "I love every square inch of your"—she kissed Tyler's neck—"very sexy body."

Alex shifted again, propping herself up with her arms to hover over Tyler. She kissed her on the lips before returning to that special place behind her left ear.

At Tyler's first moan, a faint voice called out from inside the beach house, "Mom? Alex?"

Alex whispered into Tyler's ear, "We'll finish this later." She then scrambled to return to an innocent position next to her wife. "Out here," she shouted.

Bree hurried out the glass door leading to the deck, eyes peeled toward the western sky. "Did I miss the fireworks?"

Tyler shook her head again. "See? Mini-Alex."

"Oh, come on, Mom. This is part of nature's concerto." Bree briefly shifted her gaze to Alex and winked.

For months after moving in, every time a storm rolled through and Bree was here, Alex reminisced about their gallery namesake and the story her mother had told her about lightning and thunder. Alex had a way of explaining the complex by boiling it down to its simplest form, Tyler supposed, just as Rebecca had. That talent would make Alex an excellent mother, Tyler thought. Maybe, just maybe, they should have a baby of their own.

Long after the storm had passed, the dogs had fallen asleep, and Bree had gone to bed, Alex and Tyler remained in their favorite spot, facing the ocean and enjoying the magnificent show in the sky. Tyler caressed Alex's left hand, staring at it as it rested on her leg. She twisted Alex's wedding band, playing back the last five years in her head.

Crossing paths on that Napa riverfront all those years ago altered their futures. From that day, Tyler knew change was on the horizon. She just didn't know how much. She didn't foresee how happy a woman, this woman, could make her. Chaos had brought them together, and blind suspicion nearly cost them decades apart. Every deep, dark secret in their lives had tested them, yet their love had survived. Tyler twisted the tiny gold band one more time, sure that she and Alex would be connected in their hearts...in their minds...in their souls...forever.

Bella Books, Inc.

Women. Books. Even Better Together.

P.O. Box 10543
Tallahassee, FL 32302
Phone: (800) 729-4992

www.BellaBooks.com

More Titles from Bella Books

Mabel and Everything After – Hannah Safren
978-1-64247-390-2 | 274 pgs | paperback: $17.95 | eBook: $9.99
A law student and a wannabe brewery owner find that the path to a
fairy tale happily-ever-after is often the long and scenic route.

To Be With You – TJ O'Shea
978-1-64247-419-0 | 348 pgs | paperback: $19.95 | eBook: $9.99
Sometimes the choice is between loving safely or loving bravely.

I Dare You to Love Me – Lori G. Matthews
978-1-64247-389-6 | 292 pgs | paperback: $18.95 | eBook: $9.99
An enemy-to-lovers romance about daring to follow your heart, even
when it's the hardest thing to do.

The Lady Adventurers Club - Karen Frost
978-1-64247-414-5 | 300 pgs | paperback: $18.95 | eBook: $9.99
Four women. One undiscovered Egyptian tomb. One (maybe) angry
Egyptian goddess. What could possibly go wrong?

Golden Hour - Kat Jackson
978-1-64247-397-1 | 250 pgs | paperback: $17.95 | eBook: $9.99
Life would be so much easier if Lina were afraid of something
basic—like spiders—instead of something significant. Something like
real, true, healthy love.

Schuss – E. J. Noyes
978-1-64247-430-5 | 276 pgs | paperback: $17.95 | eBook: $9.99
They're best friends who both want something more, but what if
admitting it ruins the best friendship either of them have had?